G000075132

FIENDILKFJELD
CASTLE

MATTHEW PUNGITORE

Fiendilkfjeld Castle
Written by Matthew Pungitore
Contact the author at: matthewpungitore_writer@outlook.com
Published by BookBaby

Cover and Interior Design by BookBaby

Printed in the United States of America
Published 2019
First Printing, 2019

(Print) ISBN 978-1-54397-692-2
(E-Book) ISBN 978-1-54397-693-9

BookBaby
7905 N. Crescent Blvd. Pennsauken, NJ
08110

With eternal love, I dedicate this book to my mother and my sister.

TABLE OF CONTENTS

ACKNOWLEDGMENTS

I want to express sincere thanks to BookBaby. I believe that I have received great kindness, patience, and guidance from the entire Book-Baby team. This book exists because of BookBaby and the entire BookBaby team.

I want to greatly thank my mother, my sister, and my father. My mother and my sister have always made me feel wonderful strength, love, and hope. I want to thank my father for the courage he helped me feel while I was creating this book.

PROLOGUE

I AM SEARCHING FOR POWER IN A WORLD THAT IS ABSOLUTELY and utterly dead. Anything that can be attained is a gray corpse of something that is not truly real. The gratifying pursuit of strength is the only ultimate form of communication I have left. The vulgar aches in my hands and mouth are reminding me that I should find a more violent type of expression.

My fingernails are scratching a very cold wall. I smell its dusty old wood as my teeth scrape against it. Vehemently, I claw against the wall. As I am biting it, my hot rank breath warms my lips. My claws inflict savage scratches into its rotting wood. I am marring it with my fangs. Snorting and growling, I continue attacking. The damage that I am doing to this wall is wicked and obscene. This outburst does not satisfy the barbaric desires of my body. My talons want to feel real quarries next time.

I stop attacking the wall and jump into a dark corner of this room. The darkness hides my entire body as I sit on the wood floor. My screams extinguish the dull silence. The silence slowly returns as I gradually stop screaming.

Moonlight slips through the window and pierces the darkness of this chamber. The Gothic arch and the bars on this window cause the falling moonlight to form into imposing shapes on the floor that are frightening and exciting. These shapes of the moonlight cast into my mind the images of looming tyrants, cemeteries and funerals, chevaliers and knights holding spears or swords, burning villages, trapped princesses, and haunted crypts.

I am now looking out through this window. I am in an uppermost room, within a high tower, that is resting high above the trees. The blue moonlight shimmers on the white skin of my hands. The full moon is hanging in the night sky. The dark world outside is a beautiful but dangerous moonlit landscape. The dark forest and distant valleys out yonder are haunting. My face presses against the cold iron bars of the window. I continue looking out the window and peer downward, and I am seeing how high up above the ground this room is. I see a small segment of the stone exterior of this tower in which I am located. Jagged ridges and peaks of mountains lean against the outside of the tower. Cold air, blowing through the holes and cracks in the glass, briefly glides across my eyes. Dizzy from the immense altitude, I flinch. If I were to drop out of this window, I would crash against the rocky ground below the tower or be impaled by the spikes and horns of the pinnacles and crags.

A gentle voice floats into this gloomy room. This delicate sound makes me forget my agonizing torment. It sounds like the voice of that beautiful woman who has been frequently visiting me in my dreams at night. Her voice is as ethereal and lovely as the moonlight gliding through the broken glass of the window. Like the view from the window and the moonlight pouring into the room, the voice I am hearing is implicitly sublime. My eyes are shut as I hold on to the bars of the window. The feminine voice is whispering my name.

She says, "Theodemir."

FIENDILKFJELD CASTLE

PART 1

CHAPTER 1

I am Theodemir Fiendilkfjeld. A remnant of my soul forced me to write about my life. By writing about the things that I remember about my past, maybe I could rescue a part of myself that has some value or goodness. I did not know who I could trust with my secrets, but I wanted the spirit of my story to spread to those who needed to know the horrifying truth about what happened to me after I went to Fiendilkfjeld castle. I did not know who could believe my story. No one listened to me. They never did.

Anyone who does not want to be connected to the evil that surrounds me or my story should turn away now and forget me. I need to tell my secrets to someone, or I will implode.

I decided that I would begin my story by writing about the events that I experienced around the time that I decided to travel to that castle. I still find it hard to concentrate on the past, so I can only show what I understand about it all. First, there are some other things that I should explain about myself.

I was born in Italy. I lived in northern Italy with my family. I always loved Italy. Another side of my family, the more mysterious and reclusive side, lived in a castle there, too. The castle was called Fiendilkfjeld castle, and it was the home of the noble relatives of my family. My father took me to Fiendilkfjeld castle only once but then never again. He said that it was a bad influence. I did not remember anything about the castle or my noble relatives that lived within it, except that the castle was always dark and the people inside of it were always sad.

There was one thing, actually, I did remember. The beautiful Gothic architecture of the castle haunted me. Images and memories of its Gothic arches, flying buttresses, ribbed vaults, and stained glass windows had bewitched me. I was enchanted by the mystery and otherworldliness that exuded from all parts of the castle. Ever since I first went there, I knew that I wanted to surround myself with that kind of majesty.

After, my family and I moved to Austria. I lived with them for many years, but then I left. When I was twenty years old, I moved to England. I made sure that my estate in England was crafted with Gothic, Medieval, and Norman styles. I Gothicized my estate and had my manor built with elements of Decorated style, Gothic revival, and Victorian architecture, too. When I was twenty two years old, I ordered a theater and chapel to be constructed and attached to my Gothic manor. I had the best builders and architects working on it. I hired the fastest laborers and the greatest workers to help them complete my manor.

When the year was 2060 CE, I was twenty five years old and I was still living on my isolated private estate in England. My manor was complete, and I did not have to listen to the noise of the builders any more. I was a wealthy man and supported by the wealth of my family. I was an art collector and also making additional money by working as a private historian. My manor and estate was hidden in a dark forest. It was great for me when I needed to be alone. I rarely had guests, so it was a fabulous place to relax or work. I loved spending autumns here. I loved living in England, but I always thought of Italy.

Earlier that year, I had sent letters to my friends who were living in England. My letters explained how I would be traveling to Italy at the end of October to help a detective find a missing woman for a while. My letter expressed that I did not know when I would be returning back to England. The messages also expressed how I wanted to see all my friends and have a fun, quiet night with them at my estate in England before I left.

One night, at the beginning of October in that year, I was having guests at my estate. My friends and I were sitting in a parlor of my manor. With me was Dean, Boris, Mildred, and Greta. They were all very rich and they came from wealthy families, too. I first met them at a funeral. I had been friends with them for five years. I was not certain whether I actually could say that they were my friends. I did not know what I should call them.

That night, I was trying to talk to my friends, but they would not listen to me. Every time I had said something, they would ignore me like they could not hear me. I asked Dean how he had been doing recently, but he was silent. I asked Mildred if she had done anything new or exciting since the last time we spoke, and she turned her back towards me without saying anything. Boris and Greta also shunned me.

I looked at my reflection in a small mirror that I was holding. Light glistened on my white skin. My dark blue eyes held a glum expression. I was filled with boredom. My lips had moved into a form that reflected my disappointment. I put the mirror down beside me.

Boris approached me, and he cleared his throat in a way that subtly expressed to me that he wanted to privately speak away from the other guests. Boris appeared nervous and impatient as he briefly tilted his head and shot a sideways look at me. I followed Boris into an antechamber.

"I need more money," said Boris.

"Do you know how much money you already owe to me?" I asked.

Boris lit a cigar.

"Do not do that here," I said. "Please, go outside for that. I would honestly appreciate that."

Boris said, "I will go outside in a few seconds. You can help me again, right?"

I said, "Ask me again after you get rid of that cigar. I do not want the smoke in here."

"Do not act tough with me, Theodemir."

"Are you drunk?"

Boris laughed. He continued smoking his cigar.

I asked, "Are you still using those gross drugs Dean gave you?"

"Why can you not just help me?" asked Boris.

I said, "I have already given you, Dean, Mildred, and Greta far too much money. None of you have ever repaid me. I cannot do it anymore. What happened to you? Do you need to pay for more booze, cocaine, or barbiturates? You need to find someone else to ask for money. Enjoy the night with me. Let us return to our friends. They are waiting for us."

"Forget it," said Boris. "Enjoy Italy. You should stay there. Stay away from me." He puffed on his cigar, inhaled the smoke, and then blew smoke from his mouth into my eyes.

"Outstanding," I said.

Boris cursed through clenched teeth as he was leaving the room. The loud impetuous sounds of his footsteps were fading away. The loud sound of the door when it was slammed shut reverberated throughout the manor.

I walked back into the parlor to be with the remaining guests.

Dean said, "Greta, your gown is stunning. You need to tell me how much it is worth. I love it."

"I never wear anything unless it is shockingly costly," said Greta. "People need to see that I only buy the best things."

"I agree," said Mildred. "I think that Dean and I are the same way, but we do not have husbands who buy everything for us. Your husband gives you everything you want, Greta."

"Which husband?" asked Greta. She winked at Mildred as she put Dean's arm around her shoulder.

They all chuckled dryly.

Mildred said, "Everything I buy must be expensive, otherwise it stops being artful. Fashion has created new arenas of competition that can only truly be mastered by those who can afford the best things. Your clothes should always be tearing down the competition and setting new standards of liberation. That is the only way to live."

By eyeing their clothes, I discerned that Greta, Dean, and Mildred were wearing expensive but immodest garments. I had spent so many years around them that I had gained knowledge and learned skills that were useful for correctly judging and examining clothing. The clothes that they were wearing now were lewd and dull. I had seen funeral shrouds that were more attractive and decent than the coverings they were currently wearing.

For years I had been trying to appreciate their postmodernist obsession with lustful indecency, but now it seemed so empty and dangerous. My guests were like all the other irksome masses of modern society. They only cared about flaunting how much money they had, what the prices of their clothes were, and how relevant they still were. I had learned that each of them was always ready to replace the old clothes with new ones every day. They would boast about how unique and different they were, but it was only for attention because they were so obsessed with conforming to the latest modern styles.

I realized that Dean, Greta, and Mildred were the type of people who pretended to be rebellious, but even their faux defiance was a modern habit they had adopted to crush anyone they perceived to be their competition. I had known them for five years, so I thought I understood them well enough to say that they were, in my opinion, absolutely lifeless. If they were shallow and narcissistic, it was only because they believed that becoming those things was fashionable and good. They did not like to admit that they even knew what goodness was. They, like modern society, pretended to be above everything, above ethics, and even above morals. They wanted to subvert and deconstruct anything meaningful, and they replaced it with the only thing they understood. Repudiation. That was not how I wanted to live anymore. I wanted to reject the mediocrity and emptiness that was around me.

I did not want to be with these monotonous beautiful beings, but I did not want to lose them. I wanted now to enjoy this night. Even though I was with them, I thought I could turn the situation into a pleasant one. I still wanted to have fun. I wanted anyone to help me break my boredom. I hated how I desperately desired to receive validation and acceptance from these dangerous devastatingly attractive people.

"How is your husband, Greta?" I asked.

Greta was now whispering and flirting with Dean beside the fireplace. Mildred walked away to gaze at a painting on the wall. She did not respond to my question, and I did not think that she even heard me. I was not sure if anyone here knew I was even in the same parlor as they were. No one made any recognizable indication that they knew I was here. Their behavior is not new. They have treated me like this for years. They have continued to act as if I did not exist.

I hated feeling so bored. I walked to Mildred and noticed that the moonlight was shimmering around her petite thin body. She was wearing a gray satin camisole that exposed her lean midriff. Her skimpy brown shorts ended above her knees and exposed the white skin of her thighs and slender legs. Her brown leather sandals were the same color as the short hair on her head. She did not even turn her head toward me when I approached her. I thought her body was very attractive.

I said, "I want to thank you again, Mildred, for coming here tonight. I was so bored. I have not seen you for months. When was the last time we saw each other?"

Still looking at the paintings, she said, "I saw you when we were in France. You got bit by a wild animal when we were looting a crypt. Your blood went everywhere; it was so astounding. You have such pretty blood. It is such a shame that you are so dull and normal, Theodemir. No, you are not attractive, but your blood is so nice. I should have taken a photograph. Did anyone ever find out what bit you?"

"I cannot help you with that stuff anymore," I said.

"We need you for another job," said Mildred.

"No. I have had enough of that," I said. "I told you this before. I told all of you. I will not help any of you rob any more graves or tombs. I am done with it. I already helped you numerous times. We plundered tombs, mausoleums, and pyramids. We raided burial vaults, stole burial treasure, and we even pilfered many human corpses, too."

Mildred's eyes really looked into mine for the first time this night. My heart started pounding faster in my chest. I smiled at her. She was frowning. Her head turned to face me. She walked closer to me.

"I am leaving soon," I said. "I am going to Italy. I do not know how long I will be gone for, so I will not be around or available for a while."

"You are really going to leave, like a little coward, when we actually need your help?" asked Mildred. She appeared so incredibly insolent and derisive. Her words were snide. She scornfully glowered at me as if she was too tired and disgusted with me to hear what I had to say. She made me feel as if she did not want to waste any of her precious time listening to my opinions that were so unimportant and meaningless compared to her needs.

I said, "I am sorry, Mildred. What can I say? Can we not enjoy the night while we have it? We are together with our friends, we have wine, and the fireplace is warm. I know that we do not agree all the time and we really are very different, but I want to have fun. We have known each other for so long, we should find a way to make a bad situation into a happy one."

"We have not known each other for long. Are you crazy?" asked Mildred.

"Is five years not a long time to know someone?" I asked.

"We barely see each other," said Mildred.

"I try to make plans with you-all, but you never talk to me," I said. "You guys never reply to my letters or messages. None of you do. You-all only see me when you want my money or you need me to help you sell more fake mummies. I do not want to do that anymore, Mildred. I helped you and Dean make disgusting drugs by combining alcohol and exotic medicines with flesh, blood, and bones of stolen mummies and desecrated human corpses. We used dead people to make drugs. We are all humans here in this room, right? Doing those things to corpses should disgust us. I do not know how I allowed myself to be convinced by you to do those horrible things."

"You liked it," Mildred said. "You loved it. It was fun. It was actually exciting. This is who we are. You cannot walk away from this. You and I spent a lot of time together with the dead."

"Are you admitting that we have spent a lot of time together?" I asked.

"True art must be destructive and transient," said Mildred.

I said, "I know what you want. You want me to rob more graves. I have to live with what I did, and I do not want to live that kind of life anymore. We destroy history every time we rob those tombs. We are erasing history."

"History?" asked Mildred. She laughs cynically. "Who actually cares about human history? The past is an illusion, Theodemir. When you see it, you should destroy it. You are wasting your life by researching folklore. You are foolish for writing books about antiquated folkways and black magic. You are exactly like those fools who we sell those fake mummies to. You are the same as the people to whom we sell those ceremonial drugs that have human flesh and bones in them. You still want to believe in magic or traditional convictions. Magic is not real. People like you create systems and religions that only enslave people."

"Are you hearing yourself?" I asked.

Mildred said, "Everything is meaningless, so we must reject traditional standards of beauty. By selling the dead and robbing graves, we have become the new artists and revolutionaries of the modern world. Art should not struggle with the past; it should destroy the past. Our actions and desires need to conform to the contemporary will of modern society. That is how we stay strong and resist tyranny. The weak ones must be eaten or manipulated so that modern society can survive."

I said, "I reject modern society."

"We should not be ashamed of what we do," said Mildred. "We provide services to the idiots and lunatics who actually want to believe that magic spirits are living in the remains of the dead. You cannot blame me for exploiting the ridiculous delusions and superstitions of those freaks."

"At least those freaks believe in something," I said. "Those people take those ceremonial drugs because they believe it will bring them closer to the people that they loved who died. They have beliefs and traditions. They reach out to the people who love them. You have nothing. You believe in nothing and have no faith in anything but your own ambitions."

Mildred sneered at me. She said, "You cannot stay away from this forever. Your hands are going to want to reach into the dead flesh. You want to smell the blood. You want to see the bones. You will be begging to join me. I know people. I am thirty years old. I might not live more than five or ten more years, but I am going to have so much fun. I need to keep living while I can. I will live dangerously, but I will always be a leader."

Mildred shoved me away as she walked past me. She was shorter than me, but her thin arms were strong. I turned around and watched her. She was leaving the parlor. I sat down. I looked out the window and saw that she had left the manor.

Greta and Dean approached me. Greta sat on my lap. I felt her soft posterior on my legs. Her skinny body was so light. I felt the soft white skin of her hands caress my neck. Greta was wearing a long brown silk dressing gown, a beige satin brassiere, and a brown silk skirt. Her silk slippers were gray. Greta's lips were painted crimson. Her whitish blond hair was very long. I was six feet tall, but she and Dean were slightly taller than me. Dean was wearing a gray sweatshirt, gray sweatpants, and beige leather boots. His blond hair is very short.

Dean said, "I think you said that you were going to Italy soon."

"Yes," I said. "I sent you a letter."

"Why would you go there now?" asked Dean.

I said, "I have been having strange dreams."

"That is what I am confused about," said Dean. "In your letter, you said that you have been having dreams about a woman who was lost in your family's castle. Do you actually believe that your dreams were real?"

I said, "The dreams feel real. I have been having these dreams for many months. I saw her trying to escape a castle. In my dreams, I saw a beautiful woman who was trapped in a castle. When I saw her walking around, it looked as if she was in a castle. After a few dreams, I started to realize that the castle that she was trapped in looked like my family's castle. I saw her running around, trying to find a way out. She often appears lost and afraid in my dreams. Sometimes, she walks down the passageways and corridors. Sometimes I feel as if she actually sees me, like she is looking right into my eyes. Sometimes she is not so afraid and sometimes she seems happy to see me, but she is often terrified. She is always incredibly beautiful, even when she is sad. Then, one day, a detective says that he needs my help finding a missing woman. The woman looks like the woman I see in my dreams. The detective said that a woman named Alison went missing after she went to my family's castle. He wants me to help him find her so that he can rescue her if she is in danger. I had to agree. Do you not think this is destiny or a prophecy?"

"I am twenty six years old," said Dean. "I am too old to believe in magic."

"I am twenty four years old," whispers Greta. "Will you take me to your family's castle so I can find a new husband? I never married a nobleman before."

"Do you really want to go to Italy with me?" I asked.

Greta pinched my cheek and cynically laughed. She slowly stood up. She rocked her ample posterior near my face as she sauntered away. She said, "I do not like castles. I have been married twice. The next time I marry someone, I want him to be fun. Castles are not fun."

"Why does the detective need your help?" asked Dean.

I said, "He wants someone from my family to help him; none of my relatives want to help. That other side of my family is very reclusive; they will not talk to the detective unless I am there with him."

Dean stared at me. His eyes were intimidating. The ghost of a suspicious smile lingered on his lips.

"You really do not want to help us rob graves?" asked Dean. "You really do not like the money?"

"I cannot do it anymore," I said.

"What about all the money we make from buying abandoned cemeteries and selling the corpses?" asked Dean. "Would you help us with that?"

I said, "I cannot do it."

"We are going to leave," Dean said. "Be careful in Italy."

Greta gave a delicate but curt wave and a short mischievous giggle.

"Take care," I said.

Dean said, "Theodemir, do not say anything idiotic to the detective."

Dean and Greta quickly walked out of the room. I waited for them to leave the manor. I felt so many strange emotions. I was glad when they left the manor, but I was also incredibly lonely. I could not understand why they were so rude. I had been trying to have a fun with them, but they only wanted to talk about what they wanted. I had always been loyal and generous towards them. I had been trying to become close with them. I wanted us to be good friends. I had wanted them to like me even though I could not tolerate them. I just did not want to be alone.

Now, I sat alone in the parlor. My servants were busy in other parts of the manor.

My guests were gone. I inferred that the real reason that any of them came here this night was to get things from me. I surmised that Greta, Dean, and Mildred only came here to find out if I was snitching on them about the grave robbing, the drug dealing, and the smuggling we had done together. I could understand if they might be suspicious about how I was suddenly speaking to a detective. If they were suspicious about me, they should have had more trust in me. They should have known that I would never do that to them, because I would never want to get in trouble either. This could also have meant that they would be watching and observing me to make certain that they would be safe. I felt like I was now in danger. I did not know whether they were going to attempt to destroy me or just ignore me. If they did think I was informing the police about them, they might want to make me suddenly disappear. I wondered if they were thinking that I was a liability now and if they would try to incriminate me. They might have decided that they would pin all of those crimes only on me to rid themselves of any guilt or culpability.

Greta, Mildred, Dean, and Boris were terrible people, but I still wanted to hold on to them. I liked how they made me feel like I was actually connected to something. I had hoped that I could still be their friend, but I did not want to help them rob any more graves. I hated the way they had been living, yet I still wanted to have their lives. I still wanted to be a part of their lives, but I did not want to join their dirty schemes. A part of me regretted pushing them away. I had thought that I could learn to live like them, but I now felt that they had never really accepted me. Another part of me was glad that I was pulling away from them and everything they represented. I did not belong with them. I needed to find people who would truly accept me. I wanted to be a part of something truly beautiful.

I remembered the feeling of Mildred's sensual hands against my body when she pushed me. I recalled the sensation of Greta's amazing skin against my neck. I thought about how great it felt to actually have physical contact with other human beings.

I shut my eyes and visualized Mildred's eyes looking right into mine. The smell of the smoke from Boris' mouth returned to my memory.

My whole body was trembling.

CHAPTER 2

As I walked into the antechamber, I saw the detective leaning against a black wall.

"What are you doing here, Roman?" I asked.

Roman was the detective who I had been talking to about Alison and the dreams. He was wearing a wide black leather trench coat that appeared slightly too big for him. He was somewhat taller than me, but not significantly. When he took off his coat, I discerned that his slender body also had a lean outline and a masculine shape. He appeared rather lanky and skinny, but his body had agile and nimble aspects. Roman was wearing a black leather doublet and a black leather shirt. His trousers, boots, and gloves were black leather, too. His short wavy red hair was lush and shiny, and it would glimmer with rich autumnal crimson colors when the lights shined on it. His hairline was low, and his brow appeared mellow but courageous. His eyebrows were long and thin, but they still had strong masculine characteristics. His irises were amber, and the lines of his eyes were elegant yet humble. The quiet stately expression of his eyes exuded confidence. When he turned his head, his profile was stunningly statuesque and majestic. The profile of his tall narrow nose is straight and sharp like a cliff or pyramid rising to touch his smooth straight forehead. His face was gaunt yet handsome. His sharp cheekbones protruded and were prominent. His sharp chin had a brave aspect, and his jawline was wide. His lips showed relaxed optimism. I had never seen that kind of good-natured mood on a person's face before.

Roman said, "Your servants allowed me to come in. I was waiting for you." His voice was low yet mellow.

"Roman, why are you here?"

He stepped slowly to me, examining me with his eyes. He smiled and said, "I needed to see if you were safe."

"You mean to say that you needed to make sure that I was not being manipulated," I said. "You have been watching me, have you not?"

"I am investigating your family," he said. "That means I need to observe them, even you."

"I thought that you were investigating the disappearance of that woman," I said.

"Alison," he said.

"Yes," I said. "Alison, the Austrian heiress."

"Theodemir, I was thrilled when you agreed to work with me, but I've been gumshoeing for too long to just neglect all my instincts now."

"What are your instincts telling you now?"

"You could be in danger. You could already be compromised, or someone could be shadowing you, too. Or, you might already know where she is. Yes, something is telling me that you have already seen this woman before."

"I had nothing to do with her disappearance," I said. "Is that what you came here for? You wanted to see my place so that you could find out if she was here?" I did not want to tell him about my dreams of her. My friends already had thought I was a lunatic for taking those dreams seriously. Saying that I have been dreaming about the woman who was missing would make me look insane or guilty.

He said, "I already discovered some interesting things about you, Theodemir. I have heard some macabre rumors."

"What kind of rumors?" I was already imagining ways to throttle him.

"Do you know why I asked you to help me find the heiress?" he asked.

"You said that you wanted a historian who was close to the family to help you do some research about the Fiendilkfjeld region while you were there," I said. "My expertise with paranormal research intrigued you. You said that my experience with researching the rampant murderous cults that have been roving across Europe for the past decade would be useful to your investigation."

"That is correct," said Roman. "I believe that someone in your family, on the noble Fiendilkfjeld side, could be the culprit and that they are linked to those cults. You know how they behave. You can think like them, and you can understand their beliefs and taboos."

"What are you saying?" I asked.

"I know that you are good at stealing dead bodies," he said. "I needed to know if you were also good at stealing living people, too."

I asked, "Why would you say that?"

"Say what?" He asked.

"What did you say?" I asked, nervously.

"Nothing," he said. "I wanted to ask you about the woman. You seemed to know her when I showed you her picture." He took out a small photograph of the missing woman from his pocket and gave it to me.

Holding the photograph, I looked at the face of the woman who had been visiting me in my dreams for so many nights. I was dumbfounded and alarmed when I saw her again. Roman had showed me this photograph when I first met him. I had stared at it for so long when he first showed it to me, and now I was staring longingly at it again.

"You really seem to have a connection with that woman," he said. "You look at her like someone would look at their wife or lover."

"I am sorry," I said. I gave the photograph back to him "You must forgive me. She is just so beautiful. I have never seen her before. I have only seen her in the photograph that you have shown me." I could not tell him that I wanted to find her because I was infatuated with her. I wanted to find the woman who looked like the woman who I had been seeing in my dreams. I needed to see this person who looked identical to her. That was not crazy. I was following my destiny. I said, "I want to help you find her. I really do."

"Will you allow me to search your estate?" he asked. "Let me look around so that I can sleep easily."

"Is that necessary?" I asked.

"Do you think that I will find something I should not find?" he asked.

"Is there anything I can do to make this go away?" I asked. "You do not need to check my estate. She is not here."

"What are you implying?" he asked.

I chuckled nervously. I said, "I do not know what I am implying."

"Theodemir, you can relax," Roman said. "Everything has already been taken care of regarding your security. Nothing bad is going to happen to you. Anything about your past, private life, and businesses is no one's concern. It is all set."

"It is?" I asked, astonished.

"The noble Fiendilkfjeld family really cares about you," he said. "They told me that they want to see you soon. They do not even want to talk to me unless you are there, too. They want to see this whole mess go away as fast as possible, and they are eager to reconnect with you."

"What is happening?" I asked.

"We should talk somewhere more private," Roman said. "We should talk about the other side of your family. You really do not know anything about them, correct?"

I said, "I know that we who are born of the Fiendilkfjeld family are descended from ancient dukes, lords, barons, and wealthy knights. I do not know much about the noble side of the Fiendilkfjeld family. I do not know what I would even call my father and mother. I am not certain what I am. My side of the family did not inherit any noble ranks or royal titles. My mother is rich and she comes from a very wealthy family. I knew her side of the family well. We drifted away from my father's aristocrat relatives who live in Italy. My father is closely related to them, but he never wanted to be an aristocrat. He did not want to be a nobleman. There were others in our family who were like him who renounced the nobility and their noble status. They wanted to live more like regular common people, but with a lot more money and property. My father and mother already had a lot of money, and then they made more money together. My father never told me why he renounced his family and the noble ranks."

We walked into a private chamber upstairs. Inside, Roman began telling me about the noble Fiendilkfjeld family. We locked the doors and covered the windows, for privacy.

Roman said, "The noble Fiendilkfjeld family does not officially control any land in Italy. The region of Fiendilkfjeld is named in honor of your family, but they hold no official power over it. They are a symbol of strength and national pride. They are a link of solidarity and honor between the main government and the people. The noble Fiendilkfjeld family does act as guardians and official advisors to the councils and committees of their region. There are many sections within the region of Fiendilkfjeld that are private property controlled by the family. They give money to many charities, they provide support with political fundraising, and they help with matters of diplomacy. They provide protection and maintenance for many historical and religious sites in Italy, too. The family gives funding and aid to museums, archives, libraries, and farms. They have influence over the police and other official figures of authority. With approval, they may even have influence over the military. The citizens of the Fiendilkfjeld region love your family because they see them as a symbol of power and bravery. Many people appreciate that your family upholds and respects the ancestral pagan traditions, holidays, and ceremonies of the region. Your family has cultivated a place where the spiritual needs of the locals are valued and recognized. Their culture is being preserved, and the people resonate with that. This has generated major public support for your family. The region of Fiendilkfjeld is a wealthy territory and it is a great place to live. There are areas within it that have their problems, but the region is a generally quiet isolated area."

"Can it really be that great there?" I asked. "You seem to really like it."

"They take care of me," he said.

"Why would you get involved with this case?" I asked. "You think one of my relatives captured a woman, and you want me to help you catch them. You think that I can guide you to where they will strike next. What happened to your loyalty to my family?"

"I never said I was loyal to them," Roman said. "I need to prove my autonomy every now and then, show them that I cannot be controlled so easily. There is nothing wrong with gaining leverage on those you are close to. I have been black-mailing your family for years."

"I understand," I said. "You think that my family will give you a much larger pay off if you actually do find evidence that could truly link them to the woman's disappearance. If you find the woman, you will be a hero. You could use her to squeeze more money from my family if it turns out that one of my relatives actually took her. If you do not find her, you could go away with the money they already gave you to handle things."

"You have a great imagination," he said. "Why would I be telling you all of that if it were true?"

"You want me to cooperate with your plans. You need me to know that I am in a similar situation with you. Roman, you are a blackmailer, an extortionist, and a crooked detective. You have dirt on me and you need me to know my place in this relationship. I need to keep quiet about what I see and hear when I go to Italy with you. You would not want me to tell anyone anything about what I might learn about you."

"We have an agreement? Each of us will never share information about the things we know or will learn about each other?" He asked.

"I agree," I said. "What do we do with the woman when we find her?"

"We will bring her back to her parents. The woman's family said that she went missing after she left to visit someone at the Fiendilkfjeld castle. So far, your family has been uncooperative with the investigation. I have several witnesses who said that they have recently seen her around the castle and the village cemetery. If we find the missing woman, we will return her to her family. We will simply say that your family was not responsible if they decide to pay me well enough."

"Why would you risk making my family upset with you when they have already been good to you?" I asked.

Roman said, "Your noble family members are not saints, Theodemir. I am sorry to tell you this, but I know that they are involved with blackmail, extortion, bribery, and many sordid dealings. They have caused a lot of trouble for me and my partners in the past, too. I am being forced to work on this case. This is my assignment. This is the kind of business relationship I have with your family. Sometimes we help each other and sometimes we fight each other. You can say it is a symbiotic relationship, but I really do not think that would apply. Sometimes I like doing the right thing, and other times I do not. They take comfort in the fact that they know what I am."

"They would rather have you investigating them instead of someone who would actually do more damage. They are familiar and comfortable with you because they understand you and your desires," I said.

"It is like how you feel with your friends," Roman said. "You hate your friends, but you understand them, so you are comfortable with them. You do not want to lose them because you recognize them and they have shared experiences with you. They provide something familiar and safe, in a strange and dangerous way. You are a little more complicated now, because you are starting to doubt yourself. You are starting to think that you might deserve better friends."

"How long have you been watching me?" I asked.

"I need to leave," he said. "I will see you soon."

I watched Roman leave as I was imagining ways to rip his face off his skull. I did not want to actually hurt him because he was a detective and there was no way I would get away with it. I meditated on what he had been saying to me. He knew about the grave robbing and looting, but he was going to keep it a secret. Someone had paid him off to keep me safe. I assumed that it was my parents or someone from the noble side of the family. Roman was afraid that I would learn terrible things about him when we were in Italy together. He wanted me to make sure that I would be silent, too. Perhaps this was just his way of staying safe and distant from people. I guessed that he was the type of person who learned everything about the people he was working with. There was something about the way he spoke that made me feel as if he actually wanted to protect me.

CHAPTER 3

Near the end of October, Roman came to my estate again. It was time to begin our journey to northern Italy. When Roman was inside, I greeted him in the parlor.

"I did some investigating, too," I said. I tossed a folder at him.

Roman deftly caught the folder and inspected its files, photographs, and documents.

He asked, "What is this?"

"This, Roman, is proof that you are not such a bad guy," I said. "You wanted me to be scared around you. You wanted to keep me in a position where you could hold all the cards and easily navigate around me. You should have been an actor."

"Get to the point, Theodemir. I am no actor, but I can tell when a bit is not playing."

I said, "Roman, you are not just investigating this case because you were forced into it. No. That was only one small part of the reason why you took this case and why you refused to back away when my family bribed you to drop the case; I am certain that they must have tempted you with a consider amount of money, on top of the money they have already paid you to be lenient with them. You have your duties to the authorities. You have your natural curiosity. You also have a heart. You personally know the missing woman. You are one of Alison's friends. You want to find her because you are attached to her. You did not want more people to see this side of you. I am curious about this. You were putting on a show to my family, and me, by pretending that you were only searching for the woman as a way to leverage more money from us. You care about that woman, and you do not want anyone to use that against you or her. You are worried that your connection with her could cause her harm if she is still alive. Am I getting close to the truth, or am I already there? Stop me when I have reached the truth."

"You have said enough," he said.

"Good."

"Are you going to use this against me now?"

"No, Roman. I respect you."

"What?"

"Roman, you are fighting for a friend. You are a man who is brave and strong. There is so much light around you. People like you are rare. I want us to be friends," I said.

"When I saw the way that you were looking at her photograph when we first met," said Roman, "I noticed that you were looking at her like she was your friend, too. I thought that you knew her. I suspected that you might have had something to do with her disappearance, but I was wrong. I realized that you also, for some reason, wanted to make sure that she was safe. I want to rescue Alison if she is in peril. I believe that she is still alive. She must be. I need to protect her."

"Why would someone take her?" I asked. "Ransom?"

"So far, no demands have been made. Her family has not been contacted, and Alison has been missing for many months," said Roman.

"You are sure that someone took her?" I asked. "Did she run away with someone?"

"I knew her. She would not run off with someone."

"How do you know that?"

"That is not who she is."

"What are you trying to tell me?"

Roman turned his back toward me. He seemed troubled by something. He sighed and lowered his head. He whispered, "Alison is pure, gentle, maidenly, and kind. Alison is twenty two years old, she loves her family, and she loves the people that also love her back. She would never abandon the people who love her."

I said, "She loves her family and respects their traditions."

He said, "Alison would be getting married, not running away with someone. She would never disappear without any traces of her whereabouts."

"She sounds too good to be true."

"Do you know a lot of woman who go suddenly and mysteriously vanishing without telling their friends or family where they are going?"

"Yes," I said. "I have known a lot of women who had many different lives. Some had no lives at all, they were just like ghosts. They simply walked out the door one day, and they were gone forever. They could walk out your life and you would never hear from them again. You would never know if they were alive or dead."

"Who have you been associating with, Theodemir? The people you have met seem to have been very weird. I guess I should not talk," Roman said as he paced around the room. "I am twenty six years old, and I have met a lot of people just like that. Everything always moved so fast for me in my life. Everything came crashing toward me, ever since I was young. I had to grow up very quickly and learn to use my mind. I grew up rich and always wanted to help society, but I do not think that I have ever met anyone I could really trust, except for Alison. We have been friends ever since we were young."

"You trust her, but she has gone, too," I said.

"She did not run away from me," he said, turning to face me. He appeared bold and stubborn. "We really need to leave."

"Roman, I want you to know that I do care about her. I do not know Alison, but I want to find her, too. From what you are saying, she sounds like someone who is worth rescuing. I guess we should leave soon so that we do not waste any more time."

"You do know her, do you not?" asked Roman.

"Pardon?"

"While I was listening to your conversations with your friends, I overheard some confusing talk about your dreams. I did not understand what you were saying," he said.

"You would think I was crazy if I told you."

"I must insist."

"Why?"

"I have worked with occultists before, Theodemir," said Roman. "I have had temporary partners who said that they were clairvoyant, psychic, telepathic, or soothsayers. Most of time they were frauds, but sometime they were right. When they were right about anything concerning a case, they were astonishingly precise and eerily accurate. Even if they were all liars, they did offer great help from time to time."

"Magic is not real," I said. "You are confused."

"I think that you are right," he said. "Only, I do not think that you actually believe that. You have written books about cultural superstitions, witchcraft, curses, and pagan rituals. A part of you must believe, or want to believe, that magic is real. If you have been having dreams about her, maybe you can provide a unique perspective that can help us find Alison."

"My dreams were not important. They were nothing."

"We are very similar, Theodemir. We are both trying to hide our connection to Alison for mysterious reasons. What is your link with her?"

I said, "What do you want me to say, Roman? Should we not leave now?"

He said, "I need you to give me a sign that she is still alive, Theodemir. Please, even if your dreams were nothing, they could really give me the determination and hope I need to keep my sanity. Even if magic is not real, I need you to give me some motivation. Help me believe that she is still alive and that we have a chance to rescue her. I need you with me on this. Tell me that you have been seeing her in your dreams."

"You care about her deeply," I said.

"You saw her, did you not?"

"In my dreams, I see someone who looks like her. I have been having dreams about her for many months."

"You saw Alison in your dreams, Theodemir. It must have been her." Roman circled around me. "What was she doing? Was she alive?"

I said, "I saw her in a castle. She knew me. She knew my name. She was trapped in a castle."

"She has been reaching out to you!" He stopped walking. His eyes appeared to be searching mine. I wondered if he was trying to find her within my eyes. A bitter expression changed his eyes. I felt as if his resentful gaze was attempting to mentally dig into my soul through my eyes, as if he had thought he could find her there, like he thought that I had caged Alison within my skull.

"You seem upset," I said.

"What gave you that idea?"

"Roman, you are jealous, are you not? She comes to my dreams, not yours."

"Your ribald remark was unbecoming," he said in a huff. "I strongly urge you to behave maturely during the investigation."

Roman might have been feeling helpless in that moment, and he must have hated me for that. My dreams might have reminded him that she was still missing. He had said that he need my visions to help him find her. He wanted me to give him hope and inspiration during the investigation. As long as I was still seeing her in my dreams, she might have still been alive. This also associated me with her disappearance and might have made me a target of his frustration. People are so juvenile, even when they are being chivalrous.

CHAPTER 4

Roman and I were driving toward northern Italy. I was letting him drive, because I had always hated modern vehicles and did not care to use them often. I thought that he would prefer to drive, anyway. He seemed, to me, like the kind of person who wanted to appear like he was always in control. His masculine demeanor exuded a chivalrous kind of devotion, as if he was proud to show that he could protect and guide others. I imagined that his ability to easily manipulate and deceive people was connected to a need for information and privacy.

It felt as if Roman was so distant from me even when he seemed to be so close. The more I knew about him, the more I felt as if he were so far away. He spoke to me about himself, he told me about how he had become a detective, and how he had studied and worked hard at an early age to become one. He had focused on that one path for his entire life. Everything he researched and studied, his education, and all his work for many years was devoted to that goal. With his dedication and important connections with people in the field, he was able to do what he had always wanted.

He told me these things, yet I was ensnared by many contradictions and inconsistencies with his personality and characteristics. The way he spoke about himself, the way he described himself, and the way he behaved were all things that were pushing me away. I could not understand him, and I did not feel as if I was actually uncovering anything about him. Every story he told opened up new questions and mysteries. Maybe I was ignorant or missing something obvious about his nature, but there were times when I questioned the validity and sincerity of everything he was showing me about himself.

Roman said, "I always wanted to help people. I wanted to use my influence and money to become someone important."

"Why did you become a detective if you wanted to be important?" I asked. "You should have been an artist or a leader."

"There are many different ways that someone can become important," he said. "Being important means being the one person who can actually see something that no one else will ever see."

"You became a detective because you wanted to get information about people," I said. "You wanted to be the only one with all the answers about the lives of others."

"I am not interested in people's lives," he said. "The more you know about people, the more their lives infect your own. You can catch their thoughts or emotions just by looking at them."

"Do you feel like you are easily influenced by other people's emotions?" I asked.

"I never stay around anyone long enough for their feelings to change me."

"What about me?"

He said, "We are going to be working together, but you and I will not be together often. Each of us will go in different directions. We will have our own responsibilities and interests. We will only reconnect when we have enough evidence or we find something important. You search in one direction and I search in another direction. I cannot have you following me everywhere, and I am sure that you would not want me to give you orders all the time."

"What do you want me to do?" I asked.

"Tell me about your dreams. Then, we will split off. You will walk around, talk to people, feel everything around you with your senses, and try to use your head," he said.

I asked, "How should I use my head? You want me to try to think like the person who captured the woman. Of course, we are only assuming that she has been captured. What if she just got lost and then got attacked by an animal or something?"

"Use your mind. You tell me what happened to her."

"Was Alison seen at the castle?"

"Yes."

"There should have been guards there to protect her. How did anyone let this happen?"

"Right, so how is this possible?"

I said, "Someone, who knew when she would be alone, had to have taken her away from those who could have protected her."

"What else?" asked Roman.

"If she went to the village, someone could have taken her when she was there."

"Remember, no one has found her body," he said. "What does that mean?"

"Either someone hid her corpse, or she is a prisoner," I said. "Do we know anything else about the circumstances?"

"We have nothing else," said Roman. "She was seen at a village and at the castle."

"Did she not have guards when she was in the village?" I asked.

"She had guards."

"This is strange. You are telling me that she suddenly vanished. No one saw anything unusual happen to her?"

"Right, so that means that some of the information we have is false. We need to know where the lies are so we can begin finding the truth."

Roman stopped the car several times, but we were always moving as fast as we could to get to the castle. We continued rolling down the roads, and I was looking at the beauty around us.

"There is so much beauty in Europe," said Roman.

I said, "Yes. Europe holds true strength that keeps people safe and sustains the values of those who hear this land speaking."

"You sound like the aristocrats in your family's castle," he said. "You all have an affinity with the land of your ancestors, especially the region of Fiendilkfjeld and its castle."

"I wish that I had truly been given the opportunity to know that side of my family better," I said. "I am glad that you found me. You have given me that opportunity."

"We found each other," he said. "It could have been our destiny."

"Do you believe that people can be destined for something? This journey, was it fate?"

"What do you mean?"

I said, "I am starting to remember something strange about a curse in my family. It could have been a prophecy. I think my family believed in prophecies, and they might have believed that we were surrounded by an unnatural destiny."

"I still do not understand," said Roman.

"I guess it was nothing. I must have been confused."

"If you are asking whether or not everything is predetermined, I would have to say that strong people change the future," said Roman.

"So, you believe that human beings can have an influence on fate," I said.

"Would that not depend on your perception of fate?"

I said, "I know that there are a lot of people who want to talk to their dead relatives. People see fate as something they can control. They try to change things about the world around them, especially when what they want to change involves death. People die so often, Roman, and people leave everyone behind when they die. There are a lot of people who still believe that there is a reason for their lives and deaths. They want to bring those whom they loved back from the lands of death and nothingness. Everyone is seeking resurrection of someone or something in many different ways, but they would never openly admit to believing in magic. The dead are silent."

Roman said, "You want to know why there is so much pain yet so little happiness."

"I have met so many people who are trying to contact the dead. They are searching for the other sides of reality or another dimension. All their effort is in vain. Sometimes it means nothing to them; some people are just searching without any reason. There are a lot of lonely people who are all in pain," I said.

"And yet, they do not reach to the people around them who are still alive," said Roman. "Some people say that they have contacted their dead loved ones."

"There is no evidence to prove that it happened. There is no formula or technique that can be replicated to get those results, if it were possible to do so," I said.

"Maybe only pain stays here on this earth," said Roman. "This is a world of emptiness and suffering. When we die, we can never return. Only the darkness and the sins remain. You have to live well and make sure that you leave nothing behind that could haunt someone else."

"Death is always haunting," I said. "Even if people knew there was a hereafter, there would still be sorrow when someone dies."

Roman said, "If we lived in a world where people knew that dying or death was not permanent, there would be chaos and mayhem. No one would fear death. No one would respect it. Everything would become corrupted. There is a reason why this world is the way it is."

"The world is already corrupt because of the emptiness around us," I said. "We live in a world without meaning. Why should we live if we are going to be erased forever one day? We cannot even talk to those who have died before us. Nothing we do has brought back the dead."

"Humans are not meant to have that kind of power or knowledge," said Roman. "You should not focus on these kinds of questions. No one has any answers."

"I do not know now if I have ever actually tried hard enough to genuinely have faith in anything," I said.

CHAPTER 5

Italy was magnificent. Its landscapes were sublime and inspiring. Ruins of Roman fortresses slouched over its hills and plains. We passed through its luscious fields, valleys, and forests. Fogbound, the rivers around us evoked a foreboding divination within my mind. Like ice dropping into my veins, this divination was an eerie suspicion warning me that we would upset something that was sacred and taboo. I wondered if somehow we had attracted something dangerous just by unknowingly looking at it.

Peculiar shadows extended across the landscape. A diffuse orange glow hung in the air like a creepy haze lingering around me and everything else I could see. Fog rolled across the ground and the surfaces of the lakes.

We drove into deep clouds of rainy darkness. Unnatural shadows flew around us as we entered a long tunnel. I thought those shadows were only swarms of bats flying away. We passed through many tunnels, and the tunnels were long and empty. I felt as if we were going farther downward because the darkness around me was so disorienting. The silence disturbed me.

There were no other cars around us. We were always the only people on the roads, and our car was the only vehicle. The ride was taking much longer than I had predicted it would. Empty tunnels stretched out for miles. The bridges over which we drove extended over valleys that were far too deep. We drove into chilly fog that was so thick. Sometimes, Roman was driving the car incredibly slowly so that we would not drive off a cliff. Other times, he was driving too fast. I wanted to say something to Roman, but I was petrified with doubt and worry. I was afraid that I would be bringing us into darker dangers if I had said something then. I do not know how long we had been driving for. It had felt like hours.

"How long have we been driving?" I asked.

"I do not know."

"Everything around us seems so unnatural, do you not think so, Roman?"

"Be calm." Roman stopped the car. He said, "I am going to look at a map."

"You do not remember how to get to the castle?"

"Strangely, no. I know I did know the way, but I forgot."

"We are in northern Italy, right?"

"We should be, but I do not remember this area. Nothing looks familiar to me."

"I do not know where I am anymore," I said. "My memories are foggy. I cannot even keep my eyes open."

Roman said, "Close your eyes and try to calm yourself. I will find out where we are."

I did close my eyes. I felt so exhausted and drained. There was only darkness around me. My body did not correctly feel like my own. My thoughts were so far away from me. Each of my senses floated out of me. I was hearing thoughts that were not mine. Sounds and even the feel of my own clothes on my body were all foreign. I was dizzy and nauseated. I felt as if I was receiving thoughts and sensations through someone else.

Alison floated out of the darkness. White light was glowing around her. She smiled. Then, I saw her running through a dark stone castle. All the windows and doors were covered by iron bars. She screamed as she was trying to find a way out of the castle. I saw her in narrow passageways and secret chambers. Alison ran through battlements and moved up and down towers. There was no place for her to go, and no way to escape the grim castle. The towers, crenellated walls, and battlements were too high up from ground; the doors and windows were all blocked; and something inside was keeping her from leaving. She looked as if she was being chased by something. Someone threw her into a dungeon, and she begged for mercy.

I woke up when I heard Roman saying my name. I opened my eyes and turned to him.

"I cannot find the region of Fiendilkfjeld on any map," he said.

"What?"

"The Fiendilkfjeld castle is not on any of the maps I checked."

I asked, "How is that possible?"

"We need to find someone who knows where it is."

"Why have we been so alone?"

"What?"

"I have not seen any other humans for hours."

"I do not want to think about anything else until I find out where I am and where we need to go."

Roman drove for several minutes before we finally found someone walking out of an old cemetery. I could see him talking to the man while I was sitting in the car. When Roman returned to the car, he said, "That man said that he never heard of Fiendilkfjeld."

"That cannot be right. He was lying."

"He said that he never heard of the castle or your family."

"We should find someone else," I said. "We need to get out of here. There is nothing around us except trees."

"We should have seen the castle by now," said Roman. "I forget how long I have been driving for. I feel like I did not sleep for days."

"Rest before you drive again."

"I can drive."

"Why have we only seen one human being during this entire ride?"

Roman said, "We are tired. We are not thinking clearly."

"Then should you drive?

"Relax."

I shut my eyes and saw Alison again. Her long fair blond hair was shimmering. Moonlight glistened across her pale white skin. She reached down from the shadows with her delicate hands and long thin fingers.

CHAPTER 6

After driving around northern Italy for what felt like hours, we finally found Fiendilkfjeld village. It felt strange to me, but I knew where we were at the very second that we arrived. I suddenly remembered this village and how to reach the castle.

I had been confused and disturbed by the fact that Roman and I were alone during the entire ride before we arrived here. The memory of those empty roads and uninhabited valleys was unnerving for me. I wanted to see another human being and forget about the journey I had experienced to get here. I had thought that we would never see other people again until we entered the village. Rising into the night sky, waves of smoke floated out of the numerous chimneys of the village homes. The smoke made me relax, because it was a signal that there were people living and cooking in this village. I felt relieved to finally see a sign that there were other human beings near me, but I did not know these people and did not want them to hate me.

Fiendilkfjeld village was surrounded by rolling hills, deep valleys, and dark forests. Beyond the forests, massive mountains rose over the village and loomed through the darkness. The mountains towered high up into the night sky. The sky rained loudly. The forceful rain battered the rooves and walls of the village homes and buildings. Thunder crackled in the air. Flashes of lightning slashed through the shadows that had settled into the village. Whistling, driving gusts of strong wind pushed against the village. The leaning, broken monuments around us were dripping wet. Strange shrieks rose out of the dark forest. Unearthly groans rolled down the mountains. Unnatural whispers fluttered around the valleys.

"I need to sleep," said Roman. "I will find a place for us to rest."

We found lodging in an antiquated pothouse. Our rooms were above a quiet little tavern. Roman had his own room, and I stayed in mine. This inn was small, but our lodgings were comfortable.

Alone in my room, I dreamt of Alison again. She was the most gorgeous woman I had ever seen in my entire life. The perfection of her attractiveness was flawless and without match. The way her nimble limbs elegantly moved exuded symmetry and poise. Her womanly figure embodied repose and propriety. The natural movements of her very skinny body manifested ease and deftness. Such consummate beauty was difficult for me to comprehend; it left me feeling inadequate but inspired. I felt as if I had seen what I was missing in my life, but I could still not define it. I meditated on the future, on how I was supposed to continue living my life without someone so beautiful beside me? The only consolations for me were these dreams; these dreams might end if we do rescue her or if she were to die. I was not sure if she was still alive. If she was dead, then I needed to know who this woman was and why she looked so much like Roman's Alison. I felt as if I had seen a vision of everything pure and good, but I knew that I could never attain those things for myself. I was certain that I could never hold her or hear her tell me that she would be mine. I wondered if she knew that I wanted to be hers. I wanted to touch her hair, but she was gone before I could move a single muscle.

Then, I was not sure if I actually ever really knew what beauty was. Alison had appeared so pure and innocent that she resembled a divine light that pushed away all the shadows around me. When she was gone, I was back in the abyss. I wondered if I had ever, even for a moment, truly walked among that kind of light before. I knew that I had seen something unique that made me think about myself. I was caught in a spiritual wave at the edge of the duality within my own soul.

I opened my eyes and saw the narrow room and tilted walls around me. Thunder crackled. Blue beams of light, from the flashes of lightning, shined into the dark gloom around me. The wind whistled as it clawed against the outside of the walls. The rhythmic sounds of all the ceaseless rain droplets hitting the building were hard and raspy. Cascading rivulets of water slid down the glass of the windows. Echoing and multiplying in my mind were the harsh sounds of the descending hooves of rain and the crashing waves of water beating the outside of the tavern. The howling night sky was now raining faster and stronger. More rain was falling, and I did not know when the rain would stop.

For hours, a profuse shower of rain fell from the sky; I was sitting in my room, listening to it crash against the inn. I could not return to sleep. The rainstorm became louder. I heard the terrifying roars of the thunderstorm.

I was pacing around the small room, looking out the windows, and sitting on my bed. When I stepped to the window, I thought I heard someone behind me. Lightning flashed and I saw my reflection on the window. I saw my skinny body and long blond straight hair. I flinched and screamed at my reflection, but immediately laughed nervously when I recognized myself. My dark blue eyes looked back at mine.

I decided to walk around. I wanted to leave this room. I feared that I would lose my sanity if I stayed here any longer. I never liked being alone for too long. When I was alone, I would feel all the loneliness and emptiness surrounding me too vividly.

I was going to touch the doorknob, but I heard something on the other side of the door. I heard scratching and eerie chuckling. An intimidating sound, like something was scraping their sharp nails against the outside of the wooden door, chilled my bones. My heart was pounding faster and I could not breathe. The sinister sounds of something gasping and gurgling behind the door oozed into my ears. I tried to scream. My knees hit the floor. I crawled away from the door. I tried to scream again, but no sound came. I did not want to shut my eyes for a second. Mocking sounds of impish laughter assaulted my senses, and I screamed as loud as I could.

I was alone and lying on the floor for a while. I was listening to the thunderstorm while I waited for the night to end. I wanted to see the blue light of morning. As more time passed, I presumed that the person who was making those noises at my door was a drunkard who had been trying to find his own room. I felt ridiculous and silly for allowing myself to be so manipulated by my own anxiety. I hated my juvenile weaknesses and fears. I told myself that there was nothing bad in the dark, but I hated being vulnerable and alone. I could not let go of my suspicions and fears, because I never really knew what or who was making those sounds, and that uncertainty was troubling.

CHAPTER 7

When I opened my eyes, I did not remember when I had last fallen asleep. I did not remember being asleep or dreaming anything. If I had been dreaming, I did not remember what those dreams were or what they had shown me. I felt as if I had blinked and suddenly the darkness around me was gone. Yellowish violet sunlight spread through the windows of my room. The room was still dim, but the light allowed me to see things clearly. The windows were not covered, but I thought that I had covered them. I remembered that I had looked out the windows the night before, but I was now not sure if I had covered them or not.

I looked out a window and smiled. From the window, I had an astonishing view of valleys, hills, sinuous canals, small paths, narrow roads, the canopy of a forest in the distance, and a faraway wall of gigantic mountains and soaring pinnacles reaching the clouds in the sky. These distant mountains curved around the outside of everything I saw.

I remembered that I had been in this village once before, but I could not recall anything but short vague images of it from my memory. It was almost as if I were seeing the village for the first time, because I knew that I was not the same person I used to be when I had first come here. I could barely recognize that person.

I was proud and felt glad to be in a place that had been dedicated to my family. I was standing in a living monument created to honor my blood. This village and the entire Fiendilkfjeld region was mine, yet it was under the true power and authority of the Italian government. This place felt, to me, like a testament to the strength and vision of the rulers and warriors who had defended this land hundreds of years ago. This village reminded me of where I came from, the purpose of those connected to this land, and the potential that this land always will have. I wanted to believe that the people of this land were like my blood, too.

From what I had been told by my parents, my ancestors were Italians, French, English, German, and Scandinavians. We had lineage and roots connected to great rulers, warriors, and conquerors of the past. As I looked at this astonishing village, I thought about the greatness of ancient Roman leaders, the grand ideals of the medieval era, and the artists and philosophers who created so much beauty on this land. I had never felt so proud or at peace with myself until now, finally here again. I could not wait until I reached the castle of my ancestors.

I wanted to clothe myself with new garments, but I did not bring anything else to wear. I had planned to buy new clothes after I reached the castle. I assumed that my family would allow me to stay with them. I wanted to ask Roman whether or not we were allowed to stay in the castle. I was sure that they would allow us to stay there, but now I was not entirely confident about it. I was sure that I would find a way to get new suitable clothes.

I began to think about what type of people the noble side of my family was. I pondered what their reactions might be when they saw me. I was afraid that they might think that I was not good enough for them. I hoped that they would not think that I was trying to insult or harm them.

I did not know what I would do if I were to discover that one of my family members was responsible for Alison's disappearance. A part of me believed that I was betraying my family by being connected with this investigation.

I was starting to wonder if I made a wrong decision by connecting myself with this case. I did not want to get in trouble, and I did not want to break any code or law. I was related to the people involved with the disappearance of an heiress. I pondered whether or not I was too close to things. Another part of me considered the fact that I would not actually be doing much except providing consultation. I would be like a mediator so that Roman could communicate well with my family. Also, Roman valued my dreams because they encouraged him. I also considered the very important fact that Roman was continuing the investigation to rescue his friend and rattle my family a tad.

I inferred that this case was merely personal for Roman, and that he only wanted Alison. He might have known that he would never be allowed to attack my family, because he was too deep in the darkness with them. From what Roman had told me, he and my family had been protecting each other for too long. If he were to incriminate them any further, he might be destroyed. That is how I was understanding the situation. If Roman was doing all of this merely for his own curiosity, that was understandable. I could not understand why anyone in my family would take the risk of capturing someone and holding them as a hostage. What this was all for was a question that burned into my heart. No one else in my family wanted to be involved with this. I had been the only one who came forward and offered services. No one stopped me. No one had warned me of any dangers.

I wanted to save Alison, too. I wanted to know who she was. I had seen a woman who looked like her in my dreams, but I did not know why I was seeing her. I wanted to understand this strange coincidence. The woman from my dreams had captivated me, and her beauty inspired me to follow this mystery.

I remembered that I should have been with Roman by now. I had lost track of time. I accepted the fact that I would need to go with the clothes I was wearing. All of the clothes I was wearing were black. I wore a long fur coat, tight leather trousers, leather boots, leather gloves, a silk vest, and a silk shirt. My black necktie was silk and my black top hat was leather. Each of my boots were pointed at the toe. The collar of my shirt was tall. My belt was black leather, too. Even the buttons of my garments were black. My clothes still looked clean and presentable enough, so I assumed that I would be forgiven for continuing to wear them until I arrived at the castle. After looking at myself, I began to wonder whether I should tell anyone in this village who I was. Obviously, I looked like an aristocrat, so I would need to come up with a good excuse. I did not want to reveal my identity to anyone in the village yet. I decided that I would ask Roman for his advice on this matter.

After I left my tiny room, I looked around me, hoping to avoid the strange person who had been at my door the previous night. The hall was empty and very quiet. I was afraid that I would attract the attention of that person if I were to make too much noise. I stealthily moved down the hall. I flinched at every creak and groan that the wooden stairs made as I walked down. When I arrived at the barroom downstairs, I noticed that there were several people already there.

A man, who appeared to be fifty years old, was standing by the fireplace. This man was wearing black garments, and he was holding a meerschaum in his right hand. His vest, trousers, and jacket appeared to be neat and humble yet morose.

A woman sat in a chair beside the man with the pipe. This woman appeared to be maybe fifty years old or older; it was hard for me to guess because she had a black veil over her face. She was wearing black garments that were mournful and somber. She wore a long gown, lace gloves, and a lace shawl. The funerary veil around her head and face was also black. Her whole body was covered by her garments. Long black silk ribbons hung from her gown. A large black silk bowknot covered her neck. She had a black cap on her head. The color of her clothes was dull and dark, but her clothing was ladylike and proper. She was looking into the flames.

A woman was standing beside the man who was holding a pipe. This second woman appeared to be forty years old, but it was difficult for me to guess because she, too, had a funerary veil around her face. She was wearing mournful garments that were identical to the other woman's clothes.

Something pulled my shoulder, forcing me to turn around. A man's hand gripped my shoulder. The man grabbed my coat. He opened his mouth and gritted his teeth. I smelled his rancid breath that reminded me of cheap booze and excrement. I pulled away from him, but he walked closer towards me. This man was lanky and dirty. He seemed emaciated and jittery. This drunkard gasped and groaned, and I was reminded of the sounds that I had heard the previous night.

He had pale white skin, and he appeared to be forty years old, maybe older. The skin on his hands looked leathery and gray. His sunken eyes were wide. The pallid flesh of his face was coarse. He wore black clothes that were loose and ragged. His jacket, vest, shirt, and trousers smelled of mud and decaying flesh. His rank moldy stench reminded me of a cemetery.

With clenched teeth, this man said, "Leave, now."

I glared at him and said, "Step away, you poor bloke."

The drunkard said, "You do not belong here."

Staring at him, I asked, "Why?"

"You are dead," said the drunk man.

"Leave the gentleman alone."

I turned around to see who had just spoken. I saw the man with the pipe staring at the drunk man. I turned to see the drunk man, but he was gone. I looked at the man with the pipe and asked, "Who was that?"

"That was Cosimo. Forget him. He is a sorry drunkard, and he always acts that way to travelers, but he is harmless. My name is Bartolomeo. Who are you?"

"I am Theodemir. I thank you, Bartolomeo, for your assistance with Cosimo, but I dare say that Cosimo might not be harmless. I do believe that he might have been the one who was clawing on my door last night."

Bartolomeo said, "Cosimo lost his mind many years ago, but he is not dangerous."

"I must disagree. What happened to him?"

"Ever since he saw Fiendilkfjeld castle, he has never been the same."

"What? How could looking at a castle cause someone to lose their mind?" I asked.

"That is not something we should be talking about," said Bartolomeo. "I am a simple barber of this village, and I do not like to speak of things that could cause anyone any sort of distress."

"I must implore you. My good chap, to tell me more about this blooming castle," I said.

"There are many strange things that are always being brought here," said the woman standing beside Bartolomeo.

"Who am I speaking to?" I asked.

"I am Celeste," said the woman beside Bartolomeo.

I asked, "What is brought here?"

"Every one of the villagers knows that spirits haunt this land," said Celeste. "Many souls of the dead wander through here. People who have died come here, even those who died far away; they all come here like pilgrims on a sacred journey. This land is a cursed place where undead people come to pass on to the hereafter."

"Why would dead people come here?" I asked.

"Spirits and ghosts from all throughout the globe travel to this land for their own reasons," said Celeste. "The region of Fiendilkfjeld attracts death and those who have died. It pulls in people who are dead or close to death. It attracts ghosts from nearby or distant lands, and sometimes it tries to keep them here."

"Not just ghosts," said the woman sitting in the chair.

"Who is she?" I asked, pointing at the woman in the chair.

"This is Linda," said Bartolomeo. "Her husband passed away. We just came back from the funeral."

Celeste said, "We always wear funerary clothes to honor and guide all the ghosts who pass through this place."

I asked, "Do you see a lot of ghosts around here?"

"Not only ghosts," said Linda, still staring into the fire. "The dreams of the dead manifest here, too."

Bartolomeo said, "While you are living here, you never can be completely certain if you are talking to a living human being or a dead person. It is best to respect those who have died, and always dress properly so that you do not accidentally offend the dead."

"All the villagers know the legends, stories, and rumors about this place, but we know how outsiders view us," said Celeste. "Perhaps we have said too much to you."

"Have you heard about the woman who disappeared?" I asked. "She was seen at Fiendilkfjeld castle."

"You should not talk about that castle," said Bartolomeo.

"Goodness, my dear fellow, can you at least tell me what you have heard about the missing woman?" I asked.

"I have not heard about that," said Bartolomeo. "None of us wish to talk about that kind of thing either. Everyone around here knows that you should never go near the ruins of that castle, and you should never speak about those who have gone there."

"Ruins?" I asked, surprised. "I want no quarrel with you, but I must insist that you stop toying with me."

"We have nothing more to say to you," said Celeste.

I assumed that they were trying to dupe me with their trifling stories, and then I decided to find Roman. Frustrated and insulted, I walked away. I almost wanted to pull out my own hair. I needed to find Roman. I was incredibly disappointed with myself because I had not discovered anything valuable by talking to those villagers. For people who acted like they were so very respectful of the dead, they certainly had no scruples about being rude to the living. I was astounded by how impudent and uncivilized human beings could be toward one another. This entire planet had been mired in hypocrisy and double standards. I contemplated the events that had just transpired in the barroom and wondered what I could have done better to get more information from those locals.

I became suspicious of these villagers, and decided that I would need to change my behavior towards them. The villagers I had met did not seem to like to talk about their own superstitions with someone who they believed was an outsider. I presumed that they did not like to talk about Fiendilkfjeld castle. I could only assume that the people here were scared of something or someone. I wanted to use what I had learned to improve my connection with the villagers.

If Roman wanted me to talk to people here, I would need to learn how to communicate properly. All I had learned was that there were people here with strong beliefs, and they feared something about my family's castle. It was not much, but it was something from which to learn.

I was impressed that there were people here who actually had a faith that connected them as citizens. They shared values that were important to them, which brought them closer together. I remembered their black funerary clothes, and I respected that they had the decency and appreciation for actually having respect for something so strongly that they would even clothe themselves with garments of their emotions and reverence for their values and standards. Those villagers appeared to always be considering the lives of the people around them. I could not stay angry with them, because they were so charming and interesting. They had faith in something here, and their beliefs connected them to others.

I assumed that these were the type of people who were always thinking about the feelings of others, their place in the world, and how to protect one another in the community. This place seemed truly grand. I understood why the people would love the noble Fiendilkfjeld family so much, because my family was supporting their ability to express these folkways and the traditions of this community. I did not understand why they would fear speaking of the castle. I considered the possibility that the villager did not speak about the castle because they had too much respect for it.

As I turned around, I flinched with fear. The barroom was empty. I slowly walked around the barroom. I stepped to the fireplace. I saw an empty chair resting before it. There was no one here. I crouched low before the fireplace. There were no flames. The wood that had been burning was now a heap of cold ashes.

The fireplace had been Gothicized and was decorated with carvings and black mouldings that resembled bones and smoke. A Gothic arch rose above the fireplace. The wide hearth was fashioned with skeletal designs. Its pillars and columns were adorned with figures of handsome men and beautiful women.

A long black andiron sat in a dark chamber inside the fireplace. This firedog had been shaped like wolves howling at crescent moons. The cold dog iron was covered by soot and ashes, but no wood. It was as if all the wood had burned away a long time ago.

The jambs around this dark chamber supported small statues depicting knights. Each of these knights wore a conical helmet and a tight hauberk, held a long spear in their right hand, and carried a round shield with their left hand.

Ornate patterns of water and wind ornamented the mantel, too. The mantelpiece had been furnished with a Gothic arch motif. Designs of thorns and vines embellished the mantelshelf. The designs on this manteltree reminded me of the ruins of an old graveyard gripped by trees and vines.

The black corbels of the fireplace were adorned with the figures of human skulls. An arrangement of monstrous figures decorated its plinths.

The overmantel was decorated with black carvings depicting flames and human skulls. The corbeled niches above the fireboard hold small black statuettes of human skeletons holding scythes and wearing cloaks.

I did not see any workers or customers in the barroom. The room was silent and colder than it was before. I did not understand how the room could have become so empty so quickly. Foul moldy air lingered in the room. A smell like rotting food cut into my senses. The awful stench stung my nose. All the architecture, walls, ceiling, the furniture, and the floor was covered by dust. I was coughing because of the dust and the bad smells.

The windows were dusty, too, but they were allowing light to pass into this gloomy room. I thought that I was hearing voices coming from the distance. I assumed that they were the sounds of all the villagers and locals working and talking outside.

I walked back up the stairs and attempted to speak with Roman. I wanted to talk to him and see if he was noticing anything unusual about this inn. I feared that I did not eat well enough. I thought I might have been sick or tired from not getting proper rest. I presumed that I should relax and calm myself. I knew that my dreams and nightmares were causing me to feel exhausted whenever I woke up.

I decided not to speak to Roman yet. I planned to rest first, then eat, and then speak to Roman. I knew that I could help him better if I was rested and fed properly. I could not be useful if I was disoriented and confused. I presumed that my mind would continue tricking my eyes unless I rested and ate. I also planned to consult with a doctor after I arrived at the castle. I had also noticed that electronic devices do not work in this village, so perhaps something in the air around here was making me confused.

CHAPTER 8

After resting, I woke up. I did not know how long I slept for. I did not think that Roman tried to contact me, so I figured that he did not need me yet. I had to eat something, so I went towards the barroom. The inn was full of very loud people now.

Revelers, diners, and carousers filled the entire tavern. I assumed that many of the people here were also travelers because I saw them holding their baggage, carrying their suitcases, and pulling their luggage around with them.

After watching and listening to many people in this inn for several minutes, I was able to discern the villagers and locals apart from the tourists and wanderers. I started to remember how the locals had dressed and spoken when I had been in this village many years ago. Memories of the natural behaviors, beautiful accents, and rich dialects of the true villagers flooded back into my mind.

Ragged drifters, loudmouthed auslanders, and suspicious vagabonds moved up and about the halls and chambers of the inn. I was amidst the loud revels and merrymaking as I was finishing my meal. Noisy merrymakers praised the season of harvest and shouted thanks to their deities of autumn. A Clangorous tumult of exaltation rang throughout the entire inn. Drinkers and partiers participated in the boisterous festivities.

I overheard several people gossiping about the strange things they have heard and seen in the region of Fiendilkfjeld. The gossipers were two men and two women. They were sharing stories with one another about how the mountains around the entire region were haunted. They said that the villagers believed that the mountains were breathing down an eldritch air that was bringing evil spirits to this land; some said that the wind was bringing strange curses that were constantly changing the people; someone said that they had seen ghosts stalking the cemeteries at night here; and another person mentioned that a wild animal had already killed several people from this village. From these gossipers, I heard that some of the villagers believed that those murders were committed by something that was not a human or a natural animal. Then, I heard someone say that they knew someone who saw a beautiful woman being taken away by cloaked figures one night at a graveyard.

I asked the gossipers, "What did you say about the beautiful woman? You spoke to someone who saw a woman being abducted?"

The gossipers scowled at me and walked away. I said, "I need to speak with you about the woman who was abducted!" As they continued to walk away, I shouted, "I am helping an investigator look for her! This is important!" The rude, impudent gossipers sauntered away and apathetically ignored me. I knew that there was nothing I could do. I did not have any authoritative power. I remembered the flippant faces of those two arrogant men and those two conceited women. I imagined how wonderful it would be to pull out their tongues and eyes.

I knew that I should get Roman's help. I wanted to tell him about what I had heard, but I did not want them to get away before I could get some more information from them. First, I followed the gossipers so that I could see where they were going or what vehicles they had. I could use this information to have Roman trail them.

Keeping a good distance from them, I walked out of the barroom. Moving through the shadows, I followed those gossipers. I moved through the fog until I could see nothing but grayness and shadows. I followed the sounds of their voices and stalked them through the village. I was careful to hide behind monuments and buildings whenever I thought that they might see me. I followed them all the way to a bridge that was covered in fog. I moved through the fog to continue stalking them.

As soon as I heard one of the women start screaming, I ran away. I ran all the way to a cemetery to hide behind one of the mausoleums. I was gasping for breath. I thought that I would faint. I tried to breathe. I feared that I would die. When I finally started breathing again, I started to calm myself. I searched for Roman. He was not at the car, and I had not seen him all day. I realized that it was already nighttime. The night sky was very dark. The moon was so bright that the moonbeams actually stung my eyes a bit.

Next, I walked around the village. I did not know what to do. None of my electronic devices worked, so I could not communicate with anyone. I knew that I should have waited at the car, but I could not think clearly there. When I returned to the mausoleum, I heard loud gunshots. I followed the sounds until I saw some villagers standing amidst the tombstones. They were looking down at something on the ground. I walked up to them and saw that they were looking at the corpses of two men and two women. I recognized the corpses because they were the same two men and two women that I had just been following, but they were now dead.

I asked, "What happened?"

One of the villagers said, "It was that wild animal. It killed these innocent people and dragged their dead bodies here. We scared it away, but it is still out there somewhere. You should go inside before it returns."

"You saw the animal that killed these people?" I asked.

"You should let the police take care of this now," another villager said. "You need to protect yourself."

I looked down at the mutilated corpses of the gossipers. I asked, "Did it try to eat them? Why would it bring them here to this cemetery?"

A villager said, "It took out their eyes and tongues, and it looks like it ripped open their bellies and ate some of their organs, too."

"What could have done this?" I asked.

"Did you know these people?" another villager asked.

"No," I said. "Why?"

"Then this is none of your business," the villager said. "You need to leave, unless you want to be another one of the creature's victims."

"The creature?" I asked, nervously. "What are you hiding from me? What did this?" I stared at the corpses of the gossipers and trembled. My hands were shaking and my teeth chattered. I slowly stepped backwards. The macabre bloody corpses dumbfounded and mortified me. Their eye sockets were bloody ragged pits. Their jaws had been ripped off. Their tongues were missing. Their teeth were scattered around their heads. Intestines and broken bones had spilled out of their disfigured torsos. Deep claw marks sliced open their limbs. I felt nauseated as the horrible smell of decay and blood exuded from the dead bodies of the gossipers.

I ran away. I thought about everything that I remembered about this night. I remembered the gossipers at the bridge. I remembered the scream in the fog. I remembered running away after I heard the scream. I assumed that the animal had attacked them on the bridge, and that is why the woman screamed. If that were true, then I could have died if I had not run away. That animal might have been attacking them then. If I had been slower, or if I had not run away, I could have been dead, too. That animal might have mutilated me, too. It was probably following me! The animal might have taken the bodies to the cemetery because it was following me there! It was stalking me, too! I considered all of those possibilities and I wanted to shut my eyes. I wanted to sleep and forget this night. I told myself that I could have died tonight, too. That animal could have taken me away and those villagers would have found my corpse in the cemetery, too. I wondered if this animal was also responsible for Alison's disappearance. If it had a habit of carrying around bodies, then it could have easily carried her away, too. I wondered what kind of animal would behave like that.

"I found you."

I turned around and saw Roman.

"Finally!" I yelled. "Roman!"

"Where have you been?" he asked.

"I was looking for you, too," I said.

"Did you hear about the murders?" asked Roman.

I said, "Roman, I could have been killed, too."

"What do you mean?"

"I was following the people who died. The victims were at the inn," I said. "I overheard them talking about legends, folklore, and supernatural rumors about this area. I also heard them talk about how one of them knew someone who saw a woman being abducted, or maybe they saw her being abducted. I do not really remember it clearly right now, but they knew about a woman being captured."

"Did you talk to them?" asked Roman.

"I tried," I said, "but they would not listen to me. They were so rude to me, Roman. You should have seen the way they looked at me. They scowled at me and their eyes mocked me. They ignored me after I tried to talk to them. They just walked away. I had to know more about what they knew, because it sounded like they were talking about Alison. I followed them to a bridge, but everything was covered by fog. Suddenly, I heard a woman scream. I ran away because I got scared. I did not know what was going to happen. I panicked. I ran to the cemetery and then I tried to find you. I went back to the cemetery and I heard the villagers shooting at something. When I went to see what was going on there, I saw the villagers standing around the dead bodies of those people I was following. The victims were those two men and the two women who I was trying to talk to at the inn, the same people who said they knew someone who saw a woman being captured around here."

Roman said, "It sounds to me like you could have been killed, too. If you did not run away when that woman screamed, you could have been attacked by the killer."

I said, "The villagers said it was a wild animal that killed them. I was right there when it happened, and I did not even know what was happening. There was so much fog that I could not see anything."

"I do not know if an animal could do that," said Roman. "Did you see what it did to those people?"

"Yes. I saw."

"I heard the villagers say that they saw the killer carrying the corpses to the cemetery."

"I think it was following me."

Roman said, "It could have been following you, but why?"

"It must have smelled me or something like that," I said. "I was there when it attacked those people. After it was done with them, it wanted me, too."

"Why would it bring the bodies with it?"

"It might have wanted to bring the bodies to a cave so that it could eat their remains later."

"I just do not know what kind of animal would have the strength to bring four adult human bodies around with it so quickly," said Roman.

I said, "It could have been several animals. Maybe a pack of wolves or mountain lions did it."

"It might have been a group of adult men," said Roman. "It might have been part of some kind of ritualistic slaughter. If they brought them to the cemetery, the deaths could have served some kind of ceremonial function."

"The villagers said that it was a creature," I said. "What do you think about that?"

"I think the people around here are too superstitious," said Roman.

"I think you might need to listen to them more," I said.

"What do you want me to believe? Say it."

"Nothing," I said, "But, I know that you are confused about this, too. You want to think that these deaths were committed by humans, but you are not certain. You do not know what to believe."

"I think that you are nervous about something else," said Roman. "Something has scared you so much that you are unwilling to face the truth of it."

"What would I be scared of?" I asked.

"We need to start thinking clearly about this," said Roman. "Yes, I am confused. I am not sure what to think about all this. We should think about what we know. You say that these people knew about a woman being abducted. You followed them. You heard a scream in the fog, but you could not see anything around you. The scream scared you, so you ran away. Afterwards, you discovered the dead bodies of the people you were following, in the cemetery. Two men and two women were mutilated, disfigured, and carried from the bridge to the cemetery. The villagers say that they saw a creature and that they scared it away by shooting at it. That is all we really know. What does that sound like to you?"

"Someone might have wanted to kill those people because they knew something about the woman being abducted," I said.

"Let me take care of the deaths," said Roman. "I want you to sleep at the inn. Relax. I will handle this mess."

"I really want to go to the castle," I said. "I need to see my family after all this madness."

"I understand," said Roman. "We will go as soon as I am done here. I need to speak with the police and local authorities, file some reports, do paperwork, and take care of a few other things."

"We can stay at the castle, right?" I asked. "My family gave us permission to live there for a while?"

"Yes," said Roman. "Your family has allowed us to stay in the castle for a few nights so that we can investigate things properly. We need to talk to your relatives who live there, the guards, the staff, servants, priests, and anyone else living there.

Then, we need to look around the castle, too. We cannot stay for more than a month, but this gives us enough time to get the information we need."

I said, "I want to rescue Alison if she is still alive. I want to help you, Roman. I want to find the woman who looks like the one I have seen in my dreams. I need to understand what has happened. If I can help rescue that beautiful woman, or be a part of her life in some way, then I will gladly help you. I am just so afraid, Roman. I never realized what kind of madness could exist in this area. There is something wrong about this place. While I am terrified, I have become even more curious. I need to investigate the sinister mysteries surrounding this region. I want to learn more. I want to understand more about this place that is so different from everything I have ever really known. There is something alive in the wind here. I can feel the energy of the land. Do you not feel as if this whole place is alive?"

"This place is strange," he said. "I just want to focus on finding Alison. I need to rescue her if she is still alive. I cannot become distracted by anything else. Something tells me that she is at the castle."

"I feel differently here," I said. "I have never felt like this before. I cannot explain it."

"Do you feel anything about Alison?" he asked. "Are you sensing anything about where she is?"

"I feel like she is still alive," I said. "We need to get to the castle."

"Rest," he said. "I will come to your room in the morning."

I said, "Roman, be careful."

He said, "You, too. This place is really creepy."

I returned to my room at the inn, but I could not sleep. I locked my door and covered the windows. I continued thinking about the gossipers and their dead bodies. I did not even know their names, and yet I was obsessed with them. They were all I could think about. Not only them, but the circumstances surrounded their deaths. It was a bizarre kind of emotion I was feeling, as if fate were speaking to me.

Reoccurring thoughts of those men and women who died continued to swirl around in my mind. I thought that it was so eerie and sinister how I had been so close to people who were actually dead now. I was near them when they were being attacked, but I could not see them because of the fog. I had not realized that a killer was near me, too. I was terrified of the idea that I was so close to murder. I had been near an actual murder. I had heard the screams of that woman as she was being attacked. I had not known that she was being attacked. I had not known that they would die. I had been following them because I wanted to learn more about who they were and what they knew about Alison. I considered the possibility that I was missing something crucial about their deaths. I wondered if they really were killed on that foggy bridge. I was only assuming that the woman screamed because she was being attacked, but I did not honestly know if that is what happened. All I knew was that a woman screamed and I ran away. Then, I had returned to cemetery and found those men and women dead.

I did not want to continue thinking about this, but there was something else that made me cold and afraid. The way that they had been killed was so similar to the way that I had wanted them dead. I had wished that they would die. I had wanted to pull out their eyes and tongues, and then that is how they died. This macabre coincidence made my whole body quiver rapidly. I felt as if I was convulsing. Mortified and paranoid, I was shaking uncontrollably. Intense guilt and suspicion clawed at my heart so terribly that I felt as if I would die from the shock.

I did not want to feel responsible for their deaths. I knew that they left after I had spoken to them, and that somehow made me feel as if I had caused them to leave the tavern. If they had not left the tavern, they might not have died. I told myself that this was not my fault. I had not known, at the time, that they would leave the tavern after I asked them questions. They were the rude ones who mocked me after I tried to communicate with them.

I tried to focus on what I was doing here. I was here to help rescue Alison if she was in danger. I was here to investigate a woman's disappearance. I was here to learn more about my family. I told myself that this is my quest, too, and I should not be scared. I told myself that the woman who I was seeing in my dreams would not want me to be scared. Alison looked like that woman in my dreams, she was trapped in a castle that reminded me of my family's castle. I tried focusing on all this information, but unwanted thoughts continued to push their way into my mind. These unwanted thoughts told me that I was guilty and stupid. I thought that I might have actually wanted them to die and somehow I made it happen.

I did not want to continue thinking these things. I told myself that my mind was only agitated because of all those rumors I heard about this region being haunted. I wanted to go to the castle. I wanted to be there now. I did not like being in this village any longer. I was not even at the castle yet, and I already felt like I was being overwhelmed. At the tavern, I had heard many rumors about how this land was haunted and cursed, so those stories must have made me nervous.

I was on my bed, thinking of things I wanted to do when I finally arrived at the castle. Those thoughts were pounded by more feelings of dread and embarrassment. It was hard to concentrate about anything.

I began to wonder if the villagers in the cemetery had anything to do with the murders of those gossipers. I had seen the villagers with the bodies, and they did not want me to linger. I thought that perhaps there was something going on in this village that was linked to the murders and maybe the disappearances of many other people, too. Roman could have been right about the killers being a group of cultists that wanted to ritually murder people. It would make sense that a large group of fanatics had come to slay people and then bring their bodies to the cemetery as a sign of reverence to the season of harvest. I had researched this sort of thing before. I knew that there were wandering groups of murderous cults and thieves who killed people in ways that were similar to the way those gossipers were killed.

I wondered if Alison might have been involved with those cults, too. I pondered the idea that she might have become connected with someone from one of these cults. If she had, they could have followed her to my family's castle. If she was in the castle, one of my relatives was hiding her there, unless she was somewhere that no one could find.

I wondered whether or not it was possible for someone to have put her in a hidden chamber, inside the castle, that was in a place that no one knew even existed. I wondered whether it was even possible that none of the occupants of the castle knew that Alison was inside. If she was inside the castle, and if the occupants did not know she was in there, then she had to be somewhere that was hidden from everyone, and only few people could have known where she was being kept.

No demands for money had been made yet, and Alison's family had not yet been contacted either. Alison had been missing for many months. With only a few days to investigate, I was not sure if we would actually discover anything valuable. If I did not find her, that would only make me look like a fool in front of my family. I already felt guilty for being involved with this, so I needed to make sure that this was worth something. I was not even sure when the dreams would stop. I had no idea whether or not the dreams would stop even if I did not find her. I meditated on the idea that the woman of my dreams and Alison were not actually the same person. Nothing made me calm, and I could not sleep. I knew that I wanted to rescue Alison because she was so beautiful and inspiring. Her beauty gave me hope. I wanted to involve myself with the woman who looked so similar to the woman from my dreams. This quest might even bring me closer to another side of my family that I never got to know. Still, nervousness and confusion plagued my thoughts.

CHAPTER 9

I slept and had another dream. Alison was in it again. I saw her running through the castle. She moved through a hidden door and entered a dark chamber. She walked down a long hallway. Knightly suits of chivalrous armor were standing around her. Long medieval tapestries dangled on the wall behind her. Torches were hung on the stone walls. All the doors and windows were barred.

After I woke up, I waited for Roman. I walked around the village during the start of the morning. Roman had not visited me like he had said he would. I really did not care, at that point.

So much had happened to me recently that I was starting to feel like I was slipping away from everything. It was hard for me to describe my own emotions to myself at the time. It was as if I was repeatedly being so bombarded and so confused by rapid strange events that my soul had actually walked out of my body, and now I was like a rusting automaton.

I had been having strange dreams; an heiress, who looked like the woman in my dreams, was missing; a detective, who was the missing heiress' friend, wants my help to find her; the heiress, Alison, was last seen alive at my family's castle; someone, or a group of people, recently murdered some other people; and I still need to reach the castle so I can investigate the disappearance of the detective's friend, Alison.

When my emotions returned to me, I was in a cemetery. First, I cried. I cried for several minutes. Then, my sobs became loud screams. I thought that someone might find me, but no one came. No one seemed to mind that I had been making so much noise, or maybe they knew that it was best to leave me alone.

I thought about Alison and the woman who looked like her in my dreams. Now, they were both becoming like the same person. I was thinking about them the way I would think about an individual. For me, Alison was the woman in my dreams. I had been watching her, but she might have been watching me, too. I did not want her to see me as someone who was weak.

When I stopped crying and screaming, I walked around the gravestones and funerary monuments. Tall waves of fog stretched across the cemetery. I heard faint crying sounds coming from some of the graves, as if there were people buried under the ground. When I investigated the crying graves, the sounds stopped. Nothing was there except the silent gravestones surrounded by tall dead grass. I heard soft whispering coming from a mausoleum. I inspected it, but it was silent when I arrived there. I could not see very far because of the fog. I could only see a yard or two in front of me, at best. These sounds could have been from people who were walking through the cemetery, people that I might not have seen because of the fog.

I left the cemetery and walked throughout the village. Fog rolled across the village paths and old roads. The village had been filled with many Gothic abodes and decrepit buildings that had been fashioned with Gothic architecture. Black iron fences partitioned the old homes from one another. Blankets of fog mantled the gloomy farmhouses. Thick mist floated over the fields and dreary pastures. Cold air whistled through the gnarled trees that were swaying over the grave-yards. The bleak winds were freezing my body as they slammed into me. The chilly air was clawing at my back as it was stinging my neck and ears. Broken statues lined the sinuous dirt paths. Wilted old homes leaned against the rotting walls of other dilapidated houses. Churches and cemeteries pervaded this village more than homes.

I waited all day for Roman. I looked for him, but I could not find him. I was starting to get worried. I did not know what had happened to him or why he disappeared again. I felt helpless and vulnerable.

My electronic devices were still not working, so there was nothing I could do but loiter around the village and putter about. I asked some locals if they could help me with this, but they all said that electronic devices usually never worked in this region.

When I needed to eat, I returned to the inn. I knocked on Roman's door, but he did not answer me. I asked people at the inn if they saw him, but they did not know who I was talking about. I asked the manager of the tavern to help me find Roman.

I said, "Please, I am worried about my friend. Roman and I have been staying here for two nights now. I do not know where he is. Can you help me find him?"

The manager said, "What does he look like?"

I said, "He is tall; he has red hair, white skin, and amber eyes. I am sure that our rooms are attached to his name."

The manager said, "I do not remember anyone like that."

"Can you check?"

"Wait here." The manager walked into another room.

I waited for the manager to return.

The manager returned after fifteen minutes. "I do not have anyone here by the name of Roman."

"That is impossible," I said. "Wait, he could have used a different name."

"Why would your friend do that?"

"We are looking for a missing woman," I said. "We are part of an investigation to find an heiress who has been missing for many months now. Maybe you know something about that?"

The manager said, "I need you to leave."

"What? I am telling you the truth. A woman's life is at stake," I said. "I can pay you for any information you have about her. Her name is Alison."

"I do not know anything. I am busy." The manager left again.

I was flabbergasted. I could not believe what the manager had said to me. I presumed that Roman had been using a different name so that our identities could be hidden, but I could not understand why the manager had been so rude to me. I felt so helpless and impotent.

I left the tavern and walked to Roman's vehicle. I sat behind it and closed my eyes.

I tried to sleep, but I heard more gunshots. Hiding behind the vehicle, I tried to see what was happening. I followed the sounds until the gunshots were getting louder. I stealthily walked through the mist.

I found out where the gunshots were coming from. Police officers were talking to several villagers nearby the tavern that Roman and I had been staying at. I asked someone, standing beside me, who was also watching the scene, about what had happened.

The person said, "Someone killed the manager of that tavern, and the police are talking to some locals who say that they were shooting at the killer."

I asked, "Do they know who did it?"

The person said, "No one else saw anything except for the villagers with the guns. They say that a large animal jumped out of the window and started attacking people. They were shooting at it, but it got away."

"Are they sure that it was an animal?" I asked.

"The villagers say that it was a creature, but no one knows what they are talking about. I think they saw a bear or something. The police had to arrest some villagers who were fighting one another, but that is all I know. Sorry."

I talked to some of the police officers to ask if they knew where Roman was. They told me that they did not know anything about it. I told them that I was helping him find a missing woman, but they did not know anything about it. I asked them to take me to a police station, but they said that they were too busy to help me.

I walked back to Roman's vehicle and waited there. I was there all day, trying to understand the circumstances around me. When night came, I walked around the village again.

Strange people populated the docks of this village that night. All these people were almost abnormally tall, maybe around seven feet tall; they were lanky, boney, and their skin was a pallid grayish white. Their eyes were red and their teeth were sharp. Their clothes appeared to be made out of black wool. Each of them was wearing a hooded cloak, tunic, shirt, and leggings. Their black gloves and black boots appeared to be made of leather. They each had long straight gray hair that hung in front of their faces. When I tried to approach them, one of them hissed at me. The others glared at me, and I walked away. I walked into a blacksmith's workshop and asked the blacksmith about the strange people I saw at the docks.

The blacksmith said, "We have so many weird people coming here these days. The whole world is so crowded with hooligans and degenerates that, sooner or later, people have nowhere else to live. There is no room for any more people on this planet. They go anywhere they can to stretch their legs, and they wind up here. That means the crazy people follow them here, too."

I said, "Do you do a lot of traveling?"

"I once did. I like my life here. Everywhere else is all the same; everywhere you go, you will only find overpopulated cities, overcrowded towns, and nowhere to work. I love Fiendilkfjeld village and I love the Fiendilkfjeld region. I do not want to it be destroyed."

I asked, "Have you ever seen those people with the red eyes that I saw at the docks?"

The blacksmith said, "Yes."

"What do they do?"

"I think that they work for the noble Fiendilkfjeld family."

"Why would you say that?"

The blacksmith said, "I have seen them deliver things to the castle. I have heard them say things about the castle, too, but they usually speak in a strange language that I cannot understand. I never heard a language like that. Do you know what I mean? It was unnatural. Look, I need to work. I am too busy to be staying idle with you."

I generously paid the blacksmith for his information and left the workshop. I had a feeling that I would find something important at the docks. I wanted to sneak onto a ship that belonged to those strange people with the red eyes. There might have been someone there who knew something about Alison's location.

I returned to the docks and located those strange people again. I stalked them as they moved from one ship to another. While hiding in the shadows behind a small boathouse, I saw them carry caskets from one boat to another. The sound of a moan blew through the air. When I moved toward the wharf, I looked up and saw many dark buildings and medieval homes rising up the cliffs and mountainsides in the village. I shadowed those strange people to a harbor and heard them speaking an unnatural language of hissing, rattling sounds that I had never heard of before. When they entered a pier, the light from the lampposts and sconces made these people appear more like corpses than living human beings. I quietly stepped across the Gothic walkways, walked through the arcade of Gothic arches, and followed these strangers to an eerie fogbound shipyard.

I trailed the hooded strangers into a large black ship. Inside the ship, I moved through narrow passageways. Numerous metal pipes, like ribs, stretched across the rusty walls and low ceilings. The sconces on the walls were blinking red light into the darkness. The pointed arches and ribbed vaults of the corridors reminded me of a crypt. Brown grease dripped down onto my hand. As I continued walking, my feet were splashing through water on the floor. The water had risen less than an inch above the floor, but the murky water smelled brackish and putrid. I knew that those people had to be here somewhere, but I did not want them to spot me.

When I heard footsteps, I rushed into a dark booth and closed the wooden door. Hidden in shadows, I heard terrifying sounds of screams and growls. I heard something horrifying that sounded like clothes and flesh being ripped apart. Some dragged against the wet floor, and then the silence returned. All I could hear was the gross sounds of something dripping.

I emerged from the darkness and opened the door. I looked around. No one was in the hall, except me. Quietly shutting the door, I continued searching for answers. I needed to know what was really happening here. I moved down a staircase and only walked in areas where there were still lights.

I wondered if Alison could have ended up in a place like this or if she had been captured and brought here to suffer. If those strange people had a connection to my family, they could have infiltrated the castle, stolen Alison, and taken her to a place like this ship. I considered that Roman could have also be a prisoner here, too. I wondered if there were more places like this were people were taken and tortured. I did not know whether people were being tortured here or not, but I knew that something evil was happening here. I had heard those screams. I heard something that sounded like someone's skin and garments being ripped open. If something was killing people here, I wanted to save anyone I could and take them away from this horrible place.

I saw a green light at the end of the hall. There was a room with a door that was slightly open. The green light was sliding out of the partially open doorway. I peeked into the room and saw a sight that petrified my mind. What I saw had terrified me so awfully that I could not move or scream. My eyes were wide as I gaped at the horrible sight.

I perceived bloody men and women eating human corpses. These ghastly creatures were wearing black robes and cloaks. They chewed on the bones of dead people who were still in their coffins. The ghoulish humanoid beings had bloody hands and fingers that they used to rip off cold muscles and bones as they pushed more dead meat into their mouths. The creatures' pale ears were long and pointed. Wisps of red light floated from their glowing red eyes. Blood was dripping down the rotting white flesh of their faces. The creatures' black cloaks were slowly transforming into black leathery wings. Their long gray hair was soaked with dead blood. The ghouls continued eating corpses and chewing on the bones of dead people.

I felt cold hands around my neck. I pushed away and turned around. I saw dozens of red glowing eyes in the dark. A group of people had discovered me. Walking out of the darkness, undead creatures moved towards me. Human skeletons and decaying human corpses were walking with their arms and hands reaching out to grab me. The undead attackers shrieked as they pushed me to the ground. Their dirty decaying hands covered my mouth and eyes.

I opened my eyes and screamed. I was shaking and flailing my arms. I slowly lowered my arms and stopped screaming when I realized that I had been sleeping in Roman's vehicle and Roman was driving the car. Breathing normally again, I slowly regained my composure and calmness. The morning sun was in the bright sky above us.

"What happened to you?" asked Roman. He chuckled.

"I do not even know what to say right now," I said. "How did I get here?"

"I told you that we could leave in the morning," said Roman. "You said that you were ready."

"No I did not," I said. "You were gone. You abandoned me."

"You must have been so drunk," he said.

"I was not drunk," I said. "How did you find me?"

"You were in your room," said Roman. "I told you that we could leave. You said that you were ready."

"That is not what happened," I said. "I could not find you. I thought that I was going to die."

"What are you talking about?" asked Roman. "Are you trying to tell me about another dream that you had?"

"I do not know," I said. "Now that I am really thinking about everything, it all feels like it was a dream. It all seems so silly now."

"You probably ate and drank too much before you fell asleep, and then you must have been having a nightmare," said Roman.

"Tell me what really happened to us," I said.

"After those people were murdered, you went to your room to sleep. I found you in the morning and we left. We are driving to Fiendilkfjeld castle right now," he said.

"So, it was a nightmare," I said.

"What did you dream?" asked Roman.

I said, "In my dream, someone else was killed. I do not know who did it. I followed some people into a ship and they were eating dead people. They were killing me."

Roman said, "You are alive, Theodemir."

"I know."

"Did you see Alison?"

"I might have."

Roman said, "Did you discover anything else that you might want to tell me about?"

"No," I said.

I was not sure what to say or do at that moment. I was afraid to close my eyes, because I might return to that ship with those creatures if I did. I wanted to believe that I knew what reality was, but everything was feeling so bizarre. On the outside, I might have appeared to be calm, but my mind was a maelstrom of worry and doubt. My memories were starting to feel more real than anything now physically around me. I flinched at every one of my thoughts, afraid that my mind would physically pull me back into that awful place with those dead people and skeletons.

"You look sick, really bad," said Roman. "What happened to you? Why are you flinching and shaking?"

"I feel like something is going to burst out of my skull," I said. "Something is pulling me apart from inside of me." I groaned with pain.

"You need to be strong," said Roman. "We can fight through this pain. Trust me, you will be all right. I am going to get you to your castle."

Burning pain pierced through my brain and stretched down to my toes. Every part of my body felt as if it were being electrocuted. My legs and arms were shaking, and my teeth were chattering. I grabbed Roman's arm for comfort. I felt as if my intestines were being cramped and stretched.

"You look so pale, like a white bone," said Roman. "What did you eat last night?"

"I do not remember," I groaned.

"I am going to stop the car. I will stop the car, and then I am going to give you some medicine," said Roman. "I think I have something that can help you. Relax. Breathe. Be calm. You are all right. Nothing bad will happen to you. You will be fine."

"I am really scared," I sobbed. "Tell me what is happening to me, please."

Roman stopped the car and walked to the back of the vehicle. When he came back, he gave me a glass vial filled with blackish purple liquid.

"What is this?" I asked, looking at the vial in my hand.

"I bought this medicine from a soothsayer in the village," said Roman. "This will help you."

"What does it do?" I asked.

Roman said, "It will help you sleep. If you can sleep, your mind might heal and your body will be calm."

"Why were you buying medicine from a soothsayer?" I asked.

"I was talking to anyone who I thought might know about any dangerous cults in the area," he said. "I thought that the soothsayer would know about if there were people in the village who were part of a cult that could have been killing people. Someone must have heard about someone who was interested in murder or sacrifices. The soothsayer knew that I would speak to her. She knew about you, too."

"Do you believe her?" I asked.

"I do not know," he said. "She warned me about Fiendilkfjeld castle. She said that it was cursed or haunted, I think. She said that we were about to walk into dangerous territory."

"What did you say about the castle?" I asked.

"I was not really paying attention to her," said Roman. "I bought this potion because I wanted to see what it was like. Now, please, drink it. Do not waste our time with more questions."

I looked at the vial. Hesitantly, I drank the potion. It made me cough several times. I felt a warm spicy sensation float into my mouth and nose.

"How do you feel?" asked Roman.

I said, "I feel calmer. I feel like the pain in my body is vanishing. There is a balmy sweetness lingering on my tongue. My mouth smells spicy, if that makes any sense to you."

"We are not far from the castle," said Roman. "We will be there soon."

I thought that the potion worked. I was calm and no longer shivering. My thoughts were calm, too. A pleasant feeling washed through my body. I breathed slowly and tried to sleep. I closed my eyes and concentrated on the wind blowing through my hair. I heard that the car was moving faster now.

Thinking clearly, I began to question what my life would be like once the investigation was over. I did not know what Roman was going to do after this. I wondered if Roman would still talk with me, if we would be friends, or if he would forget about me. I did not want to be with the friends I had now. Dean, Boris, Mildred, and Greta were not my friends. I wanted to escape them. I wanted to be friends with Roman. Roman seemed like someone I could actually respect. At the same time, I really did not know Roman. I only knew about some things, but he was still a mystery to me. I was not sure exactly why I wanted to be his friend, but I knew that there were things I liked about him, things that made him different from normal people. Maybe that is why I wanted to be his friend. He was different and interesting. I prayed that he would not abandon me.

"Do not ever leave me alone again," I whispered.

"What?" asked Roman.

CHAPTER 10

I WAS NOT SURE FOR HOW LONG I HAD BEEN SLEEPING. I HAD another one of those dreams where I was aware that it was a dream, yet I was observing myself and not actually participating. I knew that I was having a dream, but I could not change anything. I did not even have control over my own actions. Those dreams are always scary, even if nothing frightening actually happens. The feeling of seeing myself live while I am not actually making any decisions on scary. My body moves, I hear its thoughts, but it is not me. Even if the other version of me is not doing anything wrong, that discomforting feeling of being separated from my body makes any mundane event in the dream so much more terrifying.

In the dream I recently had, I was in a dark chamber. Moonlight came in through the Gothic arched windows. The walls, rib vaulted ceiling, and floor were made out of black stones. I was standing in front of a pointed arched mirror. I was wearing only my black trousers. I watched as my two pale hands tug the white glistening skin and fat of my thin abdomen.

Alison's very skinny body was behind me. I saw the reflection of her womanly figure in the mirror. Alison had green eyes, small shoulders, pale white skin, and long blond hair. She was shorter than me, and I guessed that she might have been, at least, five feet tall. She was wearing only a gossamer white chemise that accentuated her ample breasts and firm buttocks. Her long chemise had long sleeves and a long train, and it had a high collar so that all of her body was completely covered. The only skin I saw was the white flesh of her toes and the pale skin of her beautiful face.

I heard a voice, in my head, asking a series of questions. "Is this Alison? Who is the woman in my dreams? Why is she trapped in this castle?"

Her delicate hands and long thin fingers moved across my eyelids.

The woman in my dream whispered, with a beautiful voice, "Save me from him."

I asked, "Who is keeping you here?" I saw only shadows.

She whispered, her soft sweet breath puffed against my left ear, "His priests"

"Which priests?" I asked.

"Those who live in the castle with your family."

"There are priests living at the castle?"

"If you come for me, you will die."

"I want to be with you," I said. "I want to be with you."

"Help me," her voice gradually became fainter and floated off in the distance, as if she was being taken far away from me.

After I woke up, I saw Roman driving the car down a path through a dark forest. Blue moonbeams swooped down through the canopy of gnarled branches and dead leaves above. Wrinkled purple and violet leaves were swirling through the air all around us. We drove over a long viaduct that took us across a deep valley.

As we passed through a dark tunnel, I felt as if that last dream had been actually very short, more like a flashing thought in my mind. A part of me felt betrayed that the woman in my dreams wanted me to save her when she knew that I would die. I did not want to die, and I did not know why I had said, in the dream, that I only wanted to be with her. I did not want to be with her if that meant that I had to die. My mouth said that I wanted to be with her, but my mind understood clearly that I did not want to sacrifice my life for someone I did not really know. I did not recognize the person that I was in that dream. Yet,

I did want to be with her. I wanted to help her, I just was not sure if I was ready to actually give my life for her security.

I started to consider if the dream was telling me that I had made the wrong decision, like a deeper part of me knew that I would be sacrificing myself for no reason by being part of this investigation. I knew that things were becoming more dangerous. People had already died, and their deaths might be linked to the disappearance of Alison. I could have died that night when I followed those people from the inn. I could not be sure if I really wanted to commit to this investigation. There were so many reasons for me to walk away from this. The only thing keeping me here was my connection to Alison. I wanted to be a part of her life, but I was starting to realize that I would be really putting myself in more danger if I continued to link our fates. I started to ponder the possibility that my dreams were actually coming from another part of me that wanted me to avoid Alison. Maybe there was a side to me that knew that I should not be involved with this. There was also the reality that I wanted to understand the noble side of my family together. They might have never wanted to see me before, and they might have never allowed me to be with them, but they wanted me now. This investigation allowed me to hold on to this opportunity to understand a part of myself that was buried in this land and that castle. I saw this as an opportunity to make something meaningful and beautiful out of my life, I just was not sure if I was ready to give up my old life for the new one. If I backed away now, I would be throwing so many things away. Alison represented something pure and meaningful, and I wanted to protect her. Her mysterious gracefulness and uniqueness actually inspired me in a way that I had never felt before. My life had always been so ugly and dark, until she came into my dreams.

Roman said, "Finally, we are here."

He stopped the car in front of the castle. Thrilled, and filled with excitement, I got out of the car and stood up. Astonished, I gazed at the gigantic castle towering above me. This castle was breathtakingly humongous and reached high into the dark clouds floating in the black night sky above. My whole body shivered as I started to recognize the castle of my ancestors. I remembered coming here and looking up at it many years ago, just as I was doing now. It was more than a castle; it was like a fortress, or a town. This place had massive walls, a moat, a medieval drawbridge, and a gatehouse too. The moat was still filled with dark water.

Fiendilkfjeld castle loomed out of the fog and shadows like a black dragon. It was incredibly tall and enormously wide. The castle was like a preternatural manifestation of a sublime dichotomy between irrationality and rationality. Its Gothic architecture manifested a clash between reason and imagination. Its designs and patterns embodied a struggle between asymmetry and harmony. The structures and elements of the castle had become like a stone embodiment of distortion versus symmetry. Fiendilkfjeld castle appeared like a building made from a duality of emotions and logic. It was like a giant beautiful monster, terrifying and mesmerizing. I felt as if this castle incarnated a dance of restraint embracing wildness. From its solid bodies and carved figures, I discerned wild emotions competing against a pattern of order. A cold, rational, comforting symmetry was alive in all its structures and elements; there was also a deranged asymmetry and a hostile mystifying characteristic loitering within them, too. While it appeared, at times, to look like a beautiful corpse, it also appeared like a horrifying living creature. While looking at the black castle, I was reminded of death, immortality, and doom. I felt an organic presence and an artificial will converging within every dimension and feature of this castle.

The numerous surfaces, edges, facets, sides, and parts of the castle were asymmetrical but organic. Like a perplexing labyrinth the castle appeared to be repositioning and fluctuating, as if it were a giant serpent slowly breathing while sleeping. Its tall black towers are like sharp horns. Dozens of spires rise out of the castle like claws. Its crenelated walls reminded me of fangs. It had many battlements and machicolations that resembled teeth. Its gnarled pinnacles, pointed bartizans and tall turrets were each like dangerous spikes. Its pinnacled flying buttresses looked like bat wings or skeletal ribs of a corpse. Its shingles reminded me of the scaly flesh of a black reptilian creature.

The main walls of the castle are adorned with Gothic arches and blind arcades. Segments of the towers display motifs and patterns of pointed arches, too. The east wing of the castle connects it to a Gothic cathedral with two bell towers. The west wing of the castle connects it to a shadowy fortress obscured by fog and darkness. Most of the windows of the castle are stained glass, and many of them appear to be barred. The main face of the castle has three large portals with black iron doors shaped like Gothic arches. The jambs and tympanums are adorned with numerous statues depicting cadaverous priests and demonic knights.

Circling the entire castle is a moat and several large spiked crenelated walls that were adorned with machicolations. To reach the castle, we walked across the bridge and through the gatehouse. We were blocked by a large black iron gate. The gate was locked, and there were many dark metal chains around it to prevent us from getting through. When we reached this gate, a windstorm had begun.

Shrieks escaped from the sinuous walls. A whistling wind was blowing around us. Loud moans appeared to be coming from the statuary. Gusts of cold air slammed against me. Groans floated through the colonnades of the castle. The gates rattled with the blowing air. I thought that a wretched snarling yawn had come from the castle. I thought that I heard the castle hiss as a breeze swooped down with the rain from the dark sky. A rainstorm had brought a gale of cold air and water that soaked my clothes. Lightning cut through the shadows. The loud sounds of rain and wind battering the castle and everything else around us filled my ears. The rainstorm shrieked and rattled as the wind howled. I thought that I heard the castle moan as thunder roared across the air. Lightning whipped through the darkness as it flashed across everything around us.

Roman yelled, "What are we going to do?"

I had to yell over the rain and thunder. "I do not know."

"Did you not tell them that we were coming?"

"I thought that you were talking to them," I yelled.

"How are we going to get in?" he asked.

"I have not spoken to these people in years. I have no idea what to do," I said.

"Electronic devices do not seem to work around here, so I think we are stuck."

I said, "Do they not want to see us anymore?"

Roman said, "I told them that we would see them in less than one week. It has only been two or three days since we left England."

"We should get in your car," I said.

As we walked away, I heard someone whisper my name. "Theodemir."

I turned around and saw lightning strike the chains around the gate. The gate swung open as a groaning breath of air blew across my face. Roman and I looked at each other with astonishment. We chuckled at each other. I was surprised but happy that we could now get to the castle.

We ran through the gate and reached the main wall. After we passed under the archway, an iron portcullis slammed down into the ground behind us. It looked as if the castle was blocking us from exiting it. We reached the main portal and knocked on the door.

"You look bad," said Roman, looking at me.

"Do I?"

"Yes. You need a doctor or something."

"How bad do I look?"

"You look really sick. What happened to you?"

The door slightly opened, revealing a cadaverous face that loomed out of the shadows. Its sunken eyes were glowing red, its skin was deathly white, and its cynical smile, dripping blood, revealed sharp white teeth. This wrinkled face had a gray pointed beard and long mustache. It looked like it was a male face, but there was a subtly inhuman characteristic about it. The hair on its head was long and gray. Brownish red centipedes and blackish crimson earwigs wriggled through the wisps of his hair. I thought I saw small black spiders crawl around his beard. Yellowish pale maggots writhed around his neck. This face reminded me of those vicious ghouls from the ship. Its heavy breathing blew out a stench that smelled of rancid decaying flesh and cemetery dirt. Almost immediately upon seeing this antagonistic head, I screamed and shut my eyes.

Bewildering fear sliced through my mind. I opened my eyes, turned around, and tried to run away, but I was blocked by the portcullis that had fallen down earlier. I felt as if the castle had known that this would happen, and it wanted to make sure that I was stuck here.

"Kill it!" I screamed. "Kill it, Roman!"

I felt hands grabbing my mouth and neck.

"No!" I screamed. "No!"

I was being dragged backwards on the floor as I wriggled my body and thrashed my legs. I tried to escape, but something was pulling my arms behind me so that they were over my head. All I could see was the portcullis getting smaller and more distant as I was being dragged into the dark castle. The doors closed, and there was darkness all around me.

Roman asked, "Where is everyone?"

I gasped and opened my eyes. I looked around and saw that we were still standing in front of the main portal of the castle.

Roman asked, "Is anyone home?"

I said, "Roman, what happened?"

"What do you mean?"

"Where are we?"

He said, "Fiendilkfjeld castle."

I said, "I think that I had a prophetic vision."

"Did you see something? Did you see her?"

"I saw danger here," I said. "There is something dangerous inside this castle."

The doors opened and revealed the rugged figure of an old man. The old man was tall and lean, but still slightly burly. He had short white hair and white leathery skin. His face was rugged and his arms were brawny.

The old man's eyes were brown, and he had many perpendicular scars circling around his left eye. Three scars above his left eye curled to the left and forked out into smaller scars. Three scars below his left eye curled across the lower eyelid of this eye and slithered down to the left side of his left cheekbone.

The old man spoke with a low, gravelly voice. He said, "My name is Wessel. Welcome to Fiendilkfjeld castle."

Wessel was wearing a black leather hooded coat, black leather trousers, and black leather boots. Three servant men were standing beside him. The servants were wearing black formal uniforms that were conservative and modest but antiquated. Wessel and the servants bowed to us. I bowed in return. Each of the servants' uniforms consisted of a silk swallow-tailed coat, a silk vest, a cotton shirt, a silk necktie, tight leather gloves, silk breeches, leather leggings, and leather boots. Each of the servants wore their hair pushed back to swoop behind the head.

Wessel said, "We have been expecting you, Mister Theodemir Fiendilkfjeld."

We were allowed into the castle, and the servants took our coats as we walked inside. The air inside the castle smelled flowery, sweet, and earthy. There was an undercurrent of harsh fleshy odors lingering in the air. The aroma became more clammy and acerbic the deeper we walked into the darkness. All I could do was follow Wessel and the other servants into the shadows, and the stench was stinging my senses. I covered my mouth because of this pungent sweet but putrid odor.

The servants were holding ornate silver candelabrums to illuminate the narrow corridor. Each of the arms of these candelabrums was shaped like a beautiful reclining woman stretching out her thin arms above her head.

Suits of medieval armor and beautiful statues lined the passageways. Many of the statues depicted princesses and lovely maidens. Vivid paintings of handsome gentlemen and aristocrats were hanging on the wall. We walked slowly under a rib vault ceiling and Gothic arches. Flashes of lightning struck the stained glass windows. A glow of lightning flashed into the hall revealing dark skeletons in the shadows around us. I flinched when I saw the skeletons. Their glowing red eyes appeared hostile. I told myself that they were not real, they must have been only the empty suits of medieval armor or the lifelike statues.

"Were are we going?" asked Roman.

"Our master cannot see you tonight," said Wessel. "So, I am bringing you to your rooms."

"How long are we allowed to stay here?" I asked, trying to distract my frightened mind.

Wessel said, "The master has been forced to allow you gentlemen to search the castle for three nights."

"That does not seem like enough time," said Roman.

"You should feel lucky that you have been given that amount of time," said Wessel. "The master did not want anyone to search the castle at all."

"I was thinking that, maybe, I might be allowed to stay here after the investigation is over," I said. "I really want to reconnect with this side of my family."

Wessel said, "That is something that you will need to speak to the master about."

"Did you guys do something different to the castle? This place looks different," said Roman.

"Nothing ever really changes," said Wessel.

"I feel honored to be here," I said. "Wessel, were you here when I first came here? I came to this castle when I was very young, so I do not remember much from that time. You must forgive me, but I do not remember you."

Wessel did not respond. I did not want to upset them, so I decided to remain silent, too. I followed Wessel and the servants up several flights of stairs. When Wessel brought me to my room, the foul smell was finally gone.

I turned to Wessel and said, "Where and when should I meet everyone tomorrow?"

Wessel said, "I will find you when it is time for you and Roman to speak with the master."

I said, "Thank you Wessel. I appreciate your help. I am sorry to inconvenience you and the master."

Wessel and the servants bowed to me. I bowed back towards them. I turned to Roman and said, "Roman, be careful."

Roman turned to me and said, "Be careful, too."

Wessel said, "Roman, I will now take you to your room. Please, follow us."

I walked into my room and closed the door. New, dry clothes were waiting for me on the bed, which made me feel thankful and appreciated.

Perplexed, I whispered, "How did you know?"

I inspected the armoire and wardrobes. Inside them all, I discovered clean, warm clothes. There were coats, jackets, trousers, undergarments, shoes, neckties, vests, and so many other things for me to wear. These garments were of the same type of style and design that I had always admired.

I whispered, "Did they tailor and choose these clothes just for my tastes? How is that possible?"

I looked around the room and found the lavatory. After showering and washing, I dressed for sleep and climbed into the large bed. I tried to sleep, but I was always waking back up.

"I might be too excited," I said. "I am finally back here, Fiendilkfjeld castle. I am really here."

Lying in bed, I started to remember the times when I was scolded by my parents, teachers, or friends. I remembered that my father had said that this castle was a bad influence, but I had never known what he meant by that. I felt different now. I felt as if something was whispering directly into my brain, like old thoughts that wanted me to hear them once again after a long time of hiding.

Now, the walls were whispering to me. I did not know what they were saying, but I heard my name. I put my ear against a wall and felt soft skin caress it. I put my hand on the wall and felt pleasant fingers curl with mine. I looked at the wall, but there was nothing there.

I walked out of the room. I heard something saying my name. I followed the voice. The voice was speaking with a lovely, soothing tone. The sincere, inviting sound of that voice was making me feel so appreciated and warm. It made me feel like I was needed. It was more than that, too. The sound of the voice made me feel like I belonged somewhere.

"You cannot tell anyone that we spoke."

"I will not say anything," I said.

"You have had a hard life."

I said, "I have."

"Do you want to talk with me more?"

"I do," I said.

"Are you sure?"

I eagerly said, "Do not leave me. I want to talk to you."

"You are so strong."

"I am strong," I admitted.

"Come into the basement with me."

"Where is it?" I asked. Nothing responded to me. I asked, "Hello?" Again, the voice did not respond to me. I thought that it was waiting for me in the basement, so I continued walking. I figured that it would not say anything to me unless I found it. I concentrated on my emotions. I let my feelings guide me through the shadows. I thought that I could sense where I needed to be. There were times that I thought the shadows were pushing me in directions that they wanted me to move. I grabbed a lantern continued walking.

Finally, I found stairs leading down to what I thought was a basement. The light of the lantern helped me safely move down the stairs. Long gray curtains of thick dusty cobwebs stretched across the walls and slithered over the floor. Dusty white blankets covered tall leaning objects and things sprawled on the floor. These things appeared not to have been touched or disturbed for many years. The walls were made out of large thick gray stones.

I stood in the basement, waiting for something to happen. I wanted to feel that soothing presence and the loving voice again. While I was waiting, I starting thinking about how things were going to be in the future. I whispered, "When this investigation is over, will Roman want to be my friend? What will happen to Alison? If she is alive, will she want to be my friend, too? I do not like my old friends. They do not like me either. Would Dean, Boris, Mildred, and Greta try to hurt me now that they knew I did not want to help them anymore? Did anyone ever really need me? Please, voice, I need answers. I do not know what my life is going to be like when I have to leave this castle. Are you still there? Hello?"

Wessel found me the next morning. I was screaming in the basement. Wessel dragged me up out of the basement as I was thrashing against him. I was screaming and kicking irrationally. I did not stop screaming or resisting until I got out of the basement.

When Wessel got me to the top of the stairs, he asked me, "What happened?"

I whispered, "This castle is changing me."

Wessel asked, "What happened last night?"

I whispered, "I do not remember. I remember nothing about last night. I went to bed, that is all. This castle is changing me. I am changing. There is something wrong with me."

Wessel said, "You are still dreaming. I will put you back to bed and then you will feel fine when you wake up again."

"Yes. Sleep. Bring me to the bed so I can sleep," I said. "I just need rest."

I thought about leaving the castle, but something in my mind forced me away from those thoughts, as if there was a part of me that did not even want to consider leaving. A part of me wanted to stay to solve the mysteries. I wanted to know what happened to Alison, and I wanted to discover what exactly was living in this castle. I wanted to know what was changing me.

When I thought about it, I knew that I was somehow different, but another part of me actually liked the new way that I was now feeling. It was actually more like I had always been feeling this way, but now I was actually expressing it more sincerely with myself, like I was letting myself feel these things. It felt like something was coming to life within me, or maybe something was dying. One side of my soul felt more confident, brave, and beautiful. Another part of my soul felt mortification, humiliation, and horror. So many extreme emotions clashed within me. I felt like I was losing control over myself. I did not know what to feel or what to think, like I was experiencing the sensation of two people in one body.

I knew that if I left now, I would never be able to control this madness. If I stayed here, I could learn what was going on and come up with a solution to reclaim my sanity. Staying here allowed me to experience new things about myself, my family, and about the woman I was seeing in my dreams. A voice inside my head told me that this was the only exciting thing I had left in my life. I knew that I would never get another chance to dive into so much mystery again. This was a chance for me to acquire knowledge about things that human beings were never meant to know. There was something here that needed me to see it, understand it, and breathe it. Yes, there was power, inspiration, and information here that I needed to claim.

I whispered, "Alison, did you discover something here, too? Did you also uncover forbidden knowledge that somehow trapped you here? Is that what has happened?"

PART 2

CHAPTER 1

Roman and I were finally having dinner with the master of Fiendilkfjeld castle. Nighttime had begun and I was so hungry. The master said that his name was Adalric Fiendilkfjeld. Adalric, Roman, and I were sitting at a long wooden table in a dimly lit chamber. The table was adorned with the most fanciful and mouthwatering food that I had ever seen. Every course appeared sophisticated and luscious. All of the dishes, antipasti, and plates were fashioned with lavish elegance and embellished with resplendent decorations. The roasted pigs and ducks were trimmed with black flowers. The cakes and other pastries had been decorated with black plumage. Each meal brought a new satisfying aroma. Candelabrums illuminated the room. The ceiling was low and the walls were a beautifully dark greenish turquoise. Servant men and servant women were silently standing around us. The whole room smelled so delicious and wonderful.

As I was looking at Adalric, I realized that he slightly looked like me. I had dark blue eyes, but Adalric had green eyes. We both had long blond straight hair. Both of us were tall and had lean skinny bodies. We had similar pale white skin. His face was handsome and masculine, and appeared more brave and dignified than mine was. The way Adalric moved and spoke was very eloquent and passionate. He looked like he was thirty years old, but he spoke like someone very old who had seen everything and had a memory full of exciting experiences from his countless years and lifetimes of significant existence.

"Where is your wife?" asked Roman.

Adalric said, "My wife Hilda could not join us. She is with our son Roland."

"How are we related?" I asked, looking at Adalric.

Adalric said, "Theodemir, you are related to the noble Fiendilkfjeld family through your father's blood. It has been our tradition, for hundreds of years, to allow anyone connected to us by blood to carry the Fiendilkfjeld name. Even though your father married a common woman, you were allowed to be a Fiend-ilkfjeld, even though you were not considered actual nobility. However, we have had relatives, in the past, who have been transformed into nobility after they completed a ceremonial test. Our blood is strong, Theodemir, and we do not want it to fade away. We mark our territory with our name and we have kept this blood alive for centuries. The monarchy is gone, but we remain. We exist. Nothing is more important to us than family."

"My family and I were not allowed to come here," I said. "Why?"

"Your father, Theodemir, was always a rebellious man, like you," said Adalric.

"What do you mean?" I asked.

Adalric said, "I have heard stories about you, Theodemir. Ever since you were very young, you were always a delinquent, always getting into trouble, always breaking and stealing things, and constantly fighting others. Your father was the same way, and he blamed us, and this castle, for his vulgar behavior. He preferred to speak to our family members who were also not aristocrats."

I said, "Why did I never hear back from you? I know that I had tried to contact this castle before. I wanted to know you."

"Theodemir, you are here now, are you not?" asked Adalric.

"You are not eating, lord Adalric?" asked Roman.

Adalric said, "I am suddenly feeling tired. I cannot eat when I get too tired. If I do, I cannot sleep. Please, forgive me. It has become a bad habit of mine.

Sometimes I do not eat anything for many nights. It can feel like I have not eaten anything in months."

I tried to continue eating, but my food tasted rotten and moldy. The food that I put in my mouth was dry and putrid. I started craving something more warm and juicy. My mouth was watering as I was ogling a beautiful servant woman who had long red hair. She was looking flirtatiously at me. Her sensual eyes and smile invited me to come for her. I walked to her and grabbed her neck. I pushed her head into the wall and bit into her flesh. The blood from her neck poured onto my tongue. My fingernails ripped through the soft flesh of her lips.

"How do you like it?" asked Adalric.

I gasped and looked at him. Roman was looking at me, too. The servant woman who I was biting was gone. I glanced at the servants, and none of them were doing anything except standing.

"Where is she?" I asked.

"Who?" asked Roman.

"There was a servant woman here, I thought," I said.

"There are a lot of servants here," said Adalric. "They do not matter. Do you request one for tonight?"

"I do not feel well," I said as I gagged.

"I did not want anyone to investigate my castle," said Adalric. "A missing woman should not be my problem. Several teams of analysts and investigators have already been here. I feel like my rights have somehow been violated. I must obey the will of the government, I assume. I am being pressured by different agencies and organizations, so I will do what I can to help you, but do not get comfortable. You must leave."

"I wanted to stay," I said. "I wanted to stay with you for a while. Lord Adalric, please, let me stay here after the investigation is over. I do not want to return home."

Adalric said, "If you prove yourself, you can stay, Theodemir."

I said, "Lord Adalric, I am so grateful." I walked back to my chair. I did not want to show anyone that I was in a lot of pain. My legs felt stiff, like rocks. My eyes were itchy, too.

Roman said, "Lord Adalric, you know why I am here. If you pay me more money, I will walk away with her, and I will not cause you any trouble."

"I feel really sick," I said. I realized that hiding my pain was somehow causing me more pain. I wanted someone to help me, but I did not want to embarrass myself.

Adalric said, "Roman, I know how much you love her, but she is not here. Firstly, she was never yours. You could never have her. She belonged here, but she is gone."

"Where is she?" asked Roman.

"Help me," I whispered as I closed my eyes. I felt my body slam down to the floor. I had fallen and slammed my head into the wooden floor. I opened my eyes and got on my feet. I stood up and the servants helped me walk to the lavatory where they splashed water on my face. I could not stand. My legs felt so limp and I could barely keep my eyes open. I thought that the servants were washing my face, but I did not understand why. I tried to speak, but all I could do was create odd mumbles.

When I opened my eyes, I was looking at my reflection in the mirror, but it slowly changed. My reflection scowled at me and its eyes were darkly sunken. Blood poured out of my reflection's mouth and nose. I started screaming very loudly. I thrashed and struggled against the servants who were trying to keep me in the lavatory. I started punching the servants. I attacked them. I was only trying to leave this place. I started wondering why I had ever wanted to stay here. The servants tackled me to the ground. I screamed and cursed as they dragged me out of the lavatory.

I hated how weak I was. I should not have been defeated so easily. I wanted to be victorious, but there were too many of them. I wondered if maybe it was better that the servants had control over me, because they could help make me feel better. At the same time, I hated how foolish I thought I looked.

I was feeling so many conflicting emotions. There was a side of me that really wanted to stay here, and there was another side of me that wanted to escape. I did not understand how I was feeling so many turbulent feelings at the same time.

The servants dragged me up the stairs and brought me to my room. I puked on several servants as they tried to bring me to the bed. I was laughing as they were punching me. I attacked them back and ran into the hallway. I tripped, fell on the floor, and then vomited on the rug. I screamed for help. Some servants came to help me walk to my room.

I saw the faces of some of the other servants looking at me as I was being taken to my room. Many of the servants did not want to come near me. I saw their grimaces and facial expressions of horror.

The servants helped me wash and clothe myself. I was locked in my room and told to stay there until a doctor could come to see me.

"Someone, please, stay with me," I said. "Do not leave me alone."

I thought about Alison. I wondered if she had experienced the same things I was experiencing. If this was another vision, I wanted it to end quickly. I prayed that this was just a dream and that I would wake up. If she was sending me these visions, I did not want them anymore.

I asked, "Is someone in the castle doing this to me? Or, am I being transformed by the castle? Is it possible that Alison was changed by the castle, too? Could it actually be alive? Haunted?"

I curled up in a dark corner of the room. Mortified and humiliated, I screamed and sobbed. I felt so helpless, shameful, and obscene. I could not control my emotions or thoughts. I pulled a long black curtain around me, trying to hide myself. The room was spinning around me. I felt so dizzy and weak. I wanted to sleep, but I did not want to be in the bed. I clawed at the walls and the floor. I grabbed the bars at one of the windows and then tried to shake them. I yelled and screamed as the moonlight poured down on my face.

When I stopped screaming and crying, I was on the floor. I turned over so that my back was on the floor. I looked up at the ceiling.

I said, "Tell me what is happening here. I must know the truth. I cannot run away from this. I need to know everything about this castle."

I concentrated on the whispers and moans I heard coming from upstairs, they sounded like they were coming from upstairs. I was not completely sure where they were coming from, but it sounded like they were coming from somewhere faraway up there. I was still slightly dizzy. The floor was the only place where I felt like I could control my sense of stability.

That awful stench returned again. I smelled a putrid odor that was like something had been decaying for many days. The rancid stench filled my nose. It smelled more bloody and earthy this time. The terrible smell made me gag. I rushed to the lavatory and tried not to vomit.

"What is that awful smell?" I asked my reflection. "Where is that awful smell coming from? How could something smell so bad in this place?"

Something was sliding up my esophagus. I gagged as I felt something slide back up my gullet. I pounded the wall as it went up my throat. I reached into my mouth and pulled out a clump of bloody red hair. My hands were trembling.

I walked back to my bed and dropped the hair. I gaped at the rancid corpse that was lying in my bed. I beheld the corpse of the servant woman that I had attacked, and her dead eyes were looking towards me. I recognized her face and hair. Something had ripped out some of her hair, as if something had been biting and chewing on her head. Her face was torn and bloody. She had been eviscerated, and her red blood dripped all over my bed. Her clothes and uniform were ragged. Her skin was white. Large wounds were on her neck, and she looked as if something had been eating her body.

A painful feeling of helplessness sank into my heart again. Deranged thoughts flashed into my mind. Irregular emotions crawled through my veins. I heard so many different voices in my head, but I did not know what they were saying. I wanted someone or something to get rid of the awful smell that was in this room. I wondered if the stench had filled up the entire castle. The odor was making it harder for me to concentrate on anything but the awful pain in my chest and my head.

The walls were beginning to flex and bend. The warped walls were undulating and pulsing. Their wallpaper was peeling like the pale skin of a snake. Their wood was rotting like a corpse. Their stones were cracking. The walls, ceiling, and floor reminded me of a human organ, heart, or a living creature's bloody intestines. The walls were sticky as they slipped off their molts. The moldings and corbels of the room were becoming like gargoyles.

I ran to the wooden door and tried to open it. I slammed into it, trying to break it open. The door was thick and strong. I kicked the door and pounded on it. I was still hearing odd moans and whispers that sounded as if they were coming from behind the walls.

I screamed, "Let me out! I want to get out of here! You cannot do this to me! I cannot breathe in here! Help me! Help me!"

Black bats were flying around the ceiling. I heard them shrieking and squeaking. I saw that they were coming down towards me. Their large wings flapped around my eyes.

"Forgive me!" I yelled. "Forgive me!"

Dismaying moans filled my ears. I turned and saw the servant woman's corpse begin to twitch. I was flailing my arms around to get the bats away from me. I slapped away some bats that were on my neck. The woman's moans slowly became demented laughs. I saw her move on the bloody bed. I kicked the door and screamed for help.

"Help!" I screamed. "Someone! Someone! Open this door! Open this door!"

Finally, I broke the pulsing door down. I ran out of the room and then down the dark hallway. The swarm of black bats swooped out of the room and flew around me. I screamed with the cacophonies of screeching bats. The bats were following me and surrounding me as I was running. I could feel some of them crawling on my head and back. Flashes of lightning came through the windows and crashed against the walls.

CHAPTER 2

I TRIED TO LEAVE THE CASTLE, BUT THE GUARDS WOULD NOT LET me exit. I feared that I would never leave this castle. I wondered if it would be so bad if I were to stay here. A part of me began to think that life would be better if I were to stay and become another piece of the beautiful mysteries within this castle. I knew that it would be dangerous to remain here, but I also wanted to remain here, and that terrified me.

Servants came to take me back to my room. This time, I did not resist them. The castle was still swallowed by the darkness of night when a doctor came to visit me in my room. The servant woman's corpse was not in my bed. My room was normal, the walls were motionless, and the bats were gone. Everything seemed peaceful here. The doctor said that I needed to sleep, but I did not trust his advice because I thought that I had been sleeping well enough.

"This castle is changing me," I told him. "Doctor, it is."

The doctor said, "Tell me what you are experiencing."

I said, "I told you this already. I feel like I am losing my mind. I do not know if medicine can help me. I think I should leave the castle. Sometimes, I do not feel like myself."

The doctor said, "I do not think that it would be safe to take you away from the castle. I think that you are suffering from anxiety and stress. You will be fine. You should rest here. I will visit you again in a few days."

"What is wrong with you?" I asked. "I need actual help."

The doctor said, "This will pass. Soon, everything will make sense to you again."

"What if it is too late for me by then?" I asked.

I gasped and realized that I was suddenly not in my room. I felt my eyes quickly open wide, like I had just woken up from a bad dream.

"Where am I?" I asked. "Hello?"

I woke up in a crypt illuminated by many candles. There were many caskets and tombs here. One of the caskets was moving. I heard scratching sounds from inside the long coffin. Its lid was shuddering. I opened the casket but saw nothing inside. I stepped inside the coffin, reclined down, and sighed.

I said, "I wish that I could find Alison. I wish that she were here with me. Where are you, Alison? Speak to me. I am here now. I am inside the castle. There must be a way for me to save you without dying. We can be together, Alison. I am here for you."

I closed my eyes for a few seconds. When I opened them, I was back in my room. I was in my bed. The doctor walked into the room with some servants.

"Hello, Theodemir," said the doctor. "I am a doctor that lives in the castle. I was told that you were not feeling well and attacking the servants. Is this true?"

I said, "Yes, but I am feeling better now. Doctor, I think I ate something bad. My food tasted moldy and bitter. I had been feeling dizzy and stressed earlier, too. I am trying to find a missing woman and the stress is manipulating my mind. I have been having bad dreams, too, so I think that is all that it was. I am fine now."

"I am very busy," said the doctor. "I do not have the time to deal with this right now. Just behave yourself and do not let stress take control of your actions. If you need anything, ask the servants."

"Thank you," I said. "I will behave."

The doctor and the servants left. After several minutes, the master of the castle, Lord Adalric Fiendilkfjeld, walked into my room. Adalric was wearing black silk clothes and a black cloak.

"What can I do for you, Lord Adalric?" I asked.

"You may call me simply Adalric," he said.

I said, "Forgive me. What can I do for you, Adalric?"

Adalric said, "You can start by telling me why you have come, and why you want to stay here."

I said, "Roman needs my help. We are looking for Alison."

"I did not want Roman to be involved with this."

"I know. I understand."

"Do you?"

I tried not to look into his eyes. "Yes, I believe so. This is your home. Everyone who does not belong here is an invader."

Adalric said, "Do you think that this castle is making you sick?"

I said, "I honestly do not know what to believe. I have been having really weird dreams. I think I have just been worrying too much."

Adalric said, "Tell me about your dreams."

"For many months, I have been having dreams where I see a woman who looks like Alison. I saw her in this castle, it looked like this castle. I think she knows me, and she wants me to save her, but she knows that I will die if I help her. I really do not understand it, and I cannot really explain it any better than that. I came here because I wanted to connect myself with the woman who looks like the woman in my dream."

"Why?"

I said, "Because, Lord Adalric, I mean Adalric, that woman inspires hope in me. She is so beautiful."

"You love her."

"Adalric, I do not know if I can say that I love her."

"You love her."

I said, "There is something about her that gives me a reason to live."

Adalric said, "You believe that your life can actually mean something if you can help her."

I said, "No one has ever accepted me, Adalric. No one has ever made me feel important. I always tried to make friends, but I always ended up with the wrong groups. Every time that I thought that I had made good friends, they always left me at some point. All of the women that I had loved all left me. I traveled around with some people that I had met. I thought that they would protect me, but they left me. I woke up and they were gone. They had just abandoned me, and I did not even know where they went. I never saw them again. I feel something when the woman in my dreams talks to me. I feel something when I see her at night. She gives me this warm presence that lets me know that I am someone. When Roman told me that he was looking for a woman who looked exactly like this girl from my dreams, I had to follow my destiny. I thought it was too much of a coincidence that she would be connected with you at this place, my family's castle. I had always wanted to meet you and all the others who live here. I thought that you all hated me and my parents. You can help me understand who I really am, and maybe help me connect with the woman who I have been seeing in my dreams."

Adalric asked, "Are you starting to doubt yourself?"

I said, "I do not know what is happening to me. I have seen so many strange things that I cannot explain. I think that I have just been worrying too much. My imagination was just making me see things that were not there. I have been trying to think like the person who took Alison, and I think it is giving me strange dreams and thoughts. I do not understand myself anymore. Do you know what I mean? I wanted to understand myself better by coming here. I am finally here, but I understand myself less."

"Finding Alison will help you understand yourself," said Adalric. "Who would be keeping her here? Who would have taken her? What will you do when you realize that she is not here?"

I said, "Finding her might make the dreams stop, and then I can find peace. If someone is keeping her here, it might be someone who is close to you. You might have a traitor inside these walls. If she is not here, I will use my experiences here to get closer to this other side of my family that I have never fully known. You are part of my family. We should want to understand each other."

Adalric said, "Trust me, I will continue to help you understand what you really are. You just have to let me into your world, as I have allowed you to walk into mine."

"What do you mean?" I asked.

"I am feeling a resisting force around you," said Adalric. "You do not even realize that you are doing it."

"I do not understand," I said.

"Why are you really here?" asked Adalric.

"Well, I do want to understand what has been happening to me, too," I said. "There might be something here that can help me understand the world better."

"What are you really looking for?"

I said, "I think that there is something here that will help me grow as an individual."

I was getting nervous. I did not want to upset or disappoint the master of the castle. I did not want him to think that I was ignorant or shallow, and I did not want him to believe that I was weak or foolish. I was not sure what I should say to him honestly and what I should conceal.

"I want to believe in something meaningful," I said. "I have always wanted to believe that magic was real, but I have known that it is not. I have never seen anything that convinced me that there was anything guiding my destiny. This castle makes me doubt everything I believed about reality."

"Do you think that we would ever share our secrets with you?" asked Adalric.

I said, "I think that I have a responsibility to do this for myself. If there is a way for me to discover something that is actually supernatural, then I need to follow that path. Even if it means nothing, I need this quest for my own soul. I need to prove myself. I need to be someone that has meaningful."

"What if you have no soul? What if there are no secrets to uncover?" asked Adalric.

"The truth would be better than the mystery," I said. "I need to know the truth. I want to learn everything about our universe and our world. I want to know what this reality really is. I do not know if I have ever really tried to be connected to anything meaningful. This will be my proof, for myself, to know that I did something special and was part of something unique. You never would have allowed me to come here if I was not with Roman's investigation. You would not have allowed Roman to be here if he did not bring me. You wanted to keep me away, but there was a part of you that wanted to see me, too."

Adalric chuckled. "Will you try to leave again?"

"Why will you not let me leave?" I asked.

"I cannot allow anyone to leave until this investigation is over," said Adalric. "I need to make sure that you are not a liability to me. You have come here, and now you will obey my rules. You and I need to completely understand each other before I can let you leave. Besides, you should stay to meet my wife Hilda. One of your third cousins, Dragana, will also be coming. You must meet her. I know that she wants to meet you. You want to understand us, right?"

"How are you and I related?" I asked.

"You do not want to know how old I am," said Adalric.

"What about our name?" I asked. "Where does that come from?"

"Our name, Fiendilkfjeld, comes from our ancestor who was a wealthy man from Scandinavia," said Adalric. "He was a powerful saint to many, but a wicked heretic to others. We are descendants of his offspring. He protected this land and its king. You should know our family's history."

"Why did my father not like you?" I asked.

"Your father hated what he was," said Adalric. "He thought that we aristocrats represented a darker part of history that should have been forgotten. He was afraid of responsibility and strength. He could never deny that he envied us, and loved us. He always wanted to be different and special. He was always searching for something to give his life a certain kind of purpose or value. I believe that he thought that he could find that by distancing himself from his real family. We always loved him, but he was afraid of us. He married a very wealthy woman, he had a son, and then he was gone. He did not want to be called a lord, count, or duke. He just wanted to be a normal wealthy man. Or, he might have just been afraid of our family's curse."

"There is a curse?" I asked.

"Do you truly believe in fate?" asked Adalric.

"I do not know," I said.

"You might not be ready for this knowledge yet," said Adalric.

"What is it?" I asked.

"When you truly want to know, I will tell you," said Adalric.

"What does that mean?" I asked. "I want to know now."

Adalric said, "I should go. You have work to do. Or, maybe you will sleep. I will not trouble you any further tonight."

"Will you tell me about the curse?" I asked.

Adalric walked out of the room and closed the door behind him. I wanted to follow him, but I did not want to earn his anger. I told myself that everything was going to get better now.

"All of those strange things that you have been seeing and hearing, they have all just been part of your imagination," I said. "Magic is not real. Curses are not real. I should not think about this any longer. But, why am I looking for Alison? If the dreams are just dreams, does that mean that it would be useless to look for her? No. I can help someone. I can do a good thing by helping her. This will be my moment to be someone important for someone. Look, I got here, did I not? Adalric would never have allowed me to come here if I was not with this investigation. I am learning so many things about my family. I am seeing my own parents from a new perspective, too. There is nothing for me to be afraid of. I need to calm myself. I need to be calm. Be calm." I flinched after I heard something creak. I turned around and said, "Who is there?" I heard the wind sighing as it blew against the walls outside. "Hello?" I asked. "The wind is so loud around here. I have never heard wind so loud before."

I was not sure if I could go to sleep. I did not want to be tired for the next morning, because I needed to be awake enough to help with the investigation. I started thinking about the things I had seen recently. I knew that they could never have actually been real. I knew that I did not kill anyone, and bats were always getting into old buildings like this, especially an old castle. I tried not to be worried about any of that stuff.

"Why did I like it?" I asked. "What? No. But, it was fun, right? I did not enjoy being chased by bats, and I do not want to be locked away in a dungeon for stupidly murdering someone. I never would have done that. I am fine. It was all a dream. I need to focus on Alison."

CHAPTER 3

Someone was knocking. I turned to the door and heard the knocking again. I was not sure what I should do. I did not want to believe that this castle could be changing me, but there was a voice in my head that said that I should be afraid of everything here. I did not want to believe in magic or ghosts, but something was keeping me from opening the door. Looking at the door, I heard the sounds of someone or something knocking on it. It sounded like human knuckles knocking on the wood, but I feared that it was something that was not human.

"This is silly," I said. "I should not believe in magic. Ghosts are not real. I should open this door and see who needs me. If someone does need me, why have they not spoken to me?" It was strange that the person at the door would knock without saying who they are or making any kind of announcement. "Why are they so silent?" I asked. I moved farther away from the door. "Who is it?" I asked. "Hello? You should stop knocking. Who is there? Who are you?"

I closed my eyes and walked closer to the door. I heard the knocking becoming louder. I did not want to be afraid. I was certain that this was only part of my imagination deceiving me. My mind must have been tricking my ears. I opened the door and saw that there really was no one there. I walked out into the hallway. I looked right and then I looked left. I did not hear or see anyone.

"I know that I want to believe that magic is real," I said, "But, I cannot allow myself to start hallucinating." I thought it was so strange how I wanted to believe in the reality of magic, but I was also terrified of it, too. There was something inside of me that wanted to block out anything that was not real or understandable. I began to think about what Lord Adalric had told me earlier when he visited me. If I truly wanted to learn about the mysteries of this world, would I need to stop trying to block out anything I did not want to accept? I was not a lunatic. I could not just accept any dream or thought that I had as truth. I needed to be able to function as a normal human being. I could not allow myself to be thrown into absolute madness. I needed facts, evidence, and clues. I needed a formula or some kind of totally tangible proof that there was truly something here that was really supernatural.

Alison and the woman from my dreams could have only been beautiful coincidences. I needed better evidence, something that was more than dreams and strange thoughts. I walked back into my room and shut the door. I heard the sounds of knocking again. I screamed and jumped with fear.

Roman walked into the room and said, "What has been happening with you?"

I said, "Roman, it is nice to see you. What can I do for you?"

Roman said, "I cannot believe what you did to those servants. What have you become?"

"I really am very sorry about that," I said. "I think I ate something bad and the stress of this investigation just made me loss my mind for a minute."

"You lost your mind for more than a minute," said Roman. "You bit a man's face and you took out someone's eye."

"What? No, Roman, please, stop that. Do not say things that are not true," I said.

Roman said, "Do you think that this is all a joke? You are lucky that you are related to these aristocrats otherwise you would be harshly punished."

"Roman, I really do not understand what you are talking about," I said. "Why are you saying these things to me?"

"What made you start attacking the servants?" asked Roman.

"Roman, I told you, I started to panic," I said. "My anxiety made me freak out a bit, but I did not do anything that was too bad."

Roman said, "What do you think has been happening?"

I said, "Roman, I think that you are the one who needs medicine now."

Roman said, "You could have actually killed people."

"I do not believe anything that you have been saying to me," I said. "I did not bite anyone and I did not take anyone's eye. Why would you do this to me now?"

"Do you know why you are really here?" asked Roman.

"Do you know?" I asked. "What about you? Do you know why you are really here?"

"Why did I bring you?" asked Roman.

"You wanted me to give you hope," I said. "You wanted me to soothe your mind and tell you that Alison is alive. You are starting to doubt everything about this case, and now you are pointing your anger and disappointment to me. I do not like being disrespected, Roman."

"The Fiendilkfjeld family is always using me to cover up their messes and hide their secrets," said Roman. "I should have known that you would not be different."

"Who do you think I am?" I asked. "Do you think that I can be easily deceived? Maybe you are the one who has been filling my head with stupid thoughts and ideas about dreams and visions. You have been using my dreams against me so that I can help you."

"I am trying to rescue an innocent woman," said Roman. "You are not innocent."

"I am innocent," I said. "Roman, I am innocent. I do not like the way that you are talking to me."

Roman said, "You are pathetic. You are supposed to be helping me, not fighting the servants."

I asked, "Where is this coming from?"

"You cannot do anything right. You are too afraid of everything," said Roman.

"I know that you do not mean the things that you are saying," I said. "Who is making you say these things?"

"The noble Fiendilkfjeld family does not want us here," said Roman.

"Then, they might be the ones who are responsible," I said. "They want us to fight. They could have gotten to us and maybe they are messing with our minds."

"How would they do that?" asked Roman.

"What do you want from me?" I asked.

"I want to help you," said Roman. "I want you to be strong. We need to be strong, for Alison."

"Do you think that I am strong?"

"You cannot help me if you are always going to be sick or delusional."

"You need me, or the investigation is canceled," I said. "The family will not allow you to be here without me. That was the deal that you made with them. This was never about Alison. I think I understand now. You just want to pressure my family for money, and they did not let you come here without me. I am your representative. The real question is, why would they need me? Why would you need me, too? The family wanted someone who was part of their blood but not actually from the castle. I am here to protect them from you. I need to make sure that you do not do anything that could hurt them while you pretend to look around the castle for clues or evidence. No one else wanted to come with you because they did not want to get involved with the case or this family, because of old rivalries or paranoia. You said that my dreams could help you, but you know that my dreams could mean nothing. Now that we are here, you want me to stop watching you. You want to push me away. What are you really planning to do now that you are here, Roman?"

"I will find her," said Roman. "I know that she is here. Someone is keeping her here."

"You do not know anything," I said.

"I know that you are a lunatic."

112

"You are, too."

"I do not want to work with you anymore," said Roman.

"If you leave me, you will need to leave the castle," I said. "You may not want to work with me, but I will be shadowing you. I will be beside you. I understand now what Lord Adalric was telling me. He was trying to tell me something that he could not actually say with words. I understand now. I am here to make sure that you are the one who does not do anything harmful. Go on, look around the castle. Look for her. I will be looking for her, too, and I will be watching you."

Roman said, "You need to remember that I am a detective. I have power. I have information. Do you remember? I know things about you and your sleazy friends Dean, Boris, Mildred, and Greta. I am sure you do not want to remember them, do you? I know that you helped them rob graves, steal bodies, steal mummies, and sell fake mummies, too. I know that you have helped them make illegal drugs that have human blood and bones in them. Remember that?"

"What is it that you need me to do?" I asked. "Tell me. What do you want from me? What has this all been for? Why are you using me?"

"You helped me get here," said Roman. "But, I do not want to work with you anymore. If you are not with me, I cannot stay here. I need to stay here to find Alison, which means I also need you with me. I do not think that the family will let us stay here any longer if you are going to continue attacking their servants. If you ruin this opportunity for me, I will ruin you."

"This is not just about her," I said. "I think that you want something else from me. You want me to help you blackmail my family. You want to use me to put pressure on them and confuse them, while you sneak around planting false evidence. You want everyone to keep believing that she is here so that you can use that as leverage to get more money from us. Now that I am not dancing along with your tune, you want to get me out of the act. You really should have been an actor, Roman. You want to blackmail me, too. You are going to continue to play games with all of us, and you will not ever let it stop. You do not want us to be free."

"You sound insane!" said Roman. "I am a detective! I am trying to rescue my friend! What has this place done to you?"

"I think that the medicine you gave me was what made me sick," I said. "You have been manipulating me. Now that I am here, you want me to cause trouble for my own family."

"You are not making sense," said Roman.

"You thought that you could use me," I said. "You know things about my past, and you are always going to try to use that against me so that I will do whatever you want. You collect information about people. You thought that you could use me to cause chaos here. In the chaos, you would get more information about us, and you would use it all to control us. I understand now. It was so simple, but you failed, Roman. I understand now what I must do. Roman, you know too much about the noble Fiendilkfjeld family. I will correct things and prove myself."

"Prove yourself to whom?" asked Roman.

"The castle," I said as I strangled Roman.

A voice inside my head told me that this is exactly what I had always wanted to do to Roman. Roman was a detective, he was fast, but he was not stronger than I was. He was not ready for the brutal ferocity and malevolent strength that was pouring through my veins and into my muscles. He was not ready for my punches and kicks that broke his bones. I throttled him before he could get the gun out. He was so pathetic that I had to laugh as I broke his hand under my heel.

Roman had been blackmailing my family for a long time, and now I got to watch him bleed. I wondered if this was my real plan the entire time, if this was not exactly how I had wanted things to get between him and me. All he secrets that he knew about us would be gone. I ripped his face off his skull with my fingers. I did not do a good job, so his face became shredded.

I was proud that I had defeated Roman. I did something good for my family. I was not going to let him take me away from this castle. I did not want him to hurt us any longer. I was surprised that I had actually killed him. I was not certain that I would actually do it. I did not know how I was going to get away with this.

After Roman was dead, I took his clothes and other possessions. I covered him in some blankets. I left my room and found one of the servants. I had him take me to see Wessel. I walked into Wessel's room and found him sitting in a chair by a fireplace filled with bright tall flames.

I said, "Wessel, someone has died."

Wessel said, "You killed the detective."

"How did you know?" I asked.

"They were hoping that you would."

"Adalric wanted Roman gone, too. Is that why I was summoned here? Was I being used to commit murder for the family?" I asked.

Wessel said, "You have done a great service for your family. Roman was a crooked detective, a blackmailer, and a thief."

"Was he right about Alison?" I asked. "Is she here?"

"That is your quest," said Wessel. "You need to find out if she is here or not."

"What? Why can you not tell me? I thought that you would be proud of me," I said.

"We will not let you leave this castle until you find out the truth," said Wessel.

"This does not make sense!" I screamed. "You cannot do this to me! I need to know the truth! I need to find her!"

"You will understand, one day," said Wessel. "If you do not find her in time, you will be trapped here forever."

"No! Do not do this to me! No!" I screamed. "No! You cannot do this. Why should I be a prisoner?"

Wessel said, "Only you can end this. You are not ready to leave. You cannot be trusted, yet."

"What is this for?" I asked.

"You must answer that question," said Wessel. "You wanted to search for meaning and truth about your world. You have taken the first step toward true power. You would not have killed Roman if you did not want to truly begin your journey."

"I killed Roman because I did not want him controlling my life," I said. "I did not want him to interfere with my family's lives. He was threatening me with blackmail, and he has been causing trouble for you all, too."

"Do you feel the life of this castle?" asked Wessel. "You know that it is alive. You want to know more, but you are not ready yet. You do not have much time. Discover the truth, and you will be free. If you are too late, you will be buried alive forever."

"What kind of game are you playing?" I asked. "This is insane! Why did I kill Roman? Why? No! No! Why did I kill him? Why?"

"You have three nights to discover the truth about Alison," said Wessel. "If you do not discover the truth before three nights pass from now, you will forever be our prisoner."

CHAPTER 4

I ONLY HAD THREE NIGHTS FROM NOW TO FIND ALISON, AND I had no idea where to begin. I hated myself for getting involved in any of this. I wished that I had never met Roman. I wished that I had not killed him. Remembering how I had strangled him and ripped off his flesh, I did not even recognize myself.

"Was that really me?" I asked myself. "Did that even really happen? How could I have killed someone?"

I looked out a window and saw that nighttime was still throwing its shadows across the sky and down upon the castle. As I was returning to my room, I could not stop thinking about Roman's death. I knew that the person who killed him was not me. Something happened to me. The memories of his death did not make sense to me. I did not want to believe that the castle was changing me or transforming my soul. If I accepted that I actually killed someone, I would have to be accepting that I might have killed other people.

I stopped walking. "No," I said. "I never killed anyone. Someone else did it. Someone knows that I am getting too close to the truth. Alison is here. Alison will help me understand everything. Alison, please, where are you? Speak to me, Alison. I am right here. Say my name, Alison. I am right here. I will rescue you."

I continued walking until I arrived at my room. I shut the door behind me and looked at the floor. There was no blood.

"See?" I whispered. "No blood. No one died here, Alison. Everything will be all right."

I decided to burn my clothes and wear new clothes. I burned the clothes that I was wearing in my fireplace. I grabbed the clothes that I saw on my bed. I put on undergarments and socks, black silk trousers, and black leather boots. I put on a black silk shirt and black velvet vest over it. My skin was already white, but I put white powder on my pale face so that my skin would look brighter. I repainted my lips and fingernails black, put some black leather gloves in my coat pocket, slicked my long blond hair and brushed it back so that it curved behind my head, and then put on a black top hat. I put on a black fur coat. In the coat was a black leather holster that hung from the inside of it so that I could easily reach in and pull the gun out. I did not have many bullets, so I was not planning on using the gun often. I remembered that the guards here had guns, too, so I would need to be careful.

I walked out of my room and searched for a servant. I tried asking them about Alison, but they ignored me. I spoke to several more servants, but they all ignored me, too. I tried communicating with the servants in many different languages, but they still ignored me. I began to wonder if they were part of the game that the family was playing with me.

I avoided the guards whenever I saw them. I did not want them to see me or hear the things that I was saying. I did not want to know what would happen if they were to discover that I was attempting to escape the castle again.

I saw a servant man walking past me. I gazed around and thought that there was a good possibility that we were alone. I grabbed him by the neck and pushed him into a dark empty hallway. He tried to scream, but I covered his mouth. He was thin, he had dark brown hair, blue eyes, and pale skin. He was shorter than me and felt very light when I pushed him.

I whispered in his ear, "Be silent or I will erase you from this world." I took my hand off his mouth. I asked, "Who are you?"

"My name is Luca," he whispered. "I am twenty two years old, and I am a servant for the noble Fiendilkfjeld family. What did I do wrong, my lord?"

"The noble family is playing games with me," I said. "I need your help. You can help me, right?"

"I will help you, my lord."

"What do you know about the heiress Alison?"

"We are being watched, my lord. There are ears everywhere."

"Where can we talk?"

Luca stepped away from me and whispered, "You have to find me when I am in the kitchen."

I grabbed Luca's arm and said, "If you say anything about this to anyone, I will destroy you." I pushed him away and faded into the shadows.

I walked through a baffling maze of hallways and narrow passages. I was lost in a labyrinth of corridors, dead ends, and winding halls. I tried to open many doors, but they were all locked. The windows had been barred, too. I was unable to find my way out. I passed under many Gothic arches as I searched for a way out. The hallways were illuminated by torchlight.

Many of the walls, ceiling, and floors were made of stone and black marble. Some of the walls appeared to be covered with black wallpaper. Large suits of medieval armor stood beside life-size white marble statues of handsome Roman warriors and Visigothic rulers. I looked up and saw the rib vaults and pointed arches.

I tried to open more doors, but none of them would open. I tried to break them open, but the doors were too strong. Walking through the halls was exhausting. There were times when I thought that these rambling hallways would never end. There were no guards here, so I wondered what this area of the castle was being used for.

I heard footsteps behind me. I turned around, but saw nothing. Looked down the hallways, but I was alone. When I turned around, I saw a man take a corner and disappear. I followed him because I thought that he looked familiar. I took the same corner and saw the man walking toward the end of the hallway. I recognized his clothes, too, and they reminded me of the clothes that I was wearing. The man took another corner. I followed him, but he was gone, and I was alone again.

It took a while for me to finally find a door that was not locked. The black door had the shape of a pointed arch and was made of thick iron. Its jambs were decorated with large statues of priests and monsters. The marble carvings on the tympanum depicted many graves and human skeletons.

I walked through the doorway and entered a Gothic cloister. I quietly closed the door and continued walking. I saw people who were wearing black cowls, cloaks, and hoods. Their black clothes were clean and neat. I could not see their faces, which were hidden in shadows. There were several of them who looked like monks, and they appeared to be talking to one another.

I spoke to them. I asked, "What is this place?"

One of the monks said, "This is a place for monks, priests, nuns, and all the clergy who belong to Fiendilkfjeld castle. You will find a cathedral if you keep walking. This area also connects to a convent and our monastery."

"Thank you for your help," I said.

The monks quickly walked away, and I assumed that they did not want to answer any more of my questions. I did not follow the monks. I walked in a different direction from them. I heard something whispering my name, so I decided to follow the voice.

The voice led me to a red door. I opened the door and walked down the stairs. I saw a room filled with many lit candles. I heard people talking. I stood still and listened the voices that seemed to be coming from behind these walls.

I did not understand what they were saying, but I thought that I heard someone say, "Theodemir, please, stop."

I heard someone crying and another person screaming. I looked around for a door, but there was none. I ran out of the room and left that place. I closed the red door and gasped for air. I found a chair and sat down. I sat for a while and waited to regain my energy.

Another monk sat beside me. He asked, "What are you doing here?"

"I am looking for a missing woman," I said. "I came here because I think that she might still be here. Do you think that is possible?"

"This is a very large castle," said the monk. "There are many places for a person to hide. This woman whom you are looking for might not want to be found."

"I think that she wants me to find her," I said. "I feel her presence."

"Who is she?" he asked.

"I do not know her," I said. "She gives me hope."

"How does she give you hope?" he asked.

"She is so beautiful," I said. "You might have seen her before. Did you ever know a wealthy woman named Alison? She came here and now no one knows where she is."

"What does she look like?" he asked.

I said, "She has long blond hair, white skin, green eyes, and she might be five feet tall. Does that help?"

"I cannot help you," he said, "I can only tell you that you have come to a very dangerous place. It is possible that she is here, but I know that there are many people here who are already hiding many wicked secrets."

"Can you tell me anything?" I asked. "I feel as if nothing I do is important."

He said, "I can tell you that this castle has always been a sacred place. Many pilgrims have come here looking for salvation, hope, faith, or even inspiration. You are looking for inspiration, too. You must understand what keeps you attached to things and what has attached to your soul. Sometimes, we get taken to a place because we need to learn something from it. You can find yourself inside a situation that you do not understand, and you will not have any choices about it. You can feel like you have no free will. All you can do is be there and learn from your experience within it. Sometimes, not having a choice can actually be valuable. When you are forced to be somewhere or do something, you can feel like you are starting to become someone different. That kind of pain and transformation is valuable. It teaches us how to become better servants so that we can become connected to the only thing that matters. Evil, pain, chaos, and death are actually gifts that allow us to learn how to connect to truth, faith, happiness, love, and eternal life."

"I thank you," I said.

He walked away, and so did I. I walked through a hallway that led me into a Gothic cathedral. I tried to speak with some nuns and priests, but they did not speak to me. I thought that they did not know how to speak my language. I tried to speak different languages, but they did not seem to understand me. Some of the priests appeared suspicious because they looked as if they were too afraid to talk to me.

I found one priest who did want to speak to me. I asked him, "Do you think that it is possible that this castle is haunted?"

The priest said, "Yes. The castle is haunted. We are here to make sure that the evil is never released."

"What evil?" I asked.

"The evil that lives inside the walls and the ground that we stand on," he said.

I asked, "What is it?"

He said, "This region is cursed, and so is the castle. The clergy are here to purify this land and all the sinners that walk upon it."

"What is haunting the castle?"

"Do you believe that you can be saved?"

I asked, "I do not know what to believe."

He said, "You must have faith that your soul can be purified. You must believe that there is still time to save your soul."

"I am trying to save a missing woman," I said. "I think that someone here is keeping her here. Do you believe that there is someone here who could be hiding her? Has someone abducted her? Where is she?"

The priest said, "You need to pray. Pray with me."

"I do not have time to pray," I said. "You must forgive me. I need to find some-one."

"Stay here. I will help you," said the priest. "I will help your soul."

"Why would you do that?" I asked.

The priest said, "Evil deities lurk within the ground. This castle pulls the damned into it. We are being punished, because we are sinners. Those who hear the voices of the deities will become doomed. We are always being watched. You must beware Lord Adalric."

I asked, "What can you tell me about him?"

The priest said, "You must let me help you."

"I need to go," I said. "I need to find someone."

I ran out of the cathedral. I found one of the libraries of this castle. I searched for books that contained research and information about paranormal occur-rences and supernatural events. I began reading books that contained informa-tion regarding magic, superstitions, and monsters. I had already been studying the supernatural for many years, but now I wanted to see if there was anything that I had missed. I hoped that something in any of these books would help me understand what was happening here. Many of these books were old, so I was very careful with them. The books in this library were broken and damaged. I could only read short segments of the old texts and information from the moldy scraps and burnt remains of the pages that were left attached.

Though I already was familiar with some of the information in these books, I was excited and enjoying reading them. I read about people who said that they saw ghosts or monsters. I learned that many people in the region of Fiendilkfjeld believe that they are being protected by deities of the forest and mountains. I read about ancient curses that prevented people from being with their relatives unless they were dead. There was a lot of information in these books about the supersti-tions of this region. Some of the books were saying that there were people in this region who hunt the monsters that have been killing people here. Another book was saying that people could be turned into monsters or evil spirits.

I lost track of time. I had to go. I returned the books in the places where I had found them. After, I left the library. I did not know what to do with the knowledge that I had gained. I was not sure how to think about anything anymore. If magic was real, if it was in this castle, it would change the way I thought about everything. I meditated on what I had learned, what others had told me, and what I had seen. I tried to understand what was happening here. I wanted to make the magic mine.

That ambition gave me an idea. I began to wonder if Alison had discovered something magical here, like I had. There was a possibility that she was also searching for a way to control the magic that lived inside this castle. If she was calling out to me in my dreams, then that might mean that she believed that I could help her control it. If she was not searching for it, something supernatural could have taken her. My curiosity to understand these mysteries was strong.

I returned to my room, but I felt strange, as if I had already been here. It was like I did not actually leave. I turned around a few times, but nothing seemed strange. I closed the door and began getting ready for sleep.

When I shut my eyes, I saw Alison again. I saw her walk into a crypt. I felt as if I was following her. She appeared to be looking for something. I tried to speak to her, but I woke up.

CHAPTER 5

MORNING HAD BEGUN, AND I WAS STILL IN THE LIBRARY. I woke up still sitting a table, with my nose deep into a book, and I was surrounded by tall crooked stacks of large books. I must have read dozens of books before I had fallen asleep. These books were written by my relatives and other aristocrats of the Fiendilkfjeld family.

For many years, I had thought that I was strange and abnormal because of my obsession with occult research, but now I realized that many people in my family also had devoted their lives to studying magical phenomena. This library was filled with books that my family had written.

It appeared that the books of this library had all, at one point in the past, been terribly damaged by fire and water. They had many wounds and damages that appeared to be caused by flames and flood. The pages of these books were frayed and ragged. The tatters of these books were blackened and sullied, but small portions of beautiful, bright red and blue colors peeked through the stains. Sunlight from the windows glistened on the amazingly elegant illustrations of monsters and creatures that still clung onto the damaged pages.

Some of the books that I thought were not damaged actually were. I remembered reading books that were clean and preserved, but now they also appeared withered, moldy, and broken. Hideous insects crawled around the floor. I crushed them under my boots. More insects were crawling on the books. I jumped away from them and decided not to touch these books again. I hated bugs and insects.

I turned around and noticed someone hurrying away behind the giant bookshelves and bookcases. The person disappeared, but I was not going to let them get away. If they had been spying on me, I needed to know what they knew.

I found someone hiding behind a statue. I chased the mysterious figure into a dimly lit room and pulled out my gun. There was nowhere else for the figure to run to. When the figure turned around, I realized that it was a woman who appeared to be thirty or thirty five years old. She gasped and looked terrified.

This woman was wearing a tight black leather skirt, black silk stockings, black leather shoes with long heels, and a green cotton shirt. Her shirt had wide puffy shoulders, long loose sleeves, and a tall lace collar that covered her neck.

She was holding books that were wider than her thin waist. She appeared to be struggling to carry the heavy books in her shuddering arms. She was squinting, and her eyes appeared to be struggling to not cry, but small tears rolled out of the corners of those frightened eyes.

"Who are you?" I asked.

She said, "I am an archivist for your family. My name is Agnes. Please, my lord, do not shoot me." When she spoke, her voice sounded scared.

Agnes was tall with white skin, a skinny body, and gray eyes. She had voluminous blond hair that was slightly wavy and very fluffy. The candlelight made her hair appear like golden sunlight. She dropped the books and put her hands above her head.

"You know who I am?" I asked. "How long have you been working here?"

Agnes said, "I am thirty three years old, my lord; I have been working for the family for five years in this castle. You look like the master of the castle, my lord, and we all were warned that you would be coming here."

I asked, "Warned?"

"Everyone in the castle knows who you are."

"What do they know?"

"We know that you are part of the family. You came to visit the master."

"I came to find someone," I said. "A woman has gone missing. She was last seen here."

"The family never allows anyone to leave this castle."

I asked, "What? How is that possible?"

I was still aiming the gun at her.

Agnes teared up, and she sobbed. She said, "Electronic devices never work correctly here, my lord. Everything is monitored. Everyone is being watched. They hear everything."

"That is not possible," I said. "My family would never be allowed to do something like that. It is just not possible."

Agnes sobbingly said, "They will kill me if I tell you anything else, but I need you to believe me."

"Why were you watching me?" I asked.

Agnes said, "I was not watching you."

She tried to punch me, but I slapped her face with my gun. She fell to the ground.

I asked, "Who are you? What are you doing here? Where is Alison?" I aimed my gun at her. I said, "No more games."

She looked up into my eyes. Her red blood moved out of her nostrils and slid down her lips. She stopped crying and glared at me.

"No more crocodile tears," I said. "Now, you show your true nature to me."

"Yes, I was watching you," she said. Her voice sounded forceful and vicious.

"Do not get up. Do not move," I said. "What is really happening here?"

She said, "No one is allowed to leave. I was telling you the truth."

"Why were you watching me?"

"I will not tell you anything." She spit blood at me.

I kicked her in the face. I screamed, "I need to find someone! Do you not listen?"

"If you help me, I will help you," she said.

"What do you know?"

"If you find a special tapestry for me, I can tell you where I saw her."

"She is here."

"She is."

I said, "How do I find her? Who has her?"

Agnes chuckled. She said, "You need to find a tapestry for me. It is hidden in a very old haunted part of the castle. I am too afraid to go. I have tried, but the ghosts there are bloodthirsty. If you get the tapestry for me, I will tell you what I know."

"What does the tapestry look like?"

"If I am correct, the tapestry should depict an evil deity being worshipped by knights," said Agnes.

"Why do you want it?" I asked.

"It can help me get out of here."

"How?"

Agnes chuckled shortly.

"Fine," I said. "Where is it?"

Agnes said, "I will give you a key. Use that key on an old door that is at the bottom floor of this library. The path will lead you to the old laboratories and archives of the castle. Many were killed there, and their souls are still trapped down there. They have become distorted and corrupted, transformed into bloodthirsty evil spirits that can now only survive in the shadows of that place. If you survive, and bring me that tapestry, I will help you. I will not say anything else to you, not even if you rip me apart."

"You would be surprised," I said. "A lot of people think that they are tough, but they tell everything they know when they start feeling the slightest amount of pain. Human beings are so weak and unfaithful."

"Why do you not torture me?" asked Agnes.

"I am trying to decide," I said. "I think that you might tell me more if I get that tapestry for you. If you disappoint me, I might just torture you anyway. Give me that key."

"You are a freak," she said.

"The key," I said.

She pulled out a key from her pocket and threw it somewhere in the shadows. I kicked her stomach. She gasped and coughed. I kicked her again. She growled and screamed.

She said, "Kill him!"

One of the walls began to spin around. A man jumped down from a hidden recess behind the moving wall. He tried to attack me with a knife, but I shot him in the head. The man was wearing a robe and cloak like the monks wore. I stepped on Agnes' hand as she tried to reach for the knife. I grabbed the knife before she could.

I said, "I think that you had something to do with Alison's disappearance. You have her, do you not?"

Agnes screamed loudly.

I inspected the hidden room, but I did not find Alison. I returned to the room where Agnes was. She was crawling on the floor and crying. I grabbed Agnes by the neck and pulled her up.

"You are going to come with me," I said. "Show me where the tapestry is."

"No!" She screamed. "I cannot go there! That place is haunted!"

"Come with me or you die here," I said. "You had something to do with Alison's disappearance. You want the tapestry, but why? You said that it can help you get out of here? What makes you think that?"

Agnes sobbed. She said, "The tapestry has power."

"What kind of power?"

"I do not know."

"You are dead."

She said, "Please! Wait! That is all I know! I was told that I could only leave when I got the tapestry."

"Who are you working for?" I screamed.

"I do not know," she said.

"Who are you working for?" I growled.

"The man who has Alison," she sobbed. "They need her blood for some ritual. They have been waiting for the right time to take her life."

I started choking her harder. I listened to her gasping for air. I threw her into a wall, and I thought I heard one of her ribs break. I aimed my gun at her.

"Nothing you have said makes any sense," I said. "You want me to believe that you are a prisoner and that the only way that you can get out is to help someone sacrifice Alison for a ritual. You want me to believe that there are people here that are keeping you as a hostage. Am I supposed to believe that my family has been keeping prisoners here and that no one has ever discovered any of this? I am really feeling like I am losing my mind, and you are not helping."

She said, "This place is not what you think it is."

I heard her wheezing and gasping.

"I do not want to hear you speak right now," I said. "I am going to find that tapestry, and then you are going to tell me everything that you know. Then, I am going to try to contact someone who can do something about this."

As I said that, I began to wonder what would happen if I were to get the police involved with this. I was not sure how connected my family was with this conspiracy. I did not want to cause my family trouble. They were the only ones who could accept me. If I betrayed them, they might destroy me. As I watched the blood dripping from Agnes' mouth and nose, I began to wonder why all of this had to happen. Not only that, I was enjoying the smell of her blood.

"Do not die before I come back," I said. "And do not leave this room. I am going to ask you more questions when I return."

I began thinking about how my life was in danger again. That monk had tried to kill me, and I had to kill him first. I was not sure if I was ready to give my life for this, but I wanted to rescue Alison. She was incredibly important to me. My family was also important to me. I wanted to help them both. I knew that I would find a way to do it. I had to find a way to rescue her without harming my own family. I wanted to belong here. I did not belong anywhere else.

With the key, I went into a long passageway that led me into a dark chamber. The torches on the wall mysteriously became lit when I entered. I moved down the flights of stairs and searched many underground rooms. Below these rooms, I inspected the archives and laboratories, but I did not find a tapestry. I leaned against a wall, to relax, but the wall leaned backwards and I slid down a long tunnel that dropped me into a pitch-dark room.

Loud shrieks filled the room. I screamed with horror when I saw glowing pale apparitions of decaying women floating through the shadows. The ghosts of dead men floated up from beneath me. They tried to grab me, but I ran away. Blindly, I tried to escape the ghosts. White glowing shrouds swooped down and covered my head so that I could not breathe. I was pulled up into the air by the white shrouds. I used my knife to stab them, but my attacks did nothing to them. I could not see anything except the white translucent figures and white skeletons of dead men and women carrying me upwards as they were suffocating me with their veils. The ghosts bit my neck. I felt them drinking my blood. I tried to grab one of the ghosts, but my hand slipped through their flesh as if they were made of smoke. I continued attacking them with my knife. I think I must have done something to them, because one of them vanished after I used my knife on it several times. The other ghosts saw that I had defeated one ghost and they dropped me.

When I landed on the floor, the fall broke one of my legs. I screamed with pain and tried to stand up. I gasped for air and started breathing again. I realized that these ghosts could be defeated if they were attacked hard enough, but there were too many of them here for me to handle. I had to escape, but I could not see anything. I limped away until I accidentally slammed my head into something hard. I fell to the ground and then started crawling. I could hear the screams of the ghosts moving closer to me. My hand touched something soft like a rug. The torches on the walls were lit again, and I could see my surroundings. There were no more ghosts, and I was on top of an old tapestry on the floor.

I woke up in my bed. My leg was not broken, and my knife was gone, but the tapestry was there with me. The pain in my body was gone. I got out of the bed and put the tapestry on the floor so that I could look at it better. It appeared to be a medieval tapestry from the twelfth century. It depicted a dark deity that was surrounded by shadows and corpses. The deity was being worshipped by warriors and priests. It appeared to tell the story of a peaceful spirit that was corrupted by evil magic and became possessed by the darker deity. The evil deity created demons and curses that transformed forests, animals, and people. A group of warriors and sorcerers, devoted to the deity, were transformed into evil spirits that were trapped in a world of nightmares and death. The cursed warriors and sorcerers could only return to the earth during autumn and only during the night or when the moon was full. The cursed beings fought against the deity many times, and they were both using one another for power. Somehow, the deity and the cursed beings were all trapped together. That is all the tapestry seemed to show me.

CHAPTER 6

I found Agnes in the library. I put the tapestry on the floor so that she could see the whole thing.

"How did you get this?" asked Agnes.

"I did what you were too afraid to do," I said. "I almost died, but the tapestry saved me. You are going to tell me what is so special about this."

Agnes said, "This is what they wanted. There is something in the tapestry that can help them complete the ritual. I think that there is a spell and ingredients that are written on it somewhere."

"Who took her?" I asked. "Who has Alison?"

"I never actually saw them," said Agnes. "They spoke to me from the shadows. I need this tapestry, or I cannot leave."

"If I let you have the tapestry, Alison will die," I said.

Agnes said, "You need to really open your eyes. You do not realize what is happening."

I said, "Tell me what is really happening. I would love to know the truth, because I am tired of the ghosts and the games."

"Do you really want to know?"

"I do."

Agnes chuckled.

"Will you tell me?" I asked.

"They took her to a crypt," said Agnes. "The people who have her are using the power of the dead to give their ritual strength. They have brought this entire castle closer to the world of the dead and the damned, because of their dark spells. The evil spirits are manipulating things. They are secretly controlling everything. They want to use Alison to make them stronger. If you join me, I can make you powerful, too. You and I will both be free."

"I do not believe you," I said. "I cannot let you have the tapestry. You will help me rescue her."

Agnes screamed as she lunged toward me. She grabbed my throat, but I pushed her off of me. I pulled out my gun and aimed it at her. Agnes cynically chuckled as she looked at me. She knew what I would do. She screamed and I shot her in the head. I knew that she would never have given me the truth, and she never would have helped me recuse Alison.

If the tapestry was useful to the people who took Alison, then I had to destroy it. I took the tapestry, but I was not sure what to do. If I destroyed it, I would lose its power forever. I decided to secretly study it and learn from it. I wanted to obtain the wisdom and power that it was secretly guarding.

I hid Agnes' body in the room with the dead monk. Then, I used the library to help me understand the tapestry. From what I read in the books and on the tapestry, this castle was used as a place to communicate with demons. Those techniques were written in books that were being hidden below in an underground crypt. If what I was reading in the books was correct, then the tapestry was also showing which crypt to look in.

The tapestry was too important, powerful, and beautiful to destroy. I wanted to hide it in my room, but I was afraid that the servants would find it. I heard the door open and aimed my gun. I heard people walking into the library. Tall monks, wearing black robes, walked into the room and surrounded me. They aimed their scythes at me. The monks towered over me as they held their scythes up high, ready to destroy me. I aimed my gun, ready to start shooting if I had to.

One of the monks said, "We will take the tapestry. You can join us or be killed here."

I said, "You want to use the magic spells that have been written on the tapestry so that you can kill Alison."

The monk said, "We need her to die for our ritual. If you come with us, we will let you live, and then you can also become one of us."

"What does that mean?" I asked.

"Your blood is strong," said the monk. "You can become a powerful knight."

"Whose knight?"

The monks spoke together, "The deity of this castle. The demon Fiendilkfjeld."

I started shooting at the monks, but they were too fast. They evaded the bullets. I did not see their scythes cut me, but I saw red blood spray into the air. I was in agony like I had never felt before, and then my eyes were closed.

When I woke up, Roman was standing over me. I screamed when I saw him and jumped out of my bed. I looked around and saw Agnes in the room, too. I ran into a corner of the room and started screaming. Roman came to me and held my face with his hands. I tried to push him away, but he grabbed my arms.

Roman said, "Theodemir, relax. Theodemir, it is only me. Be calm."

"My good man," I said. "Roman, you are alive."

"Was I dead?" asked Roman. He chuckled.

"Roman, what happened?" I asked. "What did I do?"

"Everything is fine," said Roman. "You must have been having a nightmare."

"What is Agnes doing here?" I asked. "We cannot trust her. She knows where Alison is, Roman. She knows. You need to arrest her before they come. They will not allow us to leave. Where is the tapestry? Do not let her get away, Roman. She is standing right there, my good man. I know that you must want to kill me, but you must get her before she can hurt Alison."

"Theodemir, everything is fine. Agnes is here to help. She has been taking care of you while you were sick," Said Roman. "Someone poisoned our food, but you suffered worse than us. We were cured. There is nothing to worry about. The poison is gone. I think that your mind was attacked worse than your body, but you are fine now."

"No, that is not right," I said. "That cannot be true."

"Try to remember what happened," said Roman. "You were eating with me and Lord Adalric. Do you remember if anyone looked suspicious? Was there anyone there in that room who could have poisoned our food?"

"There was," I gasped. "The servant woman. I was looking for her. I think that she had red hair, or something like that. I saw her, but she disappeared. It must have been her."

"There is someone here who is keeping Alison hidden from everyone," said Roman. "Someone is keeping her locked away from everyone. They do not want us to find her."

"Did Lord Adalric see anyone suspicious?" I asked.

"We did not, no," said Roman. "None of us saw anything, except for you."

"Do you not remember the woman with the red hair?" I asked. "It must have been her. She tried to poison us. She put something in our food and then left. She could have been working for someone else, someone who is still here."

"We might need to make all the servants with red hair come meet us somewhere," said Roman. "We can see which one you recognize. If you see that woman, we can ask her questions."

"I do not remember," I said. "She might have had red hair."

"So, what you are telling me is that we still have nothing," said Roman. "We cannot find her like this. We need something better to follow. Did your dreams show you anything?"

"I really do not want to talk about my dreams," I said.

"I brought you here because of your dreams," said Roman. "Your dreams show you things."

"I know that you do not believe that," I said. "You do not believe in magic. What am I supposed to believe? I do not want to talk about my dreams, Roman."

"Can you at least tell me if Alison is still alive?" asked Roman.

I said, "Do not ask me that."

Roman said, "I want you and Agnes to go to the archives. I need you and her to find some maps of this castle. I want to know everything about this place. I want to know where all the secret rooms and hidden doors in this castle are. I need to know what the interior is. If we are going to find her, we are going to need to know where all the possible recesses and corners are. I want to see dungeons, towers, hidden rooms, anything. I want to know everything about this castle."

"Do not make me go with her," I whispered. "Please, let me do this alone."

"We need special authorization to get that kind of information about this castle," Said Roman. "We need Agnes' approval on this."

"Who has the real power here?" I asked. "You are working with the government. You should be able to do whatever you want."

"It does not work like that around here," said Roman. "These people have influence, power, money, and they are the ones who can basically do whatever they want. We need to fight hard when we are dealing with the noble Fiendilkfjeld family. They know politicians, lawyers, and a lot of scary people. They themselves are scary people. They might as well control the police. What am I supposed to do? I can only work with what I have, Theodemir. Every second, they are trying to find new ways to kick us out of here and end this investigation. I told you already, all I want to do is rescue Alison. My job is to believe that she is alive. I do not want to hurt your family, but I will put pressure on them to save my friend."

"I need new clothes," I said. "I cannot wear these clothes. I need new ones. Give me time to clean and wash myself. I feel really dirty."

"There are many clothes in here for you to choose," said Roman. "Do what you need to do to get clean and handsome, and then talk to Agnes."

"What are you going to be doing?" I asked.

Roman said, "I will be looking for that woman with the red hair."

"Everything will be fine?"

"It will be."

When everyone left the room, I washed and cleaned myself. I checked my hands. No blood. I had no wounds on my body. I wore black silk trousers, a black silk shirt, a black silk vest, and black leather shoes. My socks were black wool. I did not paint my lips and fingernails black. No powder was put on my white skin. My long blond hair was straight, clean, but slightly messy. I had no knife and no gun. I knew that the castle was really dark, so I took some matches with me so that I could light some candles or torches if I needed to.

"I knew that I never killed anyone," I said. "That is not me."

I walked out of my room and saw Agnes leaning against a wall. Her arms were crossed around her chest. I flinched when I saw her and gasped.

"Forgive me," I said.

"Did I scare you?" asked Agnes.

"I did not expect you to be right there as soon as I left my room," I said.

"You are so pale white," said Agnes. "You look terrified. Am I that ugly?" She chuckled.

"No, you are an attractive woman," I said. "Please, forgive my behavior. I should not have been so presumptuous. Forget what I said."

"I like compliments," said Agnes. "People do not say nice things to one another anymore. Everyone is so afraid to say anything to anyone these days."

"I agree," I said. "Modern society has taught people to be afraid of everything."

"You and I do not belong to modern society?" asked Agnes.

"You live in a castle, and I study magic," I said with a chuckle.

Agnes said, "I do live here. I have lived here for five years. I am thirty three years old now. I do not know if I will ever leave this place."

"They do not let you leave the castle?" I asked, nervously.

"I did not mean that," she said. She chuckled again. "I meant to say that I do not know if I will ever move. I do not know if I would ever want to move. This castle is really more than just a castle. It is connected to its own little village on both sides. It has a cathedral and a hospital. It is really more of a mental hospital now. That is one of the duties that the noble Fiendilkfjeld family has. It takes care of sick people, and people who are lost or need a sanctuary. They just find people and take care of them. This really is a lovely place to be. There are places for the monks and the nuns to live, there are places for the servants to live, and then there are places for people like me to live. I am not really a servant, but I do consider your family to be my masters. Do you want me to call you my lord, too? I know that you are related to them."

"I do not know what I am. I am related to nobility, but I do not think that I am noble," I said. "My father renounced his noble title, so I have never been called a lord or count by anyone before."

"They might make you a true aristocrat after this investigation," said Agnes. "They might give you back your noble title." She smiled at me.

I smiled back at her. I said, "That would be nice. I think that I would like to be connected with this place. There is something here that I cannot escape. I want to know more about this place. I feel like I am at home."

She and I walked down the hallway and continued talking to each other. I looked out a window as I passed by and saw that it was nighttime.

"Thank you for taking care of me," I said. "I could have died."

Agnes said, "Someone wanted you dead. I needed to help. I am an archivist, but I am also a doctor. My team got that poison out of you quick enough so that you did not die. I only wish that I could have prevented your nightmares, too. I hope that you did not suffer. You might experience some more bad dreams, but that will all pass."

"What did they poison me with?" I asked.

"It was something new but mysterious," she said. "I had never seen anything like it before. I think that it was something that someone created unprofessionally. It was not anything sophisticated, is what I mean, if that makes sense. It was strong, but we defeated it."

"That is scary," I said. "I am glad that you were on my side."

"You have interesting dreams often?" asked Agnes.

"Roman is a detective, but he is an unusual one," I said. "He wants to believe that my dreams can help him find the missing woman. I have been having dreams about a woman who looks like Alison. The dreams show me places that look like parts of this castle. I remember seeing those places here when I was younger, and I think that I have seen them again when I was walking around the castle. Roman thinks that he can find her if I keep dreaming about her. Maybe I will start thinking like the person who took her. We can use that to bring us to her. Then, we can catch the person who did this."

"Have you been able to think like the person who took her?" she asked.

I said, "I do not know. All I can think of is that someone needs her for something. If they took her, then they would be hiding her. If they are hiding her, they need to keep her alive until something special happens. If she were dead, the killer would want us to know. None of that could be true, but it is all I have thought of so far."

"Do you think I am in any danger? Will you protect me?"

"I will," I said. "I do not want anyone else to suffer."

"I am really scared. I do not like thinking that there is someone in this castle who could be keeping that woman as a prisoner," she said.

"I know. Someone here is hiding her. She could be in a wall or under the ground. We could have seen her and not even realized it," I said.

"That is too awful," she said.

"Some of these halls look familiar," I said. I looked into several of the open rooms. "These rooms look familiar, too. I think I have seen them in my dreams. Alison might have been here."

"Should we investigate?" asked Agnes.

I started looking around the rooms and the halls. Agnes followed me. She slid her hands across the walls, and I did the same. There was no trace of her anywhere.

"Nothing," said Agnes.

"Nothing," I said. "I cannot believe this."

"Do not be angry," said Agnes. "You will find her. I believe in you." She smiled at me.

A brief smile appeared on my face. I continued walking. I thought that I knew where I was going, but the castle looked so much different now. I remembered that I had been dreaming about walking in the castle and that I really did not know what this place actually looked like inside. I had to follow Agnes so that she could show me where to go.

"Do you have friends who also work or live here?" I asked.

"I do not have any friends," said Agnes. "I only work with other archivists and historians. I speak to the master and the servants sometimes. I respect everyone here. They respect me. We do our work."

"Is that lonely?" I asked.

Agnes said, "No. Friendship is not really something I care about. I believe in showing respect and being kind, but people are just too much work. I would rather work with people than be friends with them."

"I guess friendship is something we grow out of," I said. "We learn to stop looking for it because the search only brings pain. I do not think I have let go. I think I still want friends."

"You do not have any friends?" asked Agnes.

"No," I said. "I thought I did, but I am realizing that I do not."

CHAPTER 7

Agnes and I walked into a long underground chamber. There were many people in this room, and they all appeared to be reading, writing, researching, and studying. I saw typists, clerks, secretaries, businessmen and businesswomen, receptionists, scribes, and copyists.

"What is going on here?" I asked. "What is this place?"

Agnes said, "I supervise and manage several teams that are each comprised of dozens of scientists, analysts, archivists, historians, clerks, librarians, technicians, nurses, and doctors. These people are collecting data and important information about the many records, books, files, and documents that are being stored in the castle. Important letters must be created, business must be done, data must be collected, copies of books and manuscripts must be made, and valuable artifacts must be inspected."

"I thought that electronic devices do not work here," I said. "I see telephones and computers in this room. My devices do not work here."

Agnes said, "The telephones and computers that we use here cannot contact anyone or anything outside this castle. We use them to communicate with other people on different sides of the castle, because it is so large and big. Sometimes, we do manage to connect to people outside the castle, but it is only for a very brief time and the quality of the messages or calls are never satisfactory to anyone."

"Why does that happen?" I asked. "And why are my devices broken?"

"That happens often to people here," said Agnes. "Some of us believe that it is caused by chaotic weather or peculiar magnetism. Others might blame radioactivity. We are still trying to understand it. That is why we have these chambers set up down here. We are trying to study the unusual phenomena that happens in the region of Fiendilkfjeld. We use machines that we have created to study them, and we take those machines all around the world to study other strange occurrences. Our machines can only operate briefly here, but they are still useful. Temporary improvements have been made to them, but nothing is conclusive. Devices work better when you use them outside of this castle or when you are in the towns and villages, but electronic devices are, even there, not very reliable. Most motor vehicles work fine, most of the time."

I said, "Agnes, was Alison involved in any of this?"

Agnes said, "Yes, Theodemir. Alison came here because she wanted to study the strange phenomena that causes electronic devices to break or malfunction here. She had come here before with her family to work on diplomatic matters with the Fiendilkfjeld family. Alison discovered our machines, and she was inspired to help our research. She worked with Doctor Reinhold Fiendilkfjeld. He must be one of your cousins, right?"

"I do not know," I said. "I never met him. I do not remember a Reinhold in my family. I would like to talk with him."

Agnes said, "Reinhold has already spoken to investigators."

"Did he?"

"He does not know where she is."

"What was he doing when Alison went missing?"

"He was in the laboratory, waiting for her."

I said, "When exactly did people realize that she was missing?"

Agnes said, "Reinhold was the one who was waiting for her. When she did not meet him that night, he knew that something was strange."

"How did he know that?"

"I do not know," said Agnes. "Reinhold made the guards look for her, but she was never found."

"Someone should have told me this before," I said.

"Our machines are a secret," said Agnes. "We have many clients who rely on us to keep this a secret. Your family keeps the unusual phenomena a secret from the rest of the world, too. No one can know about the phenomena."

"I understand," I said. "Because this region is a dead spot, it is easy for people to hide secrets here. No one can access the information that you bury here because no one from the outside can hack in. The region of Fiendilkfjeld, including everything in it, is completely isolated from everyone and everything. I am sure that a lot of wealthy people are paying my family to keep their dark secrets here in this dead zone. This castle is being used to bury things that should be forgotten."

I turned around when I heard someone walking towards me. I saw a figure suddenly get close. It was a very tall man, taller than me, who appeared boney and very thin. He had black hair that was straight and reached his shoulders. He had blue eyes, pallid white skin, and a long narrow nose. The thin ridge of his nose was like a cliff that reached up to his brow. His forehead was small, like mine. We both had a low hairlines. He had a gaunt face, and he appeared to maybe be thirty or forty years old. He was mysteriously handsome, but his demeanor and physical characteristics were still somehow eerie.

"Lord Theodemir Fiendilkfjeld, this is Doctor Reinhold Fiendilkfjeld," said Agnes. Her hand motioned toward me and then to the doctor.

"Just Theodemir," I said, trying to appear humble.

Reinhold scowled at me. He appeared to cast his gaze up and down my entire body, as if he were judging and silently criticizing me. His hands were behind his back. He was surrounded by several beautiful female assistants.

Reinhold was wearing a black rubber coat, a skintight black latex bodysuit, black latex gloves, black leather pants, and black leather boots. His clothes made his thin body look thinner somehow. His assistants were wearing similar clothes and uniforms that were identical to his.

"You must be my cousin," I said. "I am happy to meet another member of my family."

"You are my cousin, but that does not give you authorization to be here," said Reinhold.

I said, "I am helping the detective find Alison, your assistant and the missing heiress."

"Whatever you need here," said Reinhold, "Agnes can acquire for you, but you are not allowed here. You must leave."

"What are you hiding, doctor?" I asked.

Reinhold said, "What we are trying to accomplish here goes beyond the insipid faculties of your feeble mind, Theodemir."

"I think that I can handle it," I said.

"You are a charlatan working for that low-life detective," said Reinhold.

I said, "I came to connect with my family."

Reinhold said, "The Fiendilkfjeld family has old traditions and rules. We are the descendants of ancient knights, lords, dukes, barons, and princes. The monarchy was destroyed, and now our family is a shadow. We are nothing but a symbol. We are ghosts. No one cares for us, but we remain here. Our wealth and our power keeps us attached here. Besides this region being named after our family, we have no power. We do not make any rules. All we can do is watch as this entire world decays and rots. We cannot control anything. We are too powerless to save the people from themselves. All we ever really had was one another. Family. Theodemir, your father wanted to separate from us. He did not want any titles of nobility or honorary ranks. Your mother was very wealthy, but not nobility. He married your mother and abandoned us. He tried to hide you from us. Why did you come here?"

I said, "I am trying to help Roman save a woman's life."

"That detective blackmails and threatens us constantly," said Reinhold. "Roman is always looking for ways to take money from us or stop our operations. Roman works with the government to harass us. He is using you and this investigation as another way to try to find something wrong with us so that he can attack us, like he always does. You want to help him find a missing woman because you saw her in a few dreams. You want to consider yourself part of our family?"

"I am proud of who I am," I said.

"You should be ashamed of who you are," said Reinhold. "Your father stepped away from nobility. He renounced his rank, titles, and his family."

"My father always had respect for the family. Maybe the family will decide to allow me to come back," I said. "They could allow me to be an aristocrat, like yourself."

"They might," said Reinhold, "But I will always know what you really are. You are a traitor."

"Whatever I am, I still need to see what is inside these laboratories," I said.

"No," said Reinhold. "You will wait outside. Walk around the castle until Agnes finds you again. She will collect the information you want."

"I will speak to Roman about this," I said. "I will talk to Lord Adalric."

"Fine," said Reinhold, "If he allows you to enter, then I will obey. Until then, you must wait outside."

Reinhold and I smirked at each other. I turned around and walked out of the room. I decided to ask some of the servants for information about Alison. There were some servant women in the kitchen when I walked in. I tried to speak to them, but they ignored me or walked away from me. The servant women were incredibly rude towards me when I tried to ask them for information about Alison. Some of them did not look at me and some mockingly laughed at me without telling me anything.

There were a few servant women who tried to speak to me. They came up to me and said that they wanted to speak to me about Alison. When I asked them for more information, the other servant woman came and attacked the women who were trying to talk to me. The women who wanted to speak to me were slapped and their hair was pulled by the other servant women.

I tried to protect the women who wanted to talk with me. I pulled the attackers off of them, but it did not help. I stopped the women from fighting one another, but now the women were all silent. Now, no one wanted to talk to me.

As I walked out of the kitchen, I saw some servant man walking past me. I followed them into another room and started asking them questions about Alison. These men appeared tired, pale and cold. They were shivering and trembling as they moved. They had difficulty lifting their bags and boxes. I noticed several bruises and small cuts on the necks and wrists of some of these boney men. I thought that maybe it was from fighting or self-mutilation, but I was not completely convinced about that. I observed these tiny red holes in their skin and saw that they were not bleeding, but they were still not truly healed. I thought that I recognized one of these men. I tapped him on the shoulder.

When he turned around, his face had a cold, dreary expression. He was shorter than me, he had blue eyes, and his hair was dark brown.

He nodded.

I said, "Hello. I am Theodemir Fiendilkfjeld. I am looking for a missing woman. You might know something about her. I am helping the detective with this. He is her friend. Anything you know about her could be useful. Her name is Alison. She is an heiress, and she was working with Doctor Reinhold Fiendilkfjeld on a secret project in the archives."

Before I could say anything else about her, the man interrupted me. He said, "No one who works here appreciates anyone talking about that woman."

"Why not?" I asked.

He said, "Alison was a beautiful and kind lady when she first came here, but she quickly became a very cruel woman after she started working with that creepy doctor."

I asked, "Why? How?"

"I do not know," he said. "It was not only her who changed. A lot of the servants began to change after she came here. Things have been very strange ever since she came here."

"How do you know this?" I asked. "Who are you?"

"My name is Luca. I started working her when she first came to this castle many months ago."

The other servant men started speaking to Luca in a language that I could not understand. The men seemed to be agitated and frightened, but they also appeared impatient and frustrated. Something about the way they were pointing and waving toward me and the boxes gave me the idea that they did not want me to keep Luca from transporting these things. The other men looked at me like I was a hindrance and a nuisance. It sounded like Luca and the other men were arguing and bickering about things that alarmed them.

Luca turned to me and said, "I need to work. Alison was a good person."

"What?" I asked. "So she was nice?"

Luca said, "I only know that she came here to see her betrothed."

"Alison was engaged to someone?" I asked.

"Yes," said Luca. "Alison was a virgin and she was going to get married to Roland Fiendilkfjeld. She went missing before the wedding. That means that she is still a pure virgin."

"Why would you tell me this?" I asked.

"That is all that I can say," Luca said. "I need to get these boxes and leave."

"So which person was she?" I asked as I watched Luca walk away with some small boxes. I yelled so that he could hear me. "Was Alison the cruel woman or the beautiful pure virgin?"

Luca vanished into the shadows. I wanted to know what those men were doing with those small boxes, but I knew that I needed to focus on more important things. I needed to understand why Luca would need to tell me that Alison was a virgin and that she was getting married to Roland Fiendilkfjeld.

Agnes found me. She had the files and maps of the castle that Roman needed.

"Thank you," I said. "Let me ask you something. Who is Roland Fiendilkfjeld?"

Agnes said, "Roland is the son of Lord Adalric."

"Who is he to me?" I asked. "How is Adalric related to me?"

"I do not know," said Agnes.

I was sure that she was lying.

"What did the servants think about Alison?" I asked.

"Some of the servants liked her, but some of them did not," said Agnes.

"Why would anyone not like her?" I asked.

Agnes said, "Alison is twenty two years old, she is a beautiful noblewoman, and she is a virgin. Many people here thought that she was the perfect woman to join the family. Some people were just jealous, I think."

I asked, "Did she get married?"

"No," said Agnes. "She was abducted before she could get married to Lord Roland Fiendilkfjeld."

"Did Alison fight with any of the servants?" I asked.

Agnes started walking away. "No."

I followed her. "Are you sure?"

"Why?" she asked, without looking at me.

"I might have heard something different."

"What did you hear?"

"I do not know what it meant, but I heard something."

"What did you hear?"

I said, "The servants here might have changed because of something she did."

She said, "I have heard things like that."

"Have you seen them?" I asked. "Most of these servants are rude."

She turned around to face me. Agnes stopped walking. She gazed at my face. She said, "I have noticed that the servants have changed. They are rude, apathetic, and often silent. They do not talk to one another. They fight against one another. Many servants have gone missing, too, yet no one investigates that. More and more servants go missing, and new servants need to be hired. Some will say that it started when Alison came, but I do not know if that is true."

I asked, "Have all the servants already been questioned about any of this?"

Agnes said, "Others have already questioned them, yes. All of them have said that they do not know what happened to Alison."

"What about the missing servants?" I asked.

Agnes said, "No one cares about missing servants. The police and the other investigators are too busy. We have had servants who were uncooperative with the police and other investigators. Some of them had to be interrogated and arrested, but they were brought back to the castle anyway."

"A cover-up," I said. "The noble Fiendilkfjeld family must have paid people to get their servants back to the castle," I said.

CHAPTER 8

ROMAN, AGNES, AND I WERE NOW IN A SMALL ROOM. ROMAN wanted us to look at the files and maps in this room, because he wanted more privacy. This room had only one wooden table, some bookshelves, and one window. The walls and floor were made of dark brown wood. Parallel brown wooden beams were extended horizontally across the white ceiling.

Agnes was talking to Roman about what the maps could tell us about the castle. I looked at the maps, too. Agnes showed us how this castle had many trapdoors. The trapdoors brought victims into dungeons, prison cells, oubliettes, and led back into the underground rivers.

Roman asked, "Is it possible that Alison could have fallen into one of these trapdoors and been dropped in the river?"

Alison said, "Yes. The trapdoors are still functioning."

I asked, "Where would the underground river have taken her, if she had fallen in?"

Alison said, "I am not sure. Those underground rivers lead to a multitude of different caves, grottos, channels, streams, canals, tributaries and waterfalls. She could have been taken anywhere."

"Has anyone investigated those areas?" I asked. "Has anyone explored those caves or the bottoms of those waterfalls?"

"The existence of these trapdoors is confidential," said Agnes. "No one should know that they exist, except for the noble family. The trapdoors have been placed around important private areas where no one should be except the family. If Alison fell into one, she was trespassing on private territory in which she was not authorized to explore."

"You did not tell the other investigators anything about this?" asked Roman.

"No," said Agnes. "We have kept it a secret."

"Why show us?" I asked.

"The family knows that Roman will keep this a secret, too, as long as he is paid correctly," said Agnes.

"What about me?" I asked.

Agnes said, "You will keep this secret if you value your life."

"All right," I said. "So, we need to investigate those trapdoors. We need to search those caves and rivers. She could be trapped in a dungeon or her body could be at the bottom of one of those waterfalls. We need to do something about this."

"The noble family already sent their servants to investigate those areas," said Agnes. "They did not find her in any dungeons or caves."

"What about the waterfalls and the rivers?" I asked.

"Her body was never found," said Agnes.

"Let me get a small team to check those rivers and waterfalls," said Roman, looking at Agnes. He turned his face toward me and said, "Theodemir, you need to inspect the dungeons, the trapdoors, and the prison cells. Have Agnes show you were all the secret rooms are."

"I will need to talk to the master of the castle," said Agnes.

"I do not know how much of the castle they are going to allow us to see," I said, looking at Roman. "They would not let me see the laboratories."

"Why?" asked Roman.

I said, "Reinhold. He said that there were things in the laboratories that we were not allowed to see. He hates me and he really hates you."

Roman said, "I know Reinhold. He does not let anyone see his secret machines and computers. We need to inspect the laboratories. Let me work on that, Theodemir. I will try to get us the authorization we need to look through the entire castle."

"There are underground crypts, tombs, and sepulchers that we should look at, too," said Agnes.

"Why would we look there?" asked Roman.

Agnes said, "Alison loved spending time here. She would pray for hours in silent."

"It could be a good idea," said Roman. "Theodemir, go with Agnes into the crypts, too. We need to learn more about her and what she was doing here."

I said, "All right, Roman. That should keep us busy for a while."

"We need to find her," said Roman. "I know that she is here. We are going to find out what happened to her. We do not have much time, but we are going to discover the truth."

"What happens if you do not find her?" asked Agnes.

Roman faced me and said, "We will find her."

I nodded at him.

Roman asked, "Theodemir, what have your dreams been telling you?"

"We will find her," I said.

Roman smiled at me, but it was not a very contented smile, and his eyes appeared downcast.

I looked out of the window and saw the brightly glowing moon suspended high up in the starry nighttime sky. I saw the village of the castle, the castle walls, the moats, and all of the beautiful fields and pastures. Fog rolled through the village streets. Gray mist loitered over the village rooftops, around the valleys, near the foothills, and at the bases of the black mountains. Orange moonlight glistened on the edges and curves of the dark mountainsides. The moonlight shined on the autumnal colors of forest trees.

I breathed in the cold air of this small room. I envisioned Alison falling through a trapdoor and getting stuck in a dark medieval dungeon. I imagined her dead body floating down a river or ending up in a canal somewhere. I thought about what might happen if someone found her body. I pictured someone seeing Alison's beautiful white dead face and her wet cold body.

"It does seem hopeless," I said.

"What?" asked Roman.

I said, "Alison's body could have been carried down a river. She might have fallen down a waterfall. She might have slammed her head and died. Then, animals could have already taken her body. She could be scattered all around the forest by now."

"Why would you say that?" asked Roman.

"I thought that you wanted us to be realistic," I said.

Roman said, "I need you to give me hope. I cannot work with your negativity."

Agnes said, "I think, Roman, that you are too emotional. You are too close to this case. You have made things too personal for you to effectively solve this."

"I am trying to find out what happened to my friend," said Roman.

"Was she really your friend?" asked Agnes.

"I am sorry that I brought this up," I said. "You are right, Roman. I need to focus on the investigation. We need to continue looking everywhere. We cannot afford to be negative right now. There are still a lot of places for me to start looking. Roman, you will look outside. Check the forests, the rivers, and the waterfalls. Also, Roman, we need you to help us get access into the laboratories. Agnes and I will check the crypts, tombs, and underground tunnels. She and I will check the caves and grottos, too. All right? We can do this. We can find her. She must be here, somewhere."

I walked out of the room and started walking.

Agnes walked beside me and said, "You are trying very hard to find someone you do not know."

I said, "She has become important to me."

"The other investigators could not find her," said Agnes. "What makes you think that you can find her? She might be dead."

"Show me where the crypts are," I said.

Agnes said, "You did not answer my questions."

I said, "Show me where the crypts are."

"Why are you doing this?" asked Agnes.

"My family, the servants, and even you are all just trying to make this go away," I said. "None of you care about Alison. Roman and I do care. We just want to know what happened to her. We do not have much time left to look around the castle. To be honest, I would love to live here, too, but I need to help Roman. I am searching for Alison for myself. This is my quest. This is something I need to do. I promise that I will not cause any trouble for you or the family, but I need to know what happened to her. This is my family's castle. There is a part of me that is in these halls, and she could be here, too. I want to be connected to this family and to her in any way that I can. Searching for her has allowed me to do those things. I feel like I belong here, but everyone else is trying to push me away. I feel a connection to Alison, but everyone else is trying to keep me from her, too. If she is dead, then she is dead, but let me find her. Let me do this for myself. Let me have something. Let me discover who I really am and maybe create something for just me. I need to have an identity."

"Did you say something?" asked Agnes.

"No," I said.

"Follow me," said Agnes. "I need to show you where the crypts are."

I followed Agnes down several flights of stairs. Large paintings, enclosed in golden frames, hung on the dark walls. These paintings depicted old aristocrats, noblemen, and noblewomen who all shared similar facial characteristics with me. I recognized my eyes or forehead on some of the people portrayed in these paintings. I saw my chin or my nose on some of them, too. I assumed that they must have been my forebears and distant relatives.

The staircases were illuminated by large candelabrums that servants were lighting as we walked past. I took a candleholder off a table and brought it to the flames of a candelabrum so that the fire would move to my candle. Agnes continued walking without me.

"Do not go into the crypt."

I turned and saw a servant man. I whispered to him, "Why not?"

"The crypts are haunted," he said.

"Haunted by what?" I asked.

"The dead who have been eaten," he said. "That place is cursed."

I whispered, "What happened down there?"

He said, "The monsters eat the dead, and the dead return for revenge."

"There are monsters down there?" I asked. "Who are you?"

The man walked away. I was going to ask him more questions, but I heard Agnes say, "Theodemir." She sounded impatient.

Once my candle was lit, I returned to Agnes.

"What did the servant say to you?" she asked.

I said, "He said that there are monsters in the crypt."

"That is rubbish," said Agnes. "It is not haunted. Ghosts and monsters are not real. Have you ever seen one?"

"No," I said.

Agnes said, "Alison used to pray there often. She was always so worried about the souls of all the dead. That was the kind of woman that she was. The family loved her."

"Why have I never seen the man who was going to marry her?" I asked.

"Roland? Roland has already spoken to investigators," said Agnes.

"Right, but now I want to talk to him," I said.

Agnes said, "Why? Are you jealous?"

"What? No."

"Why else would you want to talk to him except to face the man who has the heart of the woman with whom you are obsessed?" asked Agnes.

"I am not that kind of man," I said. "I am not jealous. You are trying to make me jealous. It will not work."

Agnes said, "There were many who were jealous. I am certain that there are people in this castle who were glad that Alison went missing."

"Who was jealous of their engagement?" I asked.

Alison smirked and turned her back toward me. She continued walking, and I followed.

We walked down more stairways that were narrow and steep. The ceiling was too low and the walls were too short so that we had to lean forward. We had to keep our heads down so that we did not bump into anything. My right hand was holding the wall, and my left hand was holding the candleholder. I felt the cold black stones and marble of the wall. The cold air here was damp and musty. Even with the candle, all I saw was darkness ahead of us.

"Why do you want to stay here?" asked Agnes.

"Why do I want to live here?" I asked.

"Yes. You seem to want to stay with us. Are you looking for work?"

I said, "I am not looking for work."

"Did you lose your house?"

I said, "No. I have an estate in England."

Agnes stopped, turned to face me, and asked, "Why the castle? Why now?"

"I tried to contact this castle before," I said. "No one wanted to talk to me. I have been trying to communicate with this side of my family, which I know nothing about. Even now, after all of this, I feel as if I still know nothing about any of you. Yet, there is something about this castle that needs me. I want to be here. Can I not try to claim nobility? Can I not be welcomed? I have always loved this castle.

What I do know is that there is something here that I understand. I hate modern society. I hate what the world has become. This castle could be my freedom."

"Do you think that Lord Adalric would ever give you nobility?" asked Agnes.

I said, "The only way I could get into this castle was to help Roman, but I want to be faithful to the family. I must be faithful to myself, too. It is like a battle."

She smiled and turned her back toward me again. She continued walking, and I followed her down. The further that we walked down, the darker the stairway was becoming. The shadows around us were becoming more and more thicker.

Agnes suddenly stopped before a black Gothic portal. This tall portal created a deep recess in the wall. Inside this recess, there is a sequence of parallel Gothic arches. These Gothic arches curved over the tympanum. Torches on the wall cast light onto this deep portal and revealed its Gothic statuary and mouldings. Candlelight glistened on the marble depictions of pointed arches and bats on the archivolts and voussoirs. The archivolts, doors, and tympanum were all shaped like Gothic arches.

Attached to the jambs and tympanum of the portal, black marble statues depicted undead knights. Their broken helmets revealed the skeletal faces and cadaverous skulls of these knights. The knights held spears and round shields. The statuary attached to the archivolts and tympanum depicted demons and skeletons holding scythes.

A black column separates two green wooden doors within the portal. Both of the doors are decorated with black iron depicting skeletal hands. The black column touches the lintel and is decorated with a large statue of a demonic figure. The black marble demon was like a man who had two large wings rising out of his back, two horns rising out of his forehead, and sharp claws.

Agnes said, "These crypts are sacred and should never be entered without authorization or supervision. You will go inside and speak to one of the guardians of the catacombs."

I asked, "You are not going with me?"

"I remembered that I have other things that I need to do," said Agnes. "I know that they need me in the laboratories. I will give you a key."

I took the key from her hand. "You trust me with this?" I asked.

"You want to prove yourself to the family, right?" said Agnes. "Besides, there are always priests, monks, nuns, and clergymen there. I really am too busy for this."

"What do they do in there?" I asked.

"They pray for the souls of those who have been buried there," said Agnes. "They protect sacred relics, too. Lock the door after you enter."

"I thank you," I said.

Agnes did not say anything else to me. She just walked back up the stairs. I unlocked one of the doors and then walked through the doorway.

CHAPTER 9

After locking the door behind me, I looked around and saw many dark caskets. There were many mysterious doorways and Gothic archways. I walked through one of them and entered inside a large mausoleum that was filled with tombs and caskets. There was an altar here, too, and its candelabrums were dark and had no flames.

I left and returned to the first room. I walked through several other passageways, and each of them was made of rocks that were gray and old. My candle offered meager light in the darkness. I walked down a stairway and found the entrance to the catacombs.

Niches in the walls held coffins and sarcophagi. The tunnels led me to sprawling cemeteries. Numerous gravestones crowded against one another. Mausoleums and tombs were protected by black iron fences. Narrow chambers led me down steep staircases. I walked through long tunnels and passed many sculptures depicting clergymen and monarchs.

The expressions of horror and sadness on the faces of these statues made me feel as if something evil was waiting for me and hunting me. The gloomy chambers and eerie shadows made me feel as if something horrifying and terrifying would soon happen to me. I began to fear that something dangerous was coming or that disaster had already struck my fate and soul.

I wondered about why I was so alone. Agnes had said that there were priests and monks here, but they were not. I was too afraid to call out for anyone. I feared that my voice would wake up the monsters and ghosts. Being down here made me partially forget that those things were not real. I turned my head side to side, and my eyes flittered in many directions.

I heard whispers, and it made me think that I had finally found the monks.

"Hello," I said. "I need help." I called out to them.

I helloed into the shadows, but no one responded. The whispering sounds were getting louder. I took a corner and was stunned by what I saw. Kneeling before an altar was Alison.

"Alison!" I shouted as I ran toward her.

Alison turned her head to face me. I tried to reach her, but she ran away from me. I chased her through the tunnels of the catacombs. Alison was wearing a black gown that was identical to the uniforms of the servant women of the castle. I shouted her name, but she would not turn her head.

"No! Alison!" I shouted. "Come back! We need you!" I did not understand why she was running. "Alison, everyone has been looking for you. Do not run away. Why have you been hiding here? Why did you come to me in my dreams? What do you want? Let me help you, Alison. Alison, stop running. Alison."

Something dropped on me and my candle died. I was blind in the pitch-dark shadows of the catacombs. I could only hear Alison's footsteps as she ran away. There were other sounds, too. I heard groans coming from something that was on top of me. I tried to crawl away, but something was pulling my legs back. I kicked at my attackers and found the candle. I used my matches to ignite the candle. With the flame, I saw that dozens of skeletons and rotting corpses were on me. Their boney bloody hands gripped my legs and neck. I screamed as I pushed them off of me. I ran away and tried to find Alison.

I discovered a room that was full of caskets. The walls and ceiling were made of human skulls. Skeletons hung from the wall. I heard wailing sounds coming from one of the open caskets. I inspected the caskets one by one until I found the source of the wailing noises. There was a man in one of the black coffins. He shouted, "Release me! Release us from this curse!"

"Who are you?" I asked.

The man floated out of the coffin. I stepped backwards. I screamed and tried to run away. I turned around and ran, but the man was now in front of me. I turned around again, but the man was again in front of me.

"What are you?" I asked.

"I am the caretaker of the catacombs. My name is Roland Fiendilkfjeld. Listen to the sound of my voice. Look into my eyes. Stop breathing, and die."

I turned around and started running away from him. I screamed for help as the man appeared in front of me again. He grabbed my throat and lifted me into the air.

"That spell should have killed you," said Roland. "Who are you?" He bit my neck and started drinking my blood. Quickly, he threw me to the floor and stepped backwards. "You are a Fiendilkfjeld."

I coughed and gasped as I stood up. "Where is Alison?"

Roland was a little taller than me. He had a somewhat lank figure. His face was a bit elongated but handsome. The candlelight glistened on his long wavy gray hair. His light white skin appeared cold. With a gloomy expression, his gray eyes gazed at me. He asked, "Who?"

"No," I said. "No. Do not do this."

"You must leave this castle," said Roland.

"Do not say that," I said. "I need to find her."

Roland did not say anything to me. He continued looking at me. I did not know what to do but look back at him, too. Roland was wearing black leather pants, black leather boots, and a black satin shirt that had silk frills and lace on the wrists and collar. Over his shirt, he was wearing a black satin dressing gown that was unbuttoned and loose. The shredded sleeves of his dressing gown were tattered so that long jagged strips of black satin were hanging from his arms.

Roland looked like he was twenty five years old. He had a tall pointed nose that was a bit steep. His long face was somewhat rigid, his eyes were a bit sunken, and his cheekbones were sharp.

"You have no idea how you really look to us, do you?" asked Roland.

"What does that mean?" I asked.

"The prophecy was true," said Roland. "We did not listen to the warnings. Doom will come for us."

"What are you saying?" I asked.

"There are many curses on this land and on the castle," said Roland. "The dreams of the dead infect this castle and all those who enter it. Our family prophecy says that you would come and awaken a horrible evil demon that sleeps beneath our castle. A great calamity will annihilate us, and the castle will be destroyed. But, how are we ever to know the truth when the past is always repeating? You cannot hear the real truth until you understand what you really are."

"What happened to Alison?" I asked. "She was here. Why is she hiding? Why are you hiding her here? I know that you have something to do with this. Let her go free, Roland. You cannot get away with this."

"The prophecy said that murders would happen here," said Roland. "Death and blood would awaken a great evil entity. This castle brings only misfortune. You wanted to know so much about your own family, but you never expected this."

"What did you do to her?" I asked.

"You have killed so many people," said Roland.

I said, "I never killed anyone. I am innocent. I am not like you."

"What am I?" asked Roland.

"Roman and I will not harm you," I said. "We only want Alison. We want to know what she is doing and what happened to her. Her family is worried about her, Roland. You were her supposed to be her husband. You are supposed to be taking care of her. You cannot keep her here. I know that I might die by trying to save her, but I must do this. It is the right thing to do."

"You are still resisting us," said Roland. "You will never be free until you accept the truth. I know that you cannot hear me, but you must fight. You are only hearing what you want to hear, but you must fight it. Fight the urge to hide from the truth."

"You want me to let you kill her," I said.

"You are not like the rest of modern society," said Roland. "Normal people are shortsighted. Their emotions are illusory. Their dreams are vacant. Modern human beings only follow their meaningless affairs and illicit amours. You are different from them. That is why you came here. You want to be part of something bigger than the real world."

"Just tell me where she is," I said. "I will not tell anyone else. It will be our secret."

Roland said, "This castle brings so many lonely broken people into its chambers."

"Why is she hiding here with you?" I asked. "No more games."

Roland said, "Leave the castle, Theodemir." His eyes began to glow with red light.

I ran away, hoping to escape him. I screamed for help. I wanted someone to find me. Roland was chasing after me. He was incredibly fast, and his claws shredded my shirt. I tried to punch him, but he grabbed my fist. He bit my hand, and I hit his nose. I continued punching his face, but his wounds always healed. It was if he could not be harmed. He bit my neck, and I felt my blood slip away. Weak and afraid, I could not keep my eyes open.

When I opened my eyes, I was crouching over a corpse. I was ripping the dead flesh of the corpse off its body and putting it into my mouth. I was eating the corpse. The monks tried to stop me. They pulled my arms away, but I lunged backward and attacked. My teeth shredded the torso of one of the monks. I laughed as the screaming monks ran away.

I woke up again. I stumbled out of the darkness and realized that I was in a dark grotto. Moonbeams came in through the mouth of the grotto. I looked outside and saw that the grotto was underneath a towering waterfall. I looked down and saw a terrifyingly high drop. To my right was a very narrow staircase carved into the cliff. Inside the grotto were many statues depicting beautiful queens and princesses. There were other grotesque statues here, too. Niches in the cavern walls held repulsive statues depicting horrific abominations, demons, and dragons. The fireplace was surrounded by statues of humanoid creatures with wings and many serpentine heads.

I heard something moving in the shadows. An iron door opened out of the darkness, and a beautiful woman walked into the grotto. The flames in the fireplace swayed with the sudden breeze. The woman who manifested into the grotto was wearing a sorrowful black velvet gown. The gown covered all of her arms, neck, and legs. She wore black leather boots and black lacework gloves.

"Alison?" I asked. "Alison, is it you?"

"My name is Sigrid," she said. Her voice even sounded like Alison's.

"You look exactly like a woman I am trying to find," I said. "Her name is Alison."

"I saved your life," said Sigrid. "Someone tried to poison you. When I found you, you had two poisoned darts in your neck. The poison was making you hallucinate, but you are all right now."

"That is the second time that I have been poisoned," I said. "Someone does not want me to find you; I mean her. Someone does not want me to find Alison. I almost had her. I know that I saw her."

"I had to take you somewhere that was safe," said Sigrid.

"What is this place?" I asked.

"This is a sacred grotto that is owned by the noble Fiendilkfjeld family. Many people come here to pray," said Sigrid.

"What do they pray to?" I asked.

Sigrid said, "The demon of Fiendilkfjeld."

"You pray to a demon here?" I asked.

"Only those who worship the Fiendilkfjeld family do."

"You worship them?"

"They are our masters. They need our strength."

"What is the demon?"

Sigrid walked to the fireplace to warm her hands. "The demon made the family."

"The family is related to the demon?"

Sigrid said, "Yes. We call them demons because they are helping us escape the light."

"Why would you want to escape light?"

Sigrid said, "The light disturbs us. We cannot survive without darkness."

I asked, "Why do you not call them your angels since they are helping you survive?"

"There are some servants who think of them like that," said Sigrid, "but many know better. Those who see them as demons understand that we must be corrupted. We need to be punished and defiled. That is where beauty and purity is found. You think that I am beautiful because I am so wicked."

"There are more people like you?" I asked.

"The castle protects us. We live in the village that is within the baileys and exterior walls surrounding the village and the castle," said Sigrid.

"Why did you save me?" I asked.

Sigrid said, "We worship you. You are a Fiendilkfjeld aristocrat."

"Worship me?"

"Follow me. I will show you so that you can understand," said Sigrid.

I followed her up the narrow staircase. "Does anyone ever fall off this staircase? There are no railings."

"Yes," said Sigrid. "Many fall and die. They crash at the bottom of the waterfall when they hit the rocks. Their flesh is food for the great monsters that live at the bottom of the waterfall. We know that we could fall and become their food. It is a good way to end."

"You believe that there are monsters down there?"

"Would you like to see?" asked Sigrid. "I could push you off."

I said, "No, please. I am not ready to die, especially not that way. I would really just like to get back to the castle. I need to find Alison. You work in the castle, do you not?"

"I do."

"So, did you ever see another woman who looked exactly like you?" I asked.

"I did."

"So, you know her?"

Sigrid chuckled. "I did know her."

"What do you mean?" I asked. I was still following her up the staircase.

We reached the top. Sigrid opened a door and walked through the archway. I followed her inside and was glad to be away from the waterfall. I was waiting for Sigrid to speak to me, but she would not answer my questions.

She brought me inside a massive chamber that had a large deep pool that was filled with red water. Beautiful women were eating men in this pool. Cattle were being decapitated, and their blood was poured into the pool. The putrid stench of the pool made me vomit. I saw massive black leathery wings fluttering and protruding out from the pool. I realized that those wings were attached to the backs of those beautiful women. Men with pitchforks were stabbing women in the pool.

"The Fiendilkfjeld family lets you do this?" I asked. "My family is involved with this cult?"

"We know that you have been following us," said Sigrid. "You have studied our cults for years."

I said, "For years, I was investigating and researching murderous cults that have recently spread across Europe. You were involved with those ceremonial murders?"

Sigrid laughed. "Drink the blood and become like us, Theodemir."

I said, "Never. You drugged me. You have made me hallucinate. I will not be a part of this."

I ran out of the chamber and then down the staircase. I found the door in the grotto and went through. I heard Sigrid still laughing.

CHAPTER 10

I DID NOT KNOW WHERE I WAS GOING. I JUST CONTINUED TO RUN through the tunnels. I ran through every archway and doorway that I could open. I opened a door and discovered that I was in a room that looked like a large laboratory. I shut the door and locked it.

"You discovered this place, finally," said Reinhold as he walked through the fog. "What do you think about my broken machines?"

Reinhold's machines looked like gigantic metal sarcophagi. These machines were giant black supercomputers joined by thick cables to other mainframes in the laboratory. Metal black openwork enclosed them. They were decorated with statues and carvings depicting humans and demons. Brackets and corbels on these supercomputers and mainframes depicted human skulls.

"These computers are failures," said Reinhold. "I created them to try to connect the castle to the outside world, but it was all in vain. These computers cannot connect to anyone or anything outside of the castle. They cannot send messages, data, or signals to anything outside. If you try to access the computers from anywhere outside of the castle, you will never succeed. If data from these computers is brought or transported outside of this region, the data will often disappear."

I asked, "You must rely on a lot of outside help to stay connected with the rest of the world."

Reinhold said, "Yes, but the people who live here like not being connected. We like being isolated, but sometimes we must reach out and bring people here to help us. Often, computers will break and stop working. Electronic devices cannot work properly anywhere in the region of Fiendilkfjeld, but sometimes they do. My teams have been studying this strange phenomenon. We are trying to understand what makes most machines and computers malfunction and break when they are here."

"Sometimes, electronic things do work here," I said. "You are not completely isolated. Vehicles and things like that seem to work."

Reinhold said, "I am working with people to try to understand that."

"You know about the cults," I said. "I saw them killing people. They said that our family is working with them. Your computers did not work, so you went looking for proof of the supernatural with those cults. You must have gotten Alison involved with them, too."

"Alison and I were studying metaphysical and supernatural phenomena, but she was never involved with cults," said Reinhold.

"I want to see her," I said.

"You are so close to the truth," said Reinhold. "All you have to do is accept what you have done and what you are. You cannot hear what we are really saying to you, can you?"

"I know that you are playing games with me," I said. "This has become a game for you."

"What will you do?"

I said, "I need to leave."

"Where will you go?"

"I need to sleep."

"What will you see in your dreams?"

I started walking away. "I do not need this."

Reinhold said, "If you walk away, you know where you will go."

"I am going home," I said. "I learned the truth."

"You want to go home?" asked Reinhold.

I said, "I told you that all I wanted to do was find Alison. I did not want to cause any trouble for the family. I just wanted to learn the truth. None of you respect me. None of you want to help me. I know that I am not wanted here. I will go. All of you want me to leave, so I will leave."

"You think you know what happened to her?" asked Reinhold.

"Yes," I said. "You killed her. You sacrificed her because she was a virgin. You wanted to study magic, and you failed. You did not speak to any great deities or see any supernatural realms. All you did was hallucinate and kill an innocent woman. You are using your power and your money to hide the truth. I wanted to be a part of your life, but none of you want to be honest with me. I am leaving."

"No one will believe you if you tell anyone about what you know," said Reinhold.

"I know," I said. "I only came here for the truth. I have it. I will not tell anyone about this."

"That would be fine," said Reinhold, "But, you are wrong. You are wrong about everything. You do not know the truth. You need to stay here, Theodemir."

I asked, "Why should I stay here?"

Reinhold said, "You do not belong out there. I thought that you wanted to be accepted by us. You wanted to live with us."

"No one here respects me," I said. "Everyone treats me like I am a fool. I wanted the truth, and no one gave it to me. I need to leave this place."

Reinhold said, "No one loves you out there, Theodemir. You have no one. You cannot leave."

"What do you want?" I asked.

"Do you not want to learn more about Alison? Do you not want to learn more about us? We are your family," said Reinhold.

I asked, "Now I am your family?"

I walked out of the room. I could hear him following him. I left the laboratories and archives. I turned my head. Reinhold was still following me.

"What do you want, Reinhold?" I asked.

"You know that we can never let you leave," said Reinhold. "You know too much about us."

"I am going to talk to Roman about this," I said.

Reinhold said, "How did you really think that this was going to end?"

I said, "You cannot hurt me. I am with the detective. Everyone knows that I am here."

"Did you think that you were going to walk in here with that crooked detective, look around, discover some hidden rooms, learn our secrets, find Alison, and then just walk away?" asked Reinhold, slowly walking towards me.

The hallway started to look narrower. The lights now were dim. The paintings on the walls began to decay and peel. The ceiling was lower. The walls and floor slanted and became crooked. I had trouble keeping my balance.

"What is this?" I asked. "What did you do to me? More hallucinations? More drugs?"

Reinhold was close to me now. "You do not realize the truth. You thought that you came to learn about us, but we have been learning about you. When you came here, you corrupted us with your evil presence. Your dreams, emotions, and thoughts changed us. You cannot expect to ever leave here. You have changed things for us, as we have changed you."

"You have not changed me," I said. "If you move closer to me, you will regret it."

"You cannot scare me," said Reinhold. "Your fear is real."

"If you threaten me, I will have no choice to be your enemy," I said. "You already have to deal with the missing servants, all those people being killed in the pools, the sacrifices at the waterfall, and Alison. Do you really think that you could get away with another murder?"

"You must stay here," said Reinhold. "You belong to us now."

"It is true, Theodemir."

I turned around and faced the person who spoke. Someone had manifested out of the shadows. Alison manifested out of the darkness. She was wearing a long black gown with long sleeves. The gown covered her entire body except for her beautiful face and head.

"Alison?" I asked.

"Do you not want to be with her?" asked Reinhold.

I asked, "Alison, what did they do to you?"

Alison said, "This castle changes you. It helps you see your own darkness and fears. It makes you become connected to the dead and forgotten. I told you that if you came for me, you would die. You must embrace your own death and become one of us."

"My death?" I asked. "What do you mean?"

"You must change and become like us," said Alison.

"What does that mean?" I asked. "What is this castle?"

Alison said, "We need you to stay here. We need your blood."

"Sigrid!" I gasped. "No! It is not Alison!"

Sigrid's hands and fingers were covered with black serpentine scales. Her fingers became claws that attacked me. Reinhold began whispering something. I evaded Sigrid's attacks, but she was getting faster.

"This is a trick! An illusion!" I screamed. "This is not real! You poisoned me! Drugged me!"

Reinhold's eyes began to glow in the darkness. I ran away swiftly and heard them cackling behind me.

I left that castle without telling Roman anything about what happened or where I was going. I wanted to put everything out of my mind. I knew that I needed to accept the truth. I needed to accept that I would never know anything about Fiendilkfjeld castle. Everything that I thought I knew about the region of Fiendilkfjeld was a confusing mess.

I presumed that people here had been poisoning me and making me hallucinate. Someone wanted me to have nightmares so that I would be too scared to learn the truth. My own family never wanted me to learn the truth about what really happened here at this castle. It was their castle. I was just an intruder and a traitor. I was involved with the detective and investigators who invaded their noble sanctuary. I was not accepted by my family.

My own parents had not spoken to me in years. All they ever did was send money to me. They paid for my lifestyles and hobbies, but they did not want anything to do with me. They had never given me any advice or guidance. No one wanted to be near me. My father wanted to forget his own family, and now I had to suffer because of it. I wanted to live at that castle, but I would never be accepted there.

I had failed Alison. I had failed Roman. I had failed my family. I never found Alison. I could not help Roman do anything. I had wanted to be a part of the history of that castle. I wanted to connect in some way to that beautiful woman who I had seen in my dreams. My only consolation was that I could say that I was there and that I helped others try to find her. That was the only trace of myself that I could leave with that castle and with her memory. I had seen Alison only in my dreams, I had tried to find her, but I had failed. That would be the only connection that I ever truly had with her. At least it was something.

I needed to forget Roman, the castle, and the horrible monsters that I saw. This was exactly what the abductors must have wanted. I assumed that Alison's abductors had a simple plan that was to make Roman's investigation and mine untrustworthy and unreliable. No one would ever believe our stories. They had poisoned our minds and thoughts so that nothing we ever said would be believable. If that was their plan, it worked, because they got me to leave.

I understood that everything that I remembered about my time at the castle was a lie. I must have been manipulated and tricked into thinking that the castle was haunted. Someone must have given me a poison that was making me see monsters. I started to believe that Roman was part of the deception. Someone must have paid him to corrupt my mind. He must have been giving me drugs that would make me believe that I was killing people. Roman could have been manipulating me even before we arrived at the castle. He might have been the one who was making me see Alison in my dreams. There might never have been an Alison. Roman might have made me think that she was real so that everyone could mock me. People would say that I was the fool who thought that he was going to save a beautiful woman from a haunted castle. The entire investigation must have been a trick or a game that the aristocrats were playing at my expense. I knew that I would kill Roman if I ever saw him again.

There it was again, my desire for blood. I felt it growing inside of me when I started thinking about revenge. I wanted to hurt everyone who made me feel embarrassed or foolish. I wanted to destroy those who used me and manipulated my emotions. I started feeling like I could really get away with murder. That was really strange. I was not usually like that. I was not sure about that.

I could not stop thinking about blood. Blood was everywhere. It was inside of everything. Blood was the cause of all the life and corruption that covered this earth. Even plants had something like it. Blood also created beauty and awareness. Souls lived in blood, as they live in everything. I was not confident that souls were real. I had no real proof of the existence of my soul. I was not even positive if I was even real. I needed to do something that was real. I needed to create myself.

"How do you create anything in this dead, fake world?" I asked myself. "How do you ever know if you are real? If all I am is this flesh, blood, and bones, then should I not take as much as I can from others? What am I saying? What am I becoming? What do I need? These are not my thoughts. These are not my emotions. My flesh is talking to me. This flesh is actually saying something to me. Am I only now becoming aware of myself? Who else is here with me? Hello?"

I smelled the putrid odor of the castle. I felt the stones of its walls. I heard the footsteps of the servants inside the castle hallways. I was now in England, but I felt as if I was still feeling Fiendilkfjeld castle inside my flesh and mind. The odors and sensations from the castle were flying into my brain and body.

"Am I doomed to only feel the castle from afar?" I asked. "I smell the earth and dirt around the castle. I hear the wind blowing through its hallways. I see the shadows on its tombs. I hear the ravens flying over its towers and spires. I hear you, Fiendilkfjeld castle."

At the beginning of November, I sent messages out to many of my associates, colleagues, acquaintances, and partners. Many of them were wealthy upper-class people whom I had met at private museums, exclusive galleries, exhibitions, and private studios. I invited my friends Dean, Boris, Mildred, and Greta. I told everyone that I had returned from Italy, and I invited them all to a ball that I would be hosting at my manor in England. I told them all that there would be a banquet, dancing, orchestras, and other troupes and ensembles. I specified that the ball would take place on the last day of November.

One morning, it was still the beginning of November, I was inside the theater of my mansion. Some of the actors and musicians were talking to me about the ball. I was telling them about what I wanted and what I expected from them. While talking to them, my servants were asking me questions about their duties concerning the ball, too. I said to the actors, "I want you to create something new, original, and truly sublime." I said to the musicians, "I want you to create something new that has a goth style." To the servants, I said, "You need to get rid of that awful smell. It smells like something died in here. What is that?"

One of my servant men asked, "Will you come with me, master?"

A musician asked, "Do I play before or after the orchestras?"

An actor asked, "Where are the costumes?"

The servant man asked, "Master, please, we found that thing under your bed."

"What thing?" I was impatient and trying to comprehend multiple questions at once. "Wait." I grabbed a shoulder of the servant man and whispered close to his ear, "Can we talk about that later?"

The servant man said, "Some servant women have it in a bag."

I said, "Just forget that."

The servant man said, "It was rather nasty, my master."

I said, "What did I say? Bury it somewhere. I am busy."

I released my grip of the servant man, turned to face the musician, and asked, "Who are you playing with?"

"There are others, master," said the servant man. "In the walls."

"What do you have in your walls?" asked the actor.

I turned my head to the actor and said, "Bats. Spiders. Snakes." I smiled awkwardly and shrugged.

The musician and the actor grimaced. I felt like I was not smiling correctly, so I relaxed and attempted to correct this. I could feel my smile quickly becoming more calm and elegant. I smiled at them, but their smiles were nervous.

PART 3

CHAPTER 1

It was the last night of November, and it was the night of the ball at my manor. I had told everyone whom I had invited to bring, or at least invite, more friends, so I knew that there would be a lot of people. There were at least one hundred guests by nightfall.

I was alone in one of the upstairs hallways of my manor. I could hear the loud noises of the revelers, the dancers, and the orchestras coming from the ballroom farther downstairs. I found a room that I did not remember having. I walked into the room, but I did not recognize it.

It did not appear to be any normal type of room. The walls, floor, and ceiling were all black marble. The walls were covered by dozens of cracked mirrors. The mirrors were all enclosed in dark brown wooden frames. These frames were gorgeously elaborate and ornate with carvings that depicted wolves and ravens.

This gloomy chamber felt eerie and foreboding. The room was illuminated only by the hauntingly dreary glow of orange candlelight produced by the dozens of red candles on the floor. The light from these candles barely brightened the room. In the corners of this chamber, these crooked candles were slowly melting. These candles had the shape of gnarled branches or old towers. They almost looked like bloody hands and fingers that were burning and decaying. The candles were bleeding and spreading webs of red wax on the floor.

I looked into a mirror, but I was not there. There was no reflection of me, only endless reflections of other mirrors and candles. I looked all over the room. The cracks in these mirrors were like webs and claw marks. It seemed like something had once smashed and cut these mirrors. Their glass was still together, but forever damaged and marked by scars.

Someone slowly walked out of the shadows. I turned around, but the figure was gone. I looked into a mirror and saw the figure slowly moving towards me. I saw my own reflection moving closer towards me. I looked at the mirror the way I would look through a window. I saw myself in the mirror walking out of the darkness. He came closer until he reached the barrier of the glass. He was trying to get as close to me as he could without stepping beyond the mirror. He moved back into the shadows and then he was gone.

"How do I make you come back?" I asked.

Someone came into the room. I saw him in the mirror. It was Valter. I turned around to face him. Valter was the playwright whom I had been working with to create a new play for this night's ball.

"Everyone is dancing," said Valter. "You will not return to your guests?"

"I am not there," I said, looking at the mirrors.

"You should be down there," said Valter. "The play will begin soon. You will love it."

I said, "Valter, we worked very hard to create this new play. Tell me that it will be wonderful."

Valter said, "I did everything that you told me to do. I remembered everything that you said to me. I took all of your advice. I remembered everything that you wanted. This performance will have everything that you said that you wanted. I hired the best actors and actresses who I thought could bring your ideas to life. I think that I have created a great new play that you will greatly appreciate. It is original, it is dark, and it is beautiful. I wrote and designed this performance just for you. You are going to love it. You have not seen anything like it before. I think that we created something truly inspiring. Everyone is going to love it."

I paced around the room. Valter was standing by the open door. I got close to his face. I looked into his eyes. "Do you see your reflection?" I asked.

"It is very dark here, and the mirrors are cracked. What are you doing here?" Valter's pale hands brushed through the long wavy black hair on his head. He was slightly taller than I was. Valter put one hand in a pocket of his black robe. He quickly scratched the white skin of his scrawny neck with the sharp black fingernails of his other hand.

"Can I be alone?" I asked.

"You have a few minutes. Do not miss the performance."

"Shut the door behind you when you leave."

I heard the door being closed, but something else, too. A cold breeze brushed against my neck. I was sure that I had heard a sound coming from behind the walls. I turned around and looked into one of the mirrors. I saw my reflection, and it was normal. I was wearing a black silk tailcoat, a black silk vest, and black silk trousers. A small spider crawled on my black silk cravat. I tried to brush it away with my hand, but it was gone. I looked at the reflection, and the spider was on my reflection's cravat. I ran out of the room. I looked at my shoulders, I checked my black leather belt and my black leather shoes; there were no spiders. My legs were shaking. I thought that there were spiders on my hands. I examined them, but they were only black iron rings on my fingers.

"Do you know where Theodemir is?"

I turned around to face the person who had spoken to me. "Are you talking to me?"

It was a woman. "Valter sent me to get him, but I do not know what he looks like. The play is starting."

"I think that he is in that room," I said. "Follow me."

I led her into the dark room that had the broken mirrors inside of it. I felt my mind going someplace filled with my own doubts and regrets. I started thinking about whether memories could actually be hiding in my blood and if it were possible for the memories of someone else to attach to my heart. If those things were possible, then cannibalism would be the only way for anyone to actually be at peace with themselves. Pain would never end until everyone had eaten one another and there was nothing left but the blood on this earth. Fire would burn this bloody earth, and then everything would be complete. I had no control over anything. Knowing this, I could only follow the will and urges of my blood. This kind of knowledge was not gratifying. I needed things to change, and I wanted to defy destiny. I wanted to reach a new path of existence so that I could better understand the truth in a new, more empowering way.

I was not worried about missing any part of the play. I was certain that the play would not start without me being in the theater. I was right. When I arrived in the auditorium, the play had not started yet. I sat among the audience and waited. When the performance started, my mind focused on something outside of myself. I felt my mind gazing elsewhere. I could not pay attention to the play. I was envisioning myself stabbing everyone in the audience. I saw my tongue slide into the ears of the old women beside me. I saw my hands strangling the men behind me. I saw flashes of bloody images like scenes depicting myself murdering other viewers. I could not hear anything except for the screams of my victims as I shredded their clothes and flesh with my claws. I smelled their blood spray into the air as I slaughtered everyone in the auditorium. Many failed to escape from me. I had locked the doors. All they could do was watch as I ripped through their friends and family. I was laughing loudly. I knew that someone would stop me. Someone would escape, and they would bring people who would imprison me.

I looked at my hands, they were not wolfish claws. They were my human hands. Everyone in the auditorium was alive. The theater was silent. The performers continued acting and singing on the stage. Everything appeared normal. No one was dead. I had missed much of the performance and I did not know what was happening or what the story was. I looked around. The beautiful women who were sitting next to me smiled at me. I smiled at them. They put their hands on my hands. I breathed with relief. Their soft skin felt incredible. Their hands were so smooth and delicate. I felt their wrists and knuckles. I slid my fingers through theirs. I felt so blessed. I watched the performance and tried to figure out what was going on.

There were musicians in the orchestra and at the sides of the stage. There were choruses on the stage and at the corners of it, too. The orchestra joined with the choirs to create dark eerie melodies. These musicians created a medieval atmosphere that filled me with a sense of longing and excitement.

Dancers and singers appeared on the stage. The dancers danced with grace and elegance, but their movements were sorrowful and gloomy. The singers were singing a melodious song that was like a medieval type of plainsong that gradually became a dirge.

I heard harps, fiddles, krummhorns, sackbuts, cymbals, tambourines, and alpenhorns. The auditorium was filled with waves of enchanting sounds from the hurdy-gurdies, dulcimers, psalteries, glockenspiels, lutes, rebecs, lyres, recorders, tabors, viols, gitterns, citharas, and shawms. The melodies of contrabassists, pipe organs, and timpani soared.

I saw performers acting like medieval pilgrims who were shivering and starving. The pilgrims were being protected by brave knights. The knights fought many bandits and defended the pilgrims.

The sounds of the flugelhornists, cymbalists, gongs, piccoloists, and cornets were passionate. The melody of kettledrums, pianists, snare drums, and vibraphones was accompanied by the tunes of vibraharpists, wood blocks, bass drums, triangles, cellos, and tubular bells.

The actors, actresses, and dancers all began to move around the stage. The scene was changing, too. The scenery had transformed beautifully. The performers were now in a dark forest. Actors dressed as knights had to fight off the giant wolves living there. Many actresses dressed as wolves began attacking the knights. Many knights died, but the wolves were vanquished, and the pilgrims were safe.

The majestic melodies of the harpsichordists, harpists, flutes, clarinetists, oboists, and bassoonists cried together. The rapturous music of the violinists, drummers, violists, contrabassoons, violoncellists, trombonists, tubists, buglers, and trumpeters was sensational. The harmonies and melodies of all the singers, musicians, and instruments created a chivalrous soundscape.

The pilgrims were walking to a Gothic cathedral. Musicians played spooky tones that wailed amidst the dreary screams of the vocalists. The cathedral doors opened, and out walked actors and actresses wearing black cloaks. The wistful harmonies and mournful melodies created a dark environment of dreamy, gloomy sounds. The eyes of these cloaked actors and actresses were glowing red and their skin was white like a corpse. Angry, neurotic tones splashed against the sublime, beautiful music. The cloaked actors and actresses grabbed the pilgrims and started biting their necks and drinking their blood. The singers shrieked and screamed with the dark harmonies and frightening melodies of the orchestra.

Knights came to the Gothic cathedral. Other actors dressed as kings and other actresses dressed as queens began to pray for the safety of their people. Wolves attacked the kings and queens. The kings and queens became wolves, too, and they all danced in the cathedral. More dancers appeared to join them. The dancers were dressed like bats and foxes. As the animals danced, the ghosts and spirits in the cathedral began to awaken.

The scenery changed again so that the animals and ghosts ran through the villages and jumped around the moonlight. Everywhere they went, the dead were waking up. The full moon was bright in the night sky. Skeletons and corpses followed the dancing animals and ghosts. As they danced, they spread plagues and curses on the sleeping mortals. The actors and actresses who were dressed as skeletons danced to the sounds of bells, xylophones, and pipe organs.

Creepy, malicious noises continued to shriek as the villagers were becoming animals. Dancers, dressed like bats and wolves, twirled and jumped around the stage. Ghosts and mortals danced together.

Valter appeared on the stage and started playing an Italian bagpipe that had large ornate chanters and drones. He was joined by other bagpipers who had beautiful bagpipes that were identical to his. Hornists stood beside Valter and the bagpipers, and they were playing horns that were made out of real goats' horns. The dancers danced around Valter, the bagpipers, and the hornists. Wolves, bats, foxes, skeletons, human corpses, and knights spun and jumped.

The orchestra created spellbinding, mystifying music that evoked in my mind thoughts of haunted gothic castles and medieval cathedrals. It made me imagine medieval peasants being tortured, murdered, and eaten by demons inside dark dungeons. Singers began chanting as the haunting music wailed. The chanters gradually sounded more and more demonic. Other vocalists shrieked and cried as the music was becoming more furious and aggressive. Dark notes clashed against wild noises. The music roared like thunder in my ears.

I heard the women sitting beside me start to giggle. I looked at them and tried to get their attention. When the women turned their head to face me, I gasped. I had recognized them. It was Alison and Sigrid. They smiled at me as they gripped my hands. I hurried out of the theater, and ran outside the manor.

Cold wind pushed against me. I looked at the edge of the dark forest that surrounded the manor. I smelled the wet, dark earth and trees. Loud howls escaped the darkness. I wanted to be with the animals that made those sounds. I wanted to see the wolves that were singing in the night. I heard the screeching of bats and the moans of owls. My ears caught the sounds of the wings of moths flying around the windows. I heard creepy noises of strange worms and bugs under the ground, too.

I heard a voice coming from the shadows in the forest. I did not know what it was saying. I walked closer to the edge of the dark forest. I heard the voice again, but I did not know who it was. "Theodemir."

I turned around, but there was no one out here but me. I looked back at the edge of the forests. I tried to look through the shadows and the trees. I wanted to see deeper into the forest. I heard the howl of the wolves again, but no voice. As I turned around to walk back to the manor, I heard something as if someone was running through the forest towards me. My body shivered, and a freezing sensation rushed down my spine. Cynical cackling and morbid laughter thundered out of the forest. It sounded like it came from something that was getting very close to me. I ran to the manor and never looked behind myself. I shut the door and locked it. I walked away from the door but noticed something staring at me from the window. Standing outside, and looking at me from the window, was me.

Horrified, I screamed and covered the window with the black curtains. I heard my double screaming outside. I ran to the kitchen to be with my servants. I did not want to be alone.

CHAPTER 2

I LISTENED AS THE PERFORMANCE ENDED. I HEARD THE APPLAUSE and the cheering. I heard the guests move to the ballroom and start dancing again. I walked into the ballroom. Everyone was wearing such beautiful formal clothes. The women wore stunning gowns. The men wore dapper jackets and pants. I could not find any of the people whom I had actually invited. I saw only people whom I did not recognize. Everyone here was a stranger to me.

Valter approached me and said, "Was that not an incredible performance that you and I created? I told you that everyone would love it. Tell me what you think. Was it not perfect? I made it just for you. I did everything that you told me to do. Tell me. It was great, was it?"

I looked at Valter and said, "We did it."

Valter said, "Theodemir, you look absolutely ghastly. What happened to your face? Your skin?"

"Nothing happened to me," I said. "What is this about, Valter?"

"Theodemir, you are so boney and white. You are starkly pallid. When was the last time you ate something?"

"I feel fine," I said.

"Do you not dance?" asked Valter.

"No, I do not, Valter."

"Theodemir, what is wrong?"

I said, "I feel like I made a mistake."

Valter said, "What do you mean?"

"I should not have returned," I said. "I should have stayed at the castle."

"You never told me about what happened there. I remember that you said that you were in Italy. I think you said something about a castle," said Valter.

"I do not know if you want to hear the story," I said.

"Why not?" asked Valter.

I said, "It would be too hard for you to understand. What happened to me was rather horrifying. You would not like to know."

"Now I must know," said Valter. "I must."

"I think I should leave," I said. "I should wait for the dancing to stop."

"No," said Valter. "Wait here. I want you to tell me and my friends all about what happened to you in Italy."

I said, "Valter, please, do not do that."

"Wait here," said Valter. "Just wait. I will be back shortly."

As Valter walked away, I could not stop myself from thinking that I was going to do something horrible to someone. I flinched every time someone came too close to me. I was worried that I would hurt someone, defile them, violate them, destroy them, or corrupt them if they got too near to me. The more I worried, the worse I felt. I gasped. I could not breathe. I walked out of the ballroom and went to the main door, but I stopped. I knew that I was waiting for me outside. I could not leave yet. I could not go like this. I had to wait for me to be gone. I did not even know what I was thinking anymore. I opened the door. No one was there.

"See?" I said. "You are not there." I walked outside and breathed in the cold air. "You were just scaring yourself."

I walked through the portico and colonnade, then arrived at the courtyard, and finally waited beside the Gothic monuments and statues. I had only the moonlight to help me find my way around in the darkness. Encircling the court-yard, large crenellated walls and battlements, covered with moss and thorny vines, towered high. I walked up the narrow stone staircase and stood on the battlements. I walked along the walkways of the ramparts and embattlements. I passed through the pathways of the parapets and battlements on the enceintes. I leaned against a gargoyle and looked at all the other statues depicting grotesque animals that squatted over the parapets and machicolations.

I gazed at the decaying crowns and dead branches of the dark forests that were hunching beyond the curtain walls. The shadowed canopies of the forests were outlined by moonbeams. So many of these trees had decayed or had already been dead for many years. Farther away were the majestic evergreen forests and pinewoods. A whistling wind rustled through the trees and pinecones.

I heard Valter's voice.

"There you are, Theodemir."

I looked down the stairs to see Valter with four people who looked very wealthy and very attractive. Valter's friends seemed to be thirty years old, and they were dressed in refined formal garments.

Valter said, "These are my friends Margaret, Ksenija, Rolf, and Giuseppe." Valter turned to his friends and pointed to me. He said, "My friends, this gentle-man is Theodemir Fiendilkfjeld. Theodemir is related to Italian nobility, and his parents are related to the noble Fiendilkfjeld family that currently resides at Fiendilkfjeld castle in northern Italy."

I said, "Yes, my blood is noble, but I am not of noble status. The noble side of my family lives in northern Italy. My father did not want the noble title, but we did keep the family name. It is very complicated. I was able to see my noble relatives when I was in Italy."

"I am honored to make your acquaintance, Theodemir. You can call me Margaret. I would love to visit Italy again. Where is your family's castle?" Marga-ret was wearing a long black gown.

"They have a region named after them in northern Italy," I said, looking at Margaret. "The castle is in the Fiendilkfjeld region, which is in northern Italy."

"You can call me Rolf, Theodemir. I am also honored to be making your acquaintance. Valter says that you have an interesting story for us, about your time in Italy." Rolf was wearing a black cape.

"Call me Giuseppe, Theodemir. I am honored to be in your presence, and I would be honored if you could tell us what it was like to be in Fiendilkfjeld castle." He bowed towards me. Giuseppe was wearing a black coat.

The beautiful woman covering her shoulders with a black shawl said, "You may call me Ksenija." She was staring at me with a mysterious expression, as if she were trying to uncover something about me with her eyes. "May I see your hand?"

"My hand?" I asked, facing Ksenija.

Ksenija said, "You were bitten on the hand by a wild animal."

"Who told you that?" I asked.

"Ksenija can read things like that," said Rolf. "She is a chiromancer. She can read the future by looking at your hands, any scars, marks, damage on your skin, or scratches."

"Ksenija only works for the wealthiest people, and she has helped to guide very rich families towards greater financial security and success," said Margaret. "Wealthy families come to her for advice concerning economic, financial, or even amorous matters. Powerful people have paid for her divinations and prophecies, especially during times of death or funerals."

Giuseppe said, "Ksenija is a skilled seeress and palmist. She can foretell the future and see into the past just by looking at scars, too."

"I am fascinated," I said, "but who said that I had a scar? Who said that I was bitten by something?" I looked at my hands and gasped. I saw something that looked like a large bite mark on my left hand. These pale scars looked like jagged, gnarled marks that slithered around my knuckles. The scars branched out and furcated into many sinuous tapering scars that coursed across my wrist. There were only scars on the back of my left hand, not on my palms.

"Those scars were not there before," I said. "This is impossible."

Giuseppe said, "I am sure that it is nothing serious, Theodemir. You must have become so accustomed to the scars that you completely ignored them and then forgot about them. You do not even notice them now, unless someone tells you that they are there."

Ksenija said, "Things like that can happen to us spiritually, too. Our ignorance separates us from the astral worlds. Our weakness blocks us from preternatural dimensions. Our individuality isolates us from the spectral lands beyond the reality we focus on. Dreams can take us places, and sometimes our souls walk in dreams while we walk in reality. The hands can tell us much about where we are and what we are holding on to."

Valter asked, "What is holding you to this place?"

I said, "To be honest, I still feel the castle. I can sense its presence within my mind."

Rolf said, "Tell us about what happened there at the castle."

"I was contacted by a detective to help him investigate the disappearance of a missing heiress. Her name was Alison. This missing woman was of a noble family, she was very wealthy, and she was going to be married soon. She was supposed to be married to the son of the master of the castle. Investigators, police, government officials, and analysts inspected the castle. They found nothing. Alison was not there. No one knew where she went. All anyone knew was that some people had seen her at the castle before she went missing. Some people had seen her in a nearby village, too. She was working with the noble Fiendilkfjeld family to study the strange phenomena that occurs there and causes electronic devices to break," I said.

Valter asked, "Why did the detective want you to help him?"

I said, "There were actually several reasons for that. The noble side of my family, living in Fiendilkfjeld castle, did not want to allow any more investigators or detectives to search the castle. The only way that they would allow someone to come investigate was if another member of the family came, too. They wanted someone who was family but not directly entangled with them. They wanted a relative who was not nobility to join the detective, otherwise they would not allow him to come look inside the castle. This detective asked my parents and close relatives on my side of the family, but no one wanted to help him. When he came to me, he showed me a picture of the missing woman. It was Alison. I recognized her. I had been dreaming about a woman who looked like her. In my dreams, this woman was inside a castle that looked like the rooms inside my family's castle. I had to accept. I knew that I had to come with the detective and look for this woman. She looked exactly like the woman I had been seeing for months in my dreams."

"What happened when you got to the castle?" asked Margaret.

"On our way to the castle, I had heard people saying that the entire region was haunted. People were saying that the castle was haunted and the whole land was cursed," I said. "The region of Fiendilkfjeld was once controlled by my ancient ancestors, and the region is still dedicated to us. When I went there, I felt like the castle was changing me. I did not want to believe that it was true, but I know now that I am not the same. I understand things differently now. Something was haunting that place."

Giuseppe asked, "Did you find Alison?"

"No," I said.

"What happened to her?" asked Valter. "Where was she?"

"I do not know," I said. "No one would say anything. No one knew anything. One day she was there, and then she was just gone. I really do not want to keep talking about this."

"What was haunting the castle?" asked Rolf.

I said, "I cannot describe it. I tried to understand it. I wanted to stay there with them. I would have lived there if I could. There was something there that was so beautiful and inspiring, but fatal and baleful."

"Why did you leave?" asked Valter.

"I did not trust the people there," I said. "They did not trust me."

"You still love that castle," said Valter.

"I always will," I said. "I know now that it changed me. I just do not understand what is different. I wish that side of my family would accept me, but they are not honest with me. They do not respect me. I was so close to uncovering something truly profound, but all I received was deception. No, the castle left something else with me. I feel something coming to me. I know that something is about to happen. It is an omen. It is a warning."

"Do you still think about Alison?" asked Margaret.

"I do," I said. "I do not see her in my dreams, but I think about her."

Margaret asked, "What was so special about her?"

I said, "She was beautiful and pure like the sky or the ocean. I wish I could explain it. She was like a storm or a fire. I thought that she could save me. I only saw her in my dreams, but she gave me hope. I felt like I needed to be with her. She was dangerous and beautiful, but she needed help. I thought that I could be more like her, maybe she could make me become better than who I was. Now that I look back on it, it all feels so strange and unfamiliar. I really do not even know why I was so obsessed with her. It is like waking up from a bad dream, and you do not know why you did the things you did in that dream. Nothing in the dream made sense. I was not even myself in the dream, but it felt real and understandable while I was dreaming. There were so many different parts of me that were taking over, and all I could do was feel their emotions. I thought their thoughts, but they really were not mine. I guess, I could say, it is like looking back on old memories of yourself and trying to understand why or how you could do the things that you did. Sometimes, you remember something awful, and you wish you could take it all back and make it go away. The only thing that makes it disappear is just to keep living."

Ksenija said, "The castle was a doorway for you. You were destined to go there. It was a part of you, and you needed to be there to reconnect with a vital part of yourself. Let me look at your scars, and I can see what the castle gave you. Sometimes, we find ourselves in places only to understand a message or a warning. You can almost think of it like a part of yourself that comes back through the future, and even the past, to help guide you on your journey."

Ksenija took my hand and looked at the scars. Rolf, Giuseppe, Margaret, and Valter crowded around me and looked at it, too. Ksenija's thin hands felt so soft on my hand. Her pale fingers were delicate and smooth. I winced, trying hard not to think about killing all of them. I pulled my hand away. Images of their corpses invaded my thoughts. I thought about biting their necks and taking their blood. I thought about how delicious their flesh would be. I did not want to kill them, but these images and urges invaded every part of my mind.

"I must go," I said.

"Wait," said Ksenija. "I have a prophecy for you."

"What is the prophecy?" I asked.

"I heard these words," said Ksenija. "I saw horrifying things in your scars. After I tell you what I have heard, you must never speak to me again."

"What? Why?" I asked. "What are you saying?"

Valter said, "Ksenija, you should not speak like that to Theodemir. He will make us leave the party."

Rolf asked, "What is it?"

As I was looking into Ksenija's eyes, I said, "Tell me."

Ksenija was looking into my eyes and said, "You will return to Fiendilkfjeld castle, and you will die there."

Giuseppe, Rolf, Margaret, and Valter gasped with shock and terror. Ksenija ran away. Valter and his friends followed her. I leaned against the rampart wall and looked up at the full moon. I heard the howl of distant wolves, and I shouted, too.

CHAPTER 3

I looked at my hand. The scars were now gone. I laughed. "Just another trick. A game," I said. "Valter was trying to scare me because I did not stay to watch his entire performance. They must have put something on my hand to make me think that I had scars. How did they know that I was bitten by something? Did Dean tell them? It could have been Greta, Mildred, or Boris. They must be behind this. This is their prank on me. The castle did not change me. I will not die. The noble side of my family probably will never let me return to the castle. They only wanted me there so that I could supervise Roman. There is no prophecy. There is no curse."

"You do not believe in magic?"

I turned around and saw a woman wearing a gray gown. She looked like she was twenty or twenty five years old. She walked up the stairs and stood next to me. "Hello," she said. "My name is Brigitte. You must be Theodemir Fiendilkfjeld."

"I am."

"I heard some people talking about you. They said that you were cursed. Is that true? Are you cursed?"

"What kind of a question is that?"

Brigitte giggled. "Why are you not inside?"

"Why are you still here?"

"I like danger, Theodemir."

I started to walk away, but she grabbed my arm.

She said, "Do you not think that I am attractive?"

"You could get hurt," I said. "I need to leave."

"You cannot reject me," said Brigitte. "Who do you think you are?"

"Remove your hand from my arm," I said.

"No," she said. "I saw you looking at me. I know that you need me."

"I never looked at you," I said. "I do not know who you are."

Brigitte said, "No. Stay with me."

I grabbed her hand and pulled it away from my arm.

"That is what I want. You rich men are so easy to manipulate. I know you cannot resist me," said Brigitte. "What else are you going to do to me?"

"You disgust me," I said. I grabbed her neck and dragged her into the shadows.

I did not know where my strength was coming from. I bit her neck and sucked the blood. I covered her mouth with my hands. She bit my hand, but I did not feel the pain. I felt no pain, actually. She screamed, but not for long. I pulled out her tongue and teeth. She was trying to fight me, but I felt absolutely no pain. I cracked her face with my hands. I broke every bone in her body.

As a corpse, she was so much more beautiful now. She was just one of those people that needed to transform. I helped her do that. People like her are unhappy with themselves. I saved her. It was destiny for her blood to move like this in the darkness.

I knew exactly where she belonged. I took the pieces of her corpse to the chapel connected to my manor. Everyone was in the ballroom, so I knew that I was totally alone. I put her broken skull on the altar with all the dead birds. I put the rest of her corpse in the underground crypt below the chapel. I was planning to use this for my family, but she was special enough now. I returned to the chapel and sat down.

"What is happening to me?" I asked. "What are these emotions that I am feeling? Will they ever stop?"

I sat there for several minutes until my entire body was in pain. I was feeling all the pain now. My hands and face felt like they were on fire. I screamed as the pain started getting worse. My head felt like it was split open. My hands and face were dripping with red blood. My clothes were bloody and stained, too. The only thing that made the pain go away was blood. I knew that I needed more, but I was not sure if I was ready. I did not want to hurt anyone. I did not want to ruin my life. I knew that I would be caught. I almost wanted to be caught. Almost.

From the crypt, I used the underground tunnels to get back into my manor. I moved through secret passageways to reach my bedroom. I changed my clothes and put on garments that were identical to the ones that I previously had on. Something in this room smelled terrible, so I left quickly.

I told several of my servants to make sure that no one entered the chapel. I said, "Keep everyone in the ballroom or in the parlor. I do not want anyone to go into any other rooms. No chapel. No courtyard." When the servants asked me why, I just told them, "It is not part of your job to ask questions."

I returned to the room with the broken mirrors. I found a door and opened it. I looked down and saw a dark staircase. I walked down with a candle and used it to light all the other candles down here. There was an archway that led me through a passageway that was bringing me upwards. I arrived in a cloister glistening with blue moonbeams sliding through the Gothic arched windows. I found a red door and opened it. I walked down the stairs.

I faced a locked door. Crying, screaming, and sobbing escaped from the other side of that door. I looked through the small window in the door. I had to put my candle up to the window to see anything inside. There was a room, and inside was a man and a woman. The man's legs were broken and the woman's eyes had been gouged out. The room was made of dark gray stones. The door was iron.

The man screamed, "Let us out of here! Let us go!"

The woman started shrieking. She was shivering in a corner of the small dark room.

"Who did this to you?" I asked.

"We need to go home!" screamed the woman.

The man yelled. He said, "Open the door! Open the door!"

"We have been here for months!" said the woman. "Help us!"

"We will never steal from you again," said the man. "We need to be free. I beg you. Let us go. Let us go."

"I have never seen you before," I said. "I did not do this to you. You have not been here for months. I have never seen any of you."

"Does that mean that you will free us?" asked the man.

I said, "I will. Give me a second. I need to find the key."

"Thank you!" said the woman. "You will not regret this."

"Thank you!" said the man. "It is finally over."

I found the key on the wall. I used it to open the door. The woman attacked me. She started kicking and punching me. The man began to crawl away. I dropped the candle, but I could smell her blood. I chased her through the dark. She tried to run up the stairs, but I grabbed her leg. I threw her into a wall. I made sure that the man was actually crippled by smashing down on his legs with my feet. The man screamed, and I heard his bones snapping. I returned to the woman. I knew that the man was not going anywhere. I dragged the woman by her hair. I brought her back to the cell and threw her in.

I bit on the wounds of the man's legs and sucked the blood. It made me feel stronger. My pain was gone again. I was healed. I bit the man's neck and drank more blood. I kicked his dead body into the corner of the cell. The woman was screaming so loudly. I was tired of listening to her. I smashed her face into the stones until pieces of her brain spilled out of her skull.

I was so upset that I had to change my clothes again. If anyone were to ask, I would need to create an excuse for why I was wearing different clothes. I could not waste more time here. I wanted to eat the corpses, but I needed to wait. The decaying meat would taste better if I were to wait a few days, anyway.

I returned to my room and changed clothes. I wore a black cloak that would keep me warm while I was walking around outside at night. I ran along the walkways of the battlements and pretended that I was flying. I flapped my arms and moved my cloak as if they were wings. I climbed to the roof where I began howling.

When I returned to the parlor, there were still many guests. Many more people were arriving, too. Valter, Rolf, and Giuseppe found me there.

"Hello," I said. "You return to meet the dead man."

Valter said, "Ksenija is gone. We are so sorry for what she said to you. We saw her leave."

"She is terrified of you, Theodemir," said Rolf.

Giuseppe said, "I have never seen her like that before with anyone ever in my entire life. She is usually very calm with people. I must apologize for her. She can be theatrical at times."

Valter said, "Theodemir, please, allow us to stay at the party. If you ever need anything from me, I want to help you. I feel so bad for what she said to you. I cannot understand why she would say that you would die."

"Your scars are gone?" asked Rolf.

"Yes," I said. "There were never any scars. She tricked me. I know that you were all tricking me. You do not need to pretend anymore. You had your laughs, I am sure."

"That was not a trick," said Valter. "If it was, we were not a part of it."

"We were shocked by what Ksenija said to you," said Giuseppe.

"Look at his hands," said Rolf. "No scars." He pointed to my hands.

Valter said, "It must have been the moonlight playing tricks on all of us."

"What if she was right?" I asked.

"About the scars?" asked Valter.

I said, "I want to go back to the castle."

"I thought that you said that you did not trust the people there," said Rolf.

"After what Ksenija said, I do not think that I would even want to dream about going there if I were you, Theodemir," said Valter.

I said, "I hate thinking that I failed. I could not find Alison. I could not make that side of my family accept me. Another part of me feels like maybe I gave up on them. You must forgive me, I really should not be talking about this. It is too painful. I wish that I could say more, but I do not even know where to begin."

"You should feel proud about the party that you created tonight," said Giuseppe. "You have hundreds of people coming to your manor. People are dancing, talking, and drinking here. You made this happen tonight. You are a man of honor and respect. You are a gentleman of the upper class. You have prestige, wealth, status, and fortune."

"I want more strength," I said. "I want more power. I want to stop feeling alone."

Valter said, "I really must be leaving now, Theodemir. Thank you for tonight's party. I had fun."

I watched Valter, Giuseppe, and Rolf leave the manor together. I started talking to other people in the parlor. It was easy to approach people and start a conversation, but it was almost impossible to keep a conversation going with my guests for more than a few seconds.

No one wanted to really talk to me. All the guests said the same things to me. "Thank you for inviting me." "I am so honored to meet you." "You have a beautiful Gothic mansion." "Can I borrow some money?" "We should work together some-time." It was always the same things, but none of them were interested in what I said. Each of them only heard what they wanted to hear, and then they walked away from me. They acted as if they could not hear me speaking.

The people here wanted my money. They wanted to attach my name to their projects or businesses. They were here for the socializing, the gossip, and the dancing; they were not here for me. They noticed me, but they quickly forgot me.

I tried to have conversations with many of the people here. They would only smile, nod their head, and then walk away after a few seconds. Some of the guests would say, "I need to see a friend really quickly, but I will come back to finish the rest of this delightful conversation." They would never find me or talk to me again. I always saw them talking to other people in the manor, but never to me.

I was not interested in their vapid ideas or their fickle interests. These guests only wanted to talk about the shallowest and most boring things that I was not interested in. They spoke so flippantly and mundanely. I was trying to talk to them about their dreams, philosophies, ideologies, and convictions.

One woman said to me, "Dreams are dead. Dreams are for poor people."

A man I spoke with said to me, "Imagination is a prison. Emotions bring wars. This is the modern world. You need to forget everything."

A different woman said to me, "You should destroy everything that you own. Books, properties, and even emotions are oppressive. You need to have fun. This is a modern world. I did it, and it changed my life. I like it." When I asked her what she was talking about, she said, "I was not being serious. You do not need to know what I really think."

For years, this is how it has been for me. I did not know why I ever thought that things would change. I had hosted balls and parties at my manor before, but the result was always the same. I tried to make friends, but no one ever really cared about me. No one ever communicated with me or wanted to really know me. No one wanted to have a conversation with me for more than three seconds. None of them ever showed that they were really concerned about me. No one ever really did anything to make me feel special or loved. It was just like my relationship with my parents. The money was there, but they were always gone. There was no emotion from them.

I sat in the parlor and listened to everyone has having conversations with one another. Their voices were just loud noise now. I could not understand anything that anyone was saying. I sat closer to the musicians so that the beautiful music could cover the racket.

I did not want to stop the party. Much as I hated these guests, I did not want to be alone. I knew that I would be forgotten the second everyone was gone. Even though these people were unfriendly, they gave me existence. I wanted to figure out a way to make them like me. I wanted to think of something that would make them want to know me.

I went to the ballroom and danced with several women, but they were never looking at me. When I was tired of dancing, I walked out of the ballroom. I walked into a lavatory, looked into a mirror, and glared at my reflection.

I said, "You do not know what you want anymore. You do not know who you are. Do you know what is real?"

CHAPTER 4

I SPOKE TO SOME PEOPLE, BUT THEY DID NOT SEEM TO WANT TO talk to me. I walked into antechamber, passed the drinkers and revelers, and realized that most of the people here were not actually talking to one another now. Conversations had ceased, and everyone was just looking at one another or dancing to the loud music of the musicians. Most of the men I spoke with walked past me when I tried to talk to them. I spoke to a woman, to try to see if I could get someone here to chat with, but she said, "Conversation is old-fashioned. This is the modern world. Excuse me, I am trying to listen to the music." That remark made me laugh rather bitterly.

"Enjoying your party?"

I turned to face a gentleman wearing a black cape. The musicians' ethereal blue lights were shining down on the white skin of his face, which made him appear like a ghost. This man looked older than me, maybe thirty or forty years old.

"What is your name?" I asked.

"Call me Pasquale."

I said, "Are you enjoying the night?"

"I am," said Pasquale. "I enjoyed the performance and the orchestras, too. I wanted to thank you. I am honored to be here. I think that it was a brave decision to invite all these people and allow them to bring anyone that they wanted. People will remember this party."

"They will not remember me," I said.

"That is the weakness of this modern world," said Pasquale. "Everyone here is afraid of emotion and conversation, yet they have been programmed to broadcast only their immature feelings. Society teaches people to uphold the new laws of promiscuity, mediocrity, apathy, and faithlessness. You cannot expect to reach out to these people. All they can do is make noise, and yet all they produce is silence. They are like ghosts. You cannot touch their minds or hearts. These people are all dead, my good man."

"Dead." I turned my head and looked into Pasquale's eyes. "Blooming dead are they."

"I have read your books," said Pasquale. "I love the work that you do. You give people so much knowledge about macabre news and evil things that are really happening around the world. Your work is educational, but you make it exciting. Your books documented and reported the real events and tragedies that surrounded all those weird suicidal cults that are still roving across Europe. You wrote about scenes of ceremonial murders and strange artifacts that were found there. You saw, with your own eyes, dead bodies and all those sacrificial victims of murderous vagabonds. You followed police, investigators, and detectives from one death to the next. You interviewed witnesses, people at morgues, and even some of the cultists who were arrested. You wrote about many recent sacrifices in your books, too. The murderers that you interview and write about in your books are very unique."

"May I ask why you like my books?" I asked.

Pasquale said, "They give me hope that there is something more interesting going on in this boring world. You report about things that are true but horrifying. The things you write about are things that are brutal but sublime. Cults, murders, rituals, witches, suicides, and monsters. No one would reveal those things except for remarkable historians and journalists like you. You show people the dark truth, and you go places that no one should go. Your books reflect the other side of human beings. You show people that this world is not dead, that something from the past still lives. There are people out there, on this earth, who want to believe in something so much that they would kill themselves or kill others for it. Your books are breathtaking journalism."

"I appreciate your kind words," I said.

Pasquale asked, "You are so wealthy that you do not need to work, so why do you do it? Why do you work as a historian? Why do you report about murders and superstitions?"

I said, "Power."

"I understand that," said Pasquale. "We are alive."

Pasquale walked away and vanished into the crowd of dancers. The manor was filled with the loud music and dreamy rhythms of the musicians. The goth rock melodies and dark beats resounded in the rooms and halls. The chanters' voices were romantic yet dismal. Macabre soundscapes were being created by the wistful moans of saxophones, the shrieking of electric guitars, the synthesizers that droned and bellowed, and the gloomy sighs of bass guitars. Morbid singing and mournful cries created a somber consonance that reverberated in the room. The musicians played eerie chords and ghostly tones. The sad voices of the vocalists were melodious yet dismal. A grim timbre manifested in the dark music that gradually became a nocturne as the harpsichordists and pianists joined. Drums began scratching and roaring. The music slowly began to sound like a morose waltz. Keyboards hummed with disturbing fury, and the spooky throbbing of synthesizers transformed the music into a dark, grieving atmosphere. The singers began weeping and shouting. Growling tones, snarling sounds, and sorrowful warbling created a wicked dissonance that echoed throughout the room.

I saw a man wearing a black cape and a black mask. His mask was shaped like the face of a black raccoon. I followed the man through the crowd of dancers as the music hissed and pulsated. The man finally stopped under a Gothic archway that would lead to the chapel.

I grabbed the man by the shoulder and said, "That area is off-limits to guests for tonight. My apologies, chap."

The man turned around and faced me. "My apologies. I smelled blood."

"You are going to see blood if you do not remove that twee mask and reveal your identity to me, mate," I said.

"You can call me Jurgis," he said. "I have been sent here to help you."

"You are the one who will need help if you do not leave this place," I said. "Guests are not allowed beyond here."

"I know what you have been doing here," said Jurgis.

"I have not done anything," I said.

"It will happen again."

I said, "Cease this jiggery-pokery, you prat."

"I know why you had this party, Theodemir. This is a distraction from the voices. You want them to stop."

"Who are you?"

Jurgis said, "One of your third cousins sent me."

"Who?"

"Dragana."

I said, "I do not know her."

Jurgis said, "You know her, you just do not remember. Tell me about your family, the noble side."

"What do you want to know?" I asked.

"Tell me what you remember about them from the last time you saw them," said Jurgis.

"I do not want to talk about them."

"Before it is too late for you, Theodemir, come with me."

"Before what?" I asked. "What are you trying to save me from?"

Jurgis said, "You must find me later. We do not have any more time. Go to the chapel when everyone is gone. I will be there."

"You will not," I said. "No one is allowed to enter there."

"Something from the castle has followed you back here," said Jurgis. "You cannot hear me, but you know the truth. Find me at the chapel when everyone is gone."

I said, "I will not allow you to go to the chapel."

"You cannot stop me, Theodemir." Jurgis clapped, which created a massive cloud of red smoke. It blinded me and made me cough. The smoke smelled like blood. I ran from it and gasped for air. When I opened my eyes, Jurgis was gone.

I commanded servants to wait by the entrance to the chapel. I did not want anyone going through. I could not get the smell of blood out of my mouth and nose. The sanguinary aroma was intoxicating and animate. It slithered up my nose and into my ears. I heard it murmuring indistinctly, at first.

When I returned to the ballroom, the aroma screamed for blood. The smell of blood overpowered all of my senses so that my vision was stained red. Everything and everyone was a different shade of blood. Crimson, violet, and black wisps loitered around everything.

When my eyesight was normal again, I realized that all of the older gentlemen and elderly gentlewomen were leaving the manor. Everyone who was still here appeared to be twenty or twenty five years old. Those who stayed were the artists, musicians, performers, heirs, heiresses, models, and dancers.

A woman ran outside. She was crying. Another woman, I assumed that it was her friend, followed her. I did, too. Hidden behind a statue, I overheard the crying woman arguing with the other woman about their boyfriends. I did not understand whether they both had multiple boyfriends or if they were sharing boyfriends, but it sounded like an utterly gormless argument. Both women were saying that they were unhappy with the men that they were with, but they also were trying to make plans. The women were talking flippantly and vapidly about what they wanted to do with their boyfriends and whether or not they should switch partners. Ultimately, what happened was one woman traded her boyfriend to the other.

She said, "You can have my boyfriend for the week, but you need to buy our cocaine." That seemed to end the argument, and the other woman stopped crying. Then, they went back to flippantly telling asinine, lewd jokes to each other. Their laughter seemed pompous and insincere.

I approached these two women and said, "I can help you with that."

The women glared at me.

I said, "I have cocaine."

One of them said, "My name is Graziella." She put her arms around my neck and looked at her friend.

Her friend scoffed and walked away. I was disappointed by this, because Graziella's friend was obviously the more attractive one. Graziella was pretty enough.

"You are so handsome," said Graziella.

I brought her to an upstairs room where we could be alone. Killing her brought me no joy. I strangled her so quickly. Even if I cut her apart now, the mood would still be dead.

There were three men in the hallway who had become too intoxicated to stand. I dragged them into the room with Graziella's dead body. The men tried to talk to Graziella. I laughed when she did not respond to their questions. They started screaming when they realized that she was dead. The men fought against me, but I was too quick for them. I evaded their sloppy attacks, effortlessly. I dodged their fists and then punched the back of their heads. They fell to the ground, so I stomped on their throats. I continued kicking their chests until I knew that they were dead.

I returned to the ballroom and observed everyone dancing. I saw Jurgis running through the crowd. I chased him through the crowd and followed him to the archway leading to the courtyard.

"Why are you doing this to me, Jurgis?" I asked.

"I am not Jurgis," he said. He turned around to face me. He was wearing a mask that resembled the face of a black fox. "Call me Taddeo."

I said, "We are alone. Why have you brought me here? You obviously wanted me to follow you."

Taddeo said, "You are still trapped. You need to release yourself."

"What does that mean?" I asked. "Why are you tormenting me like this?"

"You need to kill more people," said Taddeo. "You cannot stop."

"I never killed anyone," I said. "I am not like you."

"What am I?" asked Taddeo.

I said, "You were sent here by my family. You are one of the cultists. You are trying to get revenge against me. You want me to think that I am crazy. You attacked me on this night to break my spirit. I just want to have a fun night with my friends."

"These people are not your friends, Theodemir."

"I do not know you. You need to leave."

"Who am I, Theodemir?"

"I know that you and the other cultists killed Alison," I said. "I was not going to say anything, but I will if you and your friends keep harassing me."

"Tell your servants to make me leave," said Taddeo. "Throw me out of the manor."

I gasped.

Taddeo said, "What?"

I said, "What do you want me to do?"

"Kill," said Taddeo. "Accept what you have done."

"What have I done?" I asked.

Taddeo said, "You are lost. You need to take control over your memories. Do not destroy yourself."

"I do not know," I said. "What do I do?"

"You are being destroyed," said Taddeo. "Awaken! Awaken it!"

"Awaken what?" I asked, frantically.

"You need to kill," said Taddeo. "Without blood, you will not be protected from it. It will fight against you. It is coming for you! You cannot see it? You cannot hear it? Awaken it before it consumes you!"

"I do not understand!" I cried. I grabbed his cloak.

Taddeo said, "You are not prepared. It is coming for you now. I knows that you are weak. Your eyes are still closed."

"What is this thing?" I asked.

"It has always been with you," said Taddeo. "You must learn to hear and see more than just the truth. You must go beyond reality."

"Where is it?" I asked. "Is it in the manor?"

"Yes," said Taddeo. "It has been watching you. It has always been here. It has been under your bed and in the shadows of the hallways. It sits behind you and smiles. It moves while you are not looking. It is ready to destroy you."

"Why does it want to kill me?"

Taddeo said, "It has always wanted to kill you."

"I will not die," I said. "I cannot die. I will not let it get me."

"You have been cursed," said Taddeo. "You need to accept that. This curse will destroy anyone whom you are close to."

I shouted at him. "No. This is wrong. Magic does not exist. Curses are not real."

Taddeo asked, "How many more times will you keep denying the truth?"

"I am scared," I shouted.

"If you keep resisting your own soul, your body and your mind will not survive," said Taddeo. "You will truly be annihilated if you give up. Do you want to wander forever like this? Do you want to keep losing your memories or do you want to find them? Awaken the sadistic beast inside of yourself, or else it will destroy you."

"I wish I knew what you were saying," I said. "When will it attack?"

Taddeo suddenly disappeared. I screamed and ran to the kitchen. I had just seen a man vanish as if he were never there. People should not be able to become invisible like that. I wanted to hide from everyone. Anyone in the manor could have been the killer that Taddeo warned me about. Taddeo's words were too confusing. All I knew was that someone was trying to kill me and I needed something to protect myself with.

I grabbed a long knife and told my servants to be prepared for anything. I said, "Someone came here to warn me that I was going to be killed. I think that there is a cult that is trying to get revenge on me for reporting about their murders. It might be one of the murderers that I had once interviewed. There were people with cloaks and masks, they came here, and they told me that something bad is going to happen here. Hello?"

I turned around and saw that blood was dripping from my knife. I gazed around the kitchen. The servants were all dead. It looked as if someone had butchered them. Some of the bodies were decapitated.

"No," I said. "That was not me. That was not me. That was not me."

CHAPTER 5

I walked out of the kitchen and realized that the entire manor was empty, dark, and silent. There was no one left, but me. Inside, every room was covered by gossamer webs. All of the windows were draped with sheets of dust. Cobwebs enveloped all of my furniture. Dust had been sprinkled across the floors. The tables and chairs were cobwebbed. Repugnant spiderwebs spread across every entrance, doorway, and archway in the mansion.

Unsettling blue moonlight seeped into the dim rooms through the dusty windows. An ethereal gauze lingered in the air. A shadowy mist clouded the rooms. The candles and lights were dead. A dark haze enveloped me everywhere that I went.

I exited the mansion, but I had to run back inside. Gruesome wolves emerged from the dark edges of the forest. They surrounded the entirety of the estate. These black wolves were dripping blood. Their eyes were glowing red light. Moonbeams glistened on the macabre human corpses dangling from their bloody mouths. Black horns, like the horns of a goat, protruded from the heads of these loathsome devils.

As I ran, the wolves chased me. I heard them howling and barking as I stumbled to the door. The wolves clawed the back of my coat. As I was closing the door, the wolves pushed against it. They were trying to keep the door open so that they could get in. Their muzzles and claws jutted in through the opening. I slammed the door against their faces repeatedly. They whimpered and howled as I used the door to attack them. Their white fangs dripped with saliva and blood. Black forked tongues were flicking in and out of their mouths. I gave another hard shove against the door to slam the wolves. They retreated, and I closed the door. I locked it and started screaming as I heard the howling and yipping of the wolves.

I floundered about the murky darkness of the chambers and hallways. As I was running all throughout the mansion, I accidentally bumbled into a spiderweb. I had not seen it, and now I had fallen in. I was caught in the web. I shoved against the web and rolled out. I grabbed a knife and used it to break the other webs.

Dozens of white large spiders fell from the ceiling. The spiders jumped on me. I stabbed them with my knife. They hissed as I fought against them. Unbelievable pain burned through my body when they stung me with their vicious fangs. The bites felt like huge rocks crushing my body. I thought that they might have broken my bones. Intense heat burned every part of me. The spiders chirped and buzzed. I groaned and cried. The stings felt worse every second.

I forced myself to use all the strength I had remaining. I knifed the spiders, slashed off their legs, and pierced their eyes. I felt my flesh melting. Screaming with pain, I crawled away. Someone picked me up and carried me away. It was a woman. She used my knife to cut the white flesh of her wrist. She put her bloody wrist to my mouth.

"Drink my blood," she said.

She was wearing a black cloak and a black mask. Her mask resembled the face of a black cat. I sucked the sweet blood from her gorgeous wrist. My pain gradually died. I continued sucking blood until she told me to stop.

"Who are you?" I asked.

"Call me Jeanne," she said.

I was tired and very drowsy. Jeanne brought me to my bed and I fell asleep.

I woke up in my bed, but I was not alone. I screamed and jumped out of bed. In the bed were the decaying, grisly corpses of Dean, Boris, Mildred, and Greta.

With my knees on the floor, I screamed. My fingers dragged against my face. I shut my eyes and continued screaming, but my screams turned into sobs. I wept loudly. I shook my head. My body was trembling. I bent low and curved my body. I rocked up and down. My hands were gripping my head. My knees pressed into the floor as I continued rocking my shivering body, as if I were bowing to their corpses.

I raced to the bed and grabbed their corpses. I threw them on the floor and started smashing them with my hands. I stomped on their bones and screamed wildly. I chewed on their flesh and ate their rotten organs. I shrieked and moaned. As I kowtowed, my fingers dragged down my face and neck. I rolled onto my back and sobbed. I breathed and then stopped crying.

"I killed them," I whispered. "I killed them. I know that I killed them, but I do not remember when or where. I do not remember killing them, but I feel like I did. No, wait. I remember something. I did not just kill them. I tortured them before I killed them. I defiled them, violated them, burned them, and made them suffer. Did I really do that? When did I kill them? Was that really me? It must have been me. This must be who I am now. Is any of this real? It feels real, but something is wrong. What am I going to do? Can I make this stop? I do not want to be like this, but it feels too good. Killing people and eating them gives me value. No, it is awful. It should feel awful. I do not understand anything anymore. This is not me. This is not really me. Who else could it be? I do not like this. I do not like this. This cannot be me. I am disgusting. I am so disgusting."

I stood up. Regret and shame flooded my mind. My heart was in so much pain that I thought it would melt. I walked down into the cellar. I grabbed a knife. "I have done this before." I put the knife against my neck. I closed my eyes. My hand trembled. I was breathing heavily.

"What are you doing?" It was Jeanne's voice.

I opened my eyes and turned around to face her. She was wearing a black cat mask and a black cloak.

I said, "Your blood gave me life, but I do not want to live. I must not live. I am evil. I am scum."

"If you kill yourself like this, you will never leave this place," said Jeanne.

"I have killed so many people," I said.

Jeanne asked, "Who did you kill?"

"I do not remember," I said. "I killed my friends, my servants, and my guests. I think I killed more than that."

"Try to remember who you are," said Jeanne. "Do you know who you are?"

"I am Theodemir Fiendilkfjeld."

"What do you know about yourself?"

"I thought I could remember," I said.

Jeanne said, "Where are your parents? What happened to them?"

"I do not know," I said. "What is happening?"

"Who are you?"

I said, "How do I not remember?"

"Try to think about everything that has ever happened to you," said Jeanne. "Grab your memories."

"What are you?" I asked.

"Where are we, Theodemir?" asked Jeanne.

"This is my mansion," I said.

Jeanne said, "Are we really inside the mansion?"

I gazed around and saw that we were now inside my chapel.

"I do not understand how this is happening," I said. "What did you do to me?"

"Is this reality?" asked Jeanne.

I said, "Stop what you are doing."

"If you kill yourself here, you will only go deeper beneath this nightmare, and that poison will destroy you," said Jeanne.

"What poison? What nightmare?"

Jeanne said, "The beast that has been following you. The great storm of night-mares that you have been trapped in."

"This is an illusion," I said. "This is another trick."

"You know that you killed people, but you do not remember when or where. You know who you are, but you do not remember your past. You are losing your identity, Theodemir," she said.

I said, "I do not want to live anymore. I have done too many vile things. I have hurt so many people. I do not know how to stop."

Jeanne said, "I am not telling you to stop. You do not really want to stop. You do not want to die. If you did, you would have been destroyed much earlier. You never would have made it this far."

I said, "I want to be a good person. I want to be good. I know that I am. This is not right. I do not feel like myself. I know that I have done terrible things, and I cannot remember everything. What do you want from me? Why would you be helping me? What am I supposed to do? What could someone like me do for you?"

"You cannot understand because you do not want to understand," said Jeanne. "You cannot hear our true words because you do not want to hear them. You will not die, because you do not want to."

"What happens if I end my life?" I asked. "You say that I cannot die."

"You will be destroyed if you die too many times," said Jeanne. "When your soul is truly broken, and your mind is fragmented into millions of tiny pieces, then you will truly vanish. Your soul and your mind are being eaten. There is a beast here that wants to destroy you, to possess you. You have an opportunity to take control of it. If you kill yourself now, you will lose more memories, and another part of your soul will die."

"This is a dream?" I asked.

Jeanne, and everything else around me, began to vanish. I floated away into a wide black abyss. There were no stars, and there was no light. I could not even see myself. White light passed through the shadows. There were pale lights moving in the darkness. They were the ghosts of men and women. I did not know where they had come from, but they were floating between the shadows. Their arms and legs blinked in and out of the void. Their cadaverous faces were translucent and shining dim white light. These spirits grabbed me. I could not harm them. My hands passed through their bodies. They were choking and attacking me. I could not breathe. I gasped for air.

I woke up in my bed. I closed my eyes. "I wish that they had killed me."

"What was that, master?"

I turned my head and saw a woman wearing the black uniform of my servant women. She was standing next to me, and she had a bloody silk bag in her hands. She looked mature but lovely. I was thinking that maybe she could be thirty years old.

"What is the bag for? Who are you?"

"I am your servant Melanie, master."

"Forgive me," I said. "You are one of my servants?"

"Yes, master. Are you feeling all right?"

I said, "No. I feel rather influenzal. I very much would like to be alone."

She put her hand on my forehead. "My master, you do not feel very warm," said Melanie. "You feel chilly."

The sensations of her soft pretty hands on my head felt luxurious and intoxicating. I imagined licking, kissing, biting, and chewing on this hand. These disgusting thoughts made me flinch.

"Melanie, you must get that bag away from my face. It smells repulsive. What is in this thing?"

She said, "You always ask me to bring this for you. We do this for you every day. Have I been wicked? Did I make a mistake, master? What did I do wrong? Will I be lashed again?"

"I never asked you for this." I took the bag and put it on the bed.

"Do you not want to look inside of it, master?"

I stared at that bloody silk bag. I could not hear anything. I saw only the bag. Everything else was blurry and dark. I felt as if the whole world was shaking. I grabbed the bag. I slowly opened it and brought it closer to my face. The world was calm again. Nothing was shaking. I could hear the ravens outside and the wind blowing against the walls. My vision was normal and I was seeing clearly.

I looked inside the bag. It was so dark in there. An eye gazed at me from the shadows. I screamed.

Melanie said, "You said that you wanted this. There are so many dead cats in the forest. It must be wolves or something. You wanted me to bring a dead cat to you so that you could honor it and give it a respectable burial. Is this cat not suitable, master?"

I pulled the dead black cat out of the bag. The smell of its blood was now suddenly familiar. I put the cat bag inside the bag, closed the bag, and then put it on the floor of the bedroom.

"Melanie," I said. "Answer my questions. Do I actually make you go out and find dead animals?"

Weeping, she said, "Yes."

"Melanie, I told you to go outside, look into the forest, and bring me a dead cat?"

"Yes." She sobbed.

I said, "Melanie, How long have you been doing this for me?"

Racing out of my room, she cried loudly, "He is going to whip me again! Someone, save me!"

Servant men came into my room. They asked me, "Is everything all right, master?"

I said, "Melanie has this ridiculous notion that I am going to hurt her."

"Your family is mighty, master. Everything will be swept away. No one has to know."

"What?" I asked, bewildered. "Surely, you do not believe that I would hurt any of you."

Bowing, they said, "No, master."

One of the servant men asked, "Will there be anything you need from us?"

"Help me get ready," I said. "I am going to my chapel. I need to bring this bag there."

"Of course, master," said one of the servants.

The servant men dressed me and then escorted me to the chapel. I walked through a gate and knelt before my private altar. There were dead raccoons, foxes, cats, and ravens on the altar. I put the cat with these other dead animals and then prayed for them.

I whispered, "Please, help these dead creatures find salvation. Do not let them become nothing. Though they are only animals, let them know peace, comfort, and a better destiny somewhere beyond this terrible world. What is a soul? Who has one? What happens to the beasts, creatures, and animals of this earth after they die? Those who become like beasts, will they suffer the same fate as these animals after they are dead, too? Do they wander this earth, restless and undead? Is there only blackness and nothingness for those who have no souls? I fear that I am losing my soul. Slowly, piece by piece it leaves me. I feel as though I have died so many times. I can never escape my torment. I beg for forgiveness. I do not know what to do. I do not know who I am. I cannot control my thoughts. I know that I have killed people, but I do not understand anything. I do not feel like I did those things. Is there no redemption for me? I pray for forgiveness, for myself and for all the animals that have died here. I want all of us to walk together in a great field of happiness."

A servant's voice called out to me. "Master, a detective is here to see you."

CHAPTER 6

"Can you make him leave?" I asked.

The servant said, "As you wish, master."

"I will wait here," I said. "No. Actually, I need to hide."

"Is everything all right, master?"

"No. I mean to say that it is all right. Yes. Everything is all right," I said, stuttering.

The servant asked, "Is there anything that you should warn us about beforehand, master?"

I said, "There is nothing to be warned about, nothing alarming."

"Will you be needing anything, master?"

"Yes. Bring me a candle, some wine, two wine glasses, and a black cloak. Can you remember all of that?" I asked.

The servant said, "You wish for me to bring you a candle, a bottle of wine, two wine glasses, and a black cloak, master. Will there be anything else, master?"

I said, "Yes. Bring me some matches and some bread with a knife. A big knife. Wait. There is more. Bring me a cuppa. We must not forget that."

"May I ask what all of this is for, master?" asked the servant.

"Do not be cheeky with me," I said. "Just get those things and bring them to me. I will be below."

"In the catacombs?" asked the servant.

"Yes," I said. "Do make haste, mate."

The servant bowed and accompanied the other servants. I watched them all leave and return to the mansion. I gazed around the estate, looking for the detective. I returned to the chapel to finish my prayers. After locking the gate, I knelt before the altar one more time.

"I know that I am not like other people anymore," I whispered. "The things that I have done, these memories of them, they haunt me. More than that, they surround me, perpetually. It is as if I am no longer here. Everywhere I go, I am not really there. These memories are always blocking me from the rest of reality. No, that is not it. I should not say that. It is as if my wicked acts have echoed into the present, past, and future. They rattle and wave all around, bending reality. My horrible crimes have separated me from this world. Where am I now? Who will hear me? Who will hear my prayers? Do I deserve forgiveness? Do I deserve to live? Please, anyone, give me some hope. Show me something. I want to hear you. Tell me that you are there. Tell me that I am not alone. Give my life some shred of decency, value, or meaning. Someone, tell me where I am. Tell me what I have done. What is real? What is happening to me?"

I looked at the rancid dead animals on the altar. Swarms of gross flies were buzzing and flying around them. Hundreds of maggots were undulating and squirming around the bones of these bloody carcasses. A wing twitched. A paw shivered. A tail flinched. My eyes widened and my mouth hung low as I witnessed the carcasses begin to become animated. Black feathered swayed. Bones rattled. Repulsive breath slipped out of the decaying mouths of these creatures. Fat creepy-crawlies scuttled across their decaying flesh.

"What unholiness is this?" I gasped.

The undead raccoons, foxes, ravens, and cats stood up on the altar. The ravens lifted their rotting wings. The raccoons and foxes groaned. The cats hissed.

"This is not reality," I said. "It is as she said. This is what they were all warning me about. I am trapped. But how? Since when? How long have I been here? How do I wake up?"

The ravens flew at me as they screeched and cawed. I ran to the door and shut it before they could wound me. The grating sounds of the animals scratching and clawing on the other side of the door made me jump with fear. I ran down into the crypt and hurried into the catacombs.

These catacombs held the bodies of most of my mother's relatives. There were bodies that had been buried here during the times of the Middle Ages. These catacombs were connected to the older catacombs that had been created and used by the Roman Empire. All of my relatives and ancestors who had been buried here had been buried beside their faithful friends, guards, clergymen, servants, and even sacred pets. Now, there must have been at least one million people buried down here. These catacombs were now private and hidden from the public.

Both sides of my family were huge. My mother had seven brothers, and so did my father. Their parents had numerous siblings, and their grandparents had numerous siblings. Only several of my father's relatives, and their families, were buried down here. My father was connected to the noble aristocrats of the Fiendilkfjeld family, so most of his family were buried in the catacombs under their castle in Italy.

My mother's family had always been extravagantly wealthy, but she was never royalty or nobility. My father was an aristocrat but he abdicated all of his royal ranks and noble titles of the Fiendilkfjeld family. These catacombs have been with my mother's family for many generations since the medieval era. I was fortunate enough to be able to live on top of it. I considered myself a guardian of the dead. I wanted to protect them and honor their memories. I knew that there were many people who would love to defile the graves, so I had them regularly inspected and defended.

My father liked my mother's family better than his own family. He never told me why. I think that a part of him had still loved his family. He wanted to keep their name, and he had brought me to the castle once. I knew that he did not completely despise them. In fact, I would even say that he had missed them. He might have longed for some aspect of his family. I think that he had always considered himself a Fiendilkfjeld, even though he did not want to be anywhere near that castle. I wished that I had known my father better. He never seemed to have time for me. We had become so distant, really. My mother was the same way. There really was never any love from her. I thought that I was terrible for thinking of this now as I was walking through the ancestral catacombs of my mother's family. These catacombs contained the corpses and graves of hundreds of ancient families, cultures, and societies. All of this had been passed down to me.

I wished that I could talk to my ancient relatives and ask them what the medieval era was like. I wanted to take out their bones and ask them questions about the Roman Empire. I wanted to speak to all the old slaves and priests that were buried here, too. They had seen so much, and they had been waiting here for hundreds of years. I hoped that at least the dead would have pity on a wretched sinner like me.

As I was looking at the skulls, graves, tombs, and monuments, I realized something important about myself. I always wanted to know why my father did not want the noble title of his family. I wanted to know why he kept the name but tried to forget them. There was still so much about Fiendilkfjeld castle and my family that I wanted to understand. There must have been a connection between myself and Alison. There needed to be a reason why she came to me. Something was pulling me back towards the castle, and yet, it was also my doom. I had been warned that going there would mean my death. Additionally, I was losing my grip on reality faster and faster.

If this was a dream, then I needed to find a way to wake up. If I have been trapped in my own imagination and hallucinations, then I needed to find a way to stop them. I needed to make this madness stop. If I was ever going to really understand who I was, then I needed to control my own destiny. The forces of destiny seemed to be wanting my destruction. I kept feeling like Alison was at the center.

I did not want to see anyone. I wanted to be down here with the dead. I waited for my servant to knock on the door. I let him in. He was carrying a large basket filled with everything I had asked for. There were several other servants who came with the tea and porcelain cups.

My servants followed me deeper into the catacombs. I wore the black cloak. We walked through the Gothic archway of a rood screen. We entered a dark sanctuary decorated with skeletal statuary. I led them to a reliquary surrounded by the cloaked skeletons of ancient vassals and priests that now were hanging from the walls.

"Where have you brought us, master?" asked one of the servants.

I said, "This is a mystery to me. We have been brought here by invisible wings."

"We should not be here," said a servant, visibly distressed. The cups in his hands were rattling and clinking in his trembling hands.

I said, "This is destiny working its magic on us. There is no reason for this. You cannot understand it. We are here only because we must be. If this life is truly just a dream, then this foreboding moment surly is a message. Something is trying to tell me something important. It wants me to speak to it."

"Why would you willingly speak to something evil, master?" asked a servant.

"Why is something like this down here?" asked another servant.

I said, "This is who I am. Look at it. See for yourselves. Let this sight be the answer to your questions. Why speak to something evil? I think you know why. What do you really see?"

Before us was a black marble altar. Behind the altar was a large black casket. The casket was supported by white statues depicting cadaverous spectres. The casket was closed, but I saw the tremors of the lid.

One servant said, "This place is haunted."

"We must leave this cursed place," said another servant.

"You may leave," I said. "I will begin the ritual."

"What will you do?" asked a servant.

I said, "I need to escape this nightmare." I grabbed the knife. "Light the candle."

"This place will destroy us," said a servant.

"Let it destroy me," I said. "Let it take us all. I must end my suffering. I can no longer live as I am. This dream is destroying me."

"What if this is not a dream, master?"

I asked, "What? Not a dream?"

"Whatever you plan to do, can it not wait, master?"

"What would I wait for?" I asked.

"Roman is waiting for you," said the servant. "He is in the parlor. Speak with him, and then decide what you want to do after that."

"This sanctuary is more important," I said. "If I fail here, I will speak with Roman."

"Do not harm yourself," said the servant. "We would be lost without you."

"Maybe this is my punishment," I said. "I have done terrible things. I want to die, but maybe I deserve to suffer here. I wish I knew what to do. I do not know what I will do next. I cannot even control my thoughts. In my mind, I see horrible things. I see myself doing despicable things. I cannot forgive myself, but I am afraid to die. What is happening to me? Do I not deserve to know the truth? Should I not escape?"

The servant said, "We can bring you to Roman. He is inside the mansion. Speak with him. Do not return to this place. This sanctuary should be destroyed, master."

"Destroyed?" I stepped back. "Destroy this place? Destroy the sanctuary of this catacomb? My mother's catacomb? This is a part of me. You want me to destroy it? But, how could I? Yet, she never really loved me. She put me in this mansion so that she would never have to see me again. This was never my home. It was my prison, and I decorated it to illustrate my torment."

"Let us help you," said another servant.

"Leave everything here," I said. "The food, wine, and everything else. Now."

The servants put the food and drinks on the altar.

"We can leave?" asked the servants.

"No," I said. "Not yet." I grabbed one of the servants and stabbed him in the stomach. I stabbed another through the face. The other servants started running and screaming. I chased them through the tunnels. I grabbed one and slit his throat. I stabbed the last servant in the back while he was opening the door. I dragged the corpses to the sanctuary and placed them on the long altar. My cloak was bloody, so I put it on the corpses. The candles were lit. I put the bread on the altar, too. I poured wine into the wine glasses. I put the knife on the altar and held the bread with both hands.

"Let this bread be the bridge connecting you and me," I said. "Souls of the dead, powers of this nightmare, show yourselves to me. I will eat this bread, and connect myself with you. Show me a way out of this dream. Let me see the truth."

I ate the bread, drank the wine, and then lifted my arms up into the air. I closed my eyes. I could hear something moaning from the casket. I removed the lid and saw my doppelganger inside. I fainted upon seeing him. The last things I saw before fainting were his feet as he stepped out of the coffin. I heard him walking out of the sanctuary. I could hear him breathing heavily before everything became covered by darkness.

CHAPTER 7

I walked into the parlor and found Roman waiting for me there. He was standing beside the fireplace and looking at the flames. He turned, smiled at me, and we shook hands. His smile became a grimace as his gaze moved from my head down to my feet. He peered into my eyes and gawked.

Roman said, "Theodemir, you look ghastly. Your skin is stark white. You look so pallid and tired. Your eyes are deeply sunken. You got so skinny. You look like you are starving. You are all boney. Look at your hands and fingers; they are so sharp and gnarled. What happened to you? Did you do something to you hair? It looks darker. Your eyes, too."

I said, "Since we are prating about whatever trifle is distracting us, I would have to say that you are daft, mate. You, Roman, are rather a sorry lot. How impudent and presumptuous of you to come here and say such cheeky things to me. That is what you have come here for, is it? Would you like it if I told you all about the things that I dislike about your appearance? I could give you a list of all your blooming flaws and shortcomings. Is that the sort of thing that you fancy?"

Roman said, "I came to tell you that we never found Alison. We never found anything."

"Is that all, then?"

"I know that you had a wild party last night, Theodemir, and you are probably really exhausted now, but do not lash out against me. You need to treat me with respect."

"Do not whinge to me, Roman. I am knackered, so pray leave if you have nothing else important to say," I said. "I have neither the time nor patience to handle any more of your prattling."

"Why are you behaving like this?" asked Roman.

"Pray leave, mate."

Roman asked, "Why did you leave me in Italy without any warning?"

"No one stopped me," I said. "My family wanted us gone. They wanted us out of their castle. No one was going to let us get anywhere near the truth. My family was never going to tell us the truth about anything. It was all a show, an act, Roman. They did what they had to do to please the government and the agencies. They made everything look nice and clean for themselves. They can act like they did everything they could to find Alison, and now that is the end of it. It was all a game, and we both got manipulated. Besides, we both knew that we really were never going to find her. Even if we did find Alison, we were never going to attack my family. I never would have allowed it. You and I just wanted to find Alison quietly. We inspected the castle, and we found nothing. The only reason why you even got as far as you did inside the castle was because you have been blackmailing my family. You know about what they have been doing to their servants. You know about their dirty secrets and their connections to those cults, do you not? Yes, I saw the cultists there. I saw the victims. But, I realized something, Roman. You have no real power over my family. You have no control over any of us. You just like to act like you do. Sure, you can make noise, you can cause trouble, and you might be able to make life a little more difficult for me and my family, but that is all you can do. So, do not tell me that I need to treat you with respect. You are a parasite. You need me and my family. You help them cover things up, and you are going to help me, too."

"So, you figured everything out," said Roman. "Congratulations. It took you long enough. But how do you think I am going to help you? I work for your family, not you."

"You will help me," I said. "There is still one big thing I need to understand."

"What?"

"How do I get out of this dream?"

"What?" asked Roman.

I attacked Roman with the knife. Roman grabbed my arm. We both pushed against each other. He grabbed my neck, and I grabbed his. We were both choking each other. The knife was in my right hand. My left hand was choking Roman. We glared into each other's eyes. I pushed Roman onto the black velvet chaise longue. My knife sliced across his mouth and nose. Hot red blood gushed out of his long wound. The savory aroma of his blood distracted me. I was bewildered and enchanted by the earthy yet sweet smell. I felt my eyes rolling backwards as he kicked me away from him. I sighed deeply as a surge of strength and passion invigorated me. My eyes rolled and my muscles started to slither around my bones. When my eyes became normal again, and I could see regularly, I ran forward. Roman had already taken out his gun. He shot me so many times. The bullets cut and slammed through my body so hard that I was blown backwards and hit the floor with my back.

An immense wave of burning hot pain scorched my bones. Intense sensations of pain and happiness poured into my mind. I was feeling extreme emotions of fear and bliss simultaneously. I could smell the rancid odor of my blood. The smell was metallic and putrid yet sweet and flowery. I grunted and roared as enraging pain sliced through my skull. I felt as if something was biting the flesh under my eyelids. My jaw felt as if it was being pulled and stretched. I screamed with agony and horror.

"Are you still alive?" asked Roman.

I staggered and stood up, slowly. I could hear Roman running for the door. My servants screamed when they saw me in the parlor. I jumped on them and ripped their faces off their skulls. I drank their blood and ate their flesh, but not for too long. I still had to get Roman. I could not let him get away like this. I felt as if I was being struck by thunderbolts nonstop. My hands and feet stretched. My head began to change and become elongated. My flesh tore and became ragged. Every part of my body was transforming and growing.

I ran out of the mansion and let myself be taken by the smell of Roman's blood and emotions. He had gotten into his car and was sitting in it. He was driving away. I raced forward, jumped into the air, and landed on the car. My hands shattered the glass and I grabbed Roman. I pulled him out and tore him apart.

The guards of my estate began shooting at me. The bullets tore open my chest. I slammed down into the ground. My body was still transforming. I waited for the guards to stand closer to me. When they looked at my body, I lunged forward. I ripped off their arms and legs with my claws. After I slaughtered the guards, their flesh became my food. I used their blood to heal my wounds. All I had to do was drink and eat their corpses, and I was fully regenerated.

I ran into a forest as quickly as I could. I jumped from one branch to the next one. Something moved inside my body, causing me incredible pain. I fell from a branch and hit the ground. My face started to become more grotesque and misshapen. I felt my bones being pulled and twisted. Black fur was growing out of my flesh. My eyeballs were being pushed out of the eye sockets and replaced with new ones. I was screaming for an hour as my body was mutating and changing.

Several more guards found me and attacked. I sliced open their heads with my claws. I pulled their corpses up onto a branch and started eating them. I felt myself growing taller and stronger. My body was becoming powerful and muscular. The pain began to fade and I was becoming accustomed to my new body.

Finally, after another hour, I felt as if my body had finished transforming. The pain was gone. All of my clothes had ripped off into shreds. I had become very tall. I must have been maybe seven or eight feet tall. My body was covered with black fur. My arms were brawny and thick. My hands were humanoid, but my fingers tapered into gnarled black claws. My legs were shaped like the legs of a wolf. My feet were long, and my toes also tapered into long black claws. I had a wolfish tail, too. My torso and chest were vaguely human, but more like a wolf. I tried to speak, but I could not. Trying to speak forced me to grunt, whimper, growl, yip, and snarl. All I could properly do was howl and bark.

I needed to see what my face looked like. I wanted to see if there was anything else on my body that I had missed. I feared what else I might have on my body. I needed to know what I looked like. I needed to know what sort of curse this was. I had to know if I had any other grotesque appendages or disgusting limbs.

I ran back to the mansion and looked into the first mirror that I could find. I was so scared of looking at my reflection. I closed my eyes. I told myself to be brave. Finally, I opened my eyes and looked at my reflection.

I did not have wings or horns. I did not have fins, scales, or spikes. I just looked like a giant black wolf. I only had two legs and two arms. I had one tail and one head. I still only had ten fingers, but the fingernails were now thick long claws. I had ten toes, but the toenails were now sharp claws.

I saw that my face was now the malevolent, bloodthirsty face of a black wolf. My head had become wolfish. My face had a malicious, sadistic appearance. My gaunt muzzle was long and menacing. My eyes were long, narrow slits that were closely set and would sometimes glow with red light. I had many sharp white teeth. Thick shaggy fur was growing out of my arms, legs, hands, and feet. This black fur covered my back, buttocks, tail, thighs, torso, chest, shoulders, and neck. My head and face was covered with this fur. Only my eyeballs, my sharp claws, and the inside of my mouth did not have any hair.

I could still stand up straight and erect like a human, but I could also run like a wolf. My tongue and nose were black. I knew that I was losing my mind to the bloodthirsty urges of the wolf. I could feel my thoughts becoming more and more primitive. I could not control myself.

I ran through the mansion and followed the scent of flesh. The sounds of their heartbeats and whispers filled my ears like a roaring din of horror. I slaughtered the servants that were hiding inside their rooms. I bit off their heads, ripped open their chests, tore off limbs, and clawed out their intestines. The guards were shooting me, but I slashed off their hands. The stench of blood only made me more excited. Their screams empowered me. Eating their flesh healed my gunshot wounds.

Human bones were easy to break with my teeth. I was capable of eating whole corpses. The dead guards and murdered servants provided me with a large banquet of skin and veins. I gulped their meat and bones. I lapped the blood and sucked on their bloody guts.

Bolting out of the mansion, I searched for more prey. I had so much energy that I needed something to do with all of it. I was feeling so bored. I needed to hunt something. I needed to cause more destruction.

I ran into the forest. I clawed at the low branches. The rocks beneath my feet were rough. My paws dug into the cold dirt and soil. My hands pushed against the wet grass. Every moment that my paws hit the ground, I could sense so many strange movements and vibrations beneath the earth. The sounds of worms and bugs moving beneath the ground seeped into my ears. I heard an owl flying high into the darkness of the night sky. The mysterious sounds of the wind moaning between the trees hurried into my ears. The fetid stench of decaying carcasses pinched my nose.

I ate all of the dead birds that I found rotting on the ground. Their blood and flesh were sour and bitter. I wanted something different than this. I wanted to kill something that was alive. I continued my search. I would never give up until something could truly satisfy my desires and urges.

I ran deeper into the forest. I continued running until I got tired. I realized that my eyes were adjusting to the nighttime darkness. When the shadows were too dark, my eyes would begin to adapt and allow me to see clearly in the darkness. I felt as if I was on fire. My body was so hot. The cold breeze felt so good when it brushed against my face.

After resting, I started running again. I discovered an old marble wall. I jumped over the wall and continued running. I was surrounded by dark gnarled trees and thorny vines. I passed large boulders and tall flowers. I ran past wide thickets and underbrush.

Finally, I smelled something delicious. The odors of smoke, flames, burning wood, and sausages slapped against my nose. These smells seemed familiar to me. I also smelled people. I smelled their fear and their hunger. Beneath the noises of crackling wood and flames, I heard blood rushing through veins. I heard heartbeats. I smelled lungs, breath, hands, and feet.

I started to move slowly. I quietly moved through the darkness. I did not want them to hear me coming. When I was close enough, I saw my prey. I discovered a group of humans sitting around a bonfire. They were cooking sausages on the flames. It appeared that they had created a fire beside an old cabin.

There were five humans here. They all appeared to be adults. Some were male and some were female. They were all rather scrawny and lean, but I needed to take what I could get. I could have killed them all so easily, but I wanted to have fun with them first. I wanted to savor this thrilling moment. I continued walking towards them. I was so quiet. I moved until one of the humans saw me. The look of fear on his eyes was utterly priceless and invigorating. It was such a short moment, but time appeared to slow down for me. He and I were looking at each other. Our eyes stared into each other's. His heart was now pounding harder and faster. His fear was growing into total horror. I hoped he knew that there was no escape for him. I wanted him to suffer and really understand that this was only going to end with complete misery and bloodshed. It was going to be exquisite.

Time moved normally again. The man screamed, "Run!" The humans screamed after they turned around and all saw me. I jumped on one of the men with outstanding ferocity and swiftness. My claws brutally mangled his skull. I ripped open his face and viciously chewed on his brain. I killed him too fast. I desecrated and butchered the others much slower. When I was finished, I howled vigorously.

CHAPTER 8

I woke up in the catacombs and cried. My hands were not bloody, but I knew what they had done. A stench that smelled like blood filled my nose. My mouth tasted disgusting. I still had on all my clothes, and they were clean. The dead servants were still on the altar. A cold breeze blew around the room. Ashamed, I continued weeping.

The casket of my doppelganger was empty. I screamed and slammed the walls with my fists. When I stopped crying, I heard strange whispers coming from the shadows.

Hearing footsteps, I turned around to see who was walking towards me. I walked out of the sanctuary. Five mysterious figures were standing in the tunnel. The flames of the lamps hanging on the walls were glowing dimly. These beings looked human. They were cloaked, and their faces were hidden by masks depicting the faces of bats. Each of them was holding a scythe.

"Why are you doing this?" I asked.

One of the women said, "Theodemir, the werewolf inside of you is growing much stronger. It wants to control your body and spirit. You have partially awoken it, but it still sleeps. It has been unleashed into your soul, yet it is still not truly free. It walks while it sleeps. You have not accepted what you are becoming, and the creature has become vengeful against you."

"What does that mean? Who are you?" I asked.

"My name is Grace. I am one of Dragana's servants. I am here to test your will."

I asked, "What does Dragana want with me?"

Grace said, "Show me all of your skills, Theodemir, and give us a thrilling battle."

The five enemies charged at me with their scythes, and I leapt back to escape their attacks. Their scythes jabbed and poked forward at me, but I jumped backwards and avoided getting hurt. I ran back to the sanctuary and moved behind the altar.

Two enemies moved to my right, and three were on my left. I turned to face the foes on my right. I looked at the enemy standing in front of me. I punched their face, grabbed their arm, and pulled them back so that they would slam into the other attackers standing behind me. I charged at the foe in front of me, evaded their scythe, and punch the center of their abdomen. I turned around and kicked the knee of the other enemy behind me.

I looked back at the enemy standing in front of me and gripped their scythe. I ripped the scythe out of their hands and swung it behind me. Without their scythe, the enemy in front of me had reached into their cloak and pulled out a dagger. I kicked the dagger out of their hand and then spun the scythe at the enemies behind me. Now without weapons, this opponent grabbed me from behind with an arm around my throat. As they were choking me. I moved back and slammed them into a wall.

Four enemies charged at me from the front. I swung the scythe at them to keep them away from me. I spun around, dropped the scythe, and used both hands to grab the enemy who was choking me. I threw them off of me and rolled away. Somersaulting, I grabbed the dagger and the scythe that were on the ground.

Two enemies jumped over the altar, but I stabbed one of them with the scythe. The other swung their weapon at me, but I evaded and then stabbed their arm. I spun the scythe and started slicing the enemies. Like a spinning wind, I cut through my foes and took off their heads and limbs.

The dead servants awoke and stood up. They jumped on me, and I stabbed them. My dagger did nothing to them. They did not seem to feel pain. I had to cut off their heads to make them die again.

I searched all of the dead bodies of the masked foes and took whatever clothes and equipment that I thought I could use. I grabbed a belt, a black leather sheath for the dagger, and gloves. I put the dagger in the sheath and attached it to the belt. I wore the black leather belt and black leather gloves, but I could not wear anything else that belonged to these dead enemies because all of their clothes were ripped from the fight.

I walked away and tried to leave the catacombs, but the ceiling had collapsed in front of me. Rocks and monuments fell down, blocking the door. The stones and marble blocks were too large to move. I tried to push the fallen rocks and monuments away, but they were too heavy for me.

I felt horrible for killing Grace and her warriors, but I did not know if they were even real. I hated myself for all the people that I had killed. I was not sure who I had really murdered, because I did not know when this dream started. I did not know why I had even defended myself. A part of me wished that they had killed me, and yet I had fought to survive. I felt so sick. I did not even want to move, but another part of me told me that I needed to escape this dream.

I heard a voice inside my head telling me that I needed to find out what the truth was. It was true that I wanted to know, but everything seemed so hopeless. I felt like I had killed people, and yet I was not sure if it was actually me or the doppelganger. I wondered if it could have been both of us. I did not want to be this way. I did not want to be a killer.

Murder was the only thing that made me feel like my life had any kind of value, and yet I knew that doing it was wrong. I did not want to feel these awful urges, and yet I could not help the way that they made me feel so powerful. I wanted to take the evil that was inside of me and rip it out of me forever. I knew that it had power over me.

I was not sure what I really wanted, to embrace the darkness or to try and fight it. I knew that if I died here, I would be lost forever. My soul would be completely destroyed and whatever was left of me would be trapped in this nightmare.

I wanted to know how this had happened to me and how I got inside this nightmare. I would never get any answers if I let myself be destroyed here. I did not know who would win this battle, the part of me that wanted to destroy everything or the part of me that still wanted to be a decent human being. Somehow, both of us were trapped in this nightmare, and we both were trying to kill each other. That was not exactly true. We were fighting over my soul, but I did not know if it was even my soul anymore. I did not know which one of was the real version of myself.

There was also this awful feeling in my heart that was making me doubt everything that I thought was true. I really was not certain if this was a dream. I was afraid that I was just completely crazy, and everything that I was seeing and doing was actually part of the real world. I could only assume that this was a dream. All of the evidence was telling me that this was not real and that I was trapped in a nightmare.

I had to find another way out. I knew that there was a way to get out of here at another end of the catacombs. I remembered that the tunnels would led me to a cave somewhere that would bring me to a forest. If I could find the cave, I could escape. I had to hope that the catacombs of this dream were arranged similarly to the way they were in reality.

As I explored the catacombs, I heard a voice. It was the voice of Grace. I turned around and saw that she was alive. She was standing alone. She was alive and she had all her limbs. It was as if I had never killed her.

"Grace, help me," I said. "You have to tell me what is happening. You said that you needed to test me. Tell me what is happening."

Grace said, "Dragana wanted to know if you had the strength to control the beast that is inside of you."

"Why?"

She said, "This is only a dream, Theodemir. If you die here, you are not truly destroyed, only a piece of you is."

"If I die too many times, then I would actually die in the real world?" I asked.

"Normally, yes, but you are different," said Grace. "That monster is trying to take your body and soul. If you let the creature win, it will own your body, and you will only be a shadow in the memories of your mind. But, it will not be your mind; it will belong to the beast. You will cease to exist as you are now, and you will only be a whisper in its ear until you fade away into nothingness."

"How did this happen to me?" I asked.

"You are not yet ready to know the truth."

I said, "I am ready. I want to escape this. Do you think that I actually like being here? Do you think that I like being like this? I am ready to leave this nightmare."

"No, you are not," said Grace. "You will not be able to hear or see the truth until you have become stronger and wiser. You need to accept what you are becoming, and you must find a way to control it before it controls you."

"You mean that werewolf," I said. "Are you saying that I have become a monster?"

"Dragana will help you when you find her," said Grace. "You have proven to her, and to me, that you are worthy."

"Worthy of what?" I asked. "Why does she need me?"

Grace said, "Dragana wanted to know if you were worth rescuing. She will try to help you escape from this world."

"Does Dragana know what has happened to me, Grace?"

"Yes, Theodemir. She can tell you everything."

I said, "How do I know that you are telling me the truth?"

Grace said, "You are still unwilling to believe the reality. When you accept what you have done, you will understand. You cannot move forward if you do not trust me."

"How much time do I have to escape this dream?"

"You do not have much time left."

"What does that mean?" I asked.

"It all depends on how strong your soul is. You have proven that you have the potential to survive this," said Grace. "Find Dragana, and she will help you."

"Has she been watching me?"

Grace said, "Yes. They all have."

"Who?"

"The noble members of the Fiendilkfjeld family."

I said, "So, they have something to do with this. They have been watching me this whole time. Where are they?"

"They are also lost in this dream, like you," said Grace.

"Why did they never say anything about this to me?"

Grace said, "They never told you about the dream because they have become prisoners to it, like you are. The more real this dream became, the more it corrupted and changed everyone who had been caught inside. Anyone who tried to tell you the truth was pushed away, and your mind would never allow you to hear or see the truth. The illusions and mirages of this dream have been keeping you from hearing or seeing what is real. This dream changes your memories, your soul, and your mind. Because the dream is alive, it does not want you to wake up. It wants to keep you inside of it so that it can continue to exist."

"This dream has become alive?" I asked. "How?"

Grace said, "This is not a normal dream. It is created from many dreams that are all connected to other worlds. This world is part of the dark deity that sleeps beneath the castle."

"This cannot be possible," I said. "How could I ever believe that?"

Grace said, "There is no more time. There is still much that you must learn. You need to become stronger. By exploring the nightmares, you will gain more strength. You must go. My time is short. I will soon fade away and return to my prison. We are all trapped, Theodemir. No matter if it is a dream or reality, each of us will be carrying our own prisons around us like shadows."

Grace vanished into the darkness. I tried to reach out, but she was already gone. I ran away, and tried to find an escape. The tunnels were taking me to places that I did not recognize. I ran until I was exhausted. I needed to rest. I sat down on the ground and waited for my strength to return to me.

I heard something moving in the darkness. I got ready to attack with the scythe. I waited for something to appear. I heard slow footsteps moving closer towards me. A strange figure manifested out of the shadows. He was wearing a green tunic and black leggings. He was whispering about something to himself. He walked past me, as if he did not even notice me.

"Who are you?" I asked.

The man flinched and stopped walking. He turned around to face me. He asked, "Who are you?"

"Are you another enemy?"

"Can you actually see me?" he asked.

"You can see me, right?" I asked.

He said, "My name is Neil. Who are you?"

"I am Theodemir Fiendilkfjeld. You are walking inside my family's catacombs."

"These catacombs belong to you? That is so amazing. I did not know where I was. You never can tell where one dream will take you."

I asked, "What do you mean? This is my dream."

"This is not your dream," said Neil. "We are prisoners."

"How did you get here?" I asked.

Neil said, "I was just walking."

"How did you get in this dream?"

He said, "I cannot remember."

"How do you know that you are dreaming?" I asked.

249

He said, "That is a great question. I do not think that I am dreaming, but this is a dream. The spirits told me it was."

"What spirits?"

Neil said, "The spirits of the dead. This dream is one of many dreams that were created from the underworld. This place is connected to the lands of deceased entities. I have spoken with some ghosts, and they taught me about these things."

I asked, "Do you know how to get out of a dream?"

"A dream like this is tricky to escape from," said Neil. "These dreams are influenced by your dreams, emotions, and thoughts. We are all dreaming together in one bigger dream, but it can take physical things, like people, inside of it."

"How does a dream like this reach into the real world?" I asked.

Neil said, "It waits for the real world to reach out to it. When reality is close to the other worlds of death and dreams, the real world can become enchanted. A season of harvest is a time when reality shifts into dreams and becomes closer to the dead."

CHAPTER 9

"Neil, how long have you been wandering through other people's dreams?"

"I do not know. I wish that I could accurately answer that. Human perceptions of time almost have no true meaning when one is in a dream world."

"Can you at least guess?"

"Give me a second to think," he said. "You know, it is kind of funny, because I do not know if I should even classify myself as a human being anymore. I have been in these dreams for a very long time."

"What do you mean, Neil? What happens if a human being stays inside a dream for too long?"

"If a human being stays inside a dream? Let me think. If one were to stay here too long, they would be disconnected from their corporeal body. As a spirit, one would wander through dreams, other worlds, and even through nothingness. A human spirit is not equipped to handle such an adventure for too long, so the soul would begin to undergo transformation as its thoughts and abilities began to mutate into something more suited to its new environment."

"What does that mean?" I asked.

"That means, Theodemir, that you will stop being human if you were to stay in dreams for too long. That is why I keep moving. I keep traveling. I have been living like this for so long that I have actually had to learn many different languages just to keep up with everyone whom I encounter."

"How would someone enter a dream in the first place?" I asked.

Neil said, "Based on what the spirits have told me, I would have to say that there are many ways for someone to truly enter a dream. Just as there are many different layers of reality, there are many different layers of dreams. Most humans dream on a most basic level. Sometimes, when fate allows it, a human's dream will cross over into a deeper level of dreams, a place where reality and magic begin to overlap. This can happen most frequently during autumn, when the living and the dead are so close to each other. Or, it can happen when a mind is filled with intense emotions that go beyond human perception. This could be the result of extreme hatred, jealousy, sorrow, or desire. Sometimes, an extreme passion, like a wish or faith can make someone believe in something so genuinely that they cross over. Or, when someone is feeling so incredibly helpless, like extreme emotions of guilt and loneliness, a person's mind can be thrown into a darker dream, and the soul follows. Basically, at any point when human consciousness begins to evolve and go beyond its natural capacity, it becomes unnatural and enters supernatural worlds. But, you must be careful, because sometimes someone else's dream can actually be the one that pulls you into it. A dream can force you to walk into it, and you can become a prisoner. Dreams like that are dangerous, because sometimes you never really wake up. All you can do is keep traveling further upward, higher and higher away from reality. A nightmare like that can become like a tower that attracts many other dreams and nightmares. Sometimes, those towers collapse downwards, deeper and farther downward into darker labyrinths of suffering and horror."

"How do you talk to the ghosts and spirits here?" I asked. "I have many questions for them, too."

"I could teach you," said Neil. "But, it could take many years for you to master this necromantic art. Do you think that you have that kind of time?"

"No," I said. "I need to get out of here now. Could you come with me?"

"Me?"

"Yes," I said. "You can help me communicate with the spirits of this dream. We can ask them more questions about how to get out of here."

Neil said, "I have asked many ghosts and spirits about how to escape, but they have never given me an answer. Everything that lives in these worlds is jealous and cynical. They do not want to see anyone happy or successful. The ghosts here pull everyone down. The inhabitants of this dream are snarky, sarcastic beings that want everyone else to be miserable and trapped here as they are. They are wise, but they will never tell us how to get out of here."

"We are surrounded by the corpses of my family," I said. "They might want to help us. There must be hundreds of ghosts here that could be willing to talk to us."

"It would take too long," said Neil. "We would need to perform a special ritual for each corpse. I cannot simply communicate with all of them simultaneously. I am not that powerful, yet. We would need to choose one, hope that they are friendly, and then talk to it. If they are not friendly, they could attack us. It would be very dangerous."

I said, "You can decide which corpse we talk to. I will defend us from the ghosts."

Neil said, "We need to find a corpse that is haunted by a soul or spirit. Even if we choose one of your relatives, we have no way of knowing if it is being possessed by the ghost of your relative or a ghost of something else."

"How did you talk to ghosts before?" I asked,

Neil said, "I found ghosts who were just wandering. Or, I found a sacred place where there were many spirits dwelling, like a holy monument that has a great magic presence. There were some corpses that I did speak with, but they were always hostile. It would be better if we waited to find a ghost that was already moving around, that way we could know for certain whether it was friendly or not."

"I do not have time for that," I said. "You must help me communicate with the ghosts that are here in these catacombs."

"All right," said Neil. "We will try one corpse. Pay attention to what I say and do. If you want to learn how to communicate with the dead, then you must follow my instructions and do everything that I tell you to do. Do you understand what I am saying? I am being completely serious about this. If you make any kind of mistake, it could cost you your soul. Especially in a dream, the ghosts and spirits here can be very fickle and nasty. Also, you must beware the dark spirits that will pretend to be ghosts. Those are demons that will only try to take your soul. Do you understand? Are you ready to obey my instructions?"

"Yes," I said.

"Follow me," said Neil. "I am going to find a grave that has a magic presence. I need to search for a body that is inhabited by a ghost. To search for ghosts in a dream, you must try to reach out with your soul. Feel the emptiness inside of you growing, and use it to pull in vibrations or sensations toward you. Breathe deeply. Use the air to help you visualize your soul stretching out and washing over everything around you like a wave. Let your soul go as far away from your body as it can. When you start to feel like something is colliding with your astral body, then use that feeling to pull it back into your mind. Concentrate on what it is showing you."

"I do not feel anything," I said. I closed my eyes. "I am trying to reach out, but I feel the same. I feel cold."

"You must believe in what you are doing. You need to have faith in yourself and in the magic that you are trying to use," said Neil.

"I do not know if I can believe," I said.

Neil said, "Faith comes from your willpower and your desire to give something back to the world."

With my eyes closed, I tried to imagine that the emptiness inside of me was growing. I visualized the air in my lungs moving out of my body and blowing out around the tunnels. I continued breathing until I actually started to feel different. My lungs began to feel warm and wet.

"I am feeling sensations of warmth," I said. "What does this mean?"

Neil said, "I felt it, too. Open your eyes and follow me. I believe that we have finally discovered a ghost that might be willing to talk to us."

I followed Neil through the tunnels. He led me to a large medieval tomb.

"This is who we need to speak with?" I asked. "Why could we not speak to someone I actually know? Where are my grandparents, aunts, and uncles? This person here looks ancient. Can we not talk to someone who died within the last century?"

Neil said, "Most humans of the modern world do not have souls. Well, technically they do have souls. It is somewhere inside of them, but it is unborn and sleeping. Most people never actually awaken their own soul, they live their lives like animals, going through life by following their thoughts and emotions. Modern people do not develop faith, intuition, passion, imagination, or compassion. As time moves forward, the people of the contemporary modern age become incredibly weaker, and their souls drift further and further away from them, which is why most people never experience magic in their lives. They block themselves off from the worlds of magic and imagination because of their ignorance and cold hearts. Thus, when they die, they leave behind no memories, spirits, or ghosts, and they become chasms of silent darkness that give birth to corruption and sin. That is why it can be hard to communicate with our loved ones who pass away, because they have no ghost to talk to anymore. They simply do not exist. That is what happens with most animals, too. Most ghosts have to be created when someone experiences a grisly death or dies by unnaturally harsh circumstances. If we are going to communicate with someone, we need to talk to someone from an ancient era. We must hope that we can speak their language or that they have learned to communicate with our minds."

I said, "I will follow your instructions."

Neil said, "Help me open the tomb and pull the corpse out."

Together, we opened the doors and dragged the coffin out. We pushed off the lid and picked up the corpse. The body had been wrapped in a white shroud. Neil gently unwrapped the skeletal corpse.

Neil pushed his finger into the dirt to cut a circle around the human skeleton. He grabbed my hand and said, "Visualize the emptiness inside of you becoming like a storm. Feel the air in your body becoming very hot."

I shut my eyes and imagined that my lungs were on fire. I felt the heat burn through my body. Suddenly, the pain was gone. I opened my eyes and gasped for breath.

"What was that?" I asked.

Neil said, "You have awakened a magical spirit within you. I used that power to begin this ritual. I will now try to communicate with this corpse."

Neil raised his hands up into the air and said, "Great darkness of this dream, bring forth the ghost that resides within this vessel. Stretch the waves of our existence into the realm of this spirit, and protect us from the influences outside. Great death and blackness, awaken with the sound of my voice, and become my shadow. Open the way to the mind of this ghost. Rise, dead being, come through the mist, walk out of the shadows, and enter our dream."

The air around us howled. Electricity slithered around the corpse. Flames spun through the air and then disappeared. Smoke circled around the corpse. A pale figure sunk into the corpse and then vanished. The smoke, flames, and electricity disappeared. The corpse sat up straight and screamed.

"Who are you?" asked Neil.

The corpse moaned, "I am the ghost of Sir Viljar Fiendilkfjeld."

Neil asked, "What were you, sire?"

Viljar said, "I was once a knight. I protected a princess on her pilgrimage but died. During the journey, I was defeated by horrid monsters in the forest. Their bites infected me with sinful poison that would have surely corrupted my body and transformed me into a monster. Not wanting to sinfully kill myself, I decided to die while fighting. I did not want my family to be dishonored. After the monsters killed me, I was buried. By night, my soul wandered. I had not escaped the curse of the poison. Because I had died after my blood had been tainted by evil, my soul transformed into an evil spirit. I killed anyone who came too close to my body. After many years, my corpse was moved to this land. I cannot die, and I cannot leave the catacombs. I am doomed to be without salvation for all eternity."

Neil asked, "Sir Viljar, do you recognize this man?" He pointed to me. "This is Theodemir Fiendilkfjeld. Is he related to you? Could he be one of your distant kin? Is he of your ilk, and does he share your blood?"

"Yes," said Viljar. "I smell his blood. Theodemir is related to me. I see that he has also been cursed the same way that I was."

"What?" I asked. "I have been cursed? I do not remember that."

Neil said, "Sir Viljar, please, will you tell us more? Can you tell us what happened to Theodemir?"

Viljar looked at me and said, "Theodemir, I have a warning for you. I wanted to speak with you because I have a very important message. It concerns the Fiendilkfjeld family. You must hear the prophecy."

"I will listen to your words," I said. "What is this warning?"

Viljar said, "During the time that you call the medieval era, a secret cult of heretics and sorcerers had offspring with witches and demons. Their broods sold their souls for necromantic powers and abilities. Over time, their dark powers corrupted the land and their own bodies. They could not control their powers, and their evil magic changed them into giant beasts. These creatures had many children, and their blood was forever cursed. Theodemir, your mother and father are both descendants of these cursed monsters. I do not know exactly how we are related, but you and I share blood. We must be connected through your mother's ancestors. Thus, you must know the truth about our blood. We are doomed to face misfortune and disasters. Even if you escape this nightmare, you will discover that you are still cursed. You can never outrun this destiny. You will become a beast."

"That cannot be true," I said. "Sir Viljar, how can this be possible when no one else in my family has ever become a monster?"

"If they did not become monsters while they were alive, then their souls became phantoms after their deaths," said Viljar. "Our blood is cursed, Theodemir."

"Where did they go?" I asked. "If all of my relatives became ghosts, then where are they? Why have I never seen them?"

"Many may have not survived," said Viljar. "Others might have become pulled into Fiendilkfjeld castle."

"Why would they become trapped there?" I asked.

Viljar said, "This castle pulls ghosts and spirits into it. It attracts evil and darkness. The souls of the Fiendilkfjeld family are drawn to that place because of the demon that lives there. The demon of that castle created our progenitors. We are the progeny of that demon. We are connected to that land and that evil place, so we are always pulled toward it."

I asked, "How have you stayed away from the castle? How do you remain safe?"

Viljar said, "Away? Do you think that you have truly left?"

"What?" I asked.

Viljar said, "This is part of Fiendilkfjeld castle. What you see is only an illusory creation of your dream."

"Are you saying that we are still in Fiendilkfjeld castle?" I asked.

Viljar said, "Yes."

"What happens to those who are pulled into the castle?" I asked.

"They become food for the vampires of that castle," said Viljar. "They are nightmares that feed on the dreams and energy of sleeping victims and lost phantoms."

Neil said, "So, this is Theodemir's dream, but his dream has become attached to the dreams of those vampires?"

Viljar said, "This world is a dream. Only the dead and undead can enter this place. However, living beings can also find this place through their dreams. The Fiendilkfjeld vampires enter the dreams of others and drag those dreams into their world so that they can eat the dreams and steal souls."

CHAPTER 10

Neil said, "Sir Viljar, certainly you must be mistaken. The entire Fiendilkfjeld family cannot all be cursed. Some relatives and offspring surely would not be targeted by doom."

Viljar said, "I have said all that must be said. I have done all that must be done by me. I have no more answers for you. There is no way to escape now."

"Please, do not leave me," I said. "Tell me, what should we do?"

Viljar dropped, and he was once again dead. Neil wrapped Viljar's skeleton, and we put him back into the tomb. We left the tomb, and I followed Neil through the catacombs.

Neil said, "What did I tell you about the ghosts here? None of them really want to help us. All they do is tell you something that will frighten you, but they never give you any real advice. We are lucky he did not attack us."

I said, "What if what he said was all true, Neil? My mother and father are both the descendants of demons and witches? What am I? What have I been for all these years?"

"Do you remember anything about what you were doing before you entered this dream?" asked Neil.

I said, "That is part of my problem. I do not know when the dream began. I do not know which parts of my life were fantasy and which were real. I have memories, but they are not complete. I am forgetting names, faces, and time. I do not know how long this dream has been going on. It could have started years ago. I do not know. Neil, you must know something. Do you not feel the same way that I do? You have been traveling through dreams for much longer than I have, right? Surely you know how I am feeling."

"I do, Theodemir. Only, I do not know if I actually want to leave the dreams."

"Not leave the dreams?" I asked.

"I know it sounds so stupid now, but it actually sounds like the only logical decision that I could make, once you really give it some thought," said Neil. "Consider my circumstance. Really let it sink in. If I go back to reality now, what would I become? Would I remember anyone? What if I wake up and I am already dead or worse? These dreams are my home now. I would not know how to live in the real world."

I said, "Neil, I do not know what we should do, but staying here is not going to help anyone. I need to get out."

Neil said, "Have you ever considered the fact that the only reason you want to escape is because you might actually want to hurt someone?"

"Why would you say that?" I asked.

"I am correct, am I not?" he asked.

I stopped walking, and Neil did, too. Neil turned to face me. I looked at him. I never wanted to believe that Fiendilkfjeld castle changed me. I did not want to accept the possibility that anyone controlled my destiny except for me. Neil was looking into my eyes. He appeared to genuinely want to understand me, but he was silent.

I wanted to tell Neil that I wanted to die, but I was not certain if that was true. I did not know if I entirely did want to die. That made me afraid. I should have wanted to die. I should have wanted to be punished and destroyed.

"I know that I am not the same as I once was," I said. "But, I have these old, dark memories of my childhood. When I was young, I was very destructive. My parents always said that I raised the devil often as a young boy. Growing up, I was a hellion and a delinquent. I could never make friends, and I was always lonely. I was never taught how to be a decent person. I had to teach myself everything. Why am I remembering all of these things now? If demonic blood is inside of me, was I always doomed to become a monster? How did I never know this? How was all of this kept secret from me? I should be the only person who controls my destiny. Why should I believe anything that I have seen or heard in this dream? Maybe I did not kill anyone. Maybe there is no curse. This is all just a really bad nightmare that I need to wake up from. I just need to wait for it all to be over."

Neil said, "I can guarantee that you will be destroyed if you do not come with me. Please, let me help you. Do not start thinking that you can simply wake up from this. I tried that. I tried waiting for the dream to end, but it never ends. One dream simply passes into another. You forget everything, you start living your life like everything is normal and clear, and then suddenly there is chaos and insanity. You get pulled deeper and deeper down into the miserable darkness of the nightmares, and you slowly die as you soul breaks piece by piece. And then it starts again, and you awaken to a new dream. You start doing things and saying things that you would never do, you live someone else's life, you think someone else's thoughts, and you start acting like someone else with someone else's memories. And then the suffering begins, and the nightmare consumes you. And this will continue unless you learn to control it. You need to learn how to traverse these lands of imagination and death. I can show you how to do that. We can be together. We do not need to be alone anymore."

"I am too scared," I said. "I do not want to admit that the castle changed me. I do not want to admit that this is real. I thought I could take responsibility for my actions, but I cannot. I do not want to die. I do not want to move forward. I do not want to do anything."

"What are you saying? Do not let the words of that skeleton ruin you."

I asked, "Do you not understand? I do not feel like myself anymore. I am different. I like killing. I like torturing people. I want blood. It is killing me. I feel like being here, trapped within the dream of this castle, is making me become more and more evil. If I just stay here, maybe everything will just stop. I cannot accept this. This just cannot be real. I am a normal man. I am a good person. I do not want to hurt anyone. I want friends and family. I want someone to love me."

"If you are a good person, than you should want to escape this dream," said Neil. "You might still have time to leave. Your soul might still be human."

"What about you?" I asked. "You do not want to leave."

"I told you why," said Neil. "I am not human anymore. I have nothing waiting for me. I like things the way that they are now. You can join me if you want to. You do not have to leave the dream, but you need to stay alive. You need to keep moving onward. We can do this together."

"I could hurt you," I said. "Do you not understand? If I stay here, I never need to face reality. I cannot hurt anyone here. You need to leave me. You should go. Viljar was right, it is better to just stay here and do nothing. I should be more like him."

"If you stay here, the darkness inside of you will destroy you," said Neil. "These dreams bring people's evil nature to life. The more you stay in one place, the stronger that darkness becomes. It will corrupt you. If Viljar was right, then there is a curse. That curse will come for you unless you fight it. Fight destiny, Theodemir."

"I cannot accept this. I do not want to believe that the castle or the curse is changing me," I said. "I will fight, but I will do it my way. I need to go. I need to get away from you."

I ran away from Neil and traveled into a deeper part of the catacombs. I outran Neil and moved up a staircase. Giant spiders and centipedes crawled on the walls. I attacked them with my scythe as I continued moving upwards. I did not let them grab me. I sank my scythe into their bellies and cut off their ugly heads.

I ran through a passageway and was attacked by undead knights. They attacked me with their spears as the undead priests lunged forward with their knives. I evaded their attacks and sliced off their legs. More knights and priests rushed at me.

The thrill of fighting these enemies made me feel truly alive. I forgot about my guilt and fear. I forgot my humanity. All I wanted to do was keep killing things. It was the only thing that made me feel important and secure. If I could see the blood, I could reach salvation. There was a lot of blood. I cut off their arms and legs. Their blood sprayed across the walls. As more knights and priests attacked me, I felt a feverish rush of emotion fill me with strength. Their blades cut into my flesh, but I did not feel pain. It was more like an aching passion for more sensations. I wanted them to rip me apart, and I wanted to destroy my enemies. The more I killed, the more my wounds healed.

I ran through the corridors, slaying more enemies. I ran across the walkways and ledges on the cliffs. Undead horses and cats lunged at me. I killed them with one stroke of my scythe. An army of undead vassals charged at me from both sides.

Unfortunately for me, I knew that I could not continue fighting forever. As the enemies continued coming, I thought of something that would help me escape. I jumped at some enemies and pushed them off the edge of a cliff with me. We fell down the dark chasm and landed in the water of an underground river. It was a truly mesmerizing and sublime experience. But, when I climbed out of the water and reached the staircase, I realized that the fighting had ended. Standing on the ground again, I realized that my hands were shaking. My body was suffering from tremendous pain.

I continued walking until I reached a Gothic crypt. There were many coffins, and I inspected all of them. They were all inhabited by rotting skeletons. Finally, one of the coffins actually contained a body that looked fresh and healthy. It was a male corpse, but he did not look entirely dead. He was a short, thin man with long black hair and white skin. The cheeks of his face were almost sanguine. The pale color of his skin was almost rosy. He opened his brown eyes and crawled out of the coffin.

"Who are you?" I asked.

"Werner," he said. "You?"

"Theodemir."

"The stench of damnation is on you," said Werner. "I know this odor."

"What is it?"

He said, "You are the one I have been waiting for. Yes, it is you. I have been waiting for you to find me, Theodemir. You have been trying to shut me out. I could not reach you. But, look. Here we are, together, finally."

"I know you," I gasped. "But, it cannot be you. It cannot really be you."

"France," said Werner. "You found me there, in an abandoned medieval crypt that looked just like this one."

"This is impossible," I gasped. I started to take a few steps back away from him. "Why did I not remember you until this moment?"

"You have been trying to forget me," said Werner. He raised out his arms so that they extended out as if he wanted to hug me. "You have been trying to forget what I made you become."

"You were eating corpses in the crypt. You looked differently then," I said. "You almost looked more like a wild animal."

"You almost killed me back then," said Werner. "I bit you, and you hit me very hard. I never forgot the smell of your rage and fear. You were so beautiful, and you were already so much like me. I wanted to eat every piece of you. I would have killed you if you had not shot me in the heart. I had not completely transformed in my werewolf body, so I did not have all of my cursed powers and magical abilities."

"What were you doing down there in the crypt?" I asked.

Werner said, "I had been badly wounded by a group of hunters that had found me in the forest. Living human beings were not giving me the nourishment I needed, so I had to start eating corpses. When I returned to my human shape, I was still bleeding and weak from my fight with the hunters. I found the crypt, and then you found me. I attacked you, instinctively, and you defeated me. Fear took over, and I ran away. I could not control myself."

"When you bit me, you turned me into a werewolf," I gasped.

"Yes. You survived the attack, I marked you with my bite, and you lived through it. A werewolf's bite carries a baleful poison. If it does not kill you, it turns you into a werewolf. First, you start attacking the people around you. Slowly, you start appreciating the taste for the dead. Later, you become a gruesome demon of the forest and the darkness. Death and blood will follow you everywhere you go."

"How are you here? How did you find me in this dream?" I asked.

"Foolish whelp, I gave my curse to you," he said. "We share it now. My poison and my blood have multiplied within your body. Do you understand? You share my blood and my curse. It was easy for me to find you once you entered this dream. All I had to do was follow the smell of blood and fear. Because I made you, I can follow you anywhere you go. I can hide inside your blood and speak to you whenever I want. This dream has allowed me to move through your blood and enter the dream with you. My spirit travels through your blood, to your mind, and into this dream."

"How did I enter this dream? Did you do this to me?" I asked.

Werner said, "No. I did not force you to walk into this dream. You trapped me in here with you. I was following you while my spirit was inside of your blood. While I was lurking within your mind, your dream pulled me in. I have been trapped here because of you. I tried to reach out to you, but you obviously did not want to speak to me. I had to wait here for you."

"Why is this happening?" I asked.

"Because our souls are damned," said Werner. "We can no longer exist in reality the way that normal humans and mortals do. When we are human, we walk in reality, but we always have one foot in the grave and another in dreams. We are barbaric creatures of darkness and magic. A part of us will always belong in the preternatural worlds of dreams and death. In our blood are the evil spirits of the wild forests, of decay, and shadows. We are the rage and horror of the savage wildernesses. We are the storms and disasters of the natural world. We are the flesh and bones of doom and the carnage that spreads across the world."

Werner began to slowly transform. He became a giant black wolf, but his body was thin and boney. He must have been seven feet tall. As I ran away, I could hear the sound of his heavy breathing and the noises of his feet slamming into the ground as he chased me.

PART 4

CHAPTER 1

Screaming, I woke up in a dark room dimly lit by torches and candles. The walls, floor, and ceiling were made of dark gray stones and black marble. There was a Gothic arched window in the room. When I stopped screaming, I got out of bed and looked out through the window.

The window was barred with black iron. The bars covering the window were ornately designed to look like bones. The clear windowpane was clean and easy to see through. Mysterious blue moonlight came into the room through this window. The glistening moonlight enveloped me.

From the window, I saw the full moon floating high up in the dark night sky. Below the moon were dark clouds hovering around the jagged peaks of dark mountains. I saw medieval baileys and battlements. There was so much natural beauty to be seen, but there was also a dangerous quality to it. The distant mountains and valleys curved around everything in front of me. Rising out of the valley was a black castle that possessed bell towers, pinnacled flying buttresses, Gothic arches, arcades, colonnades, cloisters, courtyards, and dark spires. Numerous towers and turrets rose up high from the castle. Hundreds of gargoyles projected outward from the walls and towers around the castle. All of this looked so familiar yet horrifying. I gasped and backed away from the window.

"Welcome to Fiendilkfjeld castle, Theodemir."

I turned around to face a gorgeous woman who looked almost identical to Alison. The graceful features of this woman's face were so similar to hers. Her lean body was just like hers, too. I could see that this was obviously not Alison. Her hair and eyes were different. There was something about the silvery tone of this woman's stark white skin that was different from Alison's, too. The seductive manner in which this woman walked, the erotic way she rocked her womanly hips, the sneery expression of her smile, and the characteristic of temptation in her sultry eyes were all so completely different from Alison.

She jumped at me, hugged me, and then whispered in my ear, "We can be together now."

I gently moved her arms off of me and stepped back from her. "We?"

"My name is Dragana. I have been trying to help you escape from your nightmare."

"Why would you try to help me?" I asked.

She hugged me again and said, "We belong together."

"Why do you look so much like Alison?" I asked. "There was another woman here who looked like her, too. Sigrid."

"I have been waiting for you to find me. You have been so stubborn, Theodemir. You finally realize that you are inside a dream, and you have accepted the fact that you are turning into a monster."

"What am I really doing here?"

"You do not need to ask any more questions. No one will harm you anymore."

I stepped away from Dragana again. "Why do I not believe you?"

Phantasmal moonbeams shimmered on Dragana's long straight black hair. Her hair hung down both sides of her face. She had thick bangs that entirely covered her forehead and accentuated her red eyes. Shaking her ample breasts and exquisite buttocks, she danced and twirled around the room. She was shorter than me so that her head reached my chest as she hugged me, but she looked like she could be twenty two years old, like Alison. Her torso was so skinny, and her body was very supple. Her collarbone was sharp and pronounced. She also had a moderately gaunt face and sharp, pronounced cheekbones. Eerily giggling, she started floating in the air. She spun upside down and sighed. She held out her hands to reach down to me, as if she wanted me to grab them. She smiled, revealing her sharp white incisors and canines.

I grabbed her hands and she pulled me up. She held my hand, and we began to fly upward. We passed through the ceiling, as if we were nothing but mist. We flew past the gables and landed on the flat roof of a bell tower. Standing on the roof, we were surrounded by battlements. Turrets, spires, towers, and pinnacles rose high above us.

"Now that you are fully aware that this is a dream, you can control your fate," said Dragana.

I asked, "What is this place?"

Dragana said, "This is our home. This is where we live."

"Dragana, why do you live here? What has happened to our family?"

"Why do you want to know so many things, Theodemir? You should be happy that we are together."

"I need to go home," I said. "I want to wake up."

"You can stay here with me."

"You said that you wanted to help me escape the dream."

Dragana asked, "How can I make you understand that we belong together?"

I said, "Dragana, I need to leave. I want to go home. I want to be in my real body again. I need to remember who I really am. The longer I stay here, the more I forget about myself."

"That is good," said Dragana. "You should forget who you were. I have been trying to teach you that ever since you entered this dream. You should embrace the darkness and become truly evil as we are. You are a monster, Theodemir. You were cursed as we were cursed. It is in our blood to become destroyers. We have the blood of the demon Fiendilkfjeld inside of us. You should accept what you are and live here with me."

"You want me to live here forever?" I asked. "Why can I not go back the real world?"

"Why would you want to go back to the real world?" asked Dragana. "Is the real world not boring and dead? There is nothing for you out there. There is no magic there. It has no beauty. Our dream is full of beauty."

"I thought that I would escape the dream."

"You did," said Dragana. "You escaped one dream. Now, you are in another one. You are closer to the family and to our deity."

"Who is the deity?" I asked.

She said, "He is the sky and stars. He is the wind and the mountains. He is this world. We live inside his tomb. Is it not truly sublime? We have our own world where we are the masters."

"You are lying to me about something," I said. "You are not telling me the complete truth. Where am I, really?"

Dragana said, "Is my love not enough for you? We can be together forever. You do not need to know anything more. Is this not what you wanted? You wanted someone to love you and to give you a purpose. Why do you not hold me?"

I said, "I love Alison."

"Alison?"

I said, "Yes. Alison. I realize that I have always loved her. I need to find her. I know that she is still here. I can feel it. I sense her presence here. Alison is still alive."

"No!" screamed Dragana. "This is all wrong! You are not supposed to love her. You are supposed to love me. Why do you not remember me?"

"Dragana, I do not trust you," I said. "I never met you before. All I know is that you had your servants attack me."

"I did that to test you," said Dragana.

"For what?"

"To see if you had the strength to rescue me."

I asked, "Rescue you? Rescue you from what?"

She said, "I am the one that you needed to rescue, not Alison."

I said, "Dragana, I need to tell you something. I am really getting aggravated. Every time I wake up, I realize that I am inside some new scenario with new dangers. I cannot understand anything anymore. Every time I open my eyes, I wake up to a new disaster. Dream by dream, nightmare after nightmare, everything keeps changing. Nothing makes sense. And every time I wake up, I feel like I am becoming someone different. Do you know what that is like? I am tired of this. I want to go home. I need to leave this dream, or whatever this is. You have not said anything valuable. No one is willing to help me, so I need to do this alone."

"Wait," said Dragana. "I will tell you one thing. I will tell you how to really escape this nightmare."

"What is it?"

"Theodemir, the reason why your nightmares continue to get worse, the reason why you keep waking up to new dreams, is because of the vampires that live here."

"Who are they?" I asked. "What do they want with me?"

Dragana said, "They are our family, Theodemir. The vampires are Adalric, Hilda, Reinhold, and Roland. They have been keeping you trapped in nightmares so that they can eat your dreams and steal your soul. They and their undead servants feed on blood and corpses, but they also require dreams and souls, which are given to the demon. They have many ghostly slaves and phantasmal vassals to help them harvest sensations of fear and emotions of horror from sleeping victims."

"I was just another victim to them," I said. "I came here because I wanted to reconnect with my family, and all they wanted to do was eat me."

"Your soul found its way here because of our connection of blood to the demon of this nightmare. You wanted a real family, and they betrayed you. If you want to really escape this nightmare, you will need to defeat them. Push them away from your mind and soul. If you can defeat them, you can be free."

"How do I defeat them?" I asked.

"The vampires are hundreds of years old. They have been alive since the twelfth century of the medieval era," said Dragana. "You are a werewolf, but you have not completed your transformation. I should say that you are becoming a werewolf. They do not want you to complete the transformation, because they know that you could become a threat to them. They want to destroy your soul here in the dream so that your body will be taken by the bestial curse and you will become a mindless dog that they can control. They have done this many times before. If you escape this dream, your soul can return to your body and you will be part man and part wolf. You would be very powerful."

"So I need to find a way to complete my transformation here in the dream," I said. "How should I do that?" I asked.

"First, you will need to defeat the spirit of the one who turned you into a werewolf. Second, you would need to fight and defeat the chief vampires here. Roland, Reinhold, Hilda, and Adalric. Third, you must conquer the beast within you and make it connect with you. You must awaken the monster within, and then tame it. Lastly, you must conquer the nightmare itself. Only then will you be able to have control over your own body in the real world."

"How do I conquer this nightmare?" I asked.

She said, "To feed on your dreams, someone needs to create fantasies and stories that keep the mind trapped within its own obsessions. They can throw illusions and phantoms into your brain to keep you locked in a labyrinth that you will think is real. While you sleep, your own fears, insecurities, memories, and emotions come to life. Different parts of your mind and soul start to be reborn and they become jealous of one another. The vampires try to separate you from your body and your mind. You need a key that will allow you to unlock the prison that they build around your dreams. When the vampires trap you in dreams, there is always a key that your mind creates instinctively. This key is a part of your soul that allows you to find closure and hear the true message that your mind is trying to send to you. This is the message the vampires do not want you to hear. When you can use that key to unlock the message, your mind thinks that the dream is complete and then you wake up."

"What happens if I defeat them here in the nightmares?" I asked. "Will the vampires actually die in reality?"

"The vampires can only exist in dreams," said Dragana. "If you kill them here, they die forever."

"What about me?" I asked. "What happens if I die here in the dreams?"

She said, "The vampires have imprisoned your soul into this dream. If you die here, only a part of your soul will die. If you die too many times, you finally are destroyed."

"What would happen to my real body?" I asked.

"The curse of the beast would become the new master of your body. Your body would become a ghoulish wolf that mindlessly eats corpses and attacks living things until it is finally destroyed with a magic weapon."

I said, "First, I need to know what my mind is trying to tell me."

"Yes," said Dragana. "You need to follow the journey that your mind wants you to be on. You need to learn what your mind has been trying to tell you."

"That means that the only way I can escape is if I find out what really happened to Alison," I said. "This all started because I saw her in my dreams. If I want to leave this nightmare and return to the real world, I need to know what happened to her."

"Yes."

I asked, "Why would you tell me all of this?"

Dragana said, "I realize now that you will never love me until you understand the truth. You need to know what Alison really is. I cannot be the one to tell you. You need to learn the truth on your own. When you realize who Alison really is, you will come back to me. You and I can be married, and then you will finally have a place inside this castle with me."

"Do you really think that I would choose to stay here with you?" I asked. "I want to leave this nightmare."

"You will change your mind when you learn the truth," said Dragana. "I know that you will. You are just being stubborn. You are blocking the truth from your eyes. When you hear the message of your mind, you will realize that there is no real reason to go back to the real world."

"Why do you not tell me what you know?" I asked.

"Would you really believe me? You already said that you do not trust me. I just want you to love me, Theodemir. I want you to know that I love you. I will always love you."

"Would you help me kill the vampires?" I asked. "Would you help me kill members of our family? Or, do you not want to get dirty?"

"I am dirty," said Dragana. "They are dirtier. They have trapped me in a prison. I cannot use my powers. They know that I have turned against them. I betrayed them by helping you gain knowledge about their identities. Now that you know the truth, they will try to do the same to you like what they have done to me. They will try to destroy you."

"How do I rescue you?" I asked. "If I can get you out of the prison, you and I can fight them together."

She said, "You must kill Sigrid."

CHAPTER 2

I woke up in a room that appeared to be a boudoir. Feminine clothing and womanly garments were on the floor and bed. Wardrobes and armoires stood beside the door. Black drapes hung from the ceiling and reached the floor. Female servants were dressing a comely woman with a black corset. They clothed her with a black satin gown. When they finished dressing her, this noblewoman appeared like a beautiful but mournful duchess.

"So, you finally found me," said the noblewoman.

"I do not know why I am here," I said.

"Is it not obvious?" asked the noblewoman. "In a dream, you do not actually travel the same way you would in the real world. Your mind takes you to wherever you want to go. Your soul wanted you to be here. Here you are, finally seeing the truth."

"What is the truth?" I asked. "Is this the truth that you have tricked me into believing?"

"Theodemir, you are so much like us," she said.

"Who are you?" I asked.

"Use your mind," she said. "Feel my presence with your soul. You know who I am."

"Hilda," I said. "We finally meet."

"Now you are learning how to use your mind in the dream," she said.

I said, "I would prefer to leave this dream. You can make that happen."

"Why would I let you escape?" asked Hilda.

"If not, I will kill you and your whole family."

"You mean your family." Hilda snidely chuckled.

I said, "I wanted to belong here. I wanted to be accepted by you. I was looking to understand my family. You are trying to destroy me. You have been eating my dreams and keeping my soul trapped in this nightmare. You can end this now. This does not need to end ugly."

"You think that you know so much," said Hilda. "You do not know anything about us."

"Why do you not tell me then?" I asked. "Tell me who you are."

Hilda said, "Adalric and I were servants of the demon Fiendilkfjeld. We became vampires when we were chosen to be blessed with the gift of unholy blood by our master. We sold our souls for more power, but the demon tricked us. The demon took us and trapped us here in his nightmare. We lost our bodies, and we were corrupted by the evil forces that lived here. Now, we are nightmares that must eat dreams. We feed the demon with souls. We have created other demons and nightmares to create more children for us in the real world, and that is how we have been able to keep our family alive."

"You created a cursed family," I said. "So the castle is possessed by the demon?"

"Fiendilkfjeld castle is haunted by many demons and ghosts," said Hilda. "The castle has become alive. It speaks for the demon, but it also has its own will."

I said, "So, really, we are inside the demon."

Hilda said, "Yes. This nightmare is the demon. We have taken living family members and turned them into nightmares or vampires, too. Not many survive. Most lose their minds. We tried to give the unholy blood to your father and mother, but they resisted our magic."

"Can you enter the real world?" I asked.

"Sometimes," said Hilda, "But only during autumn. We mainly just get our souls and blood from the dreams of sleeping mortals. Sometimes we are forced to jump into the brains of sleeping animals. We try to stay away from the dreams of other supernatural beings, because their dreams can sometimes poison us."

"Is that what happened with me?" I asked. "You did not realize that I had become tainted by supernatural forces. You did not know that I was bitten by a werewolf and cursed to become one. I had not completed my transformation, so you did not see it. When you bit into my mind, you realized the truth. You were eating the cursed dreams of a cursed man. My dreams poisoned you, and you lost control of the dream. That is why things have become so chaotic here."

"You are clever," said Hilda. "It is true that your dreams did attack us back. We did not expect that you would actually come to us. Normally, we pull dreams to the castle. You brought your dream here. You were looking for something or someone."

"You created all those fantasies and illusions to make me believe that everything was normal. You did not want me to realize that I was dreaming. You created all those characters, those people, just to keep me dreaming so that you would have more time to eat all my dreams and take my soul," I said.

"Correct," said Hilda. "But, your mind also created its own characters, too. Things you wanted to do, people you wanted to meet, your mind created those. In a way, you trapped yourself in your own illusions. You created your own labyrinth. You never escaped because you did not want to escape. The castle was changing you. You did not want to admit that the castle was manipulating you. You did not want to admit that this world you created was false. As you started to change, you started to like what you were becoming. You liked the feelings you got from killing people. You wanted to see death and blood. You wanted to lose control and destroy everything around you. Another part of you did not want to admit that this was true. While this helped us feed on your fear and anger, it was also dangerous for us, too. The beast that was growing inside of you was not only attacking you, but it was also attacking us."

279

"That is true. You and this castle have helped me learn a lot about myself. You may have destroyed the man that I was, but I am starting to like the man that I am becoming. This castle has showed me many dreams and illusions, right?"

Hilda said, "Yes. This castle tried to transform you into something more diabolical and wicked. The castle wanted you to become as we are. That is what this castle does. This castle corrupts souls and destroys innocence. Fiendilkfjeld castle creates monsters. It wanted you to truly get lost in your dark fantasies. It wanted you to experience murder, death, and mystery. It showed you blood, catacombs, and darkness. It is not done. The castle is still changing you. Soon, you will totally become like us. You can join us, Theodemir. Forget about the real world and become a nightmare."

"The warnings were true," I said. "Someone told me that I would die if I came here. Now, I understand it. I may not physically die, but a piece of me will die. I will die, and something evil will replace me. The nightmares or this werewolf curse. I really do not have a choice about this. I cannot escape this destiny."

Hilda said, "There are so many things that we can never control. We only like to pretend that we can control everything. Mostly, to survive is to accept limitations and to follow laws. We wear chains so that we can actually be free, otherwise we lose everything. Pain and emptiness can actually be incredibly valuable armor. There are so many times in life when we must submit to the will of a higher authority. True greatness can only be obtained by the strongest. The weakest will always be destroyed or used as slaves. Sometimes, we can actually evolve by following the orders of someone or something stronger than we are. Theodemir, sometimes strength does not come from making choices but from what we experience when we are forced to do things that we do not want to do. Servitude, humility, submission, and imprisonment can actually make us more powerful. If you accept the demon Fiendilkfjeld as your master and father, you will become more powerful and loved than you have ever been before. Your life will have meaning, and you will be able to give meaning back to the world."

"That is what this is about," I said. "This demon has lost control over his children, and now he wants them back, so he traps them in a nightmare when he can trick them into making deals with him and his servants."

"Fiendilkfjeld only wants to be loved," said Hilda. "Is that not what you want? Your parents never really made you feel loved, did they?"

"You have tortured me," I said. "You have been eating my dreams."

"Did Dragana tell you all that?" asked Hilda. "Did she also tell you that she is also a vampire? She has been eating your dreams, too. She only changed her mind when she decided that she could use you to usurp control over this castle away from us."

"I will destroy you all," I said.

Hilda chuckled. "This castle has many more nightmares to show you. It will corrupt you and transform your soul. You will become our slave, and we will hold your memories."

I asked, "What will it show me?"

Hilda said, "The castle will change you. It knows where you are. Soon, you will become as we are. You will be one of us."

"I think that you are scared," I said. "You realize that my mind and soul are getting stronger. I will escape this nightmare, and I will never see you again."

Hilda vanished, and her female servants attacked me. Spears and whips appeared in their hands. I evaded their attacks, dodged away from their spears, and somersaulted away from the whips. Two servants jumped off the walls and stabbed me through the arms. I fell to the ground as the others whipped me. I screamed as they lashed me. The pain of my impaled arms was awful. I knew that they would destroy me with their spears if I did not do something quickly. I jumped in the air and bit one of the servants' necks. Drinking their blood, I started healing the wounds on my back. I used my arms to pull the spears away. My arms were shredded, but I was free. I kicked the servants coming towards me. After they fell to the ground, I bit their throats and drank their blood. The other servants tried to stab me, but I dodged and ripped open their chest with my hands. When all of the servants were dead, I had to eat their flesh to regain my strength and heal my wounds.

I walked out of the room and saw my doppelganger standing in the hallway. He was torturing a servant man and ripping out his intestines. I watched him slowly rip the man apart. The screams were almost musical. If this is what the castle wanted to show me, it was beautiful. I moved closer to stand beside my doppelganger. I watched him pull apart the bones and meat off the corpse. Each limb was yanked off without hesitation. When the doppelganger was done, he stood beside me. We looked into each other's eyes. Both of us were covered in dripping blood.

He said, "The castle wants you to stay here."

I asked, "Why is it showing me this?"

"The castle brought me here to show you how powerful you can become," he said.

"How long have we been like this?" I asked.

"We have always been like this," he said. "You tried to refuse your nature. You wanted to mix in with normal modern society. You denied me. The castle wants you to become truly demonic. Let me wake up. I can show you immeasurable bliss and carnage."

"Is that what the castle wants or what we want?" I asked. "We should be working together. You have taken the side of this castle. You and I are the same."

"We are not the same," he said. "You want to go back to reality. I want to destroy reality. I know that you hear the whispers of this castle talking to you. Listen. The castle has always been talking to you. Hear its voice. Be silent and listen."

Both of us became silent. I visualized my breath crawling out of my mouth and reaching back into the castle. I wanted to make a connection with it. Suddenly, I heard whispering coming out of the darkness of the hallway.

I heard a guttural voice come out of the shadows. "Destroy yourself, and change your soul, Theodemir. Let the dreams of the dead into your mind. Forces of death and emptiness will grow inside of you. Destroy yourself, and join this castle."

"Was that the voice of the castle?" I asked the doppelganger.

"Yes," he said. "It wants you. You can become one with it."

"Why would you want me to stay here with the castle?" I asked.

"I want your body," he said. "You can stay here, and I will be inside your head. I will become the real Theodemir. You hate reality. You want to be somewhere that you actually have value."

I said, "I am starting to understand what these emotions are. I have been feeling like I want to be destroyed. There is a part of me that does want to destroy everything, including myself. I have been feeling like this more and more, I just never really realized it, like this, until now. I almost feel like I want to lose my memories and my soul. I do not know if that is really want I want, but there is a howling void inside of me. This darkness is eating me alive. I want to live a meaningful life, and yet I also want to be reduced to complete nothingness."

"We are unhappy with ourselves," said my doppelganger. "Things need to change. That is why I know that you want to stay here."

"What would I do here?" I asked. "I cannot be a slave."

I realized that this castle had always been speaking with me. It was always telling me things or showing me something. Sometimes it used words, and other times it used thoughts. He was right about the castle trying to communicate to me.

"You can attain great power. You can destroy many lives. You can discover meaningful truths about the worlds beyond reality," he said. "They can teach you how to properly use magic. There is so much knowledge that you can gain here."

"What about you?" I asked. "Why would you not want to stay here?"

"I want a real identity," he said. "I want to feel real emotions and have substance. I am exhausted with these dreams and shadows."

"I think that you and I can have both," I said.

"What?"

"Yes. I can take you with me."

He said, "No. I want to be in control, not you. I do not want to listen to your commands any more. I want the body. You will stay here and become a servant to the demon."

I said, "This castle might be changing me, but I will never give up my own soul to this place. I am going to get my body back. I can feel the emotions of this castle pouring into my body. I feel its hatred and its hunger. It makes me want to see blood and hear the screams of my victims. I know that it wants me to become a monster, but I will live for myself. Maybe this is just the blood of the demon talking, or maybe this is the werewolf curse. If I am going to become a monster, I will be free."

CHAPTER 3

I WANTED THE CASTLE TO CHANGE ME. I KNEW THAT IT COULD make me powerful. I wanted to become the werewolf and finish my transformation. The idea of becoming a nightmarish vampire servant for the castle and its demon was revolting. I was not going to allow my doppelganger to take control over my body. I wanted to escape this dream and then go back to reality. This curse would be mine. I would embrace these urges. I would remember what the castle told me and the things that it showed me through these dreams, and I would use it to become a powerful creature. I needed to be free. I needed to live for myself. I could not do any of these things if I were to become stuck here.

I decided that I would try to control the doppelganger before anything else. If I was going to attempt to kill the vampires, I would need more power. The castle was sending me its dark emotions, and I could use that to give me strength. I needed to focus on the hatred and the thirst for blood. The castle was allowing me to focus on the thrill of fighting. I was thinking that the emotions it gave me would be like energy for my abilities. I had to start thinking about this differently. Because this was a dream, things were not the same as they would be in the real world. Passion, emotions, and desires would need to be my strength here. I had to concentrate on what I wanted. My willpower would help me control my destiny in this dream.

"Do you really think that finding Alison will save you?" asked the double.

I said, "Finding Alison will get me out of here."

"I could tell you what happened to her," he said. "You gave that information to me because you were too terrified of the truth."

"I am not going to listen to you," I said. "I will defeat you, and your power will become mine."

"You will never control me," he said. "The curse of a werewolf means that you lose your humanity to the beast. I will always be inside your mind. I am in your blood."

I said, "That does not mean that I cannot stop you from getting what you want. You want to completely get rid of me, but I will always return. I am the leader of my own mind."

"Even if you complete your transformation, you will never truly be in control of this curse," he said.

"You are not the beast," I said. "You are just another part of me that came to life because of this dream. You have attached yourself to the beast, but you will not survive for long. I will end you."

The doppelganger quickly transformed into a giant black wolf. I knew that he was trying to keep me away from that power. I knew that if I could defeat him, I would be able to have more control over the beast. I could never get rid of the curse, but maybe I could make this more of a partnership instead of a struggle. Realizing this, I started to understand what I really needed to do. I needed to make contact with the beast, not the doppelganger. My double had been keeping it from me, but I needed to communicate with it now.

The horrifying wolf was massive and muscular. It roared as it started clawing at the walls. I knew that running from it would only get me trapped deeper into the dreams. I needed to face this monster and take control over it. This was a dream, so I needed to start thinking about this as less of a battle. I needed to feel all the emotions here and see this situation for what it truly was. I knew that fighting it now would also destroy me. It was too powerful. I needed to reach inside of the beast and master it.

I looked into its glowing red eyes and visualized myself inside of them. He and I were already bonded by blood. Now, I needed my soul to penetrate through the chaos. Crimson flames encircled me. I floated through a storm of lightning, fog, and rain. I had succeeded in locating a pathway to the beast inside of me. I was moving through the ocean of blood and emotions within my flesh. The forces of the dream world allowed me to travel through my own soul and locate the area within me that was haunted by this wolf.

When the flames and the storms were gone, I started walking through a forest. I saw Werner standing in front of me. He walked close to me. He seemed to be examining me with his cold stare.

I said, "I found a way to use this dream. I created a doorway that allowed me to walk into my soul."

"Do you think that you have found a way out of the dream?" he asked.

"I am going to talk to the monster inside of me," I said. "This curse is alive. It is a part of me now. I can communicate with it."

"Is that how you think that this works?" he asked. "You cannot just talk to it. It does not want to talk. It wants to use your body as tools to destroy everything that it sees. It has been sending you its thoughts. It tells you what it wants. Your dreams show you what it really is? What do you see? You see yourself killing people. You see blood, death, and devastation. That is all this is. That is the beast inside of you."

"How are you still here?" I asked.

He said, "My soul is trapped here with you. I was following you in your mind, watching your dreams, when suddenly you pulled me into this nightmare. I have not been able to get back to my body ever since. I do not remember how long we have been here."

"You should help me get out of here," I said.

He said, "I do not know about that. I was watching your dreams for a reason. Because I gave this curse to you, I have the ability to send my soul into your blood. I can look into your mind. We share a special connection."

"What were you hoping to see?" I asked.

Werner said, "First, I wanted to understand you. Then, I realized that you were different from other people. I do not mean that you were physically or emotionally different. I mean that your blood was unnatural. I started hearing thing and seeing things inside of you. There was something there that was already inhuman, and it had nothing to do with this werewolf blood. There was something already demonic about you. Now, I realize that I am learning a lot from you. I want to see more. I have realized that I just need to wait for you to die. When you die, my soul goes back to my body. While you are here, I can see so many new things that I never would have been able to see. I am learning about these vampires, the demons, the ghosts, and their dreams. It is fascinating."

"Do you not care about what is happening to your physical body?"

He said, "My beast is taking care of that. Let him use it."

"You really have no power," I said. "All you can do is try to scare me."

"Wait," he said. "What are you thinking?"

"If you have no use for me, then I should just kill you and take the power of your soul."

"Theodemir, wait. Do not start thinking like that."

I said, "I need all of the power I can get to defeat these vampires. I will take it from anyone, including you."

Werner took several steps backwards away from me. "You do not know how to steal souls."

"All I have to do is defeat you. You cannot return to your body. What would happen to you? You are already connected to my blood. What would happen to a soul like that?"

"I can help you," he said. "I can give you some information."

"What information?"

"I learned how to handle the beast inside of me. There is no way to totally control it, but you can learn how to direct its rage, and sometimes you can control when you transform. Also, if you have power over the monster of the blood, you can even control the way it dreams, sometimes."

"What do you mean?"

Werner said, "Supernatural beings, like us, do not dream the way natural creatures do. Most people sleep and then wake up. For cursed creatures like ourselves, our souls drift into the dreams that we are connected to. Because we are created from the darkness, we return to that darkness, which is filled with ghosts and spirits. Those worlds are connected to other dreams and worlds of unimaginable torment. So, controlling the werewolf inside of you can help you regulate where you go when you dream. If you can control it, you can stay away from those worlds and dream normally. Like I said, you can never truly control this monster. When your transform, you are no longer in control of your body. The werewolf awakens, and it will do what it wants to do. However, what you can do is learn how to push it in certain directions that it want it to go. Never forget, it is not your friend. You cannot bargain with it. It will destroy everything you love. I can, at least, teach you how to control is a little bit more. I can train you."

"Then you should help me speak with this monster," I said. I grabbed him by the throat. "This is still my dream. You do not have any power here. You are going to help me talk with this monster. I do not know how much time I have left before I really lose my mind. This castle is shredding every piece of my humanity second by second. The werewolf is trying to attack my soul. The vampires are eating my dreams. I really do not think this is going to end well for me, but I will keep fighting as long as I still have my own willpower. If that means that I have to talk to this creature, then I will, and you are going to help me do it."

"What do you want it to do?" he asked.

"I need it work with me to shatter this dream," I said. "I need its power to help me get out of the nightmare. That means I need to fight the vampires that are keeping me here. They want me to get lost in these dreams so that they can continue eating my dreams. They will take my soul if we give them enough time. If I die, you die, too."

"Let go of me," he gasped.

"This is only a dream," I said. "We can wake up. We still have time." I dropped him and continued walking forward.

With Werner following me, I followed the path. I did not trust Werner, but I knew that he did not want to die here. If I was going to die here, I was going to take Werner into death with me. I was so exhausted with these dreams. I just wanted to wake up. To really wake up, this time. I needed to get to Alison. She was my key to the real world.

I may not have liked reality, but at least it was real. I could protect my soul if I got out of these dreams. That was not entirely true. If I did wake up, I would still be a werewolf. I would have to live my life as a cursed creature of blood and darkness. I would still be doomed to imprisonment, in the animal or in the dreams. I did not know how often I would transform. I did not know if it was permanent or if I would only transform once a month. I only knew that my life would still be painful. I would forever be hunting and killing. My body would be controlled by a creature. That would be the kind of life that I would be waking up to. I did not know if I could even hold onto my soul if I were to live like that. I was starting to doubt myself. I began to think about what Dragana had said to me. I was reconsidering everything.

Then, I remembered the vampires. If I were to stay here, they would be eating every piece of me. At least, in reality, I would be free to be my own master. I may be a wild beast, but I could still express myself. Being a werewolf would be torment, but it would be a better fate than having my soul and dreams destroyed in an eternal nightmare. I even considered the fact that there may be a cure for this curse somewhere out there. I began to consider the idea that maybe someone knew how to handle these things. There had to be a reason why normal people did not know about werewolves and vampires. There must have been some kind of barrier between our world and the world of mortals. And, maybe there were people who hunted things like me.

There were too many possibilities and factors to consider. There was also one big factor that suddenly came into my mind, and it made my bones shiver. There was the possibility that I could wake up and forget about all of this. There was no way for me to know if I would remember all of the events that happened in these dreams after I woke up. If I ever woke up, I could be someone completely different. I might look back at the memories of these dreams and laugh, thinking that it was all so silly and strange. If that were to happen, then that would really be like dying. To lose all of this knowledge would be so tragic. And, forgetting these dreams would mean that I would not be prepared for them if they ever tried to drag me back. I would be unaware of the dangers that were lurking while I slept. I might even forget that I was a werewolf, and I would have to deal with the shock of experiencing the transformation. Or, all of this really was a nightmare, and everything that happened and will happen here was all meaningless.

Yes, these ideas made my entire body tremble. At least, they felt like they were trembling. This was a dream, so sensations were strange here. It was like everything was real, but they were illusions, and illusions could become real.

Werner and I reached the mouth of a dark cave. Werner pointed into the cave, and I walked inside. Massive swarms of large bats flew out of the cave. The sounds of their screeching rang in my ears and echoed throughout the interior of the cave. Werner and I screamed as the bats swarmed around us. I swatted at them and flailed my arms to keep them away from me. Werner grabbed a large rock and used it to attack the bats that came near him.

When the bats were gone, we continued walking through the pitch-dark cave. Something growled in the darkness. I tried to look back at Werner, but I could not see him. I only heard him whisper, "We should not be here."

CHAPTER 4

WERNER AND I HEARD THE GROWLING SOUNDS ECHO ACROSS the shadows in this dark cave. I could hear running away, so I had to jump at him and grab his arm. I pulled him back towards me.

"You said that you can help me make a bond with the monster inside of me," I said. "If you do not help me, I will destroy you. You cannot run from me while you are inside my dream. I will always find you."

"We both know that this is not only your dream," said Werner. "I will go talk to the vampires. They can help me escape from your mind. I should have done that before. I never should have let you convince me to come here."

"I convinced you? What happened? Are you suddenly too scared? Too terrified to face the werewolf this close?" I asked.

"Do you realize how insane this is?" asked Werner. "We are not talking about speaking to a ghost, a vampire, or some imaginary aspect of your own mind. This beast is an invader. Whatever is inside this cave is completely inhuman, and it cannot be bargained with. This thing, whatever it is, is part of the curse that makes us werewolves. It is a demon, Theodemir. Do you understand? This thing is a thunderstorm, a flood, an earthquake. It is worse than those things. You might as well be trying to talk to a hurricane before it hits you. Nothing can stop whatever this thing is. It will never help us. If we get too close, it will destroy us. We are not equipped for this kind of expedition. If you want to control the beast, you need to do it from a safer distance. We should leave this place, now."

"Why should we leave?" I asked. "So that you can go to my family and ask them to kill me before I kill you? You are going to die with me here."

"You have lost your mind, Theodemir. You cannot make me do this."

"I will make you do this," I said. "You are now my prisoner. I will destroy you here if you test my patience."

Werner kicked me, and I fell to the ground. He ran out of the cave, and I pursued him. Werner transformed into a wolf and lunged at me. I grabbed a large rock from the grass and smashed his face with it. He bit my arm, but I continued hitting his face with the rock.

Werner may have been a strong werewolf in the real world, but his mind was weak in the dreams. He was still stuck inside my head. He was inside my blood. Here, he did not have access to all of his physical abilities. He was only a foreign pest that was completely out of his element. Fighting in a dream was much more different from fighting in reality. This combat would be decided by willpower, emotion, imagination, memories, and the clash of our souls. I realized that if Werner did have more power than I did, he would have already destroyed me and found a way to escape. He was trapped in here with me because he was helpless. I accidentally brought him into this dream, and now he was stuck. The vampires could have also been eating his dreams, too. He and I were both prisoners here.

I hit Werner so hard that the rock shattered against his left eye. He tore off my left arm with his teeth, but I had damaged his eye. I tried to forget the pain and my fear. I needed to visualize myself winning this fight. I breathed and focused on the air moving around me. I imagined that the air was becoming like a shield to protect me. This did not help, and Werner smacked me into a tree.

The pain was becoming too real for me. My broken arm burned with agony. Werner roared as he jumped on top of me. As he bit my throat, I bit his. I pushed my fingers into his flesh and sank my teeth in, too. Both of us started shredding each other's skin with our hands and drank each other's blood. I could feel his thoughts move into my mind. I knew what he was going to do next. Both of us punched each other's chests. He pounded on my chest with his fists.

I knew that his wounds were already rapidly healing. This was not a fight I could win if I did not think of a different way of defeating him. I tried to ignore the pain. I tasted his rancid blood in my mouth. I remembered that I had actually damaged him. My teeth cut through his impregnable flesh. I knew that I was getting stronger. I was able to penetrate the skin of this werewolf. I realized that this might have been a signal from my own mind telling me that my will to survive was still strong and alive. If I could actually do damage to Werner, I could kill him. If I tasted his blood, I had found his weakness. I had to realize what my mind was trying to tell me. I had to think of a way for my own soul to conquer his.

I pondered the flavor of Werner's blood. It was decaying, rotten, and putrid. I had to think about what my mind was telling me about this. I thought about what this might symbolize about Werner and about how I had damaged him. Then, I recognized the significance of this blood in my mouth. My mind was trying to tell me that I had been able to understand Werner. I was starting to think like him. If I could think like him, I could become him, and destroy him. His blood was in my mouth, just as he was inside my blood. The blood was the answer.

I focused on his abilities and decided to take them away from him. I felt his spirit in my blood. I had to stop being afraid of him. I did not focus on the pain or fear. I had to stop believing that he could control me. I could feel my own soul pushing him away from me, as if he were hit by a strong wind. I visualized my hands taking away his control over my strength. I reached out and grabbed his arms. His blood and flesh was melting.

"What are you doing?" He screamed.

I said, "Werner, you are inside of my blood. You invaded my soul. You are trying to use my own power against me. I am reclaiming the strength that you took from me. I am not afraid of you anymore. I am using my own blood to steal your power and make it mine. I learned this from you. I tasted your blood. You thought that you could hide inside my blood and slowly take my power, but I am taking your power now. Your soul will belong to me."

"How are you doing this?" he groaned.

I said, "Your soul is attached to mine. You connected your dream to mine, too. Also, you are in my blood. You made a huge mistake by trying to get inside my mind. I just realized that this is what you were doing to me. You were stealing my powers, too. I am absorbing you into my mind and destroying you. I am channeling the power of my blood from my physical body to this dream and using it to boil you inside of my blood. I am taking all of your power."

Werner began to change back to a human shape. I attacked him and bit his neck. I drank his blood to heal my wounds. I knew that I would need to destroy him here. If I gave him more time to live, he would find a way to betray me. I needed him to help me train the werewolf inside the cave, but he had become too dangerous now. He could not be trusted, and I did not want to depend on him anymore.

I ripped off his head, and Werner vanished. I felt his presence leaving me. Suddenly, I was feeling stronger, more alive, and more confident. I realized that the existence of Werner's soul in my mind was like a poison. With him finally gone, my mind and soul had more power.

Werner's powers were now mine. I could now drain energy from my victim's souls, just as he was doing to me. I planned to use this ability to destroy the vampires. I ran back into the cave to find the werewolf. Translucent ghosts illuminated the cave with their glowing white ethereal bodies. Inside the cave, there were many of these ghosts floating through the darkness. They looked like dead wolves. I followed the ghostly wolves, and they led me to a large black wolf sitting at the back of the cave.

I looked at the wolf. "Are you the primeval beast that haunts my blood?"

The wolf was silent.

I asked, "Are you the cause of my curse? Are you the demon that is turning me into a werewolf?"

The wolf looked into my eyes.

I said, "I need your help to escape this nightmare. We need to go back to the real world. I need your strength. This nightmare has given life to another part of my mind that is trying to destroy me. He wants to replace me and control my body. I need you to support me, not my double."

The wolf remained silent, but it was still looking at me.

"What are you?" I asked. "Allow me to understand you, please."

I started to feel as if I was floating. I became very dizzy, and the room was spinning upwards and downwards all around me. The black wolf was growing larger. It began barking at me. I tried to leave, but I could not move. I was paralyzed with immense fear. It grabbed me, and I could feel that it was sinking into my flesh. The wolf and I were becoming united. I felt the pain of my bones breaking and connecting with its bones. I could hear more voices as our brains began to combine.

The voices said, "You cannot control us. We are the chaos and hunger of your blood and soul. We will have your flesh and your mind."

I screamed, "What are you?"

The voices howled into my mind. Hundreds of voices screamed within me. I was paralyzed by the noise. I could feel myself being burned away by the noxious sounds of their howls.

"You will obey me!" I screamed. "You all will obey my will!"

"We want to bring destruction! We want to feed!" screamed the voices.

"You will obey me!" I screamed. "Now!"

I transformed back into my normal human shape, but all of my clothes were ripped and torn. Blood dripped down my body. The black wolf was inside my blood. The ghostly wolves moved around me and then vanished. Blood dripped out of my body and then began to turn into shadows.

I was suddenly back in the hallway of the castle. The blood and shadows on my body were gone. I was wearing new clothes. I was wearing a black fur coat and black leather pants. I had no socks, gloves, shirt, or shoes. My double was standing in front of me. He looked like my normal human self, not a wolf.

"What did you do?" he screamed. "I cannot hear the wolf! What did you do?"

"I took the power of this curse away from you," I said. "The monster will be helping me, not you. I learned how to direct its rage on my enemies in this dream."

"How did you convince that beast to help you?" he asked.

I said, "I found a way to communicate with it. We both want to escape this dream, and we both do not like being manipulated. I can hear its voice right now. It needs flesh and blood, which cannot be gained in a dream. Also, it believes that I am more superior to you. It sees my potential."

"Please! Do not destroy me!" he begged.

I grabbed him and bit his neck. As I drained his blood, he tried to attack me. I pushed him into a wall and grabbed his neck. I pulled him back and then snapped his neck. As his body disappeared, I felt myself becoming stronger. My muscles were not bigger, and I was not taller, but I felt more alive and confident. My pain and wounds were gone. I felt an electric wave of vitality pushing through my body. My senses had evolved and were now much stronger. I felt faster and lighter, too. I felt more healthy and free. I was more aware of everything around me. I almost felt like this was not my body, but it looked like me and it still felt like me. Without my doppelganger trying to destroy me, I could now focus on finding Alison and getting us out of this dream.

I started to sense that this was all wrong, like I had been caught in a trap. Maybe I was looking at things the wrong way. I had killed my doppelganger and taken back the strength that it took from me, but I was feeling like I had just committed a grave sin. Maybe I had done exactly what those vampires wanted me to do. It did not matter how I looked at it or why I chose this path. I had just destroyed a part of myself. My double was my enemy, and he did betray me by trying to keep me locked in this dream, but this was our dream that we had been sharing together. He was still me. As much as I tried, I could not shake away this feeling like the castle really had been changing me in ways that I did not even consider. I had been acting so differently. I knew that this was not really me, but I had no way of knowing who I really was. These were my actions, and I had to own them.

Destroying another part of myself made me feel disgusting and in the raw. I actually felt less like myself now, as if the double had been holding a piece of me that was necessary for the completion of my identity. Without him, I was beginning to feel more and more like a puppet or an evil automaton blindly falling into the same traps. I felt his death in my heart and his disappearance from my soul. Something grievous was happening to me, something that I never could have expected, or maybe I did not want to admit it like how I did not want to really admit that the castle was changing me. I was really beginning to feel like destiny was doing whatever it wanted to me. There was no way of avoiding my own demise. I could not escape my own doom and torment.

Perhaps, it could have been this nightmare that was slowly taking away every last piece of my human self. Maybe the werewolf curse was the thing that had been eating away at me. It could have been the vampires eating my dreams and destroying my sanity. My own insanity could have been destroying my brain. Or, in a diabolical sense, maybe it was all four of those things happening at the same time. All I really had was Alison. I had to hope that I could find her in time before the dream, and this castle, destroyed me. But, I was actually losing interest in Alison. I was struggling to care about leaving this dream. All I wanted to do was destroy everything around me. I wanted to see people hurt, to see their bloody faces, and to hear their cries for mercy as I slaughtered them. Maybe I did not need to find her anymore. Perhaps the real world was truly not worth it. I was considering staying with Dragana. I still needed to rescue her from Sigrid. This nightmare could offer me many opportunities to steal dreams and souls. I could become like one of the vampires here. I could become a nightmare and destroy as many lives as I could from this world of dreams and the dead.

I could not think straight. My thoughts were vulgar and obscene. Painful heat clawed into my heart. Dark impulses flickered against my mind. Unwanted thoughts throbbed and thundered in my skull. It took a lot of concentration and mental strength to finally pull back from my obsessions and focus on my one real goal to escape. I remembered Alison. I wanted to find her and put an end to this dream, but I did not know how much longer I would still feel like this.

CHAPTER S

When I entered the library, I saw an entranceway that had not been there before. I passed through it, and the path led me to the underground chambers of the archives. There, guards appeared from the shadows and started shooting at me. Black fur grew on my hands and feet as they became the black claws of a wolf. I spun through the air and dodged most of the bullets. Others cut through my body, but the wounds healed instantly. With demonic speed, I rushed around the guards and cut off their heads. Their blood became rivers that sprayed upwards into the air like curtains of red mist. I gorged myself on their bloody flesh and then continued my journey.

I walked through an archway that led me to the beginning of a dark maze. I moved through the labyrinth and destroyed the hostile skeletons that protected the exit. These skeletons had luminescent white bones that were connected to one other with shadows and black smoke. They appeared to be the boney remains of human corpses that were now possessed by a sinister type of sentient magic. After being destroyed, they regenerated; their bones reconnected so that they were wholly remade. Shadows and smoke moved through the air to collect the bones. The angry skulls of these undead enemies cackled with unearthly, terrifying voices. It was the black smoke and those moving shadows that put these skeletons back together. The skeletons bit my arms and neck. They were chewing through my flesh with their sharp teeth and fangs. I cracked open their skulls with my hands and then ran away before they could regenerate again. As I ran, my wounds were slowly healing.

The stairs were taking me upwards. I arrived in a large dreary garden of dead flowers, tall pale grass, withered weeds, and black thorny vines. I looked up at the nighttime sky above me. The garden was surrounded on all sides by large black walls of marble and iron. The weeds slithered over the ground and squeezed my legs. The vines lashed me with their thorns and spikes. I cut away the vines and weeds with my claws.

More guards appeared at the top of the walls. These guards were wearing black leather bodysuits that entirely covered their bodies, except for their heads. Over the bodysuits, they wore black hauberks. Each of them wore a black leather hood. They began shooting at me with their rifles. Their bullets blasted away my arms and parts of my jaw.

I jumped into the air and screamed with intense fury as I felt the great pain of my bleeding wounds. I ran up the staircase and used the claws of my feet to cut off the heads of these enemies. Drinking their blood regenerated my arms and face. My wounds healed, and even my clothes were regenerating. My black fur coat and my black leather pants were soaked with blood, but they were no longer torn or damaged. Red streams of blood dripped down the locks of my long blond hair. The pain vanished, and I continued walking.

I followed a staircase downward to a passageway that led me underground. I arrived at a tunnel guarded by a giant black serpent. This creature moved with undeniable speed and attacked with bewildering agility. It was getting harder and harder to evade its fangs. Its tail squeezed my body and crushed many of my ribs. With my claws, I ripped open the flesh of its tail. When it opened its mouth, a stream of blood poured out of its mouth and sprayed onto my body. Its blood burned my face and started melting my flesh. I screamed as my eyes melted, and I had to blindly attack it. All of my other senses became stronger. I could hear the serpent in ways that I could not before. I felt the air move around us. When my eyes regenerated, I saw that the serpent had swallowed me. I ripped its flesh open and crawled out of its body. It tried to strike me with its fangs, but I evaded its head. I tore open its face and slashed through its neck. Relentlessly clawing into the serpent's head, I finally destroyed this monster.

My body and my clothes had just finished healing and regenerating when the skeleton guards finally found me. They surrounded me. I ripped off a fang from the serpent and used it to attack them. After defeating them again, I knew that I had to think of something to finally stop them from returning. With the fang, I struck the shadows and ended the spell that controlled these bones. I dropped the fang and walked down the tunnel.

At the end of the tunnel, a group of knights ran toward me. It seemed as though the darkness had created them to stop me, but I would never let that happen. I slashed through the iron bands protecting their shoulders. I sank my claws into the lames and plates of their black armor. I was too fast for their swords and spears. They cast clouds of darkness around me as if they were pulling black nets from the shadows around them. I tried to run out of the darkness, but these black clouds followed me everywhere I went. I decided to stand still and wait. The swords cut into my flesh, and the spears sliced through my body. I now knew where these warriors were. I followed the sensations of the air around me and the sounds of my enemy's armor. I used the pain to show me a path through the darkness. I calculated the direction of these attacks from the wounds that they had given me. Suddenly, I could see in these shadows. Knowing where the knights were, I sliced through their bodies. After destroying their armor, these spectres vanished back into the shadows. I waited for all of my wounds, my coat, and my trousers to heal.

I continued down the tunnel and found a narrow path that led me up the side of a mountain. I crossed an old bridge and discovered Neil walking with a group of people who were also moving up the side of this mountain. Walking slowly, and staying far behind the group, I shadowed their movements. Observing this crowd, I noticed that they looked different than Neil. There was something about them that seemed like they did not belong here, like they did not complement the environment around them. These people seemed more material, yet they were surrounded by strange blurs and distortions of lights. There was something more dull and drab about them. Neil seemed to appear hazy, yet he had a dark flickering aura around him. These travelers appeared more corporeal and lackluster compared to him. They had no auras, and their eyes were colder. They were wearing dark gray robes and sandals.

Following Neil and the group brought me to a large, wide plateau. The people who were wearing robes were now looking up into the night sky. At first, I thought that they were looking at all the bright stars and the full moon. I saw fingers pointing up at something in the sky. Then, I saw a shadowy figure fly across the moon. I did not know what this dark shape was. It appeared to have two wings, and they were flapping so fast and hard. It looked like a giant black bat.

Gasps and utterances came from the crowd. They exclaimed and suspired with sounds of dread and longing. The entire throng of people sounded awed by this flying creature in the sky. Many kowtowed towards it and others bowed. Some waved their hands as if to signal to it. Several people started humming or chanting. I did not understand their words, but the sounds of their voices were droning and guttural. Neil was standing away from the crowd and observing things from afar.

I stood beside Neil and asked, "What is this?"

Neil turned his head to face me and asked, "Is it not obvious? These people are from the real world. Have you lost your ability to distinguish between the world of reality and the worlds of dreams?"

"How is this possible?"

"It is possible for mortals of the real world to interact with the lands of death, imagination, and dreams," said Neil. "Their faith brought them here. They were guided by the stars, the positions of planets, and the constellations. The season of autumn and harvest opened the astral doorways for them. Wherever these people are, their land has become touched by preternatural darkness. For a very brief time, the worlds of the dead and reality are very close to one other. For these travelers, their zealous beliefs and their arcane knowledge allowed them to see this place and move within it. They do not even realize that they are walking between the edges of death and the valleys of dreams. They might still think that they are in the real world. We see them here because they have become so close to our dream. They cannot hear us, see us, touch us, or sense us in any way unless they learn how to become more aware of the deeper eldritch presences lurking within this realm. Their ignorance of us and our natures keeps them protected from us, but it also keeps them cold and without meaning. These mortals appear to be more intelligent and spiritual than most other people in the real world, but they are still so heavy with doubt."

"What do they see?" I asked. "What are they doing?"

"They are worshipping their great deity. They want to see it fly."

I asked, "Who is that? Who is this deity?"

Neil said, "That is the giant creature flying in the sky. It is their master. The demon Fiendilkfjeld, creator of this nightmare. They have said that it is an incubus and an eater of dreams. Others say that it is a succubus and a destroyer of souls."

"Why would anyone pray to it?"

"They want to become devils, as it is."

I looked up and dark shape flying across the bright full moon. "That thing is supposed to be my creator? The blood of my entire family was made by its blood? Then, what created it? Does it see me?"

"Were you saying something?" asked Neil.

"No," I said. "I need to leave this place. I need to find Alison and Dragana."

"Not yet," said Neil. "I believe that the demon wishes to show us something. You cannot leave until the vision is over."

"What?" I asked. "No. I need to continue."

Neil said, "The vision has already begun. It is communicating to us. It is sending us a message."

"It wants to destroy me," I said. "It knows that I am trying to escape from its nightmare."

"I think that the demon is trying to talk to all of us," said Neil.

Immediately, we were inside a dark forest. Neil was the only one standing beside me. I looked around, but it appeared that we were alone. We were standing in front of the entrance to a tall cave. Two lit candles were sitting on a rock. I grabbed a candle, and Neil grabbed the other one.

I said, "What is happening?"

Neil said, "The spirits are telling me that this is a vision. We are being shown something that happened in the past. The year is 1194 CE of the medieval era. The spirits are telling me that we need to go into that cave. I can hear the whispers of that demon, but I do not know what it is saying."

"This has to be a trap," I said. "We should not go in there."

"I do not know why it has brought us to the past, and I do not know if we have any other options. If we resist the vision, we could end up stuck here," said Neil. "We need to see the events unfold and keep following the flow of time here so that we can get to the end of the vision."

"There should be a way to break this spell," I said.

"Do you know how?" asked Neil. "How do we escape an enchantment like this? All we can do is obey the will of the demon's message. If we do what it wants, it will release us."

"You do not know that," I said. "It has only trapped us within a deeper layer of this dream."

"We must do something," said Neil. "Follow me. We can do this."

Exploring inside the cave, I saw a group of medieval pilgrims holding candles. They slowly walked deeper into the cave. Neil and I followed. The pilgrims could not see or touch us. They could not hear us or sense us in anyway. I was only witnessing things that had already happened and could not be influenced. I did not have any weapons with me. I only had my body, my coat, and my pants. The pilgrims were wearing brown robes and hoods. Their faces were covered by shadows. Their candles gave more light for us to see the way. The candles that Neil and I were holding also were spreading light into the darkness of this cave.

I whispered, "Neil, are you noticing something strange about our candles?"

"What do you mean?" asked Neil.

"Look at the light of our candles. Look at our shadows. Do you feel the sensations of your feet hitting the ground as you walk? Smell the cold air? Feel the wind and smoke? It really feels like we are actually here. I do not think that this is only a vision. We seem to be interacting with our surroundings. Our shadows move on the wall. We move the rocks and dust with our feet. The light of our candles moves as we move. Are we really only in a vision, or are we actually in the past?"

"It is impossible for us to be in the past," said Neil.

"Suppose that these pilgrims entered the dream," I said. "Imagine that they crossed the edge between reality and darkness. What if they moved across time, too?"

"If that were true, then we would be inside a dream that was also in the past," said Neil. "Traveling through time is absolutely impossible. Look, they cannot hear us. We cannot touch these people. The spirits are telling me that they are pilgrims looking for a sanctuary. Watch my hand. I will now attempt to put my finger on the shoulder of the man in front of me. Observe."

Suddenly, Neil's finger poked the man's shoulder. Neil flinched and gasped. The man turned around, looked all around him, and then whispered something. I could not understand what that man was saying. The other pilgrims started whispering, too. Then, they began running away from us.

"I felt the pilgrim's shoulder with my finger," said Neil. "How? What has happened?" He looked at the tip of his finger as if it had turned into something hideous.

I said, "What does that mean? What happened?"

Neil said, "I know what the pilgrim said. He could not see us, but he felt my finger on his shoulder. He told his friends that he had been touched by the ghosts of this cave."

"He thinks that we are ghosts?" I asked.

"Yes," said Neil. "The pilgrims ran away because they could not see us, but they saw our shadows. They believed that the ghosts of the cave were following them."

"We are following them," I said. "We are here. We are actually in the past."

"Not exactly," said Neil. "We can make slight influences, but we are still in a dream. We seem to be able to interact with our environment and the things around us, but we do not actually exist. Mostly, anything we do or say will be forgotten. To them, we really are ghosts. They cannot hear us, but they can sense us. If we try hard enough, we can actually touch them. We can touch the ground, and gravity can hold us, too. We seem to have entered a dream in the past. Imagine that we are at a window and we can reach our hands inside, but we cannot actually walk in to the other side. This cave must exist between worlds and supernatural dimensions. That must be why the pilgrims believe that this cave is sacred."

I asked, "Why have we become ghosts? Why are we in the past?"

CHAPTER 6

Walking deeper into the cave, I saw the pilgrims standing before an altar. I arrived to the sanctuary with Neil. We were still standing behind the pilgrims, but we could see that there were others here, too. There were noblemen and noblewomen, and they all appeared to have respect for the statues standing beside the altar. Many kissed the feet of these statues while others gave food.

There were male warriors who began praying to the statues. All of the pilgrims knelt before the altar and its statues. The pilgrims were praying, too. The statues surrounding the altar depicted angelic men and women holding cups and wands. The walls around us were decorated with Gothic blind arcades and relief carvings depicting wolves and bats.

Neil said, "I understand some of the languages being spoken. These people worship the deities represented by the statues. The warriors, pilgrims, and the nobles are all praying to the statues of all of their sacred spirits. They believe that communicating to them will send their wishes out to the deities of the skies and forests. I remember this night. I was here. This is not just a vision. This is my memory. I forgot who I was because I had been staying in dreams for too long. My soul wandered in darkness and was corrupted by the dead. I still do not know who

I used to be, but I remember something about it. I remember that I was someone in this cave. I was one of the pilgrims. I was one of them, in a previous lifetime."

I said, "I never thought that I would ever see anything like this."

Neil said, "I remember what was happening here. I know what they are doing. These people were heretics. They are secretly praying to the deities that they believe are their true saviors. They worship the forests, earth, sky, and wild animals of this land. They are begging the animals for strength. They are asking the angels of the sky to protect them. They pray to the earth for food and vitality. They want the forests to hide them from danger. These people have many enemies, and they do not want people to know about their heretical beliefs. Some of these men are actually sorcerers. Some of these women are secretly witches. They are trying to conjure a peaceful deity of the forest to speak with them. They want to build a new world, a paradise, away from reality."

The cave was filled with the sounds of crying and lamenting. Men and women were weeping. Warriors, pilgrims, and nobles were all shouting and mourning.

"Why is everyone crying now?" I asked.

Neil said, "The spirits have ignored them. Their deities are silent. Their prayers are unanswered. They are imploring the deities to help them. They want to hear their voices, but the spirits do not wish to help them with their requests. These mortals are forsaken."

Darkness covered the cave. I was lost and blinded by shadows. When light returned, I realized that the vision had ended. I recognized the towers and walls around me. Neil and I were in a courtyard of Fiendilkfjeld castle. The light of the stars and the full moon glistened in the air.

Neil said, "I told you that we would return to our own time in the present. We have now returned to the year 2060 CE. How very strange that the demon wished to show us that event of the past. I hear the demon's voice, still. Now, I can understand what it is saying. The demon says that it wanted us to understand the importance of this dream world. Everyone is trying to change their fate, but the demon believes that only the strongest deserve to have dreams. I think that the demon wants us to believe that this world is actually a paradise. It is saying that it is an honor to be given a throne here. If we obey it, it will give us power in this dream, and we can become strong, too."

"You can obey the demon, but this place is not for me. This is a nightmare," I said. "I will never give up my soul. I will never stay here. I am going to escape."

"I want to leave, too," said Neil. "This nightmare is too dangerous for me. I have other dreams that I would like to travel to."

I heard Sigrid's voice behind us. "Did you truly understand the message of the demon?"

I turned around to face her. Sigrid was wearing a black trench coat. Her eyes were red, and her long straight hair was white. Sigrid's luminescent white face was beautiful, and it still looked very similar to Alison's face, but her teeth were sharp, wicked fangs. She was still shorter than me, and her body appeared very skinny and supple. She was wearing a black leather bodysuit that was covering her legs and torso. She also had on gauntlets, sollerets, and vambraces.

"You should stay here with your family, Theodemir," said Sigrid.

Wasting no time, I lunged at her. All I wanted was for this nightmare to end. Black fur grew on my arms and legs. My feet became wolfish paws with black claws. I felt my eyes glowing warm red light. My fingers grew into black claws. Sigrid evaded my swift attacks and then pushed me away.

"Where is Dragana?" I asked.

She laughed bitterly and then smirked.

I asked, "What is this castle, really?"

Sigrid said, "This is a prison. You should know."

A cloud of smoke rolled into the courtyard. Hilda sauntered out of the cloud and stood before me. There was something different but more alluring about her. Her stark white skin was very smooth, firm, and beautiful. She moved with more grace. She seemed to have more vitality. Eerily gazing at me, her green eyes had seductive shapes yet held a sinister characteristic. The forms of her eyelids and eyelashes were lovely yet haunting. Even her slender neck was charming and appeared smooth.

Hanging loosely from her head was long straight black hair. Her hair did not obscure her beautiful face in any way. Waves of hair slid down from the back of her head and slithered down her spine. Her hair was so long that it reached her hips. Thick curtains of hair hung down from both sides of her head, covered her ears, and swayed around her arms. Shrouds of hair hung from the top of her head and moved down the sides of her face so that her charming forehead and the front of her lovely face were revealed and pronounced.

Hilda wore black leather boots, and she was wearing a black gown that was tight on her lean body. The gown revealed her collarbone and neck. Her gown covered her arms and legs, too. Her tight long sleeves covered her arms, but she did not wear any gloves, so I could see the soft pale flesh of her delicate, slender hands.

Hilda reach out a hand, and Neil was absorbed by shadows. I tried to stop the darkness from taking him. I attacked the shadows with my claws, but they were too powerful. My attacks did not work on them. His screams quickly faded, and he was gone.

"What did you do to Neil?" I asked, looking at Hilda.

"You do not need friends," said Hilda. "You belong with us. We are your family. No more distractions. No more emotions, except for lust and vanity. The only feelings you should have are your passions and desires for power and pleasure. You should live here with us and take the dreams of every living creature on earth. Your desire for meaning and value is absolutely foolish. Friendship and tradition are poisons. Love and compassion are illusions. Here, there is only devotion to the true master. You need only worship the demon Fiendilkfjeld, and you can have everything. Your blood calls out to us. Stay here with us."

I said, "Hilda, you are wrong about everything. When I escape, I will never come back."

Hilda chuckled bitterly. "If you were to escape, you would only wake up to a reality of emptiness, Theodemir. Do you still not realize that your mind and soul brought you here to our castle? Deep within your heart, you knew that it was already too late for you. The curse of the werewolf's bite has been slowly eating at your body and soul. It is taking your flesh and your humanity, Theodemir. Soon, you will not have a physical body to call your own. If you were to escape, you would wake up in a body that would never truly make you comfortable. You would not feel or act like yourself. That curse is poisoning you, slowly making you more and more of a beast. As much as you try to fight against it, you could never win. You came here to escape all of that. This castle has been trying to change you so that you can fit with us in this dream. The castle wants you to become a nightmare, as we are. We can awaken the vampiric essence that the demon passed on to you in your blood. We can teach you how to become more powerful than you could have ever imagined. Do you not see how the spirit of the werewolf has already followed you here? Look at your body now. You are a monster even in your thoughts and dreams. We just want to help you embrace the monstrosity that you are becoming. Stop resisting. My words can never leave you. You can never forget what I have told you. The memory of us, this dream, this castle, and your experiences here will forever haunt you and transform you. All of us have already eaten so many of your dreams. Your soul is almost ours. Whether you escape or not, you will die. Something else will become Theodemir Fiendilkfjeld."

"You people are truly evil. What created this vile place that you call your home?" I asked. I was trying to delay and stall for as much time as I could earn. I needed to focus and harness all of my strength. The longer that I could talk with them, the longer that I could generate more energy and power within me. I focused on breathing and the sensations around me so that I could meditate on my strength. More talking gave me more time. This allowed my mind and body to rest, which granted me more time to visualize more strategies.

Sigrid, Hilda, and I were circling around one another. I observed them closely, trying to examine and remember their behaviors. I studied the way that they walked and their mannerisms. Sigrid displayed a ravenous, spiteful smile as she stared at me. Hilda was leering at me.

Hilda said, "I was born in France near the end of the twelfth century. Sometime around the year of 1194 CE, I was twenty two years old. I joined a secret group of heretics and pagans. Together, we searched for the meaning of our lives. Together, we looked for truth and beauty in all things. We asked for proof of salvation. We wanted to escape death and live forever. We wanted to build a sanctuary for our eternal souls. Most importantly, we wanted to create a world of peace where we could be together with all of the people we loved who had died. I searched for ways to communicate with the dead, but I never saw a ghost or heard the voice of any one of my family who had been dead. We wanted to hear the voices of the spirits and deities whom we worshipped and nightly prayed to, but they had scorned us. Suddenly, we felt as though we had been abandoned. We no longer felt love or admiration from the deities we cherished. When we asked them to help us communicate with the dead, they were silent. When we begged them to protect us from our enemies, they were silent. When we asked the spirits to speak with us and give us answers to our questions, they were still silent. We needed a new deity to help us."

I asked, "What did you and the other cultists do after that?"

Hilda said, "We found hope with a man who said that he could talk to a dead demon that was trapped in dreams and looking for resurrection. We offered our blood to this man, and he gave it to the deity. It was the demon Fiendilkfjeld. It was now alive in the real world, and it turned us into its undead servants. We became vampires. We offered many sacrifices to it, but some members of our group did not like the transformation. They hated what the deity had changed them into. I was forced to fight my friends who had betrayed our new master. And, during the battle between members of our group, our deity was destroyed. However, the demon took us with it into a dream. Escaping total annihilation, it became a dream."

I asked, "How did you survive that?"

Hilda said, "I sold my soul to Fiendilkfjeld and became one of its faithful nightmares. Others did, too. The evil forces of this nightmare corrupted our souls and bodies. Instead of drinking blood, we had to eat dreams and souls. Blood would no longer be strong enough for us. We could never exist in the real world. Those who became nightmares were given the blood of Fiendilkfjeld. We created many offspring with the demon. We created new children with other devils, too.

Our demonic descendants had the blood of Fiendilkfjeld, too. When they were mature, our offspring went into the real world to spawn with humans and animals. Our blood created a large family of mortals and beasts that continued to multiply throughout time. Our blood survived for centuries, and still does."

I asked, "What was it like living here?"

Hilda said, "The longer we stayed here, the more we depended on the dreams. After hundreds of years, things changed for us. We began to be influenced by the dreams we took from our victims. We were easily trapped in their thoughts. We became haunted by their emotions. Their dreams became real for us. More ghosts and spirits were being drawn to this castle. More ghosts brought more dark energy and forces that harassed us. I created new children, but they were very weak and could never leave the dreams. More time passed, and the dreams of humans were becoming dull and lifeless. Their dreams were not satisfying us. We tried to not eat the dreams and souls of other supernatural creatures because those were harmful to us and trapped us in hallucinations. We had to adapt and learn how to become stronger. We learned how to survive by eating the dreams and souls of other supernatural beings. As a consequence, we became more monstrous and evil. We became even more like shadows and less like natural living things."

I said, "You and your family are the ones who are eating my dreams. Correct?"

Hilda said, "Yes."

"You have the power to make this stop. Release me. Do not take my dreams or my soul. Let me escape with Alison. Why do you need us? You do not need me, and you do not need her. Find other people to torment," I said.

Hilda asked, "Do you still care about Alison?"

"I do," I said. "I love her. I saw her in my dreams. She wanted me to help her."

"Are you sure?" asked Hilda. "How can you say that you love her when she is not even real?"

CHAPTER 7

I said, "No more lies. Alison is real. I am going to release her, and we are getting out of this nightmare."

Hilda resentfully chuckled. "So, you actually heard me that time? This whole time, we have been trying to tell you that she is not real. We wanted to know when you would finally start accepting the truth. It appears that you really have become stronger, Theodemir, and your heart is becoming colder. You are no longer allowing your emotions to imprison you."

Circling around me, Sigrid said, "Theodemir, did you not want to join your true family? Did you not want to really know us? You wanted a real family. You found us. This is who we are, and it is who you are, too. Stop being stubborn, and freely give your soul to us. You can even offer it to the demon Fiendilkfjeld. You must stop struggling. This can be over quickly if you would only submit to the truth. Kneel before our demon master. Offer your soul to the castle of this nightmare. You will finally find a place to which you can belong."

Hilda asked, "Theodemir, have you really asked yourself why you really want to leave our dream? We can teach you about who you really are. If you are looking for the truth, you have found it with us."

"You will suffer for what you have done to me and what you did to Neil," I said. "Give me Dragana and Alison. We are leaving."

Hilda and Sigrid began scornfully laughing, both of them fixed their eyes on me. They sneered, and their spiteful eyes displayed a mocking look towards me. Hilda was closest to me, so I jumped at her with my claws ready to rip off her face. My claws only moved through air as Hilda instantly teleported and then vanished. She was gone, and I was alone with Sigrid. I evaded her fast strikes. Sigrid began throwing numerous punches and kicks at me with such incredible speed that I did not have time to do anything else except dodge or block her attacks.

Sigrid started screaming horribly loud. The frightening sounds of her voice echoed in my head. I thought that the noise would break my mind. Her shrieks paralyzed me, giving her an opportunity to hit me. Her attacks were so fast that she must have punched me at least twenty times each in the face and torso. My face and body were shredded, but my wounds were rapidly healing. As my body was regenerating, I rolled away and avoided her kick. She continued shrieking with her devastating voice. She created malicious sounds that filled me with dread and pain. When I felt that my body was paralyzed, I closed my eyes and meditated on my strength. I visualized my body shaking out of this trap. I imagined my arms flailing out. I imagined that I was free from this prison of sound. Suddenly, I began to move. I evaded Sigrid's kick and somersaulted behind her. I grabbed her neck and tore off her head. I drank the blood from her neck. A pale light floated out of her eyes, went through the air, and then entered my body. I could feel my body become tougher and faster. My mind was clearer and calmer. I observed her body as it slowly faded away into a cloud of dark smoke. Her armor and clothes faded away with her so that there was nothing left of her. The harmful sounds were gone. My body was fully healed and regenerated.

Dragana ran out of the smoke and hugged me with her thin arms. She was wearing a black formal gown that was snug on her skinny body. Her gown revealed the stark white skin of her dainty shoulders, and slender neck. Locks of her long straight black hair slid down past her sharp cheekbones and protruding collarbone. She looked up at me with her gorgeous red eyes. When she smiled, I could see her sharp white teeth. Her gaunt face revealed a melancholic expression. She spoke with a harmonious, beautiful voice that was elegant and sweet.

She said, "Thank you. I am finally free from her awful spell. But, you seem so unhappy. Are you not joyful to see me?"

I said, "You need to tell me everything, Dragana. The truth. Was Alison never real?"

"Why must we still talk about her when I am here now?" Dragana asked. "Why is this the first thing you ask me now that we are together?"

"Alison was my key," I said. "Finding her was the reason why I came to this dream. I needed to be with her. I fell in love with her when I saw her in my dreams. She is the reason why I am here, and I thought that finding her would help me escape this nightmare. Can you not help me escape? If you ever cared about me, you would have wanted me to be happy. I need to leave."

Dragana said, "Now that I am free, I can tell you everything. Your mind and soul are ready for the truth. Alison is not real. She was only created by Adalric and Hilda to keep you trapped here in the castle. The vampires used the illusion of Alison to trap you in this nightmare. You and I were supposed to be married. Do you not remember me? You need to remember how we met. You met me when you came to the ruins of Fiendilkfjeld castle. You wanted me to help you restore the ruins and rebuild the castle. You wanted to bring it back to life. You were going to build a mental hospital here. This was supposed to be our project. You and I fell in love with each other. We planned to marry each other. One night, you left to go to France. When you returned to me, you were different. You became very sick. I could see that you were becoming a monster, but your transformation was not complete. I tried to help you. I wanted to stop your curse, but I could not make you wake up. As I slept beside you, Hilda and Adalric invaded my dreams. They captured me and turned me into a vampire. They captured you in the dream, too. I wanted to rescue you, but I was so far away from you. These vampires created Alison as a hallucination to manipulate you and your feelings for me. They took your memories, and now they want your soul. They have been deceiving you and warping your true emotions so that they can keep you here in a labyrinth of mysteries and investigations that you can never solve. Now that you know the truth, you know that we were always meant to be together, Theodemir. We do not need to go back to the real world. There is nothing for us there anymore. We have each other in this dream. We can learn to live here. We can obey the great will of the demon Fiendilkfjeld and rule this castle with the Fiendilkfjeld vampires and nightmares. Stay here with me, Theodemir. I love you more than anything else, and I only want to be with you forever. I do not care if we are not human or if we have no souls. I just want to be wherever you are."

I said, "I do not know what to think or what to feel. Dragana, forgive me, but I need time to think about all of this. I feel like everything in my mind is exploding right now. Nothing makes any sense. I just do not know what to do. Every second, my heart dies piece by piece, and I do not know if I can ever be the kind of person I once was. I do not remember any of the things you told me. Please, Dragana, let me be alone."

"You want to leave me alone in this dangerous nightmare?"

"You love this place," I said. "Get used to it. We might be here for a while."

"How can you treat me this way?" she asked.

I said, "Right now, I want to have faith in someone. I cannot withstand this nightmare alone. I am losing my ability to have faith in anything. Dragana, I really want to love you. I keep losing people and I hurt everyone around me. I do not know what I have had to become just to arrive at this moment. I want to be with you, but I need time to really think about everything that has happened. I cannot continue my journey until I know who I am and what I really need. You make me feel important, but I just cannot be near anyone right now. I do not know if I can trust myself. I do not remember who I was, and that is really painful. For so long, Alison was so important to me. I do not know how I could be able to just move past her. Rescuing her was one of my biggest concerns. Now, I do not know what to believe any more. I promise you that once I am done figuring everything out, I will return to you. Dragana, I will be the man that you need me to be. We will learn to love each other truly once again. I want to believe that you can really give my life meaning and purpose. I need to figure myself out."

"Why must you leave me alone?" she asked. "I am scared to be here by myself. I need you with me."

"I might hurt you, too," I said. "Please. Let me be alone. My heart is tormented by intense pain and grief. You should hide somewhere in which the nightmares cannot find you."

Dragana asked, "How will you know where I am?"

"If our love is real, we will find each other," I said.

"This castle has truly made you cruel," she sobbed, and then ran away.

I wanted to apologize to her. The look of sorrow and helplessness made me want to run back to her, but I needed to be alone. I needed time to really think about everything that had happened so far. I hated myself for being so cold to Dragana, but I feared that I might hurt her. I did not want to harm her because she might have really loved me. If her love for me was true, I could not betray that. I needed to know if I should trust myself. I did not know who I could really trust. I was uncertain if I should belief what I had heard about Alison. Alison could be real, and she could still be waiting for me. I started to realize that I really knew nothing about Alison. I began to wonder if my emotions and love for her were all fabrications of the nightmares, too. If she was not real, then I needed another way to escape. If she was real, there was no way I could abandon her. Dragana appeared to love me. She seemed real, but Alison seemed real, too. Dragana's love could give my life value, but staying here would take my soul. I would become a slave.

I continued to ponder my options and thoughts as I walked the desolate halls of the grim castle. Realizing that Alison could not have ever been real, I screamed and moaned. She must have only been a specter of a dream that haunted my mind. I realized that she truly was the one thing that was keeping me here. As long as I continued to search for her, I would always be ensnared within the black walls of this dismal castle. Everything was starting to make more sense. Alison was a diversion and a phantom created by the nightmares to keep me here long enough for them to take my soul. My real life had no more value. I could only find purpose of my life in this dream. Without Alison, the real world made no sense. I knew that there was something about the real world that I did not want to return to. Something happened there that I did not want to remember. If the nightmares took my soul, I could become a new person. I could throw away the man I was and live together with Dragana. I could forget about the curse of the werewolf's bite, and I would become a nightmare as they were. Everything else could fade away. There would never be any more pain or fear. I would have Dragana's love and the love of my creator, the demon Fiendilkfjeld. I would never have to feel anything else but peace and bliss ever again. Every part of me that was ever human would be obliterated. I could stop being weak and begin being powerful. I did not need my soul any more. I had finally found the place that I belonged. I would have everything I ever wanted. My family would accept me here, and I could create a new family with Dragana. We would revel in pleasure and debaucheries. Every second of our monstrous lives would be total carnal euphoria. All of the agony I was feeling would be spread upon the dreams of my victims so that I would never need to feel pain ever again.

I did not even realize where I was walking. I stood before a large black door. I felt as if something had pulled me here. I looked down and saw a small black wolf standing beside me. The wolf looked at me and then looked at the Gothic arched door. I looked at the door, too. The doorway was obstructed by chains with padlocks. This padlocked door was breathing and throbbing as if it were made of supple flesh. I looked down to where the wolf was standing, but it was gone.

"What are you doing here?"

I turned around and saw Dragana glaring at me.

I said, "The spirit of the wolf within me brought me here. Why did it want me to see this? What is behind this door?"

"You should not have left me alone," said Dragana.

"I said that I needed time to be alone," I said. "I needed space. Besides, I have finally decided to stay with you here. You were right, there is nothing waiting for me in the real world."

"Something is different about you," said Dragana. "You do not really want to stay here."

"I just said that I want to be here with you," I said. "I want to be with you."

"Do you really love me?" asked Dragana.

I said, "Yes. I love you."

She said, "If you love me, obey my rule. Never visit this door again, and you must never look inside."

I said, "You are the one who seems different. There is something different in your eyes. What is behind that door?"

Dragana yelled. "Never ask me about that. You need to come with me." She grabbed my hand and started pulling me away from the door.

I pulled my hand out of her grasp. "What is wrong with you? Why are you keeping this secret from me?"

Dragana said, "If you are ready to give your soul to the demon, we should do it now. We do not have much time left."

"I hear the voice of the werewolf," I said. "It tells me that I need to see what is behind that door. What is there?"

Dragana smiled and said, "Nothing."

CHAPTER 8

I said, "This is nonsense, Dragana. You and I are not supposed to keep secrets from each other. I want to give away my soul to be with you, but you are not being honest with me."

Dragana said, "Theodemir, I love you. Is that not enough? You must obey me. Do not think about things that will only complicate our future together."

"Why must you have secrets?" I asked. "I am already giving my soul. I have given up on my own future. I am willing to throw away my identity to be with you in this place. How can I do that if I know that you are not being honest? What more are you hiding?"

Dragana said, "If you truly love me, and you are ready to surrender your soul to the demon, then you should not care about what is behind a door. You must surrender yourself to me. Let me tell you what to worry about. Nothing else matters. I want to be the only thing that is important to you. Forget about everything else. Forget about the truth, secrets, and doors. Why are you letting this bother you so much?"

"I do not want to be a slave, Dragana."

"That is all you can be now, Theodemir. I thought that this is what you wanted? Your life has no more value or purpose. Stay here with me and let me tell you what matters. I will give your future meaning. The demon will be our master. She will reward us with endless treasures and eternal life."

I said, "I thought I was ready to give up my soul, but now I am starting to feel like it might be a mistake. If I give up my own identity, how will I exist? Why should I let you tell me what to think about? I do not want to be a puppet. I thought that giving away my soul would only make the pain go away, but now I am feeling like it would only cause me more pain. I thought that giving away my mind to the demon would help me forget the loneliness and torment growing within me. I would never be your equal if I were to surrender my soul. You would hide more and more things from me, and I would never be able to have any control. I thought that your love would be all I need, but I need more than that. I need to have trust and your honesty. Show me that I am wrong. Show me that I can trust you. If I am meant to stay here forever, I should know what is hidden within this castle. Show me everything."

Dragana said, "You are an idiot. You could never be my equal. You are a sadistic, worthless fool who deserves nothing. You are being given a great opportunity here. Come with me and forget this door. Give me your soul, and offer your body to the demon goddess Fiendilkfjeld."

I said, "I can feel a strange sensation within my heart. Something is guiding me to that location. The voices inside my head are telling me that I must see the room behind that door. Fate has brought me here. You will show me, Dragana, or I will leave you here alone. I have already lost everything. I am being forced to accept that Alison was a lie, a mirage, and a fantasy. What am I supposed to care about now? Look where we are. You are supposed to be someone I can finally trust. How can I relinquish my soul to the demon when I know that there are things that even you are hiding from me? Do not disappoint me. Do you realize what I am willing to throw away for you? My soul. Right now, you are making me question that decision. Stop acting like a brat, and continue this impudent secrecy no further."

"Still you talk about Alison. All you care about is Alison," said Dragana.

I grabbed Dragana's arm and squeezed. "Show me what is behind that door, or I will break it down myself."

"I like this darker side of you," said Dragana. "This nightmare is truly turning you into a monster, as we are. You would become a perfect demon for the master if you would only give up your human soul."

I pushed Dragana toward the door and released her from my grip. I glared at her as she smiled mischievously at me. I watched her wave her hands across the door. The chains vanished, and the door opened. I walked through the open doorway and entered the massive room. The darkness here was deep and freezing. It was so dark here that I could not see a thing inside.

Dragana walked out of the room. I turned my head and watched her as she grabbed a lit candelabrum from the outer corridor. She returned and handed the candelabrum to me.

"Do you now see? Look around," said Dragana. "This chamber is empty. This medieval hall has been locked for centuries."

With glowing candles, I could now see inside the room. It was a dreary, desolate hall. The floor, walls, and ceiling were all made of black marble. A frigid wind was blowing around the gigantic room. I smelled the aroma of blood in the air. The ceiling had Gothic rib vaults. There were no windows. The floor and walls had many cracks.

The wolf appeared beside me. He walked into the darkness, and I followed. A large altar emerged out of the shadows. The candlelight revealed a human body sleeping on the altar. I walked closer and gasped. Sleeping on the altar was my doppelganger. I recognized his long straight blond hair, his fair white skin, and skinny body. I felt the soft smooth skin of his clean-shaven face and wide jawline. My fingers glided down his straight, tall nose. He had a low hairline and a small handsome forehead. The features of his face were charming and displayed a noble characteristic. He was wearing the same clothes that I was wearing now. A black fur coat and black leather pants. He was me.

As the black wolf howled, torches on the wall became illuminated. The flames threw away the shadows and revealed the grisly reality of this abominable hall.

The magic that masked the true appearance of this room was now dispelled. I was standing inside a horrific dungeon of dreadfulness and despair. This was a chamber of torture and nightmarishness. This dungeon was filled with horrifying devices of torture and frightening implements of cruelty. Here, there were gallows, iron maidens, pillories, stocks, racks, and stakes.

Dozens of ghoulish hobgoblins and nightmarish devils were torturing human victims in this dungeon. Horrific white phantoms, terrifying pale spectres, and bizarre monsters were punishing people with wicked daggers and whips. Hideous monsters used hammers, nets, and cudgels to torment their captives. The cadaverous hobgoblins tortured the humans with pitchforks and scythes. The repulsive devils used spears to agonize the damned victims. Bloody creatures with black scales, glowing red eyes, and sharp teeth were chewing on the limbs of the enslaved.

Hundreds of prisoners were being restrained by chains, shackles, fetters, and irons. Humans were being boiled in massive cauldrons. People were being thrown into burning pits of hissing fire. Human beings were burnt on the stakes. Victims were being hanged. The damned were being broken, bound, impaled, or eviscerated. The prisoners were being lashed, flayed, sliced, disemboweled, staked, or burned. The condemned were being executed, decapitated, torched, or beaten in gruesome ways.

The flayers and afflicters cackled as the prisoners screamed and begged for mercy. The hobgoblins, devils, and monsters laughed as the damned were groaning and sobbing. The captives moaned and screeched with agony. This abyssal dungeon was filled with the howling, yelling, and shouting of the enslaved. Cries of misery and anguish echoed throughout this nightmarish chamber. The victims' screams of malediction and suffering reverberated across the bloody walls.

The prisoners were not allowed to die. Their bodies would be repaired by the malefactors. The condemners remedied and renewed the bodies of the victims. When the prisoners were restored and resurrected, they would be tortured again. It was an abysmally malicious and dreadful cycle of enslavement, torture, and regeneration. The dead would be resurrected so that they could be restored and then tortured again. The prisoners would die again, be renewed again, and then be forced to endure more pain. The captives were eternally suffering, and not even death could release them from their agony. Their souls were trapped here, unable to move away from this dungeon.

The black wolf looked up at me, and I heard a voice in my head say, "This is where they get their power."

"Is this the voice of the werewolf?" I asked.

"Yes," It said. "I am the wolf inside of you. I needed to show this to you. This dungeon is where the vampires keep the souls of all their supernatural victims. They harvest the pain and fear of their prisoners here. Magical or inhuman prisoners produce hazardous but powerful dreams that the vampires can eat. They use the power of the souls they trap here to feed their demonic deity and master. This dungeon traps the souls of human beings with strong dreams, but it also traps magic creatures. The souls and dreams of ghosts, spirits, damned souls, and werewolves are here. Their sleeping minds are trapped here. The souls are captured and cannot escape the nightmare."

I said, "I think I understand. There are not only human victims here. There are inhuman prisoners here, too. The dreams of magical creatures, supernatural entities, bewitched beings, and cursed people are here. I am here. My body is here. It has been here all this time."

The wolf said, "It is hard for them to capture a dream or a soul. When they do, they never let it go. This is what they do to beings like us. They eat and torture our kind. They will never accept you as a part of their family. You still have your soul and your freedom, Theodemir. Escape from this nightmare."

"Why would you help me?" I asked. "Do you not want my soul?"

"I do," said the wolf. "I will be the one to claim your soul, not them. Freedom is most important to me, to us. We need to live wildly. We cannot do that if we are stuck here. I hate enslavement. If you stay here, I cannot be free. I need you to wake up so that we can complete the transformation."

"I will be a werewolf," I said. "Either way, I will be trapped."

"Who do you trust more?" asked the wolf. His voice was low and raspy, but somehow also familiar. There was something honest about the way he spoke. I could hear him growling and snarling, but I felt emboldened by his confident tone. He said, "We will get out of here, together."

Wessel appeared beside me. He smiled and said, "Your mind has become far stronger than we ever anticipated, Theodemir. You have actually awakened much more than expected. You have joined with the cosmic forces of these nightmares. Your astral will has allowed you to see the abyssal layers beneath the darker levels of this realm. Now, you are here. You have found the dungeon where we take the precious souls and enchanted dreams of the magical creatures and bewitched humans whom we have captured. These dreams are different from the dreams of normal humans. They are much harder to capture, harder to hold, but they are powerful if caught. We can never let them leave, because they are too satisfying, too delicious. You must understand."

"Were you always going to keep me here?" I asked.

"No," said Dragana, standing beside me. "I wanted this to be a surprise for you. It was only a test. We wanted to make sure that you were ready to see this place. Now, you are ready to join our family in the castle. You can become a king. You will live with us. You will be free of this dungeon when you offer your soul to the demon. Are you ready?"

"I do not believe a word of that," I said. "You were never going to let me go."

"Believe us," said Wessel. "We are your friends. Your family. We love you."

"I love you," said Dragana. "This is your body on the altar. Take the soul and throw it into the air. Give your soul and your identity to the demon."

"You all love me?" I asked. "All right. Prove it. Let me live here for a few more days."

"We do not have time for that," said Dragana.

I said, "Give me more time. Allow me to keep my soul. I will live with you for a few more days, and then I will make my decision."

"You need to surrender, now," said Wessel.

Dragana said, "Obey me. You must."

I said, "No, I do not need to obey you. I still have a soul. I think I know why you need my soul so quickly. The season of harvest is going to end. Autumn will die and turn to winter, and then your powers will weaken. My mind will become stronger, and I will be able to leave whenever I want."

"That is not how it works," said Wessel. "You are making yourself look like a fool."

I said, "No. I think I know exactly what I need to do."

"Why are you doing this?" asked Dragana.

"I began thinking about why you wanted me to do this all with such haste," I said. "You must be afraid of something. You must feel like you have no time. I continued thinking about it. Everyone must wake up at some point. Everyone with a soul. My soul has become stronger. You have lost your power to control me. What happens when autumn dies? What happens when the seasons change? How does time work here? I think your spells are weakening. The magic is fading. I could be wrong. I admit that I really do not understand anything about this castle. I do know that I can feel my soul becoming more and more powerful every second. I have feeling sensations within my skull. I can hear voices telling me that it is time for me to awaken. I will see the morning, but it will be in the real world."

Wessel said, "Theodemir has become too powerful. His mind is strong. His soul is confident. He could really destroy us. We would finally die. He could actually destroy our souls if he defeats us in this dream."

Dragana said, "We cannot let that happen. Wessel, keep him here. I will call the others to help you. Destroy Theodemir."

I said, "I am not afraid of you. I fear none of you. Give me my body, and I will not destroy you."

Wessel said, "You have ruined everything, Theodemir. You could have had a great life with us."

I said, "I told you to give me my body. I will escape, and then you never have to see me again."

Wessel said, "We can never let you escape. We need to eat your dreams and your soul. You will be our prisoner, and you will never escape!"

I jumped toward my body, but Wessel grabbed my leg and tossed me to the floor. Dragana grabbed the sleeping body of my doppelganger, and then they both vanished. All the devils came to attack me. The diabolical hobgoblins and the monsters surrounded me. Roland and Reinhold appeared out of the shadows. I heard the door of the dungeon slam shut.

As I slowly stood up, I looked around at all the enemies around me. It appeared that there were thirty or forty nightmarish creatures ready to attack me. Twenty or thirty diabolical hobgoblins swarmed around me. Another twenty devils charged toward me. Roland and Reinhold grew massive membranous black wings on their backs and started floating in the air high above me so that they were near the ceiling. I howled at the oncoming enemies as I painfully but rapidly transformed into a giant black werewolf.

CHAPTER 9

I ATTACKED THE SPECTRES AND PHANTOMS, BUT I COULD NOT damage their phantasmic forms. My enemies stabbed and pierced me with their weapons. They hammered me and whipped me mercilessly. The foes poked and wounded me with their spears and talons. My wounds were quickly healing, and my body was automatically regenerating constantly.

I butchered the grim hobgoblins with my hands and took one of their scythes. Black shadows oozed like oil from the blade. A pale mist of phantasmal skulls floated out of it, too.

The frightening spectres were shattered by the scythe, and it banished the shadowy phantoms. I devoured the malicious tormentors, killed the dreadful hammerers, and ravaged the repulsive beasts. I endured grievous injuries and maddening pain as teeth and claws were sinking into my flesh. I barked and growled as knives were driven into my bones.

With my hands, I pulverized abominable enemies and slaughtered detestable creatures. I eviscerated wretched entities while I was being speared and clubbed from all sides. Their weapons could no longer pierce my tough regenerating skin. After decapitating the vile condemners, my claws shredded the ghoulish executioners of this dungeon. The devilish enslavers were devastated by my attacks. The horrific monsters and nightmarish beings were annihilated by my scythe. The crimson blood of my enemies sprayed on me as I disemboweled the grotesque torturers. I obliterated the deranged demons with my fists, and then I finally destroyed all of the loathsome devils in the dungeon.

Roland and Reinhold were flying above and throwing thunderbolts at me while Wessel was jumping around me. While I was evading the lightning, Wessel was throwing knives at me. I grabbed Wessel and smashed him into the ground. I bit off his head and spat it at Reinhold.

Reinhold said, "Why would you ever want to leave this dream, Theodemir? Do you not see how much power you have here? Look at what you have done to our servants and friends. Some of the devils that you killed were your own relatives. Look at the destruction that you have caused. In the real world, you will never have the same kind of abilities, strength, or potential that you have when you are here in this world of dreams. In the world of mortals and reality, you will only be a barbaric beast. You will not be the unstoppable monster that you are here. If you wake up, you will only be a psychotic sadist with nothing meaningful to live for. If you stay here with us, you can have all of these amazing magical powers and weapons. Do you not want to always feel this way? The way that you feel at this very moment is the feeling of true freedom and power. All you need to do is give us your soul."

Hearing something move behind me, I turned around immediately. Roland's face and hands manifested out of the shadows on the wall. I attacked, but Roland was gone. My fist created a massive hole in the wall where Roland had been. I turned around and saw Reinhold fly above me. I jumped and grabbed his leg. I crushed his bones and smashed him into the wall. His body was regenerating, too. When he grabbed me, I became shocked by electricity. I was paralyzed by the pain.

The pain in my body was too intense. I thought that I would die. Suddenly, the pain quickly vanished. The electricity was gone, too. All the flames, the crying prisoners, and the noise of the dungeon faded away. The dungeon was dark and silent. I was a human being again with human form. I was wearing my black fur coat and black leather pants. I was healed, clean, and unscathed.

I said, "This is only a dream. This fear will not stop me. You are nightmares, but you have no more control over me. This dream is ending."

Reinhold and Roland screamed as their attacks did nothing to me. They could not even fly any longer. Now that they were both on the ground, I used the scythe to destroy them. When they vanished, I left the dungeon.

Through stairways and passages, I continued walking upward. I found a window and jumped out. I could see that the nighttime sky was now being burned by sunlight. Morning was arriving. Before I could hit the ground, Dragana flew down and grabbed me up. She squeezed my ankle and dropped me on the roof. Dragana had two large black wings protruding from her back. Hilda and Adalric were standing beside her on the roof. When I stood up, I realized that my doppelganger was sleeping on the roof, too.

Adalric's green eyes sullenly glared at me. His long straight blond hair swayed with the cold breeze. A gust of chilly air howled across the roof, and Adalric's black velvet cape fluttered around his tall, lean body. His countenance held a dour, melancholic expression. Even though he appeared so morose, he still looked so handsome and dignified. The fair white skin of his face was clean-shaven and unblemished. The blond hairs of his eyebrows were neat and comely. He wore a tight hauberk over a sleeved black tunic. His leather pants and leather boots were all black. He held a long black spear with his right hand.

Adalric said, "Theodemir, you have killed so many members of our family. You murdered the demons and devils who were our ilk. You even killed Reinhold and Roland. Your dreams and thoughts have spread throughout this castle like a noxious venom. Your presence here has brought desolation to our world. Everything that remains of the Fiendilkfjeld family is us. The beings standing here on this roof are the only things left of this family. Hilda, Dragana, you, and I are the only ones left. We were trying to destroy you in your dream, but you have destroyed us. Now, you have finally made it here after so much time has passed. You are ready to know the truth about everything, are you? You want to leave, do you?"

Hilda asked, "Theodemir, how did you become so powerful? How were you actually able to attack us from your dream? We have been taking souls and dreams from others for hundreds of years, and no one has been able to defeat us. People have escaped from us in the past, but no one has actually ever been capable of harming us in this dream. You attacked our souls and destroyed many of our family."

I said, "You invaded my dreams. I invaded yours. While I was sleeping, you entered my brain and brought me into your nightmares. You created a cage that I would fill with my thoughts and emotions. You surrounded me with worlds of suffering and fear. You never thought that I could learn how to follow you into the castle. I was never supposed to be able to enter the castle. You wanted to take my soul from the prison of nightmares that you created for me, but I escaped and followed you into your world. I found this place. I came to this castle, and you wanted me to leave. You wanted to keep me trapped in my cage of dreams, but I returned to your world. You wanted to take my dreams from a safe distance. You thought that you could hide behind the illusions of this nightmare."

Hilda said, "All of that is true. The darkness around your heart and the insanity in your mind was a terrifying force that we were unprepared for. We only wanted to eat your dreams. We never realized that you would attach your soul to ours."

I said, "My mind attacked you. I brought illusions of my own. Your evil spirits live in this world. You cannot exist in the real world. This is the only place where you can survive. You are real here. There is nowhere else for you to go. I could feel my dreams, mind, and soul slowly fading away. The longer I stayed here, the weaker I became. Now, I am taking your souls. The curse of the werewolf's bite allowed my mind and soul to become more protected against your curses and spells."

"We poisoned your soul, but you still retaliated against us," said Hilda. "You found a way to steal our energy."

I said, "The blood of the demon Fiendilkfjeld protected me, too. A piece of the spirit of that evil deity is inside me, inside all members of the Fiendilkfjeld family. You ate my dreams, but they were poisonous to you, because of the darkness and madness already around my soul. The more you squeezed, the more of my venom and malice paralyzed you, too. You lost control of the dream, but you could not get rid of me. I could not escape, but I was getting stronger. You tried to manipulate me. You continued to control my thoughts and my soul. You gave me fake memories and false emotions. You wanted me to get stuck in an endless cycle of stories and mysteries that were bizarre and grotesque so that you could eat my fear. You even tried to make me fight myself. You brought other evil spirits to attack me, but I learned how to take their powers. That is when you all started to notice that something was wrong with your schemes."

Hilda said, "Yes, that is true. But how did you avoid death so many times?"

I said, "When I stopped being afraid, I learned something about myself that allowed me to dispel your magic. As my heart was fading and my mind was melting, I was losing my identity and passions. My emotions were vanishing, but my rage was alive. I learned to fight my insecurity. I do not need to be accepted by you, the family, or anyone. I once wanted to be loved by other people, but not now. Not any longer. I do not need to be accepted by others. When I learned to be confident and believe in my own value, I started to learn how to use the magic of these dreams to my advantage. I stopped being afraid of you. I do not want anyone to control my destiny."

Adalric said, "Yes, Theodemir, you have certainly learned how to manipulate the forces of these dreams and nightmares to your advantage. You have learned how to use the magic of dreams as we do. The blood of the demon master has allowed you to awaken astral abilities of nightmares and curses."

Dragana asked, "How do you know so much, Theodemir? When did you learn the truth?"

I said, "There has always been a strange presence inside of me that I can still feel. It is cold and dull, but it has always been there. I was slowly becoming more and more aware of it. Now that I feel truly connected with the beast inside of me, that cold feeling has become more apparent to me. Now, so many things have finally become clear to me. I suppose you could say that I am finally waking up. My physical body in the real world is alive, and my mind has become aware of what is really happening. I can no longer be tricked by you. This dream is mine again. But, I still have you in my grasp. I am going to destroy you so that you can never come into my dreams again. When you enter someone's dream, you also become vulnerable to the power of those dreams. This time, the dreamer is eating you."

Dragana said, "You are insane! You are a complete lunatic! This is impossible! This has never happened before! This cannot be possible! We eat the dreams, not you! This is not fair! Only someone with a truly psychotic mind and evil soul could be capable of doing something like that to us!"

Hilda said, "We never should have tried to eat the dreams of someone as insane as you, Theodemir. This is outrageous."

I said, "I will not only eat your dream. I will take your souls, like you have been trying to do to me. When I wake up, I will forget all about you. This will only be a shadow in my memory. You will be completely erased. You wanted me to become a monster, and you blackened my cursed soul. My mind is now completely protected against devils and nightmares like you. In a way, I am thankful for this experience that you forced me into."

Adalric said, "It has become so much harder to capture souls and dreams. Our souls are being eaten away by darkness and emptiness. Madness and passions control our minds. It has become increasingly more difficult each year to survive. Everyone's dreams are so much weaker and duller than they once were. Our hunger and suffering only grows. We need more and more dreams to survive. We have become infected by these dreams. We had to eat the souls of our own relatives. We ate the weakest of our children, grandchildren, brothers, sisters, and cousins. We enslaved the rest of our family. Anyone who revolted was consumed. We were corrupted by our own sinister magic powers. The magic began to take control of us. We become more like haunted shadows year by year. We do not know how to be really alive anymore. We do not know how to stop it. We do not know how to change things. Our master Fiendilkfjeld demands more and more dreams from us. It eats more and takes more from us. The demon has become lazy, greedy, and impatient. It does not want us anymore. I knew that this day would come. The shadows told me about a prophecy of our destruction. For a while, I have known that a time would come when Fiendilkfjeld would choose someone to finally destroy us. It wants to pass on this castle to someone else. Our world, this nightmare, is finally ending. Our souls can finally rest. We have been trapped here with the demon for a long time. It has been too long. Yet, I do not want to fade away like this. I cannot simply surrender this castle. I will not give the master what he wants so easily. Theodemir, you and I will fight. I know that you have always loved the empty ruins of our castle. In the real world, you wanted to purchase and rebuild it. Now, give this old ghost a chance to see if you truly deserve to possess our home."

"I will defeat you, and you will have your destruction," I said. "Whatever is left of you, I hope you find peace in the hereafter."

Adalric and I circled each other. I felt as if someone was clawing at my heart. My emotions burned through my body. I felt overwhelmed by horrifying fear. I could feel that Adalric was trying to control the dream. I felt my mind being squeezed and tugged. Shadows and flames danced around the blade of his spear. Both of us were fighting for dominance over the dream. Every time that we wounded each other, our injuries would instinctively heal. He pierced and stabbed me with the spear, but my wounds vanished and my body regenerated. I attacked him with the scythe and ripped open his flesh, but his body would magically be repaired. I threw away the scythe and transformed into the form of a black were-wolf. I used my claws and fangs to rip him apart, but he would not die. His body was magically restored, repaired, and rejuvenated every time that I thought that he was dead. He cut and impaled me, but the wounds vanished. I felt as if our fearsome battle lasted for more than five minutes. He screamed and I howled as we both were wounding each other. He stabbed me through the throat. I broke the spear and decapitated him with my claws. Finally, he was truly defeated. As he vanished, Hilda and Dragana screamed. I pulled the spear out of my neck. Hilda and Dragana attacked me, but my claws ripped off their heads. When they vanished I heard something flying around me.

A gigantic monster swooped down from the sky, and landed on the roof. It towered over me and screeched. This devil appeared to be like a nightmarish dragon that was repulsive and mystifying. This abominable monstrosity was a horrifyingly grotesque and inhuman entity. It must have been maybe ten or twelve feet tall. This despicable creature had the body of a gigantic black crocodile. It had two heads. One head was a gigantic black head of a bat with two goatish black horns on its forehead. The second head was a slender black head of a diabolic serpent. Black horns protruded out like spikes from the forehead of the serpentine head. When the serpentine head opened its mouth, it revealed its terrifyingly disgusting tongue. This tongue was covered with human faces and flesh. This devil had two black reptilian legs. Its feet had sharp black claws. The demon had a massive black serpentine tail with a blood red fin at the end of it. The demon had two black membranous wings that were enormous. It also had two long arms that were covered with black scales and had black scorpion claws.

It opened its mouths and I heard a deep, menacing voice coming from the monster. When it spoke, it almost sounded like many voices speaking in chorus, but I could still understand what was being said. The demon said, "I am the master of this nightmare. I am Fiendilkfjeld. The family served their purpose, but they were doomed to die this way. You are my only living descendant. You were the one I chose to bring destruction to the family."

I asked, "Why did you want them destroyed?"

It said, "They were always disobedient, weak, and foolish. They worshipped me because they wanted my power, but they did not love me. They did not respect me. They were constantly attacking one another. I forced them to collect dreams and souls for me. Most of the family was still planning to overthrow me. I decided that all of them should die."

"Why was I chosen to destroy them?" I asked.

"I had trapped my worshippers and children in this nightmare many centuries ago, because they thought that they could control me. They cast curses on me to make me weak, so I cursed them," it said. "I told them they would be destroyed by themselves unless they learned to be completely devoted to serving me and finally stopped fighting one another. They obviously thought that they were too powerful to be destroyed by my curse. I chose you because I believed that you would not fail me."

"Why did you trap them here?" I asked. "Why were so many of my relatives in this dream?"

It said, "Many centuries ago, a group of mortals begged me for power and arcane knowledge. I gave them what they wanted, and they created children with me. After many decades, they stopped caring about me. They started fighting one another. They did not worship me, but they still wanted more power and wealth from me. When I refused to obey them, they tried to destroy me. They banished me and sent me into the world where I came from, so I took many of them here with me. I was dying. To survive, I became the fog, mountains, and sky of this world. The spirits of wickedness and evil that live here corrupted all of us. Even my loyal followers became deranged and diseased. There was a time when we could enter the real world at night. We created many more diabolic children and imps with humans and animals in the real world. Some of my offspring could only leave the dream at night, too but that changed. Later, none of us could escape this nightmare. We could only exist here or in the dreams of others. We were here like this for hundreds of years."

"What did you think about your children who had families in the real world?" I asked.

"They were related to the people and creatures who escaped my wrath centuries ago," it said. "When I was being banished to this nightmare long ago, I did not have time to capture every one of my children and their children. Many years passed. My blood passed on into the blood of their offspring and their descendants. Darkness and curses followed them until all of them died. Now, you are the only one left."

"What are you going to do with me?" I asked.

It said, "You will die."

CHAPTER 10

"No!" I screamed. "No!"

Extreme horror oppressed my tortured mind. I ran out of my narrow bed and clawed against a black wall. I shouted repeatedly, louder and louder. I was frantically crying. Tears poured out of my eyes and slid down my face. I heaved and gasped as I pounded my fists against the cold marble. I coughed and sobbed while punching the stone floor. My fists were bloody, and the pain was searing. I slammed my head against a wall so that I could feel more pain. Real pain. I wanted to feel a physical type of pain that was actually piercing and corporeal. Weeping, I continued hitting my head against the wall until red blood dripped down my eyes. Suddenly, everything became darkness.

When I woke up, I crawled to a corner of the room and continued weeping. I was shivering from the dreadful fear throbbing throughout my entire body. I was in a room that had four walls. The floor and ceiling were made out of smooth black stones. The black walls were marble. There was only one window, and it had a Gothic arch. The window was barred, so I could not throw myself out of it. I was so exhausted that I shut my eyes and slept. Abruptly awakening, I flinched and shouted. I whimpered and moaned with grief and weariness. I could still feel the hot pain in my hands and in my head.

The door of my room opened and four guards entered the room. It was Roman, Luca, Neil, and Valter. They were all wearing white uniforms. Each of them wore a white shirt, white trousers, and white shoes. They appeared with other orderlies who were all peering into my room or staring at me. They wanted me to move, but I could not even stand. I was grabbed and dragged out of the room. I could not keep my eyes open. Everything was darkness again. I slept.

When I woke up, I was in a different room. I was sitting in a small white bed. I looked at my two hands. I looked at my two feet. The walls were covered with violet wallpaper, the room had a white marble floor and ceiling, and blue satin curtains decorated the windows. Sunlight came into the room through the windows.

There were four beautiful women in the room. I recognized these women instantly. Ksenija, Agnes, Graziella, and Brigitte. They appeared to be nurses. All of their clothes were white. Each of them was wearing a coat, a shirt, an apron, a skirt, tights, and shoes. Their shoes had kitten heels, their aprons reached down to their thighs, and their skirts reached down to their knees. Silent and nervous, they were staring at me. When the doctor entered the room, they left.

I remembered this doctor. He was familiar to me. It was Pasquale. He was wearing a long white coat, a white shirt, white pants, and white shoes. He walked closer to me and looked at my head. Then, he looked at both of my hands. My left hand had many scars on it.

Some of the scars had the shapes of teeth and tiny round holes. Long, slender scars slithered across my knuckles and curved up to my forearm. Looking at these scars, I remembered how a wolf gave them to me. It had happened one year ago. Memories of when that black undead wolf bit my hand and slashed my arm returned to my mind. I remembered shooting and stabbing that vicious wolf until it had finally died. More memories came back to me. I remembered how that demonic creature had looked when it died. As I escaped the crypt, I had seen it begin to move again, like it could never truly be killed. I had never seen that beast again after that, except in my nightmares.

Pasquale said, "Theodemir, tell me how you are feeling."

I asked, "How long did I sleep for this time?"

"You slept for four days," said Pasquale. "Why did you hurt yourself after you woke up? Luckily, all of your wounds healed. Your body has regenerated rapidly."

I said, "I had another nightmare."

"Was it the same as the nightmares you have been having? Was it like the ones you had before?"

"Yes," I said. "It was exactly the same."

Pasquale looked at my eyes. "You saw the vampires again? The demons? The wolves?"

I said, "Yes. It happened again. I saw all of them. They were eating my dreams and my soul. The wolf was there. He was helping me fight them, but he was still hurting me, too."

Pasquale said, "Theodemir, you have been having these recurring nightmares every night ever since the beginning of October. It is now the end of November. What do you think is causing this? What are you not telling me?"

I asked, "How long have I been here?"

Pasquale said, "Theodemir, you have hidden yourself here in this castle ever since August. You did not have these nightmares until October."

I said, "I remember now. Yes. Some more of my memories are returning to me, Pasquale. I purchased the ruins of Fiendilkfjeld castle. I paid for the construction of a mental hospital here, and had it attached to the castle. I was going to rebuild the castle after construction of the mental hospital was finished. One year ago, I was with my friends and family in the woods near my estate. They died there. All of them. Everyone said that wolves did it. I lied, too, and said that we were attacked by wolves. I knew what really happened, but it was my secret." I got out of bed and stood up. I grabbed Pasquale's collar and said, "I killed them. My friends. My parents. It was me."

Pasquale gasped. "Why would you tell me this now?"

I said, "I am going to kill you and everyone else here."

"How will you do that?" asked Pasquale.

"I will transform into a wolf," I said. "No one will be able to stop me."

"You have been talking about werewolves for months, Theodemir," said Pasquale. "You have been saying that you are a wolf, but you have never turned into a monster. I have never seen you grow fur, claws, or fangs. You do not even have a tail. Look at yourself in the mirror, Theodemir. You are a human being. Look. You are a human. This is reality. This is not a dream. You have been threatening all of us ever since you hired us. This is your mental hospital. Your castle. You hired everyone here to take care of you. You wanted us to observe you. We have. We have never seen you become a monster. You only think that you are a monster. This curse is only in your mind. You want to believe that you are a monster because you feel guilty for not being able to protect your parents or your friends."

I walked to the mirror and saw my reflection. I was human. I had human shape and form, but I did not feel human. I did not feel like myself. I feared that I would suddenly disappear.

Pasquale said, "I saw the corpses, Theodemir. I saw the cabin where the bodies were found. They had wounds that could never have been created by a human being. We found wolf blood and wolf hair all over the dead bodies. You had guards with you in the cabin that night, and they said that they were attacked by a giant wolf. They said that they did not even see you. They thought that you were hiding in the woods to escape the wolves. Your servants said that they saw a large wolf running around your estate. You even said that you were attacked by a group of wolves in the woods and that you ran away. That is why you think that you are a monster. You feel shame for running away when the wolves came and attacked your friends and family. There is no werewolf curse."

I said, "I paid a lot of people to lie for me. I destroyed anyone who was a threat to me. I was so scared of people knowing the truth. Now, suddenly, I do not care what people know. None of you will survive. I do not care about anything anymore. All of my emotions have become stained with blood and violence. Everything inside of me is pulling me towards greater carnage. I was hiding in the ruins of this castle because I did not want to hurt anyone else. I did not know that this castle was haunted. The nightmares made me realize what I really want. I did not know that the land was cursed, like me. My transformation will be complete when the moon is full. Then, I will no longer be human. It has taken a long time, but I am finally ready. Honestly, none of that matters to me anymore. I do not even need to rebuild this castle. Let it rot. Let the ruins be a reminder of what has really died here. Let that death grow and multiply into an absolute nightmare. I think the castle looks better like this. All I want is to kill and to hunt." I smashed the mirror with my fist and then turned to look at Pasquale.

It was fun watching him die slowly as I strangled him. The groans and the sounds of his gasps were delightfully gruesome. The guards came, but they could not stop me. I had learned how to control the strength of the wolf within me. I could summon up its power whenever I wanted. The guards were easy to kill. All I had to do was break their skulls with my hands. I grabbed a scalpel and slowly wandered around the mental hospital. As I walked down the halls, I attacked the orderlies and porters with the blade. I killed everyone I saw, and I was not going to allow anyone to leave this place alive. Everyone here had to die. I butchered the nurses, guards, and attendants until none of them were left. There were no other patients, because the mental hospital had not been completely finished yet. It never would be.

I washed myself and then changed into new clothes. I wore black leather shoes, black leather pants, and a black fur coat. I left the mental hospital and walked among the desolate ruins of Fiendilkfjeld castle. I left the scalpel on the floor. I did not do anything with all the corpses. I would hide them later. The hospital was connected to the castle by a long hallway. I was so glad to be here. I walked through the empty corridors and broken rooms of the castle. Now that it was morning, I saw how this land was so beautifully sublime. The valleys and mountains around me were large, grim, and foreboding. Fog shrouded the land. There was no one here but me. I was alone. I felt magnificent.

As I left the castle, I realized that the sky was black and it was nighttime. The full moon emerged from the shadowy clouds in sky. I saw Alison walking towards me. She appeared so beautiful. She was wearing a long red dress and black shoes. Her long hair was blond. Her skin was white. Her fingers were long and beautiful. She was still very lean and skinny, and still had a womanly figure. She was five feet tall, and moved gracefully. She approached me. She gazed at me with her lovely green eyes. When she spoke, her voice was elegant and charmingly feminine.

She said, "I am glad to see that you finally walked outside the castle."

I asked, "Alison, where have you been?"

She said, "Where have I been? I have been waiting for you to leave this place. You never talk to me anymore. You are always here. You have become a different person. I do not know you anymore."

"Alison, I begged you to help me. When I got sick, I needed you. I wanted to talk to you. I wanted you to be beside me. I never wanted to leave you," I said.

Alison said, "I do not like how you hid yourself in this castle. All you cared about was building that mental hospital. You talked about rebuilding the castle. You wanted to live here. You wanted to live here with me, but I never liked this place. I never wanted to live here. If I lived here with you, I would be so far away from my friends and family. Ever since you got bitten by that dog in France, you have become more and more despondent, distant, morbid, and paranoid. It was like I was watching all of your emotions die slowly until all that was left of you was a morose shadow."

I said, "Alison, do not try to rewrite the past. You were spending all of my money on drugs and gambling debts. You were buying drugs from Pasquale. Those drugs were corrupting your soul. I begged you to stop, but you were apathetic. You were the one who became distant. You used to look at me as if I should never exist. You only wanted my money. You only wanted to spend time with those people who could give you drugs. I begged you to help me, but you did not care about my problems. I told you that something was wrong with me, but you did not pay attention to me. After that, I went to France with my friends. I was trying to do anything I could to make more money so that you could be happy. I got bit by something, but it was not a dog. I tried to tell you what happened to me, but you mocked me."

"You said that a werewolf attacked you," said Alison.

"After my friends and family died, you were never there for me. You did not want to be near me," I said. "You said that my problems were only troublesome and inopportune. You wanted to travel. You wanted to meet new people."

Alison said, "We never should have been married. That is why I came here. I knew that I could find you here. I wanted to tell you that things need to improve, or I will leave you. I am hoping that I can convince you to stop acting crazy, or I want a divorce."

I said, "For months, I have been having nightmares. They have always been identical. Every night, the nightmares were always the same. Every night, the nightmares would kill me. They would take my dreams and pieces of my soul. However, things finally changed. I recently had a nightmare that was different from the others. I was able to change things. In the most recent nightmare that I just had, I actually changed things. I defeated the demons. I destroyed the nightmares. I spoke with the master of the nightmare."

"This is what I am talking about," said Alison. "Why do you talk like this? Why can you not just be normal?"

I said, "In a dream, Alison, you might see amazing things. Everything you see or feel is a message. What you see in a dream is not actually what it really is. For example, a flower. In the dream, you see the flower, and you treat the flower like it is a flower. Simple. Then, you wake up. This is important. After waking up, you might not remember everything about the dream. If you remember the flower, you might also realize what it really was. It was a message. What did it say? You might realize that the flower was actually a dagger. It was poison. You start thinking about your life, and you might realize that the dream was warning you about something. Something that you loved was actually destroying you. Or, maybe the dream was completely nonsense. Either way, life is really unfair."

Alison screamed as she witnessed me quickly transforming into a black wolf. I bit her throat and tasted her sweet, delicious blood pouring down my throat. I eviscerated her with my claws and devoured her slowly. I was finally ready to begin my new life in the real world.

She was not my last victim. I consumed the living and the dead. The blood of mortals and corpses was my food. If someone escaped from me after I wounded them, they would also become a werewolf, too. The nightmares would come for them until their damned transformation was complete.

I was always partly here in the real world and lingering on the edge of annihilation and emptiness. I wore on me a dark fog that carried the tortured souls of the dead and forgotten. Remorse became a living darkness that circled my every action and every thought. My pleasure was, at best, fleeting and dull. I had to hide from everyone. My loneliness became more ominously corporeal and stinging. I felt overwhelming bursts of regret, humiliation, and despair more and more frequently. Every one of my extreme emotions brought hallucinations of violence and violation. I was forgetting who I was or what I wanted to become. The man whom I formerly had been was now dead, but I died every night I became the wolf. I suffered agonizingly slow deaths with every transformation into this monster. My pain only made me want to destroy more. I wanted to kill more brutally each time. No one should escape the abyss that I would bring with me.

EPILOGUE

I was not as powerful as I thought I was. I was not as fast or brave as I had been in the nightmare. I was not as strong or unstoppable as I had been in my dreams. Pain hurt so much more in the real world. Every emotion I had was like a knife cutting through me. My flesh could still regenerate and my wounds always healed quickly, but not as rapidly as they had in the dreams.

I wanted respect, but all I created was dread and terror. I wanted pleasure and happiness, but all I felt was bloodthirsty rage. I slowly began to lose my sense of existence more and more. I began seeing ghosts all around me more frequently. Sunlight distracted and angered me. The sight of flames and lightning made me furious and lethal. Rain and snow brought turbulent emotions inside of me. I was never able to return to my human form. I was only a wolf. I destroyed graves and ate the corpses. My bite became so haunted and wicked that some of the dead bodies that I would chew on would then rise and mindlessly move after I was done eating them. Many years passed like this.

One day, I finally became a human again. I woke up in a dark bloody cave somewhere. It was snowing. I tried to remember everything that I could about myself. I returned to Fiendilkfjeld castle, and then I began writing about all of this so that I could remember who I was and what I had been. To be truthful, I do not know why I am writing this.

There is a memory in my head that tells me why I must write this. There are voices in my brain telling me that my story can become a flame that warns others. I think that I am writing this because I want these words to create something beautiful that gives value to the lifeless world around me. Maybe I want to see these words become something special that will save my soul and end my suffering. I want to spread this story out across the world and see what happens. I do think that it is strange that someone like me would want to write about things that I think I remember about my cursed life and past. This could be the last echo of the part of me that might have been decently human.

Now, living beings are only food for the cataclysmic anguish that penetrates every part me. I do not relate to anyone or anything. My animosity towards everything has become more disturbing. I have heard the emptiness beneath my skin. I have seen nightmares and horrific beings that exist in macabre nebulae beyond this world. There are demons in my mind, and a beast is in my blood.

All things that live on this earth will be shredded until there is nothing left but morbid reflections in the haunted darkness. Fate and life will take away everything that we love. Living creatures and all mortals are infected by the passions and curses of others. My hunger for blood soars like my hunger for beauty in this repulsive world. My story is a curious reverberation of my own screams as I am brooding in the ruins of Fiendilkfjeld castle.

THE END.

ABOUT THE AUTHOR

Matthew Pungitore is the author of Midnight's Eternal Prisoner: Waiting For The Summer.